# SLOW HEAT

## Leta Blake

An Original Publication from Leta Blake Books

Slow Heat
Written and published by Leta Blake
Cover designed by Getpremades.com
Formatted by BB eBooks

First Edition, 2017
Print Edition

ISBN: 979-8-88841-020-2

# Other Books by Leta Blake

## Contemporary

Will & Patrick Wake Up Married
Will & Patrick's Endless Honeymoon
Cowboy Seeks Husband
The Difference Between
Bring on Forever
Stay Lucky

### Sports

The River Leith

*The Training Season Series*
Training Season
Training Complex

### Musicians

Smoky Mountain Dreams
Vespertine

### New Adult

Punching the V-Card

### Winter Holidays

*The Home for the Holidays Series*
Mr. Frosty Pants
Mr. Naughty List
Mr. Jingle Bells

## Fantasy

Any Given Lifetime

### Re-imagined Fairy Tales

Flight
Levity

**Paranormal & Shifters**

Angel Undone
Omega Mine

**Horror**

Raise Up Heart

# Omegaverse

*Heat of Love Series*
Slow Heat
Alpha Heat
Slow Birth
Bitter Heat

*For Sale Series*
Heat for Sale

# Coming of Age

*'90s Coming of Age Series*
Pictures of You
You Are Not Me

# Audiobooks

Leta Blake at Audible

# Discover more about the author online

Leta Blake
letablake.com

## Gay Romance Newsletter

Leta's newsletter will keep you up to date on her latest releases and news from the world of M/M romance. Join the mailing list today and you're automatically entered into future giveaways.
letablake.com

## Leta Blake on Patreon

Become part of Leta Blake's Patreon community in order to access exclusive content, deleted scenes, extras, bonus stories, rewards, prizes, interviews, and more.
www.patreon.com/letablake

# Acknowledgements

Thank you to the following people: Mom & Dad, without whom I couldn't be following this dream. B & C, my lights to travel home to after visiting made up worlds. My patrons Sadie Sheffield, SB Fournier, and all the wonderful members of my Patreon who inspire, support, and advise me. Keira Andrews for constant cheerleading. Amanda Jean for the amazing editing work. Devon Vesper for additional edits. Annabeth Albert for cover advice and general awesomeness. And thank you to my readers who make it all worthwhile.

**A lustful young alpha meets his match in an older omega with a past.**

Professor Vale Aman has crafted a good life for himself. An unbonded omega in his mid-thirties, he's long since given up hope that he'll meet a compatible alpha, let alone his destined mate. He's fulfilled by his career, his poetry, his cat, and his friends.

When Jason Sabel, a much younger alpha, imprints on Vale in a shocking and public way, longings are ignited that can't be ignored. Fighting their strong sexual urges, Jason and Vale must agree to contract with each other before they can consummate their passion.

But for Vale, being with Jason means giving up his independence and placing his future in the hands of an untested alpha—as well as facing the scars of his own tumultuous past. He isn't sure it's worth it. But Jason isn't giving up his destined mate without a fight.

This is a **stand-alone** gay romance novel of 117,000 words with a **strong HFN ending** and a well-crafted, **non-shifter omegaverse** with alphas, betas, omegas, male pregnancy, heat, and **knotting**. Content warnings for pregnancy loss and aftermath.

For Punny and Mimi, two of my favorites.

# CHAPTER ONE

**Definition of** *Érosgápe*
: an alpha or omega's biologically and spiritually determined mate

**Example of** *Érosgápe* **in a sentence**
: Some alphas and omegas are not just contracted mates, but are *Érosgápe*, bound deeply by spirit and flesh.

**Origin and Etymology of** *Érosgápe*:
Old World Greek, literally sexual love (*erōs*) and spiritual love (*agapē*) combined.

**First Known Use:** Year 32 of Wolf

THE VOICEOVER FROM the educational video echoed around the classroom. Jason slouched near the back with his best friend, Xan, at his side. Like all the other alphas in the room, they sat in complete stillness, erections aching against the front of their trousers.

The film displayed a naked omega already deep in heat. He was beautiful with dark hair, pale skin, and long muscles. The film wasn't of good enough quality to determine the color of the omega's eyes, but they looked pale, perhaps blue or green. He was exactly the type of boy who caught Jason's eye. Seeing him on display in the film, eager and vulnerable, left Jason breathless with arousal.

On all fours, back arched, the omega lifted his ass. His crack and hole glistened with the slick of his arousal and need. Jason's mouth watered as the omega in the video frantically moved his hand over his swollen dick and cast desperate glances over his shoulder toward his young but thickly muscled alpha. The word 'please' was easy to read on the omega's ripe mouth, as he squirmed and arched.

His alpha, dark and powerful, stood to the side of the bed, his massive cock engorged, and fixed his omega with a commanding stare. As he climbed on top of the boy's straining back and pushed inside, the voiceover droned on:

*"When in the throes of heat, the omega presents himself to his alpha shamelessly. Instinct pushes him to be bred, and he will go to any length to achieve his biological goal. It's important to remember an omega in heat without an alpha to meet his needs is a danger to himself. If you must restrain your omega to prevent him from running, do so. This is applicable to a contracted mate as well as an Érosgápe mate."*

Jason's cock leaked pre-come against his boxers, and he didn't dare move for fear of spontaneously orgasming in the middle of his first college-level Alpha-Omega Relations class. He glanced toward Xan and was relieved he wasn't alone in his consuming arousal.

Xan shifted subtly in his seat, big blue eyes glued to the screen, as a trickle of sweat slipped down the side of his flushed face. His dark hair had gone limp in the humid stillness of the room, and his long, pale fingers, normally moving or tapping, were still on his desk.

Jason smelled Xan's pre-come and the spicy quality of his pheromone-drenched sweat. He was familiar with all the sensual qualities of Xan's arousal from the three years they'd bunked together at St. Marjoram's Prep School for alphas. And after two months apart over the summer, he'd eagerly reacquainted himself with them over the last four days in their shared dorm at their university, Mont Nessadare.

Practice made perfect, and they'd both agreed to practice a lot with each other in preparation for the day they'd meet their omegas. *If* they met their omegas. While over sixty percent of alpha/omega *Érosgápe* pairs did eventually find each other, forty percent of each group never met their bond-mate. Jason went cold imagining an unbonded future without his *Érosgápe*. Though a contracted omega would still be better than no mate at all.

Because no matter how much he and Xan practiced together, they'd never reach the heights of ecstasy the alpha and omega in the educational film had already achieved. And the heat was just beginning.

Over the course of the class, they'd be presented with educational films of omegas at all stages of heat, pregnancy, and delivery. He'd heard from older alpha friends, a grade level above him at university, that the films of omegas in Stage 2 and Stage 3 were so intense that alpha students regularly ejaculated in class. Rumor had it they provided tissues for cleanup and advised the alphas to bring an extra pair of underwear to change into.

*"Omegas are capable of multiple orgasms of a variety of types—oral, anal, uteral, and penile—but the omega will climax both with his penis and with his receptive cavity most commonly. If his womb has descended and opened, then he can reach states of unbearable pleasure. Expect your omega to be overcome by ecstasy, especially as his womb takes the crown of the alpha's penis in preparation for Stage 2 and the beginning of insemination."*

Jason's balls clenched and he closed his eyes, reluctant though he was to miss a second of the filmed omega's pleasure and the alpha's strong command of it.

"That's all, class. We'll see more after we've learned more about Stage 1 in alpha and omega breeding. In the meantime, are there any questions?" Professor Shriner's voice was high-pitched for a man, and it cut through the room shrilly, shriveling Jason's desire almost as effectively as a splash of cold water.

"Yes, Mr. Monhundy?" Professor Shriner pointed at Wilbet Monhundy in the second row, tall and muscled, a dreamboat of an alpha if Jason had ever seen one—the exact opposite of his own scrawny, lanky, *c'mon-puberty-give-it-another-shot* body.

At least Jason had some hope for a brighter future in his swooping blond hair that lay across his forehead like a fall of wheat, blue eyes that reminded people of the sky or cornflowers depending on what colors he wore, and a pretty face that his father swore would grow into a handsome visage of alphahood eventually. Still, what Jason wouldn't give for Wilbet's biceps and abs.

"Go on, Mr. Monhundy, speak up."

"Why does the omega shoot from his dick?" Wilbet asked with a leer. "He can't impregnate anything. The come is just made of the same slick as from his ass, right? So what's the point?"

"Language, Mr. Monhundy," Professor Shriner scolded. "The omega climaxes with his penis, ejaculating an amount of liquid similar to that of the human men of yore. Before the Great Death, there were no alphas or omegas, just human men and the females of the species, known as women, and they engaged in intercourse in a similar, though not exactly the same, fashion as we do now. Human males ejaculated into a human female's orifice, known as a vagina, and impregnated her in the muscled, robust womb she carried within. The amount of the ejaculation was much less than today's alphas, but similar to the ejaculate expelled by betas who copulate for pleasure but never produce offspring."

"But why do omegas do it?" Wilbet asked again. "I mean, don't get me wrong, it's hot, but why?"

Professor Shriner rolled his eyes. "I should no longer harbor even a tiny bit of surprise at the things you ripening alphas will say." He heaved a sigh. "The omega's ejaculation is a holdover from our forefathers. But don't underestimate its power. The pleasure it brings to the omega is great, though not as powerful as some of his other orgasm potentials—of which there are several. He will relax afterward though remain eager for more. More importantly, it signals his womb to descend and soften, so it will open and accept the crown of the alpha's penis for insemination."

There was nothing sexy about hearing these words from Professor Shriner's mouth, and Jason's dick softened rapidly. He shifted in his seat, able to breathe again and strangely grateful for Professor Shriner's long nose, bald head, and harsh voice.

"In addition, the scent of the omega's ejaculate during heat is strong. Between that and the noises of pleasure he emits, an alpha will enter full rut as soon as his omega's fluids spurt from his penis. He will not stop until he has deposited his semen as deep and as far into the omega's womb as he can." Professor Shriner's jowls shook as he spoke, and his cheeks flushed.

Jason grimaced, his cock going utterly flaccid. Hopefully their teacher wasn't getting aroused talking about these things. He was too old now to rut and inseminate and *own*, wasn't he? If Professor Shriner's omega still lived, if he hadn't died in childbirth as so many of the older generation had, the poor thing must be far too elderly to bear children now. Professor Shriner surely hadn't dealt with an omega in heat in over twenty years.

But perhaps he remembered it fondly.

Jason's nose wrinkled.

Professor Shriner motioned toward his helper, a chubby beta in his forties. "Open the windows, Robston. The smell in here is pure lust. These boys are balls of hormones and my nostrils are burning with their pheromones."

Jason had to agree. While he could still easily pick out Xan's familiar scent, he was also flooded by the smell of the other nine alphas in the room. Their pheromones were sharp and challenging, egging him into a state of mild aggression, ready and willing to fight should his omega come onto the scene.

Though, of course, no omega would.

Only older omegas, either already bonded or past the age of hope, were allowed on Mont Nessadare's campus. The young omegas, from whom Jason, Xan, and the others could hope to locate their *Érosgápe*, were kept until the age of majority at Mont Juror's campus the next county over.

In two years—wolf-god, it seemed forever from now—they'd go to meet the latest crop of omegas. Ideally, they'd imprint on one, a biological response that marked the omega as their *Érosgápe*, and a contract would be struck. If not, they'd try again the next year and the year after that, before they'd choose to contract with unmatched omega.

If, however, he found his *Érosgápe*, the omega would be weaned from the heat suppressant used during adolescence, and once he was itching for a mate, greedy with need, and all sense of self-protection or self-interest dampened by the excruciating lust burning him from the inside out, they'd consummate the imprint.

Jason had heard whispers that his parents had consummated their imprint in the antechamber of his grandparents' attorney's office home shortly after his parents had signed their contract. But time and loss had quieted Father and Pater greatly, and the men Jason knew now were beyond pragmatic about their physical relationship, while maintaining a deep *Érosgápe* love.

For his omega's first time, though, Jason wanted to hustle him back to his own room at his parents' home to take his time exploring the man's needs and wants. He didn't want it to be some animalistic, semi-public event. Still, he wasn't foolish enough to assume if his omega begged him on the steps of the courthouse itself that he'd have the power to deny him.

Everyone knew that despite their passive position in the act of creation, omegas held great power over alphas. That's why there was an old saying: *a dissatisfied omega will be an alpha's noose.*

"Wolf-god, you'd think they wanted us to jizz ourselves," Xan said as class broke up. "C'mon, let's get back to the dorm. I need to do something with all this energy before I lose my mind."

Jason slung his backpack onto his shoulder, admiring Xan's tight ass in his dress pants and the way his shoulders stretched the perfectly tailored blue oxford shirt on his back as he followed behind. Yes, getting back to the dorm was a great idea. Xan was usually full of those.

XAN TOSSED HIS backpack onto the desk on his side of the dorm room and immediately started on the buttons of his shirt. "Don't make me wait," he hissed. "I'm so horny, I think I could turn a beta into an omega if I fucked him hard enough."

Jason admired Xan's hairless chest as it was revealed, his own cock waking up again. He worked open his belt buckle and kicked off his new-for-university leather loafers before asking, "How will we do this?"

Xan smirked. "Like you're going to offer up your ass?"

Jason laughed. "Never."

"I can't deal with just hand jobs today and I don't want a mouthful of your spunk."

"Sounds like you wanna play my omega again."

Xan's pale cheeks flushed, the light freckles on his nose glowing with his skin. "Make me." He toed off his own shiny shoes and shoved his pants down. "I want to see you try."

Xan was good at playing the greedy, inciting omega. His wide blue eyes and sweetly shaped red mouth, as well as his hungry asshole, were perfect for the part.

"I'll fuck you until you come screaming and begging for my knot."

Xan groaned. "You make promises you can't keep."

Jason lifted his brows.

It was true he couldn't knot Xan, as it took omega heat phero-mones to activate that biological function, but he'd make him come screaming all the same. He'd done it before and he'd do it again. Their room in high school had been cited five times by the dorm monitors for afterhours rowdiness. But really Xan had just been coming his brains out on Jason's plunging cock.

"Get on your knees," Jason barked, finally naked. "Bend over the bed and show me your hole."

Xan's lips twisted up in a mocking smirk. Not surprising since he was an alpha, too. He had to curb his own instincts to play this game with Jason. But that was what Xan loved about it, in Jason's opinion—the challenge of submitting when he had every right to say no, every right to challenge Jason to a fight instead of throwing himself across the bed, ass up, and spreading his cheeks wide.

What a view.

Xan glanced over his shoulder, making his eyes as round as possible, a pretense at the inciting guileless innocence many omegas exuded in the throes of heat. "It hurts. I need you."

Jason's cock flared to life at the words, so common among ome-gas that they were more a cliché than a real seduction, but apparently that was all it took. Nineteen, horny, teased by pretty damn great pornography in the guise of an educational film, and Jason was easier than adding two plus two.

He tweaked his own nipples, gazing down at Xan's naked form, lithe and beautiful, spread over the bed just like Jason's own omega's body would be one day. He needed some faux slick, though. Xan didn't make it, and to plunge into his hole dry would be painful to them both.

He slammed open his desk drawer and found the oil he kept there. The small bottle was still greasy on the outside from having used it the day before—the last time they'd played this particular game.

"You mine?" he asked, thrusting his voice into a lower register, pleased by the rumble in his growl. He wished he had the bulk to back it up. A glance to the mirror showed his beardless face looked as young as ever, and his naked chest lacked more than a scraggly promise of eventual chest hair.

"Always," Xan said, arching his back and shoving his ass out.

Jason grinned, dragged Xan fully up onto the bed, and kissed his mouth.

As they made out, he ran oil slick fingers over and into Xan's hole, getting him slippery, making him pant. An alpha's prostate wasn't as large or sensitive as an omega's, but it still brought pleasure when stroked.

"I want you to come in me," Xan muttered, his wide lips pressed against Jason's throat. "Need your seed. Fill me up."

Jason growled, his balls throbbing. "Shut up. You'll make me jizz and I'm not even in you yet."

"Some alpha you'll be if you can't even wait until you're inside your fake omega before coming."

"Watch it, asshole."

Xan laughed. "Why? You'll spurt all over the face of your real one if you don't get some control. Then what'll he do? Fuck himself silly on a dildo, crying and begging for you to get hard again? Pathetic."

"You know rebound isn't a problem for me." And it really wouldn't be a problem with an omega's pheromones surrounding him. "But if you don't shut up, I won't let you come on my dick."

"Like I care."

"Like that isn't your favorite thing about this game."

Xan grinned. "Get it in me and we'll see if you can be a good alpha and let your omega come first."

Jason narrowed his eyes, flipping Xan onto his back easily. Penetration was always delicious. He loved the sensation of it. So much so that he put off actually doing it a little longer in order to imagine the hot, squeezing flesh parting around his alpha cock first.

He was proud of his dick. It was the only fully-grown part of him, as far as he could tell. It was fat and long, and alpha-sized. Jutting out from his body, all thick and meaty, it looked like it belonged on Wilbet Monhundy. Or on Xan's massive father—a man with even more muscle than money. And the man had a lot of money.

Jason rubbed his giant cock against Xan's, pleased, as always, that it was half an inch thicker than Xan's and a three-quarters of an inch longer.

He didn't have a lot of alpha cocks to compare his own to, especially not hard ones. But over the summer he'd stumbled onto a small pile of old pornography films in the basement of his parents' summer cottage by the beach. They'd probably been left behind by his cousin Jamil, when he'd spent six weeks at the cottage studying the life of salamanders for his doctoral studies. He'd been without his omega for the first time since they'd met, and likely he'd have been horny as hell all alone like that.

Regardless, Jason had looked at the films every chance he could over the summer, and he'd been thrilled to find his cock was bigger than both the alphas in those movies. He'd be able to reach farther into his omega's womb and bring him more pleasure, not to mention increase the likelihood of impregnation.

Staring down at Xan's enraptured face, Jason stroked his cock. "Open up for me, omega."

Xan shuddered, spread his legs, and stared up at Jason feverishly, quivering as Jason pushed inside. "Fuck, you bastard," he hissed. "You're big."

Though omegas often commented on size as a way to egg their

alpha on, Jason knew Xan wasn't playing. His eyes shaded darker as he strained to accept Jason's girth, so Jason backed off. He slid out and then pushed against Xan's slick sphincter, groaning as it opened around him like a tight, gripping sleeve.

"Fuck," Xan whispered again. This time his head tilted back, exposing his pale throat and pounding pulse. "So good. You feel so good, Jason."

Flicking his blond hair off his forehead, Jason grinned smugly down at Xan. "Omega, that's an alpha cock in your ass. Show me how grateful you are for it."

Xan shuddered hard. "So grateful."

"Show me."

Xan clenched around him and threw his hips up to catch Jason's thrusts.

"Yes, that's right." Jason tugged Xan's cock, something he'd never have to do for a real omega: they came anally from omega gland and prostate gland stimulation. He whispered, "Look at your slutty hole all open for my come. Want my babies, omega? Want me to fill you up?"

"Give it to me," Xan muttered, his chest flushing and his nipples budding up tight. "Give me your jizz."

"Mm, you want it bad."

"So bad."

"You want my knot?"

"Yes!"

Jason closed his eyes, blocking out Xan's familiar face. He wanted an omega, a real one, a slick-assed, whining, begging, writhing omega beneath him, crying real tears for his come, pleading for his babies, begging to belong to him, and be owned by him, and to come all over his dick, screaming, riding, convulsing in helpless—

"Jason!" Xan cried out, his body jerking as thick wetness splashed between them.

The grip of Xan's asshole and Jason's urgent fantasies swamped him. Come rocketed from his balls and pumped out of his dick in massive wads. He felt it load up Xan's ass and spill out around his cock. He'd be able to jizz so much more when he finally had an omega in heat and knotted in an orgasm that went on for minutes, not just long seconds like this one. He grunted, thrust hard one more time, and felt a final spurt of pleasure.

He moaned, collapsing on Xan's sweaty body. "You okay?"

"Yeah," Xan said, his voice quiet and his body quivering. "Fine."

"Feel good?"

Xan shrugged, and Jason knew the post-orgasm guilt was settling on him like it did every time Jason fucked him.

"Shh," Jason said. "No one knows. No one will ever know. It's just you and me. When we get our omegas, we'll be glad we practiced."

He left it unsaid, and so did Xan that the only one really practicing was Jason. Xan, if his predilection was discovered, would be an outcast among alphas. Only betas and omegas got fucked. Everyone knew that.

But Xan liked it. And Jason didn't think it meant a damn thing. Liking it didn't make Xan less of a man or an alpha.

"We have fun; that's all that matters," he whispered, snuffling into Xan's hair. He wrapped an arm around him and pulled him close. "Tell me what you want your omega to be like."

Xan was quiet a long minute, but he finally answered, "Tall, blond, handsome."

It was his usual answer, but Jason wasn't satisfied. "Give me more than that. What do you want him to be *like*? On the inside?"

Xan shrugged. "I dunno. I never think that far. I just think about putting my cock in him. Breeding. That's it. It doesn't matter what I want anyway. Our bodies will choose, if we're lucky. We'll react to some stranger's pheromones, imprint, and that will be that."

Jason frowned. "Why sound so hopeless about it?" He thought it was romantic, himself. Finding his *Érosgápe*. Knowing immediately. Feeling that surge of lust and ownership. He patted Xan's arm lazily. "It's the way it's always been." At least since the Great Death.

Xan shrugged again before rolling up onto an elbow to reach for tissues on the bedside table. "Exactly. It's the way it's always been. So why think about it? We'll get what we get and we won't pitch a fit."

Jason let Xan move out of his arms to clean up, his lips set in a small frown. He didn't feel that way at all, and he wished Xan didn't, either.

Meeting his omega would be the best thing that ever happened to him if he were lucky enough to find his *Érosgápe*. No matter who that omega was, if he was his *Érosgápe*, then Jason knew he'd be happy. Thrilled. In love. They'd live happily ever after in their bond. Like his parents and grandparents before him.

What could there ever be to pitch a fit about?

# CHAPTER TWO

"Yes!" Xan pulled his head out of the return bin at the university library and held up a red-spined text triumphantly. "I knew some nerd would have completed the assignment early."

"That's the wrong edition," Jason said, shaking his head. "The spine on the latest one is blue."

He knew that because *he* was a nerd who'd completed the assignment early. As in a week early. An omega would want a smart, resourceful, educated alpha, and he wasn't going to fall down on the job. He'd been a good student his whole life, but especially ever since presenting as an alpha at fifteen. There were expectations to be met.

Earlier in the week, when he'd finished the assignment, he'd offered the text to Xan, but the dummy had waved him off and said he'd get his own copy from the library later.

"Dig a little deeper," he suggested. "It might be at the bottom if someone turned it in late last night."

He admired the way Xan's neck reddened in his irritation as he dug around in the bottom of the bin. It brought to mind how his body flushed when they played alpha and omega—like they had yet again that morning.

He'd lucked out in a roommate all those years ago. Other alphas either spent a ton of quality time with their hand, or they had to cultivate close friendships with willing betas, because once the storm of puberty hit, so did nearly torturous peaks of horniness.

Jason used to have beta pals in his neighborhood at home, and some of them had been willing to accommodate his needs when he was younger. But now that his cock had grown into its full alpha size, most had decided the pain wasn't worth the pleasure anymore. Betas were more like Old World men. Their anus wasn't as robust or elastic as an omega's and their pain tolerance not as high as an alpha's. Luckily, over the summer at his parents' beach cottage, he'd met a few slightly older betas that enjoyed alpha dick. He hadn't liked the casualness of those encounters, though. There was no foundation of friendship for role-play, or laughter, or fun.

With Xan, he had all that and more.

Xan's high pain tolerance made the penetration pleasurable for him, as far as Jason could tell, and he loved to play in every sense of the word. Jason smiled slightly, remembering Xan's helpless laughter that morning as Jason had licked his hairy armpit, demanding his 'omega' submit to a tongue bath.

"Shit." Xan chucked another book to the side and dug even deeper into the pile, his ass up in the air as he bent deeply into the bin. "Why doesn't wolf-god love me? What have I ever done to offend him?"

*Oh, just ridden another alpha's cock and begged for more.*

Jason bit his cheek. It wouldn't do to say anything in public about the games he and Xan played in private. Xan had enough internal conflict over it. He didn't need more, even as a joke.

What Xan allowed Jason to do to him violated half a dozen commandments of the Holy Book of Wolf. Being unmanned— that's how the holy book referred to an alpha being penetrated. It wasn't just unseemly or unusual; it represented a loss of status, as evidenced by the use of wrestling and rape between alphas in the early years of Wolf to establish power and dominance or to exert authority and claim lands.

Now, power and dominance were all in a family's name, reputation, and holdings in today's world. Thank wolf-god for that. With his long-scrawny limbs, so like his Pater's, he'd never be able to take down someone like Wilbet Monhundy. No, if he had to fight for his place in society, he'd be on his stomach in a heartbeat, ass up, taking a massive alpha cock, and resisting every second of it.

Good thing the world was more civilized now.

The door behind them opened and closed, letting in the cool fall air. Jason shivered beneath his light jacket.

"Maybe this one is close enough," Xan said, pulling the red-spined book out again. "How different can one edition be from another, really?"

Jason snatched the book from his hand, flipped through the pages, and tossed it back into the bin. "Different enough."

"Hey! I need that."

"I'm telling you, you don't. The first chapters on reproduction and the stuff about omega glands and the production of slick are totally different."

"How?"

"They used to think that the omega glands swelled painfully during heat solely because the extra slick was needed for the alpha's knot, but now they know the alpha's pre-come and semen play a role in reducing the inflammation as well, changing the pain to pleasure for the omega. That's why alpha dildos and fists only go so far in relieving the pain, and why omegas aren't as easily satisfied when alphas use condoms. The new theory states that the pain of overly swollen omega glands and the anti-inflammatory properties of alpha semen serve as yet another way of propelling the species to come together and procreate. Anyway, all of that's totally different in the new book. Dr. Romaire Epstar had that big break on all of this last year, remember?"

"Why would I know that? Why would *you* know that?"

Jason rolled his eyes and glanced at his watch. "Because I'm an enormous nerd, Xan."

He was a nerd with a pretty face, wealthy parents who owned a busy shipping company, and a trust fund to keep him in style until he inherited the rest, but a nerd all the same. Jason resented his social standing, though he knew he was lucky to never have to worry about money. When it came to society parties and the like, he'd rather stay home and read lame science journals for fun, and Xan knew it. They were both powerful men's sons, and yet they were both barely on the edge of their school's social sphere for a reason.

Jason went on, "Besides, who has the photographic memory here? Me or you?"

"You," Xan agreed reluctantly. "And I hate it. Living with you for four more years is going to be insufferable." He shot Jason a hot look from under his lashes, and Jason's dick twitched.

"Yeah, insufferable. If we're lucky, it won't be four years," Jason reminded him. "Only two more until we meet with the first group of available omegas at Mont Juror to see if any are our *Érosgápe*."

And if they didn't find their bond-mate, they had four more years of meetings with Mont Juror mature omegas before they'd be pressured to contract with an unbonded omega through one of the Philia Committee soirées.

Xan gave a tight smile and nodded. "Right. No more need for roommates then. Or not like now." He paused and cleared his throat, his blue eyes darkening as he searched Jason's.

"If we're lucky," Jason agreed.

Xan's gaze fell back to the pile of books in the book return bin. "Shit." He chewed on his bottom lip. "How am I going to write this paper?"

Jason tugged on Xan's soft jacket sleeve, smiling at the expensive fabric and stylish cut of his friend's clothing. Never a penny spared to look as smart as possible where Xan was concerned. Jason didn't spare expense either, but he kept things simpler. No fancy fabrics or bow ties, like Xan enjoyed—just nice-fitting pants, a solid navy button-up shirt tailored to fit well, and new leather loafers.

"C'mon," he said kindly. "You can read what I wrote and I'll help you write something almost as good."

"Almost, huh?"

"Yeah, almost." He slung his arm around Xan's shoulder, turning to leave the library. Contentment pooled in his gut. "Can't have you doing better than me when you didn't even read the assignment."

Afternoon sun shone in through the clear glass windows that scaled up to the ceiling at the library's entrance. A collection of professors and their graduate student assistants gathered around a large round table a few yards from the entrance, papers, pens, and notepads scattered everywhere. A lively conversation was underway in urgent, hushed voices.

Jason spotted Dr. Obi, the upper-level professor he hoped to land as his advisor for the research he wanted to do on the expression of the engineered wolf gene in post-Old World humans. Specifically he wanted to explore the role it played in instigating heat in omegas and mounting urges in alphas.

He'd already checked out theses on similar topics from the library, discovering that a lot of his original questions had already been answered. But there was still so much more to understand about the Great Death, the advent of alphas and omegas, and the role their engineered genes played in post-Old World human behavior.

Jason was grateful the Wolf Above Party had been defeated seventeen years prior, allowing scientists in the universities to extend and expand their research on post-Old World humanity. Science had finally been freed from the tyranny of religion, and Jason was ready to get on board. Though to express that opinion publicly was a risky thing. The Holy Book of Wolf was still considered a more important document then their government's Constitution. But no one could deny science and technology had grown in leaps and bounds in the seventeen years since the New Wolf Reform Party had taken charge.

Unfortunately, in Jason's opinion, the New Wolf Reform party didn't go far enough in the civil rights department to challenge the strict laws regarding reproduction and omega rights, but at least they'd opened the door for advances in technology and science.

Dr. Obi was a real pioneer in the study of post-Old World genetics, and Jason admired his work greatly. Optimistically, he steered Xan toward the group of professors, hoping he might steal an opportunity to ingratiate himself in a brief conversation with Dr. Obi and win his favor.

His gaze swung from the frowning, grizzled face of Dr. Obi to a handsome omega standing beside him, and his heart stopped. Sheer beauty assaulted his senses: pale skin, dark hair, green eyes, and flesh that smelled like bliss. The omega stood tall and sharp-dressed in navy trousers, a black belt, and a moss-green oxford shirt, and he gripped the arm of a tall, muscular alpha in a tweed jacket.

One moment Jason had his arm around Xan, and the next his life as he knew it ended.

A raw, musky scent flooded Jason's nose and throat, coating his mucous membranes. His eyes rolled up in his head as the scent drilled deep into his brain, awakening him with a soul-deep shiver. Pounding, urgent lust peeled his humanity away, leaving only animal instinct. His cock roared with blood. His body screamed with raw need and yearning.

Shrieks of shock barely registered in his pheromone-focused drive to get his hands and mouth on source of that mind-warpingly perfect scent. He grabbed his delicious-smelling omega, buried his face in the curve of his neck, and rutted his hips against him, growling as strong hands tried to pull him away.

His omega fought, shoving desperately, until Jason gripped his throat, stilling his struggles. He smelled his omega's terror and confusion, rolling off him in waves of stench that nearly overpowered the sweet, musky aroma that had triggered Jason's whirl of madness. Needing to touch skin, he tore at his omega's clothing, his cock pulsing wetly in his pants, echoing the musky scent of slick slipping from his omega's ass. He wanted to drown himself in that smell, rub it all over himself, die with his cock buried deep in his omega's sweet ass and dripping with his omega's slick.

His omega let loose a wild cry.

Jason released his hold on his omega's throat, color and sound spinning around him, torn between comforting his terrified omega and lashing out in rage at the hands still trying to tug him away.

"Shh." The hushing sound cut through the whirlpool of his mind. His omega gripped his hair and tugged at him, trying to meet his eyes. "Calm down now. Shh. I've got you. You're all right."

That *voice*.

Like honey and sand pouring over him, gritty and warm, sweet and itchy. Jason wanted to hear that voice every second of every day for the rest of his life. He wanted to strip this man until he was naked and pleading beneath him, begging for his cock and crying to carry Jason's babies.

But hands kept grabbing at him, voices kept calling to him, and he was really starting to get pissed off.

"Let him go!" his omega snarled. "Or he'll rip me to pieces, for fuck's sake."

"Jason, buddy. Not here." Xan's desperate voice rang in the air around him. "You need to calm down now. This isn't how it's supposed to work."

Who gave a shit about supposed to? He had his omega right beside him, and he was never letting him go.

Xan put his hand carefully on Jason's arm, and Jason growled at him, barely hearing his words. "You have to register first, contract with his family, or he can press assault charges. You know the rules. You need to calm down. Right now."

Jason's cells screamed to possess the man he held protectively in his arms and had backed up to the table. He wanted to kiss his omega's pink, lush, gaping mouth. He wanted to rip his pants down and get his fingers drenched in the slick seeping from the man's anus in readiness for Jason's cock.

It was the fear in his omega's arresting moss-green eyes that held Jason back more than Xan's tugging grip, or his sensible words, or the strong arm of another alpha laid across Jason's chest. More than the security guards hustling into the library with syringes at the ready to prick him with alpha sedative, more than the quelling lull of the drug rushing into his system as they reached him and jabbed those sharp points into his neck, arm, and thigh. No, it was the glint of terror in those beautiful, perfect, soft green eyes that made Jason stand down.

He couldn't look away as his knees went weak and he collapsed onto the stretcher the security guards had rolled up to catch his fall. He held out his hand, a cold horror enveloping him as the room grew fuzzy and distant, like in a dream. Fingers took hold of his, and he blinked his eyes open again, grateful to see his omega holding his hand.

"Get his information," Xan said to one of the guards harshly. "We'll need it for his alpha's parents."

"Wolf-god," the alpha standing next to Jason's omega whispered. "How the hell...?"

Jason snarled at the man groggily, tried to lift up from the stretcher to tear the alpha's eyes out for daring to speak to his omega when he was slick and opening for a cock. He'd rip the man's eyes out and then tear his testicles to shreds. He'd kill him for looking at his omega, for smelling his aroma.

"Shh," his omega soothed him. "He's a friend."

Jason didn't like the sound of that, but his omega's calming hand on his shoulder was almost as soothing as the alpha-sedative the guards had hit him with.

"How is this possible?" the other alpha asked, and Jason lunged again, but his omega stilled him by pressing him back onto the stretcher. "He can't be old enough for you."

"Apparently, he is, Urho," his omega murmured, stroking his thumb soothingly against Jason's wrist. Jason shuddered at the lush, velvet heat of his omega's voice, and he offered up a grateful smile that felt like it was going to melt off his face and slide to the floor. His omega smiled back tentatively, his teeth white and straight, his eyes still glinting with fear. "It's fine. Don't say anything more right now."

Jason tried to get a good look at his omega, but the world was hazing in and out now. He gripped his omega's fingers and let his eyes fall closed, listening hard to what he could make out around him.

"Name and address where you can be reached for the next few days?" a security guard asked, and Jason peeled his eyes open to see the beta standing close, a notepad in hand, and a serious expression on his face.

"Vale Aman," his omega said.

*Vale.*

Such a beautiful name. Jason's heart constricted and released, a twisting ache that made him gasp.

"You don't have to give them any information," Urho interrupted, placing his hand on Vale's arm, until Vale flinched back from him with a pointed look down at Jason.

"But I do, don't I?" he said. "It's the law."

"He's just a child. He can't be yours. He's too young."

"Don't you mean I'm too old?" Vale sighed and closed his eyes, releasing Jason from their spell. "I'm still of child-bearing age. His claim is valid." His cheeks reddened, and Jason was on fire for him. "Now let me get this over with. I'm Valendo Aman, known as Vale, of 981 Oak Avenue, and I'll be happy to entertain this young alpha's parents as the law commands." He swallowed hard and squeezed Jason's hand reassuringly. "Is that all?"

"Don't you want to know *his* name?" Xan asked.

Vale glanced his way, startled. "Yes. I suppose I do." He gazed down at Jason appraisingly. "And who are you?"

Jason opened his mouth, but the alpha-sedative had made his tongue numb. His lips trembled on an inarticulate groan.

"He's Jason Sabel, son of Yule Sabel and Miner Hoff. A good family." Somehow Xan's tone implied that Jason's family was better than his omega deserved, and Jason tried to shoot him a glare of warning, but his eyes could barely stay open.

As the guards secured Jason to the stretcher, preparing to take him out of the library, he fought to stare up at Vale, mesmerized by his green eyes.

"And here I thought I was in the clear," Vale murmured, almost to himself, but Jason heard him clearly through the mess in his head. Vale pressed his bow-shaped mouth into a line and cleared his throat. "It's not the first time I've been wrong. It won't be the last."

"You mean you thought you were free," Xan said, a little nastily, crossing his arms over his chest. Jason slurred a snarl at him, but Xan ignored him. "You hoped your alpha was dead."

"Hope isn't quite the word," Vale said softly, his gaze gratifyingly fixed to Jason's. "And it appears he's only slow to arrive." He smiled down at him, a bitter-tinged, sad thing that Jason wanted to erase and replace with radiance. "Took his time."

"In what? Getting born?" Xan sneered. "Or maybe you were fast. I bet you're one of *those* omegas. I bet you're not even pure."

Jason launched at Xan, tugging against the restraints the guards had secured only moments before. He'd pummel his friend, pound him, break his face for his insults.

"Take him," a security guard called out.

Jason clung to Vale's fingers, tugging him along, until Vale bent low and whispered, "Let go now."

Eager to please, Jason dropped Vale's hand and then crowed in misery as the guards ripped him away, carting him out into the blinding afternoon sun.

# CHAPTER THREE

"YOU DESERVE BETTER," Xan said, clenching his jaw. He lounged in the chair beside Jason's bed in the university health clinic waiting for the alpha-sedative to be cleared from his system and for Jason's parents to show up. "He's old. Used up."

Jason shoved the mop of blond hair off his forehead and glared at Xan. "I will end you if you don't shut your mouth."

"Didn't you see him?" Xan's lips curled up disdainfully.

"Yes. He was beautiful."

"Gray on his temples. Wrinkles around his eyes. He's thirty-five if he's a day and maybe even forty."

A strange, unsettled feeling wriggled into Jason's stomach. As the sedative had worn off, he found he couldn't remember much about his omega except for his moss-colored eyes and mouthwatering scent.

Oh, and his voice.

Such a sweet, delicious voice, like honey and sand, rhythmic and crashing in gentle waves against his soul. The memory of that voice made him quiver. But he couldn't recall how tall the man was, or the color of his hair, or the shape of his face, or anything to indicate his age at all.

Jason lifted his chin. "He's beautiful," he declared again.

"Pheromone delirium," Xan said dismissively.

Jason's fists balled up. "What did you say?"

Xan's voice was terse with frustration. "You heard me. I'm trying to protect you here. That's all."

"By insulting my omega?"

"He's not yours yet, is he?" Xan's blue eyes pleaded with Jason. "Be sensible here."

"I am. You're just jealous."

Xan's eyes flew wide. "I'm not. We're just...you and I aren't...I don't have feelings for you."

Jason stared at Xan, the meaning of his words chilling him like a cold blanket of snow. "Of course you don't. You're jealous I got my omega early." He crossed his arms over his chest and tried to convince himself he didn't see the hurt deep in Xan's eyes.

"Yeah, right. You're not going to get to consummate the imprint with him for a long time. You know that, right? He has to contract with you first, and your parents will drag that out if they know what's good for you. And they do, so they will." Xan nodded decisively. "Hell, they'll probably suggest a surrogate, because that only makes sense. He's too old to risk childbearing, even if he's fertile still. And they'll want you with an omega who can give you more than one."

"I'll never take a surrogate."

"Oh yeah? Just wait. When you're not blinded by pheromones, you'll see what a bad risk this omega is. He'll never give birth to healthy offspring. You'll be doomed to an old, sickly omega with no future for your name."

The Sabels weren't one of the most prestigious families in the upper crust of society, but they weren't without their reputation. He needed an heir or two. Maybe three.

"Shut up. You don't know what you're talking about."

Xan shrugged. "Fine. Have it your way."

"Mr. Sabel, Mr. Hoff, your son is right in here."

Jason struggled into a fully seated position, dizziness plaguing him as his father and pater hustled into the small room.

Father's bright blue eyes, always tender and loving, were dark with worry, and Pater's hazel ones were tired and ringed with darkness. They were both dressed more casually than usual: Father in a pair of khaki trousers with the sleeves of his white oxford shirt rolled up, and Pater in a soft shirt and winter-brown cardigan over well-worn, comfortable pants. They both had fresh haircuts. Father's blond hair was shaped into a neat style close to his head, and Pater's light brown was in a looser cut, a fringe draping clean and straight against his forehead, in a style like Jason's own.

Jason remembered that Pater had just gone through a heat several weeks earlier. A pang of guilt hit him at being the reason he'd left his doctor prescribed post-heat month-long respite. Pater was fragile, and Father usually zealously protected his rest period for the full four weeks. But apparently, Jason accosting an omega in the middle of the university library was enough reason for Pater to be out and about, health be damned.

"I'll leave you alone," said the nurse who'd taken over Jason's care once he was awake, mainly providing him with water to help wash the sedative out of his system. "Chancellor Rory will be here soon—any moment, I'm sure—to discuss this situation."

The nurse clearly didn't want to be in the room for whatever conversation was going to take place. He was a beta, like most non-doctor healthcare providers, but the idea of lingering for gossip clearly didn't appeal.

"Yes, thank you," Father said.

"Jason, are you all right?" Pater asked, full of worry, sitting on the side of Jason's bed to slip his fingers through Jason's hair.

Father crowded behind him, somehow hovering protectively over them both. Anxiety for his family poured off him in sour-scented waves Jason's sensitive nose recognized from times when Pater had been sick after a brutal miscarriage.

Xan said, "You should wonder if his omega is all right."

*His* omega, huh? Hadn't Xan just said he wasn't Jason's yet?

Asshole.

Pater's eyebrows drew down. "Oh, son. What happened?"

Jason tucked his chin down, wanting to wrap his arms around Pater and seek his solid warmth for comfort. But he was a soon-to-be contracted alpha now. He couldn't act like a spoiled little whelp.

"He was just *there* and I couldn't—I didn't mean to—it just took over." Jason didn't want his fragile pater thinking he was a brute.

Pater squeezed his hand reassuringly. "That's the reason young omegas and alphas are introduced under close supervision." He turned his gaze to Father. "What was a juvenile, unbonded omega doing on an alpha campus?"

"He's old," Xan said with a sniff.

"What?" Father darted a confused glance Xan's way and then back to Jason. "What does Xan mean by that?"

Jason shrugged. He didn't want to explain even though his parents would discover the truth eventually. But he didn't want their minds poisoned by Xan's opinion, so he shot a glare at Xan again, daring him with his eyes to speak another word against his omega.

Xan glared back.

"We're here for Jason now, Xan. You can go," Father said shortly. His tone was tired and thin. Jason knew how careful he had to be during Pater's heat to fulfill his own alpha needs without hurting or impregnating Pater, and then afterward he took care of Pater through his respite as diligently as an omega with a newborn. As tired as Pater looked, Father was probably equally exhausted.

"Xan can't go," Jason said. "He's a witness." Humiliation burned like a coal in his belly. "He has to make a report to the police, too."

"The police are coming? Here?" Pater glanced around the room. "Did you injure him, son? Or give him reason to file for assault?"

Jason shook his head, remembering the way he'd gripped Vale's throat, torn his clothes, and bent him over the table. But the man had been on his feet when they'd carted Jason away on the stretcher. He hadn't said anything about filing for assault despite Jason's out-of-control behavior. He'd given his information willingly and said he'd be awaiting contact from Jason's parents. Surely he wouldn't change his mind now, would he?

Jason's nostrils flared.

There'd been that other alpha on the scene. Urho. He hadn't heard the man's last name. He'd encouraged Vale *not* to cooperate. What if he'd gotten under Vale's skin once Jason was gone? Convinced him that Jason was too young, too unpredictable? And what if he persuaded Vale to claim assault to the police?

Jason's gut curled tight in fear and self-loathing. Some alpha he was: he hadn't controlled himself and had been carted off like a lunatic. He'd made a horrible first impression. He'd be amazed if Vale wanted to submit to him now or ever. *Of course* he'd probably file for assault. Why shouldn't he? And that other alpha...if he touched Vale, if he had a role in keeping Vale away from him? Jason would have no choice but to tear his throat out or die trying.

Gritting his teeth, he squeezed his eyes shut and tried to get a grip on his emotions. He was not going to be a child about this. He was going to be a man, an alpha, and woo his omega into falling on his knees willingly. Where he belonged. He just had no idea how to even start with that. None of what was happening was by the book.

"Did you hurt this omega, son?" Father asked, gently touching Jason's chin to bring his gaze up. His father's eyes were tender and blue, soft like a sky, with a wheat-colored ring near the pupil. "I understand how hard it can be to control the impulse. And taken by surprise like that, in your first week of university, it's a wonder you didn't do more damage. But I know you'd never intend to hurt him."

Jason's throat grew too tight to talk, but he shook his head.

"The omega was fine," Xan interjected again. "Not for lack of Jason's barbarous attempts to disrobe and mount him, mind you."

Shame curled in tight, and he pulled his hand out of Pater's grip to hide his face.

Xan went on, tone irritated. "The omega was calm enough about it. Got Jason to unhand him, at least."

He wished he knew why Xan was so mad. Jason's life had exploded into a big mess and Jason could use a friend's gentle support right now.

"His omega's name is Valendo Aman, by the way. Goes by Vale, apparently. Lives on Oak."

"Those are nice homes, Yule," Pater said to Father, hope threading into his tone, despite the worried crinkle on his forehead. "He must come from a good family. We'll need to speak to his parents."

"Good luck with that," Xan said under his breath.

Father's eyes narrowed on him again. "What the hell is going on? Jason?"

Chancellor Rory's bald head poked into the room at that moment. Another alpha added to the mix, and when his eyes narrowed on Pater, Father straightened up sharply. Pater averted his gaze to the floor.

Chancellor Rory adjusted his vest and cleared his throat, taking a moment to adapt to Pater's post-heat pheromones, and then he entered the room with a warm smile for Father. "Good evening, Mr. Sabel, Mr. Hoff. It seems we've run into quite the situation, doesn't it?"

"It does indeed," Jason's father said roughly. "I think the first question I'd like answered is what was a young, unbonded omega doing on campus to begin with? What fool brought him here?"

"I see Jason hasn't told you much about his omega." He ran his hand over his shiny dome. "Mr. Sabel, Mr. Hoff, your son's omega is not from this year's crop—"

"Next year's?" Pater said quietly. "So young!"

"No, Miner," Father said, obviously putting the pieces together. "He's older than Jason."

"Oh!" Pater frowned. "Then he should know better than to be on campus. How did he ever get in?"

"Vale Aman is a professor here," Chancellor Rory said, raising his eyebrows and letting that sink in. "He's thirty-five. Well past the expected imprinting age. He never found his *Érosgápe*." He shrugged and pulled air through his teeth. "Assumptions were made." He flicked his gaze to Jason. "It's an unusual situation. We'd assumed Vale's alpha was dead or otherwise incapable of finding his omega. Professor Aman has lived alone as an uncontracted omega for nearly fourteen years."

"Wolf-god, what a mess," Father whispered, pinching his fingers between his eyes and sighing.

"He's healthy?" Pater asked.

"Quite. As far as I know. Never missed a class outside of heats and always available for students and other professors alike. Intelligent. Educated. Fantastic work ethic." He clucked his teeth. "That will have to change, obviously. A newly imprinted alpha isn't going to react well to his omega teaching classrooms full of virile young competition. Vale will need to make arrangements, and so will the school. I'll be down a professor."

"You say that like it's Jason's fault," Father said, crossing his arms over his chest.

"Everyone knows imprinting between alpha and omega carries no fault. If we're lucky, we find our *Érosgápe*. If we're not, we settled for a contract, or go single in the world. It's as simple as that." He sighed. "I do fear for Jason. His omega has been on his own for quite some time. It won't be easy to bring him to heel. And Jason's so young, unschooled on control…"

Father's eyes narrowed. "Does this Vale Aman have ties to omega freedom groups?"

The chancellor shrugged. "I have no idea. But I do know Vale is a fiercely independent man. It's going to be a challenge no matter what."

Pater's eyebrows furrowed as he peered at Jason with worry. "Did he seem resistant?"

Jason shivered, his mind trying to encapsulate the way Vale had at first fought him, then subdued him, and finally cooperated with the law, but words failed him. His omega had been perfect, doing everything just the way he should have. Jason was the one who'd screwed up.

"He was surprised," Xan said. "But law abiding." He handed over the slip of paper with Vale's information to Father. "He said he'd wait to hear from you and Mr. Hoff."

Pater brushed his fingers over Jason's cheek again and whispered, "Don't worry. It's going to be okay."

"I've spoken with Vale," Chancellor Rory said. "He's at home, where he plans to stay until the police take his statement. Speaking of, they should be here soon for Jason and Xan's."

Jason's bladder ached after the many glasses of water he'd had since arriving at the university health clinic. His head was clearer than it had been since he'd first scented Vale, and he stood slowly on shaky legs to go take a leak.

Pater followed him like he was a toddler again, one hand on his elbow to keep him steady. Father was at Pater's side, watching *him*, and Jason huffed a laugh at the little trio of protectiveness they made together.

After he pissed and washed his hands, he got dressed slowly in the clothes he'd been wearing before arriving at the clinic. There was a slight tinge of his omega's scent lingering on the fabric, but he girded himself against going into another wild state. He refused to be in a doctor's office gown when the police came for his statement, and he *would* control himself. One bout of alpha madness was enough for the day. Jason assumed they had injected him with a dose of alpha quell when he arrived. That was supposed to help.

Pater stood by the window, arms crossed over his chest, looking out at the river. It flowed by the campus medical center, and Jason could make out the blue-and-gray waves with caps of white, rising and falling in the oncoming autumn wind. Pater's shoulders rounded tiredly, but he held himself with a pride that Jason wanted for his own omega one day. Miner Hoff knew who he was, whom he lived for, and who lived for him. It gave him a steadiness even his fragile health couldn't break.

Father stood by Jason's bed, watching him dress. He kept his hands shoved into his pockets and tilted back on his heels. His broad shoulders stretched his shirt. "Thirty-five years old," he whispered. "Childbirth will be problem—"

"Hush," Pater said over his shoulder. "Not now."

Father nodded his agreement in the way he always did when Pater made his desires explicitly known.

"The police have arrived," the nurse said, sticking his head in the door again. "They're checking in now."

"Good. Let's get this over with."

"And let's take Jason home right afterward," Pater murmured. "We'll decide how to proceed from there. Xan, you're welcome to join us if you'd like. I'm sure Jason could use a friend."

Xan glared at Jason from his seat by his bed. "No. I'll go back to the dorms and field the questions there. Everyone will want to know what's going on. Rumors will start if I don't put the record straight."

"If I hear later that you insulted him—"

Xan held up his hand. "I thought we trusted each other. With everything." His brows lifted, and Jason wondered how it could have only been this morning that he'd fucked Xan and played their dangerous game together.

"I trust you."

"Good," Xan said. "Because we need each other."

Before Jason could ask what he meant by that, two police officers entered the room, notepads in hand, and noses twitching at Pater's lingering post-heat scent. Jason watched his father place an arm around Pater's shoulders, shielding and announcing at the same time. He yearned to be that man for Vale. He hoped he'd get the chance.

If only he could remember what Vale looked like. If only he knew for sure Vale wanted it, too.

Then the questions started. Jason had to relive his humiliation, his near-assault of the man he hoped would bear his children, and to make it worse, he was fully aware that it was only the first recitation of many to come.

He'd have to tell the police, then tell the attorneys, then add a description in their contract, and in addition, he hoped to have a chance to tell Vale to his face what it had been like for him. So he could beg his forgiveness.

With any luck, Vale would grant it and fall to his knees in willing submission.

# CHAPTER FOUR

V ALE STIRRED THE fire with a brass poker.
It was early in the season to need additional warmth, but the study he'd created from his pater's old gardening room was poorly insulated and drafty. It was also crowded with books, loose papers, sketches, and notes he'd made over the years, and which he never knew how to file away. The furniture was all fairly new, purchased by his own earnings with his first check after making professor at Mont Nessadare. The floor was carefully laid polished brick, and the windows along the back of the room looked out on the overgrown garden, abandoned to nature since his pater's death.

Vale loved his study. But he couldn't bring himself to sit on the leather couch or to collapse at his wide, wooden desk. Instead, he paced by the fire, leaning against the mantle now and again to peer into the flames. He glanced toward Urho, who sank into the leather wingback chair they both preferred, swirling a tumbler of bourbon with a thoughtful expression. He couldn't be more opposite of the boy who'd grabbed Vale in the library: dark skin to Jason's pale, gray-dusted black curls where Jason's hair was straight and blond, and older than Vale by five years while Jason must be fifteen years younger.

"What are you thinking now?" Vale asked, though he was sure he'd regret it.

"He's too young for you," Urho said gently, rubbing a hand over the fuzz on his cheeks. Vale remembered Urho's taut ass as he'd stood naked at Vale's bathroom sink that morning, scraping away his salt-and-pepper stubble with the sharp razor blade he carried back and forth between their houses as needed.

Vale sighed. He was going to miss seeing that ass.

"Did you hear me?" Urho asked.

"You said he's too young. Since when does that matter with *Érosgápe?*"

"It's always mattered. It's why they created surrogates in the first place."

Vale poked at the wood hard enough that a few logs shifted, sending up a whirl of sparks. "Not really. The original surrogates were alphas like you—left uncontracted through death or other circumstances. They were brought in to help likewise uncontracted omegas through the pain of heat."

Vale hated to bring up Riki, Urho's long-dead omega, even in a roundabout way, but he also couldn't allow Urho to deny what had happened today. Even if he did it out of a misguided fear for Vale, or a realistic sense of loss for what they'd shared for almost ten years now, they couldn't avoid the truth.

But Urho seemed unaffected, only saying, "Or when an omega suffers from nymphomania."

"Interminable heat," Vale corrected. "Nymphomania is an outdated term these days."

Urho grunted.

Vale took that as acknowledgement and went on. "It was only later that omegas were taken as surrogates when an 'unsuitable' social match occurred with *Érosgápe.*" He sniffed in disdain.

"Or when a contracted omega proves to be infertile," Urho corrected, obviously determined to paint surrogacy in a positive light.

"Yes, well, all of that began at a much later date. The courts simply referred to the precedent set by alpha surrogates to approve it."

Though, really, despite Urho's resistance to the situation, what was his alternative to accepting Jason as his alpha? An accusation of assault? Easily overcome with all the witnesses and the lack of actual harm or rape. Throwing himself into the arms of one of the omega freedom groups? Possibly, but he'd have to give up his life, and he rather liked his home and his job and his friends. Suicide? No.

Vale had seen kindness in his alpha's eyes, deep beneath the wild lust and possessive rage. Perhaps that was something he might rely on. And perhaps it wasn't. Only time would tell. And maybe it would all come to nothing. He wasn't unattractive, but he was older, well past the time to be a good or reliable breeder. He wasn't going to contract for a live birth anyway, come hell or high water. So it was possible, even likely, that his young alpha *would* choose a surrogate, and Vale would be fine with that.

A pang hit him, and he took a sharp breath.

It was ridiculous how the imprint dictated everything, against all logic or intelligent interrogation of the situation. His attachment wasn't real, not based on affinity or commonalities like what he shared with Urho, and yet he couldn't deny the ball of pain in his gut, weighty and burning, at the very thought of his absurdly young alpha claiming a surrogate in his stead.

"You'll have another heat coming in six weeks," Urho said, his kind brown eyes shining. They'd both been looking forward to it and had even planned to go out to Urho's vacation house in the country for extra privacy. "Who will help you through it? The boy's unfit. Too young, too wild. At the very least he'd hurt you, and, in the worst-case scenario, he'd impregnate you against your will."

"You're so sure my alpha is a rapist, huh?"

"No. He's not a rapist," Urho bit out. "He's a child. I remember being nineteen. If I'd met Riki then, I'd have filled him up with a baby before he knew what hit him. I'd have been unable to stop myself. The drive at that age is intense—even at later ages it's more

36

intense between *Érosgápe* than with a contracted pair. Why else do you think they keep the genders separated until the age of majority? To help keep omegas safe."

"It's intense on the omega's end as well, you know." Vale flushed.

He didn't have to remind Urho of the way he begged for babies when they fucked during a heat, how he pleaded for him to take off the condom and give him what they both wanted. And Vale certainly didn't need to be reminded how steady, honest, old-fashioned Urho would deny him, and deny him, and *deny* him until the heat had passed.

Because they both knew that neither of them really wanted a child together, and they both knew Vale wouldn't ever bear children. It was just instinct talking.

With Jason, however...

"But you're right that it would be hard for a boy to resist me in a heat. It's a fair problem."

"Oh, yes. You're quite compelling," Urho said, eyes lighting with memories. "Some heats I've nearly given into you. And I'm not even imprinted on you. Imagine what a young, out of control, imprinted alpha would do? He'd fuck you to death trying to get you with child."

Vale sighed.

"So you'll let me help you with the heat?" Urho said, brows low and voice gruff. "Even if you've determined to contract and bond with another?"

"You know I can't. It would be unlawful."

And immoral. As far as Vale was concerned, that was the deeper problem.

"You'll suffer if you don't let *someone* help you."

"I know."

"You could try another round of heat suppressant."

Vale shuddered, shooting Urho an angry look. "Because that worked out so well the last time."

"It's been many years now, Vale. It's a different formula. You might not have the same reaction."

"And if I did?"

Urho groaned and rubbed at his face. "I would help you through it."

"You and how many other alphas? No. I'll never try the heat suppressant again."

He'd only given in to that temptation twice since he'd been weaned from it as a young omega. Both times had resulted in the dreaded rebound heat: longer and more intense than a regular heat.

The second time, he'd lost his mind in the haze of lust, slipped the care of his beta friends, Yosef and Rosen, and ended up the ragdoll fuck toy of a band of alphas in the kind of establishment quality people never visited.

It was a memory he'd worked hard to forget. But now it all came roaring back.

He turned away from Urho, staring into the fire, seeing it all again in his mind's eye.

He'd been there three full days taking strangers' cocks, the object of more than one alpha challenge and fight, when his friends had finally found him edging down from the heat. Humiliated, bruised, injured inside, and pregnant with an unknown alpha's child, he'd never imagined himself capable of such a low place in life.

As soon as possible, he'd endured a painful and highly illegal abortion and sworn off heat suppressants forever. The only good thing to come out of it all was meeting Urho in the midst of it all. They'd agreed to an arrangement, and his heat problems had been settled.

But humiliation and horror stung him anew as the memories

played, and he scrubbed his face with his hand, trying to banish them.

Urho knew everything about that incident, but neither of them ever talked about it.

While Vale trusted Urho with his life, the man was conservative in some of his beliefs. He'd been a medic in the military, alongside alphas who fought against omega freedom groups. And his opinions on omegas were shaped by that experience as well as the intense bond he'd shared with Riki, who, from all reports, had been a demure and quiet man.

But Vale's life was different.

"He can't know about that," Vale said.

"This young Jason Sabel, you mean?" Urho asked.

"Who else? You'll keep what you know about my past to yourself."

Urho swirled his drink and nodded, a frown creasing his forehead. "As you wish."

Vale hoped he could count on his friends Yosef and Rosen's discretion, too.

A new alpha like Jason would never understand what'd happened and what Vale had been through. He'd never know the insanity of the rebound heat, and the desperate, instinct-driven choices Vale had made. As for the helpless realization that he was carrying an unknown alpha's child? The risk and pain of the abortion? The shame that still consumed him when those memories surfaced? No matter how their contract negotiations went, Jason couldn't know about any of that.

Vale groaned. In so many ways, it would've been better if Jason had never found him at all.

"I could suggest you're carrying my child," Urho offered in that unusually canny way he had of coming close to reading Vale's mind. "We could stage a miscarriage once the damage to your reputation and desirability is done."

Appalled, Vale shook his head. "Besides the fact that I'd never agree to lie because I do, in fact, value my reputation, it wouldn't hold up. A simple examination from a doctor, or, wolf-god, a sniff from any alpha, including my own, would confirm I'm not pregnant."

"I *could* impregnate you on your next heat if you hold off contracting that long."

"Putting protocols aside, and the many ways impregnating me at this juncture would violate them, you don't want a child with me."

"I don't *not* want it." Urho's voice was tender, affectionate.

"Well, that's a compelling reason to reproduce if I've ever heard one!"

What they shared had been good for them both—affection, sex, friendship. But neither had ever wanted more than that. Vale had his own life and so did Urho—and of course, Urho had his memories of Riki. Reproducing with an alpha who'd known a true bond seemed an insult both to Vale and to Urho's lost omega.

"If it's about the scar tissue, I know ways to induce the labor early and you'd probably live through the event." Urho frowned again. "It would be risky for the babe, though."

Vale scoffed. "As if I'd put you in that position after all you've been through? No, Urho, I won't risk any of that. You told me once that giving birth was not in my cards now, and that opinion has been confirmed by every doctor I've seen since. Let's not go to drastic measures."

Urho sighed. "You're important enough to me to try anything."

"You're trying so hard to help me, going beyond your usual comfort zone, even, and I appreciate it." Vale smiled at Urho, affection burning in his heart. "But has it occurred to you that it's possible I don't need your help?"

"So you're going to just submit?"

"Like the omega I am?" Vale challenged him.

Urho sighed. "You're not just any omega, Vale."

"*Every* omega is not just any omega. Even if we all abide by the same laws and the same nature."

"You've built a whole life! To see it dashed at the feet of this young idiot is—"

"That's my alpha you're insulting," Vale said quietly, poking at the embers again.

"How can you roll over and leave it all up to him? How can you let him choose whether or not he wants you?"

Vale shot Urho a wry glance. "Those are nearly revolutionary questions, my friend."

Urho huffed, looking away and out into the dark, overgrown garden. "I know my usual stance is that omegas belong with alphas, and vice versa, and that our laws exist for a reason, but dammit, Vale, that's when things work out the way they should."

"The way they did for you and Riki."

"Yes."

Vale let the words hang in the air for some time, letting the truth set in without having to say it aloud: not everyone got to be Urho and Riki. Some, like Vale, got years of unbonded independence and now this mess. Finally, he reassured Urho the best way he knew how. "I'll have some say in it. The law doesn't require me to sign a contract holding terms I can't abide—and he'll want me to be happy with the terms."

"Omega persuasion," Urho said.

It was a kind of slur, the implication that omegas used their sexual thrall over alphas and their alpha's intrinsic need for omega approval to get their way. But Urho said it with an affectionate remembrance that took away the sting. He'd obviously enjoyed being in Riki's thrall.

"He'll have his parents to argue for his best interests. I'll have only myself."

"And me. And Yosef. Rosen would likely come to be at your side, too."

"Yes. I can't imagine he wouldn't."

"Don't be so stubborn as to go face this child's parents and attorney alone. You against a wall of them? Omega persuasion only goes so far. He's a pup. He'll cave to whatever his parents want."

"Maybe. You never know."

Urho grunted.

Vale pondered. "Have you ever known of another incident like this? I know they exist in the records, but, personally, have you known an alpha and omega pairing this distant in age cohorts?"

"In the military, when I was a young medic, there was a commanding officer whose omega was twenty-five years his junior, and not a surrogate. *Érosgápe.*"

"And?"

"And the omega was a hot piece of tail. A sweet-looking thing, and—"

"Urho, if this is going to be a lurid and offensive tale about interminable heat in an omega, I will stab you with this hot poker."

"Well, the older alpha did have his work cut out for him. He enlisted the aid of some alpha friends when his stamina ran low. It cut into his ego, but he did it out of love for his omega. I imagine you wouldn't have that same trouble as the receiving partner, so long as you make enough slick."

"Wolf-god, you bring it around to sex every time. I meant more than that. Were they happy? Did they love each other? You say your commanding officer loved his omega, that they were *Érosgápe*, but was it everything any other bond would be?"

"I don't know. I didn't ask. I was obsessed with getting back to Riki at the time, so I didn't spare much thought outside of the titillation of their sexual situation. I guess they were pretty much the same. I always wondered what became of the omega once his alpha died. There's no way he didn't outlive him."

"Unless he died of an illness or accident."

"Or took his own life."

"Wolf's own hell! What's that supposed to mean?"

"I just know when Riki went, I thought about it. It's a common thing with bonded pairs when one dies. I'm sure it would go the other direction, too."

They'd never talked so much about Riki's death in all the years they'd been friends. Most of Urho's mentions of his omega were of happy memories or funny stories. He usually steered away from the gloom.

"Well, I suppose if Jason Sabel chooses to contract with me instead of taking on a breeding surrogate, then I'll discover the strength of this attachment for myself."

Urho went quiet again, his expression moody and distant.

"What now?"

"*Érosgápe* isn't what you expect."

"How do you mean?"

"It's not instant. It's a gradual thing. He's already imprinted on you and that's the most instant part. And you've felt the pull of the bond, but the actual ties of it? They only strengthen over time, even if you contract. *Érosgápe* is just another word for deep love."

"Oh?"

"In my experience, anyway, and others I've talked with."

"I find that hard to believe." He already felt the answering tug toward his alpha. It didn't feel like love. It felt like an unexpected addiction—needful and cloying.

"Imprinting isn't love at first sight, but it's close. *Érosgápe* is what happens after, when you've signed the contract, consummated, and learned who the other person really is. Or, in some cases, when the contract draws out, *Érosgápe* can happen over the courtship time, which, in your case, I encourage you to make as long as possible. Give the kid time to grow up and make smart choices with his brain, not dumb choices with his dick."

"Are you calling me a dumb choice?"

"I'm calling this a complicated situation that jumping your bones won't solve."

"Fair enough." Vale sighed, placed the poker back into the fireplace utensil holder, and finally sat down on the sofa. The fire had warmed the leather so that it felt cozy against his back. "Another word for love, huh? Why did we create a different one? Wasn't love enough?"

"Nah. Love's a lot of things. Hell, you and I love each other, even if we have no instinctual urge to bond. And you loved your parents and you love your ugly cat." He nodded toward the ball of silver fur beneath Vale's desk where Zephyr slept—very much beautiful and entirely female, as only non-human creatures still were. "But *Érosgápe* is forever and it's written into law. When you're *Érosgápe*, it's love at a new level, a new, unbreakable permanence. But there's no click or sudden shift for omegas. It creeps up on them until they realize, damn it all, I'd die for him. Not just theoretically, but actually. Both alphas and omegas would tear out their guts for the other and put them on a platter if it meant their partner's life and happiness."

Vale closed his eyes. "My pater died trying to save my father from being run down by a fire truck. It hit them both." He'd never told Urho that before. He'd only said his parents had died in an accident. Urho, experienced with grief, had accepted that as enough. "But he'd have done the same for me. The love can't be that different."

"I don't have more words to help you understand," Urho said thickly. "It's different than any other love, it's instinct-driven, and it's coded into law. It's physical and it's spiritual. That's why it needed a word. When you've experienced it, you'll know. It's slow and sudden all at once."

"Do you feel *more* afterward?"

"What do you mean?"

"Do you feel more whole?"

"Ha." He swirled his drink and took a large swallow. "No. It's more like walking around all the time fully aware of your deficit and greedily hungering to fill it with your *Érosgápe*, but never fully accomplishing a melding of souls. But you come so close during heat and breeding that it's like heaven for hours at a time."

Vale asked the question he'd held back for years. "How did Riki die?"

Urho stilled, and for a long moment Vale thought he wouldn't answer. "Miscarriage. The child was quite far along. Malformed with a large head. The babe wouldn't come free. Riki hemorrhaged to death. I couldn't stop it."

Vale shuddered at the burden Urho must carry. "I'm sorry."

"Birth is always dangerous for an omega. No matter their age. When I was a full-time medic, I saw plenty of omega births go the wrong way. And when I volunteer in the slums now, I see all kinds of outcomes."

"I don't know how you do it. How do you stand to see so much gore and death?"

"Birth is beautiful when it goes well. And when it doesn't go well, I'm needed." Urho shrugged. "Like I said, it's always dangerous for omegas. I can't turn my back on that. What would Riki's life be worth if I didn't try to help?"

Vale's heart warmed, and he swallowed down a lump in his throat.

Urho went on, "Omega bodies were created, not by wolf-god like the holy books say, but by humans. Had the divine had a hand in it, no doubt he'd have made omega bodies more durable and childbirth easier. Your hips aren't wide enough for large babies to pass through easily. And the rectum has a terrible tendency to tear. And then it's all too common for an omega to go septic.

"The odds of a healthy live birth for you at your age and with your scar tissue are a bit terrifying to consider. Especially if you don't induce early, as I suggested."

Vale's heart clenched, even though he knew it was true. "Tell it like it is, Urho. Spare no thought for my feelings."

"I spare plenty of thoughts for your feelings, my friend. It's your life I'm frightened for, and I don't know if that young alpha will understand the loss to the world at large if you were to die in childbirth."

"So dramatic. The world won't miss my little poems."

"Dammit, I meant your friends and students missing their friend and teacher. But when it comes to your poetry, of course the world would lose out. Your poetry is the highest expression of what it is to be human, Vale. Don't underplay its importance."

"You're so in love with me." Vale laughed. "Don't deny it. Not as *Érosgápe*, obviously, but as something deeper than a friend. No one who wasn't in love with me would feel so passionately about my scribbles. And, yes, I share your attachment after all these years. But seriously, Urho? My poems are just one of thousands, if not millions, of so-called 'high expressions of humanity'. The man studying the 'language' of woodland rats, spending years on his stomach with a tiny microphone hoping to make sense of their chatter, is every bit wildly, deeply human as the idiot in his study making words fit together prettily by night and by day teaching students not to slaughter basic grammar. Probably more so."

"Promise me you won't contract with this child without show-ing him your poems, and if he doesn't appreciate them, if he can't see their value, don't give yourself over to him. Refuse. Say the terms aren't tolerable. It's your right by law."

The idea of showing the vibrant young alpha who'd accosted him in the library his poems seemed absurd, more absurd somehow than contracting with and fucking him. Maybe that was what Urho meant about the bonding of *Érosgápe* being slower than the instinctive imprinting between omega and alpha.

"Promise," Urho urged again.

"I love you, too, dear friend." Vale said, smiling tiredly and pointedly not promising a damn thing. "I love you very much."

# CHAPTER FIVE

J ASON WOKE UP in his old room at his parents' house and stared at the blue sky outside the window. His heart kicked against his ribs rapidly, as his mind scrolled through the events of the day before.

Rolling onto his side, he curled up in a ball as a gripping rush of excruciating joy and longing hit him. He'd been dosed the night before with alpha quell. A drug created to help alphas remain civilized through the first wave of imprinting should they be unable to secure their omega's contract immediately.

It wasn't an unpleasant drug experience, though not as fun as the low-key hallucinogen he and Xan had scored off upperclassmen a couple of times in high school. That'd been hilarious and weird with little dancing flowers following him around and birds that spoke to him in Old World Italian.

Alpha quell, on the other hand, was like a calm, cool breeze in his veins. It made the world less intense now that his alpha imprinting hormones had been triggered, but it didn't make him useless like the suppressant used by the security guards at the library. Just relaxed. It'd definitely helped him put his excitement and fears aside last night so he could fall asleep, but now it was wearing off.

Energy trembled inside him. He wondered what his omega was doing, where he was now, how he felt about what had happened.

Chancellor Rory hadn't seemed too optimistic the day before, and the police who'd interviewed Jason for his statement had seemed to pity him in some way he didn't fully comprehend. Then there had been the heated, urgent whispering of his parents the night before. He'd wanted to stay awake to eavesdrop on their conversation, but after they'd plied him with multiple doses of alpha quell, he'd been so drowsy he'd let Father lead him up to bed.

He remembered the way Father's handsome face had lined with sudden exhaustion as he'd tucked Jason in with his usual gentleness.

"It's going to be all right, son," he'd said, smoothing a hand into Jason's hair and dropping a kiss onto his forehead, just like he had when Jason was a little boy. "We'll make this right for you."

Pater had appeared in the doorway, a drink in hand—whisky, which meant he was stressed—and Father had risen to join him. They'd both stared in at Jason from the open doorway, black silhouettes illuminated by yellow hallway lamps. He'd fought to stay awake, wanting to climb out of bed and follow them through the house, to their wing, and listen outside their door.

Even in his groggy state, he'd known he was an alpha facing an unusual situation, and he couldn't let them treat him like a child. No omega would be impressed by that. Especially not an older one. He'd need to be strong and ready to lead. But to do that, Jason had to know things, and his parents weren't giving him all the facts. Just the ones they thought he needed to hear.

But sleep had gobbled him up greedily and spit him out in the morning light. The same light that now crept across the floor of his room. Shadows of tree limbs tossed in the autumnal breeze filtering in through the open window and cooling the room.

He sat up cautiously, but the alpha quell hadn't left him with a tender head like the bottle of brandy Xan had stolen from his father's liquor cabinet and snuck into their dorm room on their first day of college. They'd drained the whole thing, then fucked, and then fucked some more. Jason had found it hard to come after consuming so much liquor, but Xan had behaved as wantonly as some of the omegas in their educational videos.

But the morning after had been awkward, with Xan vomiting everywhere and Jason's head a bruise on the inside.

Not to mention Xan's usual guilt…

He turned to his bedside table and discovered a glass of water and four more alpha quell pills. They glinted in the sunlight. They were blue, and the size of small beads strung on a child's necklace. He first wet his mouth with the water and then took the pills in hand. He studied them.

What would happen if he didn't take them? Would he be so overcome by the pull of the imprint, the desire to be with his *Érosgápe*, that he'd do something insane? Would he climb out the window and race the many streets over to Oak Avenue to pound on Valendo Aman's door until he was either allowed entrance or he made a spectacle of himself? Or the police came again?

He squeezed his eyes shut, clenching the pills in his fist. He let the sensation wash over him, the tug of desire, the need to mate and bond. Was it pain or pleasure? Was it both? It felt like an open wound, something that needed treatment, and the only salve was Vale's presence.

Vale.

Who was he, anyway? What did Jason really know about him?

A professor.

A man with black hair (gray at the temples, according to Xan).

A man with moss-green eyes.

A voice that curled into Jason and gripped him hard, yet sweet.

But all of that wasn't real. It was instinct and pheromones and imprinting.

Who was Vale? What kind of person? He'd been on his own a long time.

Vale wouldn't be like some young omega straight out of Mont Juror. The kind of omega Jason had assumed would be his *Érosgápe*, and with whom the only obstacles to overcome would be potentially differing opinions on sports teams and vacation plans.

No, Vale would have life-sculpted opinions and unshared experiences Jason would need to reconcile.

Jason took one of the pills and washed it down. He waited a few minutes, curious how quickly it would take effect and if the smaller dosage would do anything at all. His gaze followed the shifting shadows of the tree limbs.

Somewhere on Oak Avenue was a man who was Jason's.

A man he knew nothing about.

A man his parents saw as a threat.

The thrumming undercurrent of alpha instinct searched constantly.

(*Where, where, where is he—he was right here last night—where has he gone?*)

As the alpha quell kicked in, the urge dulled a little. Like turning the volume on Pater's new radio down a notch. Did he really need all four pills? Was he such a slave to physiology that he needed to dial himself down four whole notches?

Maybe just one more.

Jason swallowed a second blue pill and then finished the glass of water.

He rolled from the bed and headed into the bathroom attached to his room. One door opened to the hallway and the other to his bedroom. He locked both, pissed, showered, and shaved.

He took his time, getting every last hair, even though his insides were shaking as a small plot grew in his mind. He knew the most important part of any plan was to have a desired outcome in mind, and his outcome was very simple: find out more about Valendo Aman.

Waiting for his parents to call Vale and make arrangements to meet, waiting for his father to uncover any dirt from the private investigator he'd no doubt engaged the night before, or waiting like a timid little bunny for a carefully arranged meeting with their lawyers and family present wasn't going to give him the information he needed now.

There was really only one way to get that.

He straightened his blond hair into a neater flop on his forehead, wished for a layer of muscles he didn't have, and then dressed quickly in the closest clothes at hand: khaki pants, a plain blue shirt, and sneakers.

Stepping back into his room, he made as little noise as possible. Then he crossed to the window, slid it open on oiled tracks, and crawled out onto the sloping roof just below, before slipping down the vine-covered trellis.

The soles of his shoes hit the ground with a *whump* and he was off, down the sidewalk, across the road, and heading north toward Oak Avenue and Valendo Aman.

He didn't need an address. As cranked up as he was, he'd know his omega's scent from five hundred feet away.

The alpha quell slipped through him gently, and he felt certain he'd be able to contain his impulses on half the dose his parents had left for him. Still, he'd tucked one of the additional pills in his pocket just to be safe.

As he walked, he admired the morning. The streets were freshly swept by the new trucks the city had bought to rustle and vacuum up debris. People hurried on their way to work or school, and it belatedly occurred to Jason that he was missing classes. He'd have to ask Xan for notes.

The latest fashion for bonded omegas was a gold circle pin on their collars, a sign to any wondering alpha eye that they weren't available for a contract or surrogacy, nor for plain old sexy fun. Jason noted that some omegas wore the circle in gold, others in silver, and one wealthy omega wore a circle of diamonds on his well-starched dress shirt, tucked into a thick leather belt, and stylishly tailored trousers.

Jason nodded at the man as he walked by. He knew his pater wouldn't wear one and found them offensive, but the thought drifted away as his eye caught on a bonded pair laughing by the bakery.

They were of the same cohort, obviously. Both dressed casually, like they were perhaps on vacation and had tumbled straight out of bed and into the city streets to procure the warm coffees currently steaming in their hands. They passed a white bag of sugared breads between them.

"My favorite!" the dark one cried, pulling out a gooey, cinnamon-scented loaf.

His alpha quivered with the implied praise and pulled his omega close, kissing his forehead. "Like I could forget."

What was Vale's favorite sweet? Or color? Where did he like to vacation?

Jason's gut twisted, a strange panic pooling inside him. What if Vale didn't like the shore? What if the cottage where Jason had spent most summers of his life was left abandoned in favor of adventurous trips to snow-covered mountain peaks and freezing-cold tents just to please a man he'd only just met?

Who was Vale? What was it about being *Érosgápe* that Jason felt so viscerally desperate to please him? What would he make Jason do?

He clenched his hands in fists and fought the whirl of emotion.

*That's what you're going to find out, idiot. Calm down.*

Oak Avenue was a nice street, though it was entirely middle class and average compared to the hulking, block-long structure in which his parents had made their home. Still, Vale's house was outfitted nicely with a shaded front porch, a clean front walk, and a bushy abundance of overgrown garden peeking around from the back. The wood slats were painted a seaside blue, which soothed

Jason's panic about the cottage. A man who lived in the house the color of the ocean couldn't hate it, surely?

There were broad windows on the front of the house, open to the cool morning air. The front door was painted an earthy brown and there was a long, narrow window beside it. To the side of the house was another window, also open, and one on the upper floor, too, with a breeze-blown white lace curtain billowing in and out of it.

But the back of the house stopped Jason's creeping in its tracks. From the edge of the property, he could smell the scent of his omega's skin on the breeze, and he took it in deeply. The windows along the back of the house were impressive and seemed to indicate that the garden had once been a place of pride. Now it was a mess, but a glorious one: red, yellow, and orange made a carpet on the ground, and the scent of crushed and dying roses mixed with Vale's omega odor, until Jason thought he'd swoon with rich lust.

He steeled himself to step closer.

*You should have knocked on the front door like a respectable person.*

The thought hissed through his mind as he inched toward the windows at the back of the house, edging into the cover of the garden and stepping on rivers of mint that wafted perfume.

He wasn't here to be a respectable person.

That's what his parents were being on his behalf at home. They'd have their attorney contact Vale's attorney, and they'd all meet in some tense, nondescript room, where they'd act like this was business and not so much more.

He was here to find out who Vale was on a primal level before the attorneys and the contracts got in the way.

The back windows were open, too, and he heard a voice as he crept in closer. *The* voice. Gritty with rage. Jason's hackles went up. What was his omega so angry about? Who did he need to challenge?

"So I have to pay the price?"

Another voice drifted out to Jason, and he had to suppress a growl until he realized it was coming from the newfangled speakerphone on Vale's very messy desk. Jason blinked, his hands shaking. This was Vale's office. He was peering into Vale's house.

Heaps of papers quivered in the breeze, held down by strategically placed books and coffee mugs. A leather sofa was strewn with a knitted blanket and a pillow, as though Vale had slept in the study instead of a bedroom. A wingback chair and bookcases filled the rest of the room, and charred ashes filled the fireplace.

Where was Vale?

"This isn't a punishment," the speakerphone rumbled, and Jason recognized Chancellor Rory's voice. "It's simply not possible for you to remain on campus as the uncontracted *Érosgápe* of an imprinted alpha. One wrong move from one of these young men could end very messily. You have to understand that. You're old enough to have seen how violent things can get. Until you've contracted, consummated, and the bond is set, you can't continue to work on campus."

Vale launched up from the wingback chair, having been hidden by it before. He strode over to the desk and leaned against the edge near the speakerphone, both fists clenched. "What would you have me do? Starve?"

"While I have serious doubts you even need your income, due to your inheritance, your alpha is quite wealthy. The Sabels will never allow you to suffer monetarily. They'll grant you a reasonable allowance, I'm sure."

Vale's pale cheeks went even paler, and Jason wanted to punch Chancellor Rory though he had no idea why. It was true that he would never allow Vale to endure any pain he could prevent.

"I am a *grown man*, used to taking care of myself. I don't want charity."

"It's not charity, Vale. It's your right as his omega."

"I like my job, Rory. What do you not understand about that?"

"I understand it all too well. It's unfortunate, but this is how it must be. Your position will be waiting for you when you've contracted and bonded, or he's graduated, whichever comes first."

"This is ridiculous! I can't be shielded from alphas simply because it might upset him. There are thousands of alphas on the streets, Rory. All I have to do is go out of my house and there'll be one right there in front of me."

"Those alphas aren't my charges. No one is going to sue me or have me jailed if Jason Sabel goes barbaric and beats them to a pulp. And most of those alphas on the streets are older, experienced, not so likely to make a misstep if you were to go into an unexpected heat—"

"I'm thirty-five years old! I've never had an unexpected heat in my life."

"You've never been exposed to your alpha's pheromones, either. It changes things."

Vale's breathing was ragged with distress, and Jason's pulse thrummed.

"I'm sorry, Vale. I really am." There was a pause, and when Vale didn't fill it, Chancellor Rory went on. "I'll have Jon Biers contact you for lesson plans and your current marks for the students. Truly, this doesn't have to be so bad, old friend. Enjoy your vacation."

"For two years?"

Vale flinched as Chancellor Rory snorted in astonishment. "So you plan to make him wait?"

"I don't *know* the boy! I was in his presence for less than ten minutes yesterday afternoon. Do you expect me to fall on the ground and present myself to him at our first real meeting?"

"Some do."

"Boys with other boys. Bright-eyed children with no pasts or planned futures except each other."

"Oh, Vale." Chancellor Rory sighed heavily. "Do you like the sound of a sabbatical better?"

"Not really."

"Write some poems. Publish them. Take the time to know your alpha and yourself. The world will wait for you."

Vale hung up the call, grabbed a round, flat paperweight from his desk, and threw it at the wall across from him with a harsh yell. The paperweight left a round welt deep in the coral-colored paint and landed on the floor with a loud thud.

"The world will wait?" Vale yelled. "Fuck you! I had a *life*, for fuck's sake."

Jason stared at his omega, mesmerized by the red heat flaring above his collarbones showing above his open collar.

Vale swung around, eyes blazing and dark hair sticking up wildly at his temples like he'd been tugging at it. His startled gasp was beautiful, like a taste of the noises still to come, one day—hopefully *not* two years from now.

Vale *was* going gray, Xan was right. But he was lean and tall, beautiful and strong. His green, soft-looking shirt made his eyes seem an even deeper shade of moss, and his black pants echoed his dark hair. He was stunning.

"I'll call the police," Vale whispered, staring at Jason wide-eyed and inching close to his desk again.

With a start, Jason realized Vale was staring directly at him, talking to him, and that his breath trembled with fear.

"I'm not going to hurt you," Jason said, putting his hands out. "I'm sorry. I didn't mean to scare you."

"Stalking is illegal. Even between *Érosgápe*." His hand was outstretched toward his telephone.

Jason's breath hitched in his throat. Wolf-god, he was this man's *Érosgápe*! It didn't stop being stunning and breathtaking and screamingly surreal. "No," he whispered. "I'm not stalking you."

"Then what?"

"I..." Jason trailed off.

He'd come here to snoop. To try to figure out who Vale Aman was, but he hadn't had a clear plan of action. He'd just known that he needed to see Vale again, to hear his voice, to see what his own senses and brain could tell him, and now he was so far in over his head, he didn't know which way was up.

"Eavesdropping on private phone calls is also a crime."

"I was..."

"You were?"

"I wanted to see you."

"I'm sure you did." Condescension poisoned the honey of his voice. "Your parents' attorney called this morning already to make arrangements. That's how it's done, Jason."

*Jason.*

He'd said his name. The shivering sibilance on the 'S' buzzed and burst at the base of Jason's skull and filled him with sparks.

"Say my name again."

Vale sighed, pinching the bridge of his nose. "We should call your parents to come get you before this gets out of hand."

The internal sparking bliss fizzled out, fireworks dulling to cold, floating ash.

"You didn't want to see me," Jason said aloud, the understanding coming along with the words. "I thought..."

What *had* he thought? He'd acted without much analysis, actually.

Vale let go of the bridge of his nose, and his arm fell limply at his side. "Of course I wanted to see you. I'm not immune to you, after all." He lifted his hand to forestall any move on Jason's part to crawl through the open window. "But this—coming here alone—is dangerous, Jason. And against protocol."

"Protocol doesn't tell us anything real about each other."

"Real?"

"Yeah. Like…" He wracked his brain, looking for the words to explain. "You know I want to see you, but do you know why?"

"You're driven by instinct to seek out the omega you're imprinted on."

"Yes! That's exactly right! And do you know how terrifying that is? How strange I feel? Not myself, aching and shivery inside, desperate to please you, but I don't even know you!"

He sounded insane, and he was giving it all away. A full deck of cards to be played against him at any time. That's what this adventure was and he'd known it, deep down, from the start, but he hadn't been able to stop himself, or to deny himself hope.

Vale stared at him. His dark lashes lined his eyes with color, like the make-up some older omegas and alphas wore out to local jazz clubs. Jason had seen pictures of them in the society section of the papers. But Vale didn't wear make-up. He was just naturally vibrant.

Or else his pheromones made him seem that way to Jason. Another thing he couldn't truly know.

"You're frightened?" Vale asked.

"Yeah!"

"Huh." Vale's mouth lifted at the edges, a bitter twist. "I admit I haven't considered it from your point of view. It's hard to be reminded of our animal natures. We like to believe we're above it all. So intelligent. Guided only by our moral compasses, but really, deep down, we're this." He gestured between them. "The first heat does an amazing job of making that abundantly, terrifyingly clear to omegas. It makes sense that imprinting has the same effect on alphas."

"I wanted to know something about you," Jason whispered. "Something for myself. Not information given to me in a report from my father's private investigator, or written into some contract."

"You could have tried the phone. Your parents have my number. Or you could have asked the operator to connect you to me. There aren't any other Valendo Amans in the city."

"I needed to see you, too."

"Why?"

"I couldn't remember what you looked like," Jason confessed. "Not truly. The imprinting came on so fast. It was all sensation, and my mind couldn't hold the whole of you."

Vale lifted his arms. "And what do you think?"

Jason's throat clenched. "You're beautiful."

"I'm much older than you must have been expecting."

"That doesn't make you less perfect-looking to me."

Vale smiled softly, eyes crinkling at the edges. "You're sweet."

"And what about me?" Jason lifted his arms wide like Vale had done. "Scrawny and just a kid. You must be disappointed."

Vale swallowed hard and darted his glance away, toward the hole in the wall left by the paperweight. "You're a handsome boy. I know you've looked in the mirror. You don't need my reassurance."

"I do."

Wolf-god, did he ever. He needed it like breath.

"Then know I find you appealing in ways I never thought I could."

Relief and a surge of lust flowed into him. He fumbled into his pocket and pulled out another little pill, popping it quickly.

Vale frowned. "What's that?"

"Alpha quell," Jason admitted shyly.

"Fair enough." Vale hesitated and stared at Jason like he was a wild thing. "Is it working?"

"Yes."

Vale nodded slowly, then leaned against his desk and crossed his arms. "Stay outside and we'll talk."

"Really?"

"For a little while. You aren't the only one who feels the pull of *Érosgápe*."

He wished he believed it, but Vale seemed so calm, and he felt so raw. He wanted to tug Vale into his arms and not let him go until he was sticky with sweat, saliva, and come. He didn't get the impression Vale wanted the same thing at all.

"How's your morning been?" Jason asked softly, trying for something basic.

"Lost my job. Gotta say, it's not off to a great start."

"I promise you won't have to 'pay the price' for this," Jason said. "It's not your fault I took so long to find you."

"You weren't even born."

"I was, actually. You were sixteen when I was born, so that means that I was six when you needed me."

Vale's hand twitched like he'd almost reached out to Jason but thought better of it. "And what would six-year-old Jason have done for twenty-two-year-old Vale?"

"Given you hope? For some kind of future?"

Vale's eyebrows tightened, and Jason wished he could grab the words from the air. His shoulders hunched, and he cast his eyes down.

"I had a future. Everything that happened until you appeared out of the blue yesterday afternoon was that future. It was *my life*."

"I'm sorry." Jason looked up, hoping Vale would understand. "I only meant that maybe it would've been less painful for you. I don't know anything about your life. I shouldn't make guesses. My professors are always saying that learning is listening. I'll get better at it. I promise."

Vale's lips twisted. "You're young, but, if that's your attitude, we'll manage."

"Will we?" Jason's heart leapt into his throat.

"There's a lot to deal with and sort through, but you seem to have a good heart, Jason." Vale's body relaxed, and he smiled genuinely. "That makes me glad."

"I want you to be glad of everything about me."

"Omega persuasion," Vale whispered with some derision.

Jason blinked at the offensive term from his omega's beautiful mouth, as well as the accusation that maybe Jason didn't really mean these things.

"Maybe. But isn't that right? How it's meant to be?" Jason asked.

"Oh, you're so young."

He'd come here to know his omega better, but now Vale grew more and more distant with almost every sentence out of Jason's mouth.

"What's your favorite color?" he asked desperately. He wasn't going to leave here totally empty handed.

Vale humored him. "Blue."

"All blues? Or is there a particular shade?"

Vale tilted his head in consideration, his lower lip tucking into his mouth. "Hold on. I have a piece of fabric, an old ribbon bookmark."

He moved deeper into the room, and Jason leaned against the windowsill, tempted to crawl in after him, to keep the distance between them the tolerable few feet it had been before. But he steadied himself and waited with his gaze glued to Vale as he sorted through a messy drawer in his desk and pulled out a strip of blue ribbon imprinted with a gold star on one side and words on the other.

Vale brought it to the window, holding it up. "This blue."

"Deeper than a robin egg, but not cornflower, either."

"It's called cerulean."

"Yeah?" Jason reached out to take the ribbon from him and

Vale let him, carefully avoiding skin contact. The ribbon was soft and worn, but the color was still vibrant. The words read POET OF THE YEAR, and Jason traced them with his finger. "Did you win this?"

"I did. My last year in Mont Juror." Vale chuckled, and sweetness zipped up Jason's spine. "The poem was entitled 'when the sun sets on your skin'. It was terrible."

"No, you won!" Jason argued. "It must have been good."

"It was student work."

Jason smiled, his heart tripping. So Vale was hard on himself and a bit of a snob. He could handle that. That was good. That was information he could work with to gather more. "And you're a professor now."

"*Was*, apparently."

Shit. Another misstep. He was an idiot. Vale would never believe Jason was actually intelligent at this rate.

"Back to poetry," he said hastily.

"Yes, it's much safer," Vale said, a sarcastic but amused tone ruffling his words.

"Chancellor Rory said you should write poems and publish them."

Vale rolled his eyes. "I've been publishing them for years."

"So I could buy them?"

Vale's cheeks paled a little. "I can't stop you from it, but I'd rather you didn't."

"Why?"

"They're personal."

"How?"

"I'd rather not say."

Jason's feet were starting to hurt, and he wanted to crawl in the room and throw himself into one of the comfortable looking chairs. He leaned against the sill and shifted his weight. "Why?"

"Wolf-god, you're annoyingly persistent."

"I want to read them, but if you don't want me to...then I feel torn. I want to know more about you, but I want to please you, too. One is the real me. The other one is instinct. Give the real me a reason not to go to the book store on my way home."

Vale's jaw clenched and released like it had on the phone with Chancellor Rory when he'd been especially pissed off. "I've written and published poems about my experiences with heat, Jason. I've been through many heats since I came of age. Rarely alone."

Jason sucked in a breath and took a step back from the window.

He'd known. Okay, so he hadn't *known*, but Vale was thirty-five. There was no denying the implication. Not to mention the alpha he'd been with the day before had been covered in Vale's scent. There was no way they hadn't...even when there was no heat to be pacified.

"Oh," he said.

Vale stared at him coldly, measuring Jason's response. "And?"

"And what?"

"Do you understand what that means?"

"Yes."

"And why you shouldn't read my poems."

"I can handle it."

"You look like you're going to pass out or run away."

Jason put up his chin. "I'm progressive. I believe in omega rights."

Vale sighed and pinched the bridge of his nose again. "You're so damn young. What am I going to do with you?"

"And you're so damn condescending, what am I going to do with *you*?" Jason snapped, irritation at being so easily dismissed charging out of his mouth.

Vale stared at him a moment and then threw back his head in laughter.

Jason half wanted to do just as Vale had suggested and run away. "What?"

"If we can both get past how incredibly strange this is, I think we could learn to like each other, Jason Sabel."

Jason crossed his arms over his chest and stood his ground. The scent of mint wafted to him from beneath his feet. "What's your favorite dessert?"

"Cherry tart. Yours?"

"Rhubarb pie."

"Oh, my. That's sour. You must have a very sweet heart. That's what my pater always said: a taste for sour foods reveals the sweetest heart."

"Is your pater…?"

"They're both long gone. It's just me in the world."

"Not anymore." Jason approached the window again to reach one hand inside, palm up. "I'm here now."

Vale slowly crossed from his desk, his eyes on Jason like he couldn't quite trust him, and then he gently pressed Jason's hand back out the window.

"Yes. You're very much here and you shouldn't be." He smiled kindly. "You should go home now. Or else I'll have to call your parents, and neither of us really want that."

Then he lowered the sash and shut the curtains, leaving Jason alone in the garden.

# CHAPTER SIX

"WHERE HAVE YOU been?"

Father jerked Jason in through the front hallway and toward the back of the house where Pater liked to relax and listen to music on their newfangled record player.

Dressed in crisp dark pants and a white shirt, Father looked like he was ready for business. In the conservatory, though, Pater was reclining on the navy leather sofa, wearing his softest pants, an old t-shirt from a trip to the zoo when Jason was nine, and slippers. He was smoking, too. That was never a good sign.

Smoking meant Pater was upset.

Smoking meant Father was going to get worried.

"Hey," Jason said weakly, as Father dragged him deeper into the room.

Neat and tidy, with every book and sheet of music filed alphabetically by author or composer, the conservatory was masculine but soft. Comfortable blankets draped over the backs of padded leather chairs and the sofa, and the windows and glass door opened out to a well-tended garden, bursting with robust autumn flowers and warm with fading leaves. Three guitars, a piano, a violin, and a tall, thin drum that produced a soothing tone when patted were all on prominent display.

The solid wood side tables and large card table, mainly used for sorting through Pater's music, leant a thick stability to the room, and the radio and record player had places of honor on a sideboard next to the piano Pater sometimes played.

A flat circle of thick vinyl spun on the record player, and the music drifting from the horn was lyric-less and moody, some dark piece with violin and piano combined. It didn't bode well, so Jason was unsurprised Pater looked even more fragile than usual when he leaned up on one elbow and focused his worried hazel eyes toward them.

"Where have you been?" Pater whispered, a tired echo of Father's earlier demand. He sat up slowly, in obvious physical pain, his cigarette dangling from two fingers.

Jason winced. "Are you okay, Pater?"

Pater ignored him. "Did you go harass that man?"

"I didn't harass him. I only—"

Pater's eyes flickered. "So you did go to him?"

"Yes, but—"

"Did you assault him?"

"What?" Jason blinked in shock.

"Did you touch him? In any way?"

"No." Jason swallowed hard, a thunderclap of hurt rolling in him. "I wouldn't...I'd never..."

Pater reached in his pocket before holding out the pill Jason had abandoned on his bedside table. "The dose we left for you was the right amount, Jason. Anything less and..." He raised his brows, letting the implication dangle.

"I'd never hurt him. Never."

Pater measured him carefully with his eyes and then glanced over Jason's shoulder to Father. After shrugging at whatever he saw there, he took a drag from his cigarette and turned to Jason again. "Sit down."

Father moved into his usual 'Jason's in trouble' position. He stood solidly behind Pater, hands on the back of the sofa, his shoulders broad, as though guarding Pater against some threat, and facing Jason with all the alpha authority he could muster. It seemed unfair—two against one.

"I didn't do anything bad," Jason said, as he took his place in the stuffed wingback 'punishment' chair—so called because it was where he'd been steered for lectures ever since he was child. "I only talked to him."

Pater threw up his hands, cigarette ash breaking off and falling onto his t-shirt. "You went and disturbed that man's peace? Out of the bounds of protocol?"

"I wanted—"

"You probably scared him to death, you realize." Pater sucked at his cigarette. "An imprinted alpha showing up on his doorstep with wolf-god only knows what intentions! He probably—"

"I just wanted to talk to him." The words burst out painfully.

"And did you?" Father asked, waving away Pater's exhaled smoke with a grimace.

"Yes."

"And how did that go?" Father's eyes narrowed.

"He was...fine with it." Jason squirmed, stubborn defiance warring with a hint of shame. Maybe he *had* scared Vale—all right, there was no maybe about it—but it'd turned out fine in the end, hadn't it?

"Start talking," Father said, rubbing Pater's shoulders.

Pater shrugged off the touch and then leaned to stub his cigarette out on the brass plate kept on the side table for that purpose.

Jason frowned. "Let me tell you the whole story before you talk over me, okay? Hear me out."

Pater waved his hand like he was being extraordinarily gracious to let Jason speak. Biting back the irritation, Jason cleared his throat and began. He told them about waking up and realizing they weren't going to treat him like an adult.

"Just like now," he pointed out. "I knew it would be this way. You aren't going to tell me the real things I need to know about

Vale. You're going to try to decide for me—what I want, what I should contract for, what's important. That's not all right with me."

"You don't trust us to have your best interests at heart?" Father said, surprise and hurt flashing on his face.

"Of course, I do. But my best interests aren't what *I'm* interested in. What are his best interests? What does he want? Who even is he, really, underneath all those stupid facts the investigator is going to dig up?"

Pater sighed and rubbed at his forehead. "Jason, you can't just go to this man's house and demand entrance."

"I didn't."

"You've already admitted you did."

"No. I didn't! I talked to him through the window."

"Wolf-god. Talked to him through a window. The man must have been terrified."

"He seemed okay, actually. Most of the time. I mean, he was scared at first, but then he realized I wasn't going to force myself on him." Jason felt a trickle of sweat on his forehead and rubbed it away. "He trusted me enough to talk to me for a while."

But not enough to take hold of his proffered hand.

Jason could still feel the tingle of where Vale's fingers had pushed against his knuckles, making him retreat so he could close the window.

"And what did you learn about him?" Father asked softly.

Jason hesitated. He wasn't about to tell them what Vale had said about his poems—or about the heats he'd gone through with surrogate alphas. Though he supposed it was only a matter of time before the private investigator gave his parents that information anyway.

"He likes the color blue. This blue." He pulled the ribbon from his pocket, smiling at the memory of Vale shifting through his messy desk drawer looking for it. "And he's a terrible housekeeper.

Which is fine. I'll hire someone."

"Oh, Jason," Pater whispered.

"And he has moss-green eyes, and really beautiful lips. But when he laughs it's like bells play up my spine, and—" he broke off, unwilling to say things that could be construed as romantic or sexual. His parents were all too ready to write his opinions off to the effects of imprinting anyway. "He's angry that he's been asked to leave the university."

"He told you that?" Father asked.

"No, I overheard, and he knew I overheard."

"It's a shame, but—"

Jason interrupted Father. "I promised he wouldn't have to pay that price. Can you get Chancellor Rory to let him be reinstated?"

"No." Father rubbed his hands over his head, sending his blond hair askew. "Son, you can't be on campus with him until you're completely bonded. That goes beyond the consummation of an imprint, beyond a contract. You must be fully *Érosgápe*, bonded, you realize. It'd be too dangerous for you and your classmates otherwise."

"I'm not going to go insane because a random alpha—"

"It's nonnegotiable.

"And you'll be living at home until…" Pater shook his head.

"Until this is all settled," Father finished for him.

"I have to live here at home? Why?"

"Because obviously you can't be trusted not to scamper off to your omega's house. We can't put that responsibility on the university. We'll have to deal with you ourselves."

"You can't keep me here like a prisoner. I'm not a child."

"No, but you're not ready for this, Jason." Pater darted a glance at Father, a request for backup, and Father squeezed Pater's shoulders reassuringly but was flung off again.

Sighing, Father moved to sit down in the chair next to Jason instead. "Miner is right. Your body is going to crave him like a drug, and you'll give in to that desire without close supervision."

"Xan can watch out for me."

"Xan is even more of a child than you are, and absolutely not," Father snapped.

"But—"

"No," Pater said quietly, blowing smoke in a long stream. "There'll be no further discussion of it."

Jason clenched his teeth. "Xan and I have plans. Back when we were fourteen years old, we swore we'd be roommates at university. He needs me."

"Your attachment to Xan will lessen as things settle with your omega," Pater said, a hint of knowing in his voice that made Jason wonder if he guessed some of the things Xan and Jason did together.

More smoke drifted up toward the high ceiling, curling and shifting in the air. It smelled like sadness to Jason.

"*If* things settle with this omega," Father muttered.

"What's that supposed to mean?" Jason asked.

"It means we have a lot to work out," Pater said, his voice cracking with exhaustion.

"It means I'm not going to allow your future to be determined by the too-random hand of Fate." Father's blue eyes tightened piercingly.

Pater glared at Father. "Stop. If you go down that path, you know where it will end up."

"What path?" Jason asked. "What are you not telling me?"

"Son, you need to trust us. We're your parents. We want what's best for you." Father leaned forward, brows quirked gently and voice urgent.

"It's all too soon for this conversation," Pater said.

"I'm not a fool, you know," Jason said.

"Of course you're not. But Miner is right. It's not time to talk about it now." Father glanced at his watch. "I have to meet Jeft Mellors in twenty minutes. He'll have the first batch of information for us to peruse. Then I'll stop by the warehouses, see how things are going with the shipments."

Pater shrugged, his bony shoulders rising and falling tiredly.

"That's the detective you've hired?" Jason asked. "Jeft Mellors? He's getting information about Vale?"

Father frowned. "You don't need to worry about it."

"You can't leave me out of this. I already told you that's the entire reason I left this morning, because I knew you'd do this to me. If you want me to behave, if you want me to act according to protocol, you can't keep me in the dark."

Pater sighed and Father's lips thinned.

"You'll show me what he brings you." Jason dared to point a finger at his father and tried to sound older, ready for what was coming. "All of it."

Father rubbed at his temples. "Fine. It's your right to know and your choice to make."

Jason narrowed his eyes. He wasn't an idiot. He knew what Father was implying and what Pater didn't like about it—he was suggesting Jason might take a surrogate in Vale's stead.

"Go then, Yule," Pater said. "I'll stay here with Jason. We'll work on his guitar skills today. It's been a while."

Jason groaned but didn't complain more. He accepted Father's hand in his hair and watched his parents kiss goodbye, then rose to get the acoustic guitar he'd graduated to once his hands had grown to adult size. He sat down again, this time on a stool near his pater's sofa, turning the golden-wood instrument over in his hands. "Which piece should I start with?"

Pater waved absently. "Something you won't butcher too badly. My nerves won't take it."

An hour later, Jason's fingers were tired, and Pater was lying back on the sofa, arm over his eyes, listening instead of instructing. But he wasn't smoking anymore, which was an improvement. It seemed a fair time to quit.

"I'm done." Jason rose and placed the guitar back in the stand.

"You played better than usual."

Jason smiled softly. He'd closed his eyes and pretended that Vale was on the sofa instead of Pater. But he wasn't going to admit that much. "Thank you."

"You were more focused. Any reason?"

"I thought maybe Vale would like it. If I play well, I mean."

Pater smiled and sat up. "Maybe he will."

Four blue pills appeared from Pater's pocket, and he handed the alpha quell to Jason. He downed them easily. The cool calmness seeped into him quickly, settling the renewed urges that he hadn't even realized were growing in him.

"I didn't mean to scare him." Jason sat down on the sofa, letting Pater drape a warm arm over his shoulders. "I didn't plan to talk to him at all."

"What were you planning?"

Jason's ears burned. "I was going to, uh, look in the windows and, well, see if I could...I don't know. I just wanted to know something about him."

"I understand."

"When he seemed scared, I tried to reassure him, but..."

"I'm sorry I accused you earlier. I'd been entertaining horrible thoughts for over an hour, afraid the police would show up on our door saying you'd assaulted the poor man. It's instinct. And imprinting is no laughing matter, love."

"I know. Did you know that he's all alone in the world? His parents are dead."

"I see." Pater frowned. "That will complicate our contracts. It's not customary to deal directly with the omega. But in this situation, maybe that's right. It'll prepare us for things to come."

Jason's mind went back to when he had stretched out his hand, vowing that Vale wasn't alone in the world anymore. "I told him that I was his family now."

Pater laughed softly. "What did he say?"

"He said I should go home."

Pater squeezed Jason's shoulder. "Romantic declarations will be more welcome when things seem less uncertain."

"He didn't hate me, though. He said I had a good heart and he thought, eventually, we could be good together."

That hadn't been exactly what Vale had said, but Jason had to believe that was what he meant.

"We're going to *make sure* your future is good, okay? We'll do everything in our power."

"Father's already considering a surrogate."

Pater shook his head. "Shush. We aren't going to discuss that now or, with any luck, ever." He withdrew his arm but patted Jason's knee and smiled, his lips wobbling. "But definitely not now. I'm too tired for it. I'm sorry."

"Your last heat was bad again?"

"My heats grow more intense as I age. But it's the pills that keep me from conceiving afterward that are the real problem."

It was slightly embarrassing to discuss this, but if he was going to be a good alpha to his own omega, he couldn't shy away from these topics. "I don't understand what you mean. In class they said alpha condoms should prevent unwanted—"

Pater shuddered. "I hate them."

"But why? The professors said they don't noticeably reduce pleasure for the omega, just keep them from getting pregnant."

Pater sneered. "Your professors leave out the fact that pleasure is about more than sensation. Instinct sees insemination as connection, as intimacy. Besides, I'm allergic to the government-approved condoms and the black-market ones are impossible to find anymore." Pater's eyes darkened. "They don't actually want us to control births, you understand."

"I know, Pater." He'd heard it hundreds of times when his pater had a little too much to drink and started ranting about omega rights.

"If it was only for a single round, then I could manage. But by the fifth or sixth knot, I'm swollen and bleeding. After five days of multiple rounds of intercourse? Well, I'd probably tear and go septic." He patted his pocket again, seeking the cigarettes, but Jason took his hand to still it.

"It's okay, Pater. You don't need to smoke."

"You hate it," he said apologetically. "I know. It's a terrible habit."

"You only do it when you're sad. Or scared. Or unhappy. And that's not that often."

"Usually just around heats, yes?"

Jason gripped his hand. "So when you say you take drugs to keep you from conceiving, you really mean that you've most likely already conceived and…"

Pater shifted uncomfortably. "Yes. The most effective abortifacient drugs are very poisonous. They do their job, destroying any fertilized eggs, but they take a toll on the system. Using them consecutively, as I have to, means the poison builds up, tearing down my immunity to other illnesses. It's why your father is so protective of me."

"But I thought taking those drugs for any reason was illegal?"

"I think we can agree that some laws are better broken. I'd have died long ago otherwise." He touched Jason's hair. "And I couldn't have that. You needed me."

"Father needed you, too."

"Of course." Pater's lips turned up fondly. "He'll always need me. But I'm not sure how long I'll continue to be lucky enough to be here for him. My health deteriorates every heat."

"Isn't there a way to stop it? The heat, I mean?"

"The suppressants have stopped working as I've aged and worse, they now often have the side effect of rebound heat." He shuddered. "And unfortunately, our government cares more about birthing children than it does about omega health. There's a surgery that could remove my womb, but it's much more difficult to obtain than the abortifacient drugs I take." He rubbed a hand over his mouth. "Besides, after all these years of heat and union with your father, I don't know what it would be like not to have it anymore. Would our bond be the same? Would we still connect on the level we do now? It's too risky."

"I'm sorry."

"It's okay. This is our burden and I'm only sorry that our pain causes you to suffer, too."

"Don't worry about me. I'm all right."

Pater drew Jason close, his arms circling him. "But you're not. This is a scary time for you. I wish I was stronger and we could hash out everything now, so you wouldn't be so afraid."

"You can tell I'm afraid?"

"All alphas are, love. Your father was shaking in his boots when he imprinted on me. Well, once the wonder was over and we were sweaty and relieved. I know you don't want to hear about that."

"I really don't."

"But afterward, he realized how much control I had over him, and it terrified him." Pater laughed. "I remember he wanted to know if I was a particular fan of pot roast—because he loathes pot roast and was afraid I'd demand it nightly."

"Vale didn't seem to expect my fear. He was surprised when I said I was scared."

76

Pater tilted his head, his smile softening. "Well, of course. Alphas don't go crowing it around to the unbonded masses, and while it's mentioned at Mont Juror they don't dwell on it. I'm sure his own fears have crowded out that information, too. But yes, imprinting is a helluva thing. Consuming, and the need to be near your omega is compulsive."

"Will I wake up every day and want to go to him?"

"Don't you want to go to him now?"

Beneath the alpha quell, he could feel it stirring. "Yeah."

"Welcome to the rest of your life." He felt Pater's thin throat constrict with a silent laugh.

"Truly?"

"Yes. No matter what choices you make."

"Even if I took a surrogate, I'd still want Vale?"

"We're not talking about surrogates."

It was clearly a sore spot and so Jason asked another question instead. "What was it like when you and Father first bonded?"

Casting back, Pater's face brightened. "Wonderful. We were a good match from the beginning." Then his eyes dulled again, as an unhappy memory pushed forward. "Before the failure of the first pregnancy, anyway, everything about our lives was beautiful. We were happy. Devoted. In love."

"You still are."

"Yes, but it's different now. Won through hardship and loss. In the early days it was pure and sweet, full of wonder and optimism." He laughed bitterly. "We had no idea how very wrong things could go. We were delirious."

Jason knew it was a painful question, but he felt it was important to understand. "And after the first miscarriage?"

Pater reached for his cigarette case again, and this time Jason didn't stop him. "Things grew very dark for us. The lulls between heats felt like living on borrowed time." The jewel of fire at the tip of the cigarette flared brightly as he inhaled. "After, with each pregnancy, it got worse. I was at the mercy of doctors trying to figure out why I couldn't carry to term. I was a science experiment to them. They tried all kinds of hormone shots, and pills, and tests. Your father was a ghost of himself. He didn't want to try any longer, but…"

"But what?"

"But Grandpater Derak was determined *he* hadn't gone through the pain of birthing your father in vain. The last Sabel to carry on the family name and genes." He sucked in more smoke and let it loose in a long stream. "Derak held me to the contract promising at least one live birth under threat of alerting the authorities. Then he tried to coerce your father to repudiate our contract and accept a surrogate after the fifth miscarriage. Your father never forgave him for the way he treated me." Pater snorted. "Derak didn't care for your father's forgiveness anyway. He wanted what he wanted. He'd never been much of a parent."

"Why did you never tell me before?" He'd known of their miscarriages and had guessed the emotional toll they'd taken, but he'd never heard a word of Grandpater's ruthlessness. It amazed him to think the old man who'd happily filled his plate with extra slices of pie at the Autumn Nights holiday feasts had been a controlling monster.

"I didn't want to taint our present with memories of unhappy times."

"But now…?"

"Now I need to know that you understand what it is to be an omega in this world. You have a responsibility to someone, Jason. A real person. A man with dreams and loves, a past, and a present." Pater stubbed out his half-smoked cigarette and turned to Jason urgently. "Promise me you'll hold nothing against him. No past action, especially those relevant to his nature." He took hold of

Jason's chin and forced him to meet his eye. "If we're to entertain a contract with him, you must be able to hold this bargain with me."

"I swear I won't hold his past against him. No matter what."

"Good." Pater patted his cheek and let out a hard breath, a sound closer to a gasp than a sigh.

"Are you okay?"

"I'm tired." He rose slowly, legs trembling. "I need to go rest in bed. Can I trust you not to dart across town again?"

"Yes."

"That's my sweet boy." Pater ran soothing fingers through Jason's hair. "You're going to make a wonderful alpha for him."

"I hope so."

"I know so, love."

# CHAPTER SEVEN

"**A**RE YOU ALL right? Did he hurt you?" Rosen's voice cut into the kitchen like a knife. He strode in with purpose, his nearly black hair piled high in a bun held into place with a stick, and his beige sweater bagged around the thighs of his tight, equally beige pants.

"Let me see you." Yosef plowed in behind his younger lover, pinstriped shirt pressed, sleeves rolled up, and his white beard and hair trimmed neatly.

"Lo, it's my strong, handsome, beta heroes to the rescue," Vale said, laughing, returning to spreading butter over the two pieces of perfectly toasted bread he'd made for himself. "Don't tell me I have to provide you with dinner as payment for this service? I'm all out of bread."

"I should think not," Yosef said, crossing his arms over his chest. "Rosen will cook. I still haven't gotten over the last so-called sandwich you compiled for me."

"The cheese was only slightly molded," Vale murmured, sitting down at his mail-stacked table with his toast. "You could have scraped the green off and it would have been just fine."

"It would have been just fine, he says," Rosen scoffed, pushing past Vale and into his fridge. "You look him over, Yosef, while I check for the makings of a real dinner."

"I'm all right. I promise."

Yosef made him stand, though, and inspected him like he was a piece of furniture he was considering for purchase, looking for any nicks or scuffing in the finish. "He's whole," Yosef called out to Rosen. "How's dinner look?"

"There's frozen fish I can thaw and some sweet potatoes that aren't entirely done in. They make for strange bedfellows, but it's better than the pickles and chicken soup we had here last month."

Yosef sighed, patting Vale all over again and then sitting down next to him. "We'd have stopped by the grocery on the way over if we weren't so worried about you."

"I told you on the phone I was fine," Vale said calmly, offering half his toast to Yosef, who accepted and then looked it over for any mold before taking a bite.

"What is your alpha going to think of your terrible housekeeping?" Yosef asked, gazing around at the crumb-strewn counters and the bags of garbage by the door—at least a week's worth that Vale had forgotten to take out to the curb.

"He's apparently swimming in a trust fund of cash, according to Rory. If he's offended, he can afford to hire it out."

Vale didn't mean to sound so blasé about the possibility of his alpha finding anything about him displeasing. He'd tried hard not to let it show when Jason had been standing outside his window lit by the sunlight like a glorious angel from the old times, but he wasn't untouched by the primal need to please his alpha. It just manifested itself differently—in a need to provide him with pleasure.

And unfortunately, a clean house was many a man's pleasure.

"Always too lost in your mind to care about things like taking out the trash," Rosen said, running cool water over the fish. "He'll appreciate your poetry, though. No doubt about that."

"Wolf-god, I hope not."

Yosef darted a glance over Vale's head toward Rosen. Vale didn't need to turn his head to know that Rosen was shooting a disapproving look his way, too.

"I'm not going to endure the opinion of an uneducated child on my life's work."

"So he's really that young, then?"

"Nineteen."

Rosen's whistle echoed in the room as they all let the reality of the situation sink in.

"Dear wolf-in-heaven. That's—" Yosef took a final bite of the toast Vale had shared with him.

"Awful?"

"I was going to say unusual."

"It's not unheard of," Rosen offered. He cut the sweet potatoes into pieces and lined a cooking sheet that he'd brought to Vale's house years ago and left in a concession that Vale was never going to buy one for himself.

"He's handsome." Vale hoped he didn't allow the true longing he felt to infuse his voice. Jason was young, but his jaw was cut, his chin dimpled, and his blue eyes were warm like the sea on a midsummer day. The swath of golden blond hair across his forehead was careless in the way of youth, and his smile, rare though it had been during their conversation, had stopped Vale's heart with its shine.

"Looks aren't everything," Yosef said wisely.

"That's easy for you to say when Rosen looks like he could be a star of stage and screen."

"But he's also an exquisite artist and can dissect the philosophical works of Jeveris like he teaches the stuff. Oh, wait, he does teach the stuff." He winked at his lover and then leaned back in his chair, sighing softly. "How could this have happened, Vale? You, of all people, deserved better than this. You've suffered too much already, what with your parents' death and then…"

It was the closest Yosef would come to mentioning the second horrible rebound heat and the illegal abortion.

Yosef went on. "And now this? Omegas have it hard, but you've had it harder than most."

Vale always knew Yosef pitied him his lot in life, but it still hurt to hear.

"We don't know yet if it's as bad as all that," Vale said carefully. "He seems kind enough."

"Kind? Stalking you at your home, making you feel unsafe, and—"

"He didn't mean to scare me. He's not in control of himself right now. He brought alpha quell with him and he took it. He didn't intend any harm."

"Hmm."

"Yosef, he's my alpha. Even if I never contract with him, that won't change. You'll have to get used to it."

"And Urho?"

"He's..." Vale trailed off, not sure how to discuss it.

"Heartbroken," Rosen said.

"He does love you," Yosef added.

"And I love him, too, but we've never loved each other as life partners. Just as friends. It's not like the two of you. And it's nothing like this beginning bond I feel growing now." He frowned.

"What's *that* like, really?" Rosen switched off the water and set up to fry the fish in a dented pan over the stove.

"Intense." Vale didn't want to say more. It was too personal and left him feeling out of control, like heat: compulsive and needful. But he wasn't going to say that either. "In other news, I've been let go from the university until I've contracted and bonded with Jason Sabel, or until he's graduated after taking a surrogate. Whichever comes first."

"What?" Yosef turned to him, brows drawn low. "Absurd. That's discrimination, surely."

"You're the attorney. You tell me."

He stroked his white beard slowly. "The law does give preference to the alpha in all things, obviously, and an alpha's education takes primacy over an omega's career. Their future is always so much more important than an omega's present," he said snidely, citing a familiar position taken by the omega freedom groups.

"Well, they do have to provide for us horny, pregnant, omega sluts," Vale said, offering up the New Wolf Reform and Wolf Above parties' counterargument as grossly as possible. He rubbed his eyes and slouched in his chair. "Alphas need a good education for that."

Yosef patted Vale's forearm. "Don't talk about it like that. You'll get yourself in trouble."

Vale laughed. What was he in now if not trouble?

"What are his family's politics?" Rosen flipped the fish and added some herbs he'd stashed in Vale's cupboards. "Do you know?"

"They have money, so my default assumption is they vote Stringent Wolf Reform, but I can't say for sure. They could be religious and go Wolf Above."

"Yule Sable is his father?" Yosef asked.

"Yes, and his pater is Miner Hoff. I know nothing about either. I'm sure they've got an investigator looking into me, but I can't afford to throw money at that kind of nonsense."

"Actually, you can. You're due an allowance now. No need to be so frugal with your inheritance."

"I'm not going to accept an allowance. That's absurd."

"What's absurd is that you won't even consider it. Look, Yule Sabel owns a company that makes engine parts for motorcars. That family is beyond well off. They've also inherited money from lands they owned and sold in the last fifty years for a sum that would take your breath away. It was in the papers. You'd know these things if you read one from time to time."

Vale rolled his eyes. Newspapers were for people who wanted to see all the ugly things in the world. Poets needed to see beauty or they'd never get a word down that wasn't ruined by tears.

"Look who's arrived for dinner," Rosen said sweetly. "It's my pookie-wookie wum-wum."

Zephyr slinked into the room, sniffing the air delicately.

"She despises baby talk, Rosen," Vale said. "How many times do I have to tell you that?"

Zephyr rubbed against Rosen's ankles and meowed adorably until he dropped a piece of fish. She ran off with it to the corner, where she ate in jerky little bites of bliss.

"Well, if you're going to bribe her, you can talk to her however you want, apparently. Some morals you've got there, Zephyr," Vale called to her. "Who knew your affections were for hire?" He turned his gaze to Yosef. "Unlike mine."

"That is ludicrous." Yosef folded his arms. "As your attorney, I can't allow you to leave that kind of money on the table."

"I won't be beholden to them. I won't be forced into a contract by profiting financially from the imprinting."

"That's not how it works legally. They owe you the money whether you contract with their son or not. For the rest of your life. Even if he takes a surrogate. It's how it's done. Period. There's no obligation on your part at all."

"Don't be asinine, of course there is. There's emotional obligation, if not legal. I can't accept funds from them and not have that play into my choices."

"If I know you, and I do, it would make you resist contracting more rather than less," Yosef argued. "You wouldn't want to feel like a prostitute."

"Not like old Zephyr over there," Vale said, eyeing his cat. "The little fish whore."

They fell into silence, both of them mulling over the situation as

Rosen finished up dinner. Vale rubbed at his eyes, imagining not having to worry any longer about money. It was tempting. And yet…

"I'm due the money even if he takes a surrogate?" Vale asked. "Why?"

"Because, as the omega, you'd be forbidden to contract with another alpha for life. He'd also have to pay the government a handsome annual fine for the loss of your potential reproductive benefit to the world at large—"

"Will he have to pay that if I contract with him?"

"Only if you refuse to contract for a live birth."

They stared at each other.

"So he'd have to pay the fine regardless," Vale said eventually.

"And the allowance to you, as well. If he took a surrogate, he'd have to file papers to the government explaining why. In your case, infertility or age would do the trick, and he could continue on with another omega for the purposes of making a family. The government approves of that. But given that you're *Érosgápe*, there would be blood on the street if the discarded omega reproduced with anyone else, thus the laws preventing you from such, and the fine Jason would need to pay."

"Why wouldn't that be forgiven if the reason for taking a surrogate was my infertility?"

"Because the government prizes two things above all else: money and babies. Period. Logic need not apply."

Rosen removed the baked sweet potatoes from the oven and retrieved plates for them all.

"Let's assume he takes a surrogate," Vale said, his throat tightening strangely. "What happens with my heats?"

"You'd have to be incredibly discreet in how you handle them from now on. Though, so long as you had minimal contact with your alpha, there would be almost no way for him to know how you got through them or with whom."

Rosen spoke up. "I've never understood why an infertile omega has to be discarded. Can't an alpha handle two? A surrogate and his *Erosgápe* can't be too much for a young, virile alpha to care for simultaneously."

Vale growled under his breath, a sick, rolling feeling starting in his gut at the idea of sharing his home or alpha with another omega.

Yosef's brows lifted in amusement. "There's that reaction for one," he said. "But more importantly, they used to do just that. Omegas in days of yore were treated like breeding stock, with important and powerful alphas literally purchasing uncontracted omegas for the purposes of spreading their seed wide and far. This ultimately resulted in a reduction of the gene pool and genetic anomalies, and some unsatisfied alphas started renouncing their contracts to sell their omegas to wealthier alphas with two, three, or up to five omegas. Eventually the government stepped in and put a stop to it. That was well before New Wolf Reform took over, obviously. Apparently, even the religious kooks in Wolf Above could see the problems of human trafficking."

Vale stared out the kitchen window, watching a few leaves float on the breeze and land gently in the yard.

"But there's no reason to assume he'll take a surrogate," Yosef said soothingly.

Vale shrugged. It shouldn't matter, and yet his stomach knotted up at the thought of being rejected by his *Erosgápe*. Logic need not apply in his heart, either, he supposed.

"How can we make it palatable for you to take the allowance you're owed?" Yosef asked, bringing the conversation back around to money again.

"You can't."

"I'll find a way.

"Dinner is served." Rosen brought plates of fish and baked

sweet potatoes to the table.

They dropped the topic of Vale's unexpected *Érosgápe* for dinner, instead speaking of Rosen and Yosef's tentative plans for the various upcoming Autumn Nights celebrations. After they'd eaten, cleaned up the dishes, and moved to Vale's study, it was clear Yosef was ready to get into it again. Just as he opened his mouth to speak, the doorbell rang.

Vale's stomach flipped and tangled as he walked down the hall toward the front door.

Would it be Jason? Did he hope it was or dread the idea? Damn the *Érosgápe* imprint. It clouded everything.

A messenger stood on the front stoop with two fat envelopes in his arms.

"Mr. Aman?"

"That's me, yes."

"These are from the Law Offices of Tissue & Freet. If you'd sign here…" He indicated a form and held out a pen.

As Vale signed, Yosef appeared at his elbow. "What's this?"

"No idea." Vale passed the form back to the messenger and accepted the packages in return. "They're from a law firm." He tucked them under his arm as the messenger stepped through the front lawn, dodging the falling leaves and dropping acorns of the oak tree by the gate. "Maybe Rory has already sent the terms of my temporary resignation, but I can't imagine it'd require two packets to get the job done."

"Ah, no," Yosef murmured, grabbing the top envelope from Vale's hands. "These are pre-negotiation disclosures. Everything about Jason Sabel his family deems important for your consideration and review before the official contract negotiations begin."

As they made their way back to the study, Zephyr darted in front of them, prancing with her tail held high. Vale turned on the hallway lights, using the dimmer his father had installed to keep the atmosphere pleasantly intimate. He rarely turned the lights to full brightness since his parents' death, preferring the gift of shadows over the stark revelations of white electric bulbs.

Back in the study, Rosen and Yosef lounged against each other on the sofa with Zephyr perched on Rosen's thighs. Vale settled in, and they all stared at the packages on the coffee table.

"Pre-negotiation disclosures," Yosef explained in response to Rosen's questioning look.

"Already? It hasn't even been twenty-four hours."

"They've probably been compiling the file since Jason was born," Yosef explained. "Most families do. Then when the time comes, they only have to add the latest information to the top, usually the alpha's final grades, specific plans for his immediate future, career goals and living arrangements, that sort of thing. But aside from those items, they've already got a nice packet put together for the family of any omega their son imprints on or considers for a contract."

Vale picked up a packet, weighing it in his hands and examining the unbroken seal. "These are big envelopes for only a few years' worth of information on Jason."

"There's probably family information as well—ancestry, accounts of the most recent live births in the family, properties Jason would stand to inherit, business endeavors. Basically everything you could possibly need to know about the Sabel and Hoff families. And given their wealth and status, that information might go all the way back to early post-Death years."

"What am I supposed to do with it all?" Vale brought the packet to his nose, smelling the sweetness of fresh paper mixed with the dust of old documents, too. Whatever was in these packets was more information than he wanted. But it was all things the Sabels would expect him to know.

"I'll be happy to sort through it with you. I've overseen contracts before."

"I can make myself scarce with a book, or better yet, hop out to the grocery to restock your kitchen," Rosen offered. "Whatever is in these packets isn't any of my business."

Vale nodded slowly. "I appreciate that. There's plenty of cash in the second drawer down in the kitchen. Below the knives."

"Because a thief should definitely have access to weapons before robbing you blind," Rosen scolded.

Vale shrugged. He used to keep his money in a safe in his father's old study—now a guest room—but then he'd forgotten the combination, locking a nice wad of cash up for all eternity, apparently. So now he just shoved whatever cash he took out of the bank into the drawer in the kitchen. Why not? There were plenty of nicer houses on Oak Avenue for thieves to hit before his. Who'd decide that a house with an overgrown garden and an abundance of dust on all the furniture visible through the windows made for a good bet?

Rosen unsettled Zephyr who protested with a screechy meow and took off for a bookshelf, knocking a few smaller volumes to the floor in her temper.

"She likes you much better than me. Just take her with you when you go." Vale frowned at the book of Calitan poetry that had landed on its spine, pages falling open.

"Yosef is too demanding of my attention." Rosen chuckled. "She's better off with you. All right, I'll be back in a hour and half with some fresh, mold-free food." He bent to drop a kiss on Yosef's head, and then headed out, calling over his shoulder, "Hire my lover, would you? Before you screw yourself over, Vale."

Vale moved from the wingback chair to the sofa, bringing the packet with him. "Yosef, you know I trust your judgment. Despite our disagreement about the allowance, will you agree to act as my attorney in this matter?"

"Of course."

"I suppose I'd be remiss if I didn't ask about your fees."

"Waived."

"I insist on paying you."

"If you accept the allowance, I'll consider it. If not, then absolutely not."

Vale sighed and held the first packet out to Yosef. "Will you do the honors?"

"With pleasure."

THERE WERE PICTURES. Vale hadn't expected that.

The first photo was of a tiny Jason on his pater's lap, face covered in what appeared to be chocolate pie, and the words "Mister Mess, age 2" printed neatly on the back. The second was of Jason as an infant, held in his Father's arms, a tiny fist pressed against his puckered lips. The third was from Jason's fifth birthday party—cherub cheeks lit by five candles on the cake. The fourth was a painfully awkward shot of Jason during puberty; his nose was too big for his face and his right cheekbone was warped by a large pimple. He was smiling, though, and Vale recognized that smile from earlier in the day when it had flashed at him momentarily and beautifully.

"He's smart," Yosef said, tapping the last picture. "That's an award for the highest marks in science for his school."

Vale hadn't even noticed the small trophy in Jason's hands. He'd been too transfixed by the gangly boy he'd once been. Well, the even *ganglier* boy. Jason was still tall, thin, and moved like a puppy growing into his bones.

"I'm sure they have his grade reports in here somewhere," Yosef said, moving on to sort through the rest of the papers.

"Why would they send these?" Vale went back to the first pictures of Jason as a baby. The parents—Yule and Miner—looked quite young in them. They almost glowed with happiness, and Jason was adorable in their arms.

"Two-fold: to show that he's been a healthy child all through his life, but also to whet your appetite for babies of your own. 'Look how cute your alpha was! Don't you want to make one of these with him?'"

Vale chewed on his bottom lip. Truth be told, if circumstances were different, then yes, he'd like to have one of these of his own—to carry on his parents' genes and to satisfy his own yearnings, and presumably, the yearnings of his alpha. But…

"Is it working?" Yosef asked quietly, reading through more papers and laying them out in some order Vale didn't understand.

"It doesn't matter, does it?" Vale shrugged and put the photos aside. "What else is there?"

"A letter from his parents." He passed it to Vale. "For the most part, it states the usual: their hopes and dreams for a good pairing with their son, desire for grandchildren, and a confidence that the families can be joined amicably. But the second page is interesting. It outlines Miner Hoff's biological condition, potentially heritable, that made carrying to term nearly impossible for him. It's relevant only in that your own offspring with Jason could carry the gene. If there's to be any offspring."

Vale's gut knotted up, anxiety-laced sadness trotting through his heart along with the memories of pain and blood. He closed his eyes. Urho's initial assessment and a subsequent visit to another physician to examine why Vale sometimes experienced pain on Urho's knot hadn't brought good news. Scar tissue had formed, and it was unlikely he'd survive a birth.

What'd seemed formlessly sad when the doctor delivered the initial diagnosis now had a shape and a name: Jason. How terrible to have a beautiful young alpha to wound and disappoint with his past mistakes. How horrible to take away the boy's chances at a life with his *Érosgápe*.

Shame twisted inside.

"Do you want children, Vale?" Yosef asked gently.

"We both know that isn't going to happen," he whispered. Yosef quietly accepted his response, and they let the sadness hang in the air between them. Finally, voice quivering, Vale asked, "How do we handle that?"

"Miner Hoff's disclosure gives us the perfect card to play, actually." Yosef squeezed Vale's knee. "An omega who's suffered like he has—and likely suffers still given the laws around surgical remedies—won't insist that another omega submit to an unwanted, painful, and potentially deadly experience. Not unless he's a terrible person, and that seems unlikely. Just put your foot down, make it clear that it's against your wishes, and either they'll cave and agree to always employ alpha condoms for contraception or they'll look for a surrogate. It'll be up to Jason at that point, I imagine."

"He's so young, it'll really be up to his parents. They'll be able to persuade him."

"What do you want to have happen?"

"I don't know." Vale ran an anxious hand through his hair. "As Jason put it to me today, there's the me that's me, and there's the me that he's awakened, and they don't want the same things. Twenty-four hours ago I was happy, content with my life. Tonight, I can't truthfully say I wish this had never happened. It'd be a lie to claim that I don't want him to choose me." Vale scoffed, stood up, and headed over to the liquor cabinet, where he poured scotch for them both. "I know nothing about him and I'm already moping at the idea that he'd make the smart choice. He *should* choose a young surrogate with years of breeding ahead. What do I have to offer him?" He handed Yosef the drink.

"Yourself. And you're nothing to sneeze at."

"I'm much older and won't provide him with a child. I know the union of *Érosgápe* is supposed to be near bliss, but can it really be worth the rest of the hassle? The social ostracization he'll have to face when the others of his cohort all have appropriately aged omegas? When they're having wild bashes and I'm more interested in a dinner party for a select few? When they're popping out babies and making families? Will he think, 'Well, at least I knotted Vale until we both couldn't see straight, at least I shot my condom full of massive amounts of jizz during our brilliant and fruitless coupling?' I think not."

"You're *Érosgápe*. No one else will ever satisfy him the way you can. That's the way it is and will always be. He'll choose you, Vale."

"I don't want him to!" He threw his drink back and poured a second as the liquor scorched his throat.

"You just said you did."

Vale groaned. "I know that. I mean I want him to have a good life. When he came over this morning…"

Yosef tossed his back as well, and his voice came out hoarse when he said, "Go on. When he came over this morning what?"

Sitting beside his friend on the sofa again the papers mocked Vale with a promise of a family he'd never make. "He's a good kid, with a soft heart, and he deserves a family and a good, normal, solid life."

"Wah, wah, wah."

"What?"

"You must stop punishing yourself for the rebound heat you suffered and what happened after." Yosef's eyes glowed with bare truth, the way they always did when he drank. It'd probably been a mistake to give him the scotch. "You deserve to be happy, Vale. If you're going to refuse to contract with him, at least do it because you genuinely believe you'd be happier alone."

"I wouldn't be alone. I'd have you and Rosen and Urho."

"You'll have us anyway. Maybe Urho won't be your lover anymore, but he'll always be in your life. You can have all of us and this thing with Jason, too. You aren't required to give us up. And you don't need to punish yourself for suppressing that heat years ago when you didn't have Urho to help you and you didn't know what else to do."

"I'd endured a rebound before, though," Vale whispered. "I should have known."

"Vale, desperate people do desperate things, and it's not your fault."

"I could have had the baby."

"Is that what this is about? Do you feel guilty about your choice?"

He hadn't felt like he had a real choice at the time. The idea of carrying a strange alpha's child to term, birthing it alone, and then raising it on his own had been terrifying. Add to that trying to manage his existence as an uncontracted, unbonded, alpha-less omega with a child in tow? In their culture? And so soon after his parents' deaths? It had seemed impossible and unfair to the child. What kind of future would it have?

Looking at his life now, he couldn't imagine it with a half-grown child in it, complicating this situation with Jason even more. No, he didn't really have regrets about his choice. He only regretted the consequences of it, and the fact that now he had so much less to offer the young, handsome alpha he desperately and illogically wanted to choose him.

"I want my whole life to have been different. I want to have met Jason when I was supposed to, when all my age mates met their *Érosgápe*. I want to have born him several lovely children by now. Or I want to have never met him at all and to have kept on happily with Urho until one or both of us grew tired of it, or we died."

"You'll be a perfect match for a nineteen-year-old after all," Yosef said. "Mooning over things you can't have and what can never be."

Vale snorted. "Is this your way of saying I should grow up?"

"Yes. Grow up, Vale. Get your head out of your ass and face the situation full on." Yosef's white eyebrows lowered. "You've got to make a plan. Everything will happen faster than you think."

Zephyr knocked another book from the shelf, and they both jumped.

"See, even your cat agrees with me. Stop self-flagellating and stop wishing. Take a deep breath. Let it out. Accept this situation for what it is, and then let's move forward together. Understood?"

Vale swallowed the last of his drink, slammed the glass on the coffee table, and nodded. "Your logic can't be faulted. I'm done moping. What's next?"

"Here's a list of their properties. Let's see what your alpha stands to inherit, compare that to what you bring to the table, and determine what kind of bargains we can anticipate and negotiate in your favor. It shouldn't be hard, especially since he's an only child. He'll be spoiled, I'm sure. His parents probably have little to no practice saying no to him."

Vale nodded, taking up the list of properties. There was nothing to be done but move ahead as if Jason might choose him despite his failures and faults.

And if Jason didn't? If he took the smart option?

Vale would deal with the heartbreak then.

# CHAPTER EIGHT

JASON STOOD BY his bedroom window gazing out over the manicured lawn to the road he knew led to Vale's house. He'd taken his entire dose of alpha quell that morning, supervised by Father who'd come into his room just before his usual waking time to make sure he downed it all.

The drug helped him keep his wits about him, but he resented its effectiveness, too. He wanted to feel the pull of the imprint; he wanted to give into it and run off down the street, past the other alphas and omegas going about their day, to see Vale again. Protocols be damned. But he knew better, and the alpha quell helped him remember all the reasons why he needed to be patient.

At least for today.

He headed downstairs to the kitchen, prepared his own breakfast of an egg sandwich, and ate it leaning against the study door listening for any scrap of information in Pater and Father's muffled tones. He jumped away and pretended to be examining himself in the ornate mirror across the hall just as the door opened. Patting at his hair and inspecting his teeth, he hoped it seemed as if he was doing nothing more than indulging in some vanity.

Pater's raised brow told Jason he hadn't fooled him one bit.

"Come in, son. We'd like to share the information Jeft Mellor brought for us."

Jason leapt away from the mirror and ducked into his father's office. The windows were open, allowing a cool autumn crossbreeze to carry away the cigarette smoke, but the brass plate on the edge of Father's desk and the four crumpled stubs spoke to Pater's continued anxiety or pain.

"Sit." Father nodded at the second chair opposite his desk. He was dressed in his usual oxford shirt and a pair of dress pants. His jacket and a tie hung at the ready on a coat stand next to his desk, but he only added those if a business associate came to visit.

His blond hair was slicked back from his worried forehead with the lemon-scented oil he used to style it, and his blue eyes seemed tired but not angry. Jason took that as a good sign.

Pater folded himself into the other open seat. He'd eschewed the soft pants of the day before for a nicer pair of trousers, cut in the latest style. A fashionable sweater was pushed up at the forearms, revealing his trembling hands. He tucked them between his legs and nodded at Father.

"You can smoke if you want," Jason whispered. "I can deal with it."

Pater smiled gently. "I've indulged myself enough. It's time to get to business."

Father slapped an inch-thick stack of papers on his desk alongside three slim fabric-covered volumes. "Hopefully Mr. Aman will have hired an attorney who can help him prepare his disclosure forms. I doubt he has an omega packet prepared and set aside. In all likelihood, any information his parents prepared is long gone, deemed unnecessary. We may never have all the details we'd like about his family."

"It's fine," Jason said.

Father's lips pressed together, but he didn't object to Jason's opinion. "The good news is that his father was a research assistant at Mont Juror, so there's no lack of intelligence, most likely. And his pater was considered a fine man by all accounts. Kept a good house. They were sociable and well-liked."

Jason kept his face neutral. He knew he was supposed to care about such things, but he didn't. The draw of social status paled in comparison to the beauty of Vale's eyes.

Father went on, "The first thing we have here is the projected value of the house on Oak Avenue. It's Mr. Aman's free and clear, inherited from his parents. Since you'll be inheriting our house, however, you won't need to hold onto his. Once you've bonded, you can sell it and use the proceeds to buy a more suitable property closer to us, and—"

"But if he likes his house, why couldn't we just live there?"

Father frowned and Pater coughed lightly.

"Well?" Jason pushed.

"Oak Avenue is in an upper-middle-class section of town. Nothing to be ashamed of, of course, but it isn't fit for a man who stands to inherit as you do," Father said.

Jason clenched his hands together, listening as his father droned on about the small cabin in the woods Vale's parents had also owned, but which seemed to have fallen into disrepair long before their deaths. "You'll sell that, too," his father stated.

"Can I have a piece of paper and a pencil?" Jason asked.

Startled, Father looked up from the documents. "I suppose so." He passed a yellow ruled pad and a pencil. "What do you need it for?"

"Just to keep track of my thoughts."

He scribbled:

*If Vale likes his house, we will live there as long as we want.*

*If Vale wants to improve the cabin, we will. If he'd rather be done with it, I'll fix it up and sell it.*

Pater adjusted his position and pretended not to be trying to read what Jason had written. Jason didn't hide it, but he didn't make it easy for his pater, either.

"Okay, I'm ready. What's next?"

"He writes poetry," Father said, a hint of disapproval in his tone.

"I know."

"He told you?" Pater sounded surprised.

"Yes."

"Did he tell you it was…" Father cleared his throat. "Did he say it was racy poetry?"

"He said he didn't think I should read it just now, that he'd written about heat, and about other alphas who'd helped him with it." His fists clenched, and the pencil jabbed into the flesh of his palm.

"It's only instinct," Pater whispered, touching his knee and nodding to his gripped hands. "Logic can rule instinct if we take command of it."

Jason forced himself to relax his fingers. "I don't like it, but it's not his fault I wasn't around when he needed me."

Father darted a glance between Pater and Jason, measuring them both, and then nodded slowly. "Agreed."

"But I agree with Vale on this," Pater said. "Knowing that he had little choice in choosing a safe alpha to help him through his heats and reading the poems about it are two entirely different things. I suggest you let go of any thought of reading these volumes."

"Why he was even compelled to write poems about it, I can't imagine." Father leaned back in his chair with a tight expression. "It simply wasn't necessary."

Pater rolled his eyes. "Yule, what's done is done."

"Will he write poems about Jason? I think we should include a ban on poems in any contract we draw up."

"That's absurd." Pater laughed.

"No," Jason said. "No ban." The idea that Vale might write poems about him was deliriously wonderful. His heart squeezed and jolted. He wanted to be deserving of Vale's attention and dedicated words. "He'll write according to his inspiration."

Father snorted but shrugged.

Jason scribbled on his notepad: *Vale is allowed to write about anything he wants.*

Pater clucked his tongue and whispered, "As if you could stop him, but that's fine, love. Write it down."

Father tugged another piece of paper out with a frown. "This one is troublesome. It's part of a file from a doctor's office he visited several years ago with complaints about taking a knot during heat."

Jason's fists clenched again, but he took a long breath and let it out slowly.

"Apparently there's some scar tissue of unknown origin that looks problematic for childbearing."

"Childbearing is inherently problematic," Pater said quietly. "Add his age, and now this? I don't think it's right to expect him to be able to—"

"One," Father said firmly.

"Yule…"

"Jason's our only son, and after all we went through with my pater, all we suffered so that the line would carry on?"

Pater covered his face with one hand, patting for his cigarettes with the other.

"Jason, this is important. If you intend to contract with this man, you need to think about this hard and long." Father peered at him, forehead crinkled. "Do you understand what's at stake? You have to take it into account. Generations of people before you have suffered in order to bring you into the world, to carry on the genetic line. If he's incapable, there are other options. You can contract a surrogate—"

"Stop," Pater said, cigarette dangling from his lips as he struck a match and lit it. "We have no idea if the man wants children or not. We'll cover this in negotiations."

"Who cares if he wants children? What about Jason?"

"Like you said, Jason has options." Smoke swirled from Pater's nose as he exhaled roughly. "The choice is theirs to make as *Érosgápe*, not ours."

Father's shoulder's rounded and his jaw clenched, but he didn't speak about surrogates or breeding again, moving on to the income Vale had lost when Chancellor Rory removed him from his position at the university.

"Obviously, we'll replace it as his allowance. It's a reasonable sum." Father picked up the papers and shoved them into a brown file folder. "Aside from gruesome reports on his parents' deaths, all of which seems unnecessary for you to hear about, that's all we have today. If we get more information about him, we'll be sure to let you know."

Jason stared at the poetry books on his father's desk. "Are those ours to keep?"

"I thought we agreed?"

"But not every poem is about heat or sex, surely?"

Father glanced toward Pater, and they had one of their silent conversations. After Father nodded, Pater reached to take up both of the books. "I'll read them and tear out the ones suitable for you, if you'd like."

Jason licked his lips. Vale had given the sexual poems as the reason why he didn't want Jason to read the books. He hadn't said anything about the other poems, had he? And while the idea of destroying the volumes to get at some of the poetry was unpleasant, it was still better than not knowing what his omega had written about all these years. "Yes. I'd like to read them."

Pater nodded and tucked the books beneath his arm. He stubbed the cigarette out and rose slowly. "I'll be in the conservatory. What's for dinner?"

Father snorted softly. "Take-out at this rate, but I did set those flanks out to thaw."

"I'll eat whatever you bring me." Pater smiled at him. "Anything I don't have to cook is always my favorite."

"Ours, too." Father laughed, his blue eyes losing their tired grimness. "Go on. Get your day started."

"What about me?" Jason asked. "I should be in political science class right now."

"Chancellor Rory has agreed you can return to your classes on Monday. It's protocol to keep you isolated until the alpha quell has a chance to settle into your system." Father frowned. "Still, it's no good for you to sit around bored. Why don't you wash and polish Miner's car and then we'll find another way to keep you busy when you're done."

"Other families of our status have beta servants to do those chores for them. And to cook."

"Other families don't have your pater as omega. He likes his privacy. And so do I."

Washing and waxing the car took a few hours and kept Jason's mind occupied for the most part. He did drift off into fantasies at several points, imagining making Vale a present of a brand-new car straight off the assembly line, then riding with him to the seaside cottage for a week of lazing together in the sand. He wondered whether he could get a car in cerulean blue.

Afterward, he went up to his room to shower again. He changed into a pair of clean trousers cut to perfection by his pater's tailor and a plain green button-up shirt. He started on a paper for Professor Rochera's biodiversity class, spending extra time drawing the wings of the Saturniid moth in detail in the margins. Then he practiced the guitar a bit more, playing some songs he knew and attempting to write one of his own. He'd never been a very motivated musician, not like Pater who enjoyed playing and composing both, but with Vale the poet as a potential future audience, he was determined to bring him something beautiful if he could.

He played on, remembering the drifts of loose paper in Vale's study, the light from the window on Vale's skin, and the thud of his pulse in his neck. In his mind's eye, it was a steady rhythm, delicate and yet firm. He played to its beat. Vale was so beautiful. Jason's fingers flew over the strings, and he closed his eyes, letting the music fill him in a way it never had before.

Another dose of alpha quell was brought up to his room by Father before he left to meet with some suppliers.

"I'll be home later with some sort of take-out. If you get hungry in the meantime, or if Miner does, go ahead and cook what I've put out to thaw."

"Yes, sir."

"You're a good boy, Jason," his father said fondly, sliding his hand into Jason's hair and smiling down at him. "I know you're overwhelmed now, but I assure you everything is going to be all right."

"I know, Father." Not because he trusted his parents, though he did, but because he was determined. He was young, but he wasn't an idiot. With every second that passed, Jason became more certain. He could be what Vale needed. He'd stand taller, be smarter, work harder. He'd do whatever it took.

After his father left, a knock came at the front door. Irrationally, Jason's heart leapt into his throat. He knew it wouldn't be Vale, but it was possible, wasn't it? He'd said he wasn't immune to Jason. Maybe he was dying to see him, too?

Jason tried to hide his disappointment when he found Xan on the doorstep with a tin of Woodenhall Candy Store's famous fudge in hand for Pater and a shy, nervous smile for Jason. "Hey, I brought my notes from school. Thought I'd help you out for a change."

Jason swung the door wide. Whatever had been stuck in Xan's craw when he last saw him in the student medical center seemed dislodged now. "Pater loves that fudge. So I guess I have to let you in."

"Even if I was a jerk the other day?"

Jason smiled and wrapped his arm around Xan's shoulder, guiding him into the foyer. "Who isn't a jerk when their best friend goes crazy and attacks an omega in the library?"

"Not me, apparently."

"Yeah, not you. You jerked it right up and without hesitation."

The joking soothed the airing of grievances, and the word *sorry* never needed to be spoken aloud. "Do you want to give the fudge to Pater personally? Or just leave it here on the table for him?"

"Here's fine." Xan scooted the box safely onto the marble-topped table next to the coat rack.

"Let's go upstairs." Jason peeled Xan's coat free and hung it up for him. "I've got new prepared microscope slides since you were here. Tree diseases this time."

Botany wasn't his absolute favorite thing to study, but it was pretty close. He loved learning about plants and how to grow them. The chemical processes within them and their reproductive functions were fascinating. And he enjoyed learning about plant diseases, too, as well as their cures.

Xan, for his part, couldn't care less about any of it, but he indulged Jason all the same. At least he usually did. Given that he was here to pseudo-apologize, Jason didn't think today would be any different. "The Cedar-Apple Rust fungus is especially cool."

"Nerd," Xan muttered, then laughed and straightened his blue-and-gold printed bow tie.

"The biggest," Jason agreed, taking Xan's hand and pulling him toward the staircase up to his room. "Wait until you see how pretty the bacteria is that causes root rot in Old World Japanese Maples.

It's the prettiest bacteria I've ever seen."

While Jason set up the microscope on his neatly organized desk, Xan walked around the bedroom looking at everything like he'd never seen it before and might never see it again. Finally, he sat down on the edge of Jason's freshly made bed and chewed on his bottom lip.

"They really aren't going to let you come back to school?"

"I can go back for classes starting next week." Jason pulled out a few slides from his collection. The butterfly wings he'd ordered at the end of summer were cool, too. He didn't think Xan had seen those yet. "But yeah, not to live."

"Ever?"

"Probably not. If I contract with him, then I'll live with him somewhere. If negotiations get drawn out, then my parents will want me to stay home." Jason sent him an empathetic shrug. "It sucks. We had a lot of plans, but, hey, look at the bright side. You get a whole room to yourself!"

Xan stared at him, his normally red cheeks pale. "How can you be so relaxed about this?"

Jason chuckled. "Relaxed? If I seem relaxed that's just the alpha quell." He slipped a glass slide under the microscope clip and took a look. It was a slide he'd prepared for himself instead of purchasing. It consisted of grains of sand from the shore next to their beach cottage. Under the microscope, they offered up an array of colors and shapes. "I'm going crazy deep down. But if I acted like I feel, it'd just make everything worse." A small swirl of translucent shell sat at the center of the slide, amongst, red, blue, and green coral, minerals, and rock. "Look at this one first," he said. "It's fantastic."

Xan didn't move from the bed even when Jason beckoned him with a smile. Instead, his fingers curled into fists and his tear-filled gaze met Jason's.

"What's wrong?" Jason asked gently, his heart twisting. "Why are you so upset?"

"What about me?" Xan's voice broke.

Jason gaped at him, mind turning over and over. "You're going to be all right."

"No, I'm not."

"Sure you will. I know we always promised to live together, but it's not like I planned it like this. And, unlike me, you have a lot of friends at school. People who'll be happy to keep you entertained now that I won't be there to make you study all the time." Jason abandoned the microscope and slides and sat next to Xan on the bed.

"I need you." Xan's mouth worked. "Why can't you come back? They've let him go from his job—your omega. I heard it this morning. So you'd be fine there. Say you'll come back."

Jason's heart clenched as Xan leaned against his shoulder. "I wish I could. I really do. But they say I'm not trustworthy. They think I'll go to him in the night and won't be able to control myself. They think they can watch out for me better at home."

Not to mention, home was about five miles closer to Vale's house, so maybe he didn't want to go back to school all that much.

Xan's blue eyes slowly rose up to Jason's. A storm brewed in them, though Jason didn't know why, and it made his stomach ache.

"What's it like?" Xan asked, his voice pitched low and his tone a trembling mix of anger and hurt. "Do you still...?" He shook his head.

"Do I still what?"

Xan sat up straighter. His eyes darted around the room, like he couldn't bear to look at any one thing for very long. "Is finding your *Érosgápe* as amazing as they say?"

"It's awful."

"Why?"

"Because I want him so much and I can't have him." He tried to think of the words to explain it. It was just so *big*. "I don't even know him. It's weird and intense and I have to take alpha quell now just to act like a normal person. I haven't seen him in over a day and I don't know when I will again, and that makes me feel sick deep down. Like I might be dying. It's awful."

"Do you only want him now?"

"What do you mean?"

Xan's jaw set. "You know what I mean, Jason."

"Oh!"

Shock rocked through him. He hadn't spared a thought for the games he and Xan played. Not since he'd met Vale. It hadn't occurred to him that Xan might miss them already. He tried to untangle his tongue enough to reply.

"Is it so hard to answer a simple question?" Xan's hand shook as he brushed a dark lock of hair away from his imploring eyes.

Jason's heart squeezed. It wasn't that he *didn't* want Xan. It was just that he wanted Vale more. And wanting Vale—the glint of his smile, the fan of lines by his eyes, the shivery way he said Jason's name—was a constant underlying itch that he couldn't scratch. It didn't leave room for much else.

Xan's voice trembled. "Do you still want me?" He tilted his head, one hand working on the buttons of his shirt to reveal his pale, hairless skin. He leaned in close, his breath ghosting against Jason's lips. "I still want you. Nothing's changed for me."

His kiss wasn't undesirable. It was good even, sweet and slick, greedy and somehow scared, waking Jason to the very real possibility of immediate sex. It was also just *weird*, because he wanted it, but he didn't, but he *did*.

Blood raced to fill his dick; it pressed between his thigh and pant leg. He shivered, arousal flooding him. It mixed strangely with the alpha quell, making his insides burn cold instead of hot. An ocean breeze against a sunburn.

"I woke up this morning wanting this," Xan groaned. "And you weren't there to give it to me."

"I'm sorry." Jason's head spun and his cock ached as he was pulled in two directions, even as he tilted his head to let Xan suck a kiss onto his neck.

"Give it to me now," Xan commanded, before claiming Jason's lips.

The kiss deepened and Jason went with it, curious about the split inside him, the way his mouth on Xan's felt so much less intimate than simply standing outside Vale's house, talking to him through an open window.

"You can pretend I'm him," Xan whispered wetly against Jason's lips, as though sensing the direction of Jason's thoughts. "Pretend anything you want."

Jason closed his eyes, but there was no way he could mistake Xan's scent for Vale's rose-and-musk aroma. But what was the harm in playing one last game? For all he knew, Vale was currently indulging in physical pleasure with that alpha he'd been with at the library. Jason knew what they did together. He'd smelled it on him that first day.

A hard ball of jealousy ached in his gut, and he clenched Xan closer. If Vale could have previous lovers to be forgiven for, then Jason could, too.

Xan's kisses became more desperate. "Don't stop," he moaned. "Please don't stop."

Breaking free of the kiss, Jason gazed into Xan's eyes. "You want this?"

"More than anything."

"Suck me." Jason deepened his voice, making it a non-negotiable command. "Get my dick out and make me come."

Visible relief rocked Xan's body as he scrambled to unbutton

Jason's pants. He opened wide to get Jason's cockhead into his mouth, sucking and moaning, letting saliva roll down the length and pool in Jason's tightly curled, blond pubic hair.

Jason played with Xan's dark, sweaty hair, and moaned softly. Xan knew what he liked. He gazed up at Jason with wide eyes, whimpering, and twisting his tongue around Jason's dick. Strength and command filled him as he thrust into Xan's open mouth.

"Take it," he grunted, gripping Xan's hair. "Suck me."

Xan groaned and quickly unzipped his own pants, jerking himself off with one hand while he tried to swallow Jason's cock.

Holding Xan's head down, pumping up into his gagging throat, Jason's eyes rolled back. The air around them seemed to grow crisp in a strange shift of consciousness he'd never experienced before. This wasn't the way they usually had sex. There was no laughter, no fun. He was dominating another alpha and getting off on the power. It had nothing to do with Xan.

Realization dawned.

Alpha expression. A power fuck. The same kind of fuck that alphas in the past had engaged in to punish or acquire, to make another man submit. Triggered by exposure to his *Érosgápe*, the urge to conquer and control was intense. He was tempted to revel in this new, brutal arousal. But it felt wrong, too. It had nothing to do with friendship and nothing to do with his omega.

He shuddered and released Xan's head. "Off. Stop."

Xan pulled away, wiped his wet lips with the back of his hand, and stared up tremblingly at Jason. "Why?"

Jason stared down at his hard, wet cock, beating with his heartbeat and pointing directly up at him. "This is wrong."

"Because of him?"

Jason frowned. *Yes.* But it was more than that. "I'm being rough with you."

"I like it."

"My exposure to Vale triggered alpha expression."

Xan's eyes went wider and—was it possible?—even more aroused. "Oh."

"This isn't how we've done this." Jason's cock didn't seem to care, though, and a pearl of pre-come glistened at his slit. He still wanted to dominate and force Xan to submit. An unknown cruelty pulsed inside him. He closed his eyes and wrestled it down. "Before. It was never like this. It was for fun."

"I don't care how it is, Jason. I just want it. I want it so bad, and if you leave, if you're not there…"

Questions Jason had never let himself entertain about Xan's future crowded his mind. What if Xan never found an omega? One he could trust with his secret needs? Would he really stop wanting to be fucked once he found his *Érosgápe*—if he found his *Érosgápe*? Or worse, what if Xan trusted the wrong man?

"I need it," Xan whimpered, gripping his own cock hard, and pulling the foreskin down to expose the head. "You give me what I need. Only you. And I'll help you, too. You can't fuck him yet, but you can fuck me. I'll be yours, Jason. If you'll have me."

A possessive thrill raced up Jason's spine.

Xan wasn't Vale, he wasn't enough, and he could never be, but Jason could take him. He could give him what he needed and own him for a time, be the alpha to make him scream and come. He could bring his beautiful friend the pleasure he needed. Alpha expression was natural. It existed for a reason.

"Yeah." Jason nodded. "Okay." His balls were tight and hard, and he didn't know how long he'd last, but Xan wanted what he had to give, and even if it wasn't right, Jason wasn't backing away. "Get your clothes off and your ass up."

Stripping down, they stared into each other's eyes, challenge given and received. By the time Jason was naked, the thudding of his cock obliterated rational thought. Consumed by a need to grab and take, to prove who was best between them, he would show who was the stronger alpha.

Their scents mixed in the room. Two alphas in lust and need. Rising above their mixed musk, though, he caught a whiff something else. Something true and right. Something he needed more than air, and he ripped his gaze from Xan's to search for the source of it.

He shoved Xan to the bed. Submission replaced the challenge he'd been giving off, and Jason's blood sang in victory.

"Yes, get your ass up," he muttered, still seeking the source of the scent that flitted around him, just out of reach. "Get yourself ready for me to fuck you."

Then his eyes fell to his bedside table.

*There.*

Jason grabbed the strip of blue fabric, the bookmark Vale had given him, and pressed it to his nose. *Yes.* Deeply embedded in the material was the scent of Vale's house—old papers, dusty books, and the sharp lead scent of pencils. On top of those deeper scents, Jason could just make out a trace of musk, a hint of mint from the garden, and the rose-scented sweetness of Vale's skin.

He groaned, his cock throbbing with blood, hard and aching.

Muddled thoughts rose. His omega was out there, just a few streets away, maybe being fucked by another alpha at this very moment, maybe not. It didn't matter. There was nothing he could ever do about the past or the present.

Just the future.

And in the immediate future, Jason was going to fuck the day-lights out of Xan. He'd make another alpha mewl and cry and come. He'd make him beg.

Jason's cock swelled harder.

On the bed, Xan was naked and in position. Reaching back, he held his ass cheeks open. His tight hole glistened with his own hastily applied spit.

"Hurry," Xan whispered. "Fuck me." His blue eyes burned urgently over his shoulder, and his red lips parted with each violent exhale of breath.

Jason tossed the ribbon aside, the scent of Vale's house and skin clinging in his nose. Spit wasn't nearly enough to slick the way, but Jason pushed his dick against Xan's hole. It gave a little, but he couldn't press inside. A shot of frustration zipped up Jason's spine, and he pushed harder.

"Please. I need it." Xan arched his back, presenting like an omega.

"Take it then," he said, gripping Xan's hips and pushing in past the resistant ring of muscle.

Xan cried out, his asshole spasming hard. Jason groaned, yearning to shove in more, but he didn't want to hurt his friend. He rubbed Xan's back, bending low to take in the sweet scent of Xan's sweat. It filled his nostrils, replacing the scent of the ribbon and Vale.

He closed his eyes, concentrated hard, and wrangled his mind back from the lust-addled field it'd been romping on. Vale wasn't here now. It was wrong to include him in this, especially when Xan was giving himself up so earnestly.

Jason had been wrong. Again.

Some alpha he was going to be.

He breathed in and out, calming himself. Beneath him, Xan shook and his body pulsed around Jason's cock. His heartbeat thundered wildly under Jason's palm. He cried out softly, a sour desperation slipping into his scent.

Guiding them both down to the mattress, Jason sunk in deeper as they went. "Hush," he said soothingly. "I've got you."

Xan bore down on him, taking Jason in to the root, and then he broke into soft tears, fingers clenching in the sheets. Jason nuzzled the back of his neck. "It's okay. I'll give you what you need. Don't cry, Xan."

Jason caressed Xan's back until he loosened around him, and then, while Xan cried against he mattress, he fucked into him with long, firm strokes. He took his time, making sure to angle just right, leaving Xan shuddering, begging, and twisting in the sheets.

"Talk to me," Xan said through his tears. "Say the things I like to hear."

Heart aching, he whispered against Xan's shoulder. "That's it. Take it like a good little omega. Open up for me, slut."

"Don't stop. Please don't stop."

"I won't. Not now." Jason sped up his strokes. "You want me so much."

"So much," Xan gasped, arching his back and groaning loudly, tears still leaking down his face.

"You want me to fill you up with my baby?"

"I do. Oh, Jason, I do." Xan shuddered hard. "I love you."

Jason paused in his thrusting and Xan went still beneath him.

"I didn't—" Xan started, his breath harsh and wet.

"Don't. Shh." Jason smoothed back Xan's dark hair and kissed his shoulders. "Of course you love me; you're my omega. And I'm gonna knock you up." His own throat clogged with tears, and he pressed his face to Xan's back.

A hard knot of resolve gripped his guts. This was the last time. It had to be. Because Xan loved him...and not as a friend. As a true lover, and that fantasy had to end. For both of them.

"Please make me come," Xan whimpered. "Please. I wanna come. Help me. *Make me.*"

Jason hitched Xan's hips into position so each thrust jammed against his prostate. Holding back his own emotions, he fucked Xan hard and fast, forcing him to take his cock to the base. Just the way Xan liked it best.

"Fuck!" Xan cried, his asshole stretched impossibly wide around Jason's dick. "I'm gonna—!"

"Do it!" Jason urged. He wanted to flip Xan over, see his face one last time as he came. "Show me how you love my dick."

Xan convulsed, his entire body warping with the grip of orgasm. A cry wrenched from his throat and he pulsed around Jason's cock. Jason closed his eyes, imagined a descended womb he could punch up into, and he pumped his ecstasy into Xan for the final time.

When the trembling high wore off, he nuzzled Xan's neck, kissed his shoulder, and pulled out slowly. Xan collapsed against the mattress, spent and still shaking. Jason's come slipped from his gaping asshole, and Jason had a strange urge to use his fingers to shove it back inside. Instead, he grabbed a towel from his dirty clothes hamper and handed it over.

"Was it good?"

Xan nodded, his cheeks flushed from tears and his chest red with exertion. He wiped at himself and then stared at the wet stain on the bed sheet. "Sorry."

"It's all right. I'm the one who made you come, so I guess it's my fault."

Xan dressed himself shakily, and Jason did the same. Their unusual silence weighed between them. Normally, Jason would be talking again by now trying to stave off Xan's descent into guilt, or they'd chase Xan's darkness away by making plans for the next time.

"I need to get back to school," Xan said quietly once he was dressed, his bow tie askew and his eyes downcast.

Words stuck in Jason's throat. There was a lot he needed to say, but he didn't know how to start. All that came out was, "Yeah."

Finally, Xan glanced up to meet Jason's gaze. "I'll see you in class?"

"On Monday."

At the door to Jason's room, Xan stopped him with a hand on

his chest. "I'll see myself out." He swallowed hard, tears welling in his eyes again. "This was the last time, wasn't it?"

Jason nodded.

"You're different now. He's made you different."

"It's not him. It's because...we're *Érosgápe*." He didn't know how else to explain.

"I understand."

But Xan didn't sound like he understood at all. In fact, he sounded like he was going to cry some more, and guilt mixed with Jason's own sadness.

"About what I said during..." Xan cleared his throat. "It was..."

"It was part of the game," Jason lied for him softly.

Xan's eyes darted to the floor. "Right."

Jason tilted his face up, stroking his chin with his thumb. Xan's mouth crumpled as he fought tears.

Jason tugged him into a hug. "I'm sorry. When you find your *Érosgápe* or find the right omega to contract with, this hurt will go away. I promise."

Xan tugged out of his arms and cleared his throat. "Yeah. Whatever, right? We're friends helping each other out. That's all."

Jason swallowed his reply.

Xan turned away. "See you in class."

Jason watched him walk down the hall to the staircase. His heart ached and his balls thudded from their recent release. As he turned to go back into his room, he caught movement out of the corner of his eye and smelled tobacco smoke. Sitting on the steps going up to the attic, Pater stared at him meaningfully.

Jason's skin went hot as fire. "How long have you been there?"

Pater shrugged and indicated the three boxes on the stairs beneath his perch. All labeled as Autumn Nights ornaments. "I could use some help."

"Of course. Sure." Jason wiped his sweaty palms on his pants and double-checked to make sure he was buttoned up. Downstairs, he heard the front door open and close.

Taking the biggest box from the attic steps, he smiled to cover his nerves. "Let's decorate a lot this year, huh? If Vale comes over for any of the celebrations, I want him to be impressed."

"Perhaps." Pater stood and ran his fingers through Jason's hair, straightening the mess. "So, that was the last time with him?"

"What?" Heat crept up his throat and suddenly he could smell it: the scent of him and Xan together wafting out of his open bedroom.

Pater sighed and lifted a smaller box of ornaments waiting on the attic stairs. "Just say it was the last time."

"Yeah. It was."

"Good." Pater shifted the box to his hip and stared into Jason's eyes. "Omegas don't like it when their alphas fuck other people without permission."

Jason swallowed. He'd never heard Pater be so crass. He usually spoke of making love or, if talking about something less emotional, just plain sex. "It was the last time," Jason repeated. He couldn't explain more or better than that. Not without giving away Xan's secret.

"There's a lot at stake here for you."

"I know. I'm sorry." Jason fidgeted, but his pater didn't seem done with him yet.

"Xan needs to be careful," Pater said. "Boyish indulgences are fine—typical even, despite the Holy Book of Wolf—when you're young, horny, and stuck together at Mont Nessadare. But if they aren't renounced, they can cause real problems when you start to woo an omega."

Jason nodded wordlessly.

Pater started down the attic stairs, and Jason followed. "If Valendo Aman hears about it, he won't like it. Contract or not." He shook his head. "Just keep what happened today to yourself and make sure you don't do it again."

Jason sighed. "Please, Pater, don't be disappointed in me. It was a goodbye thing. I promise. It will never happen again."

Pater lifted a brow. "I'm glad to hear it. Now, go shower and open your windows to air that room out. It reeks of sex."

The roots of Jason's hair burned, and he wished the floor would open up and devour him whole.

"Then bring these boxes downstairs to the conservatory to help me sort through them." He gave Jason a pale smile. "We'll decide what we want to put out for the first Autumn Nights celebration this weekend."

Jason smiled. "You'll invite Vale to The Feast of Alpha's Blessings?"

"I had planned on it." Pater shifted the box in his arms. "And yes, we'll make everything very nice. For your Vale."

THAT EVENING, AFTER Jason had taken his final dose of alpha quell and before he headed up to bed, his pater pulled him aside and handed him a small stack of papers with ragged edges. "These are the poems I thought appropriate for you to see right now."

Jason took them, his head swimming. "Thank you."

Father shuffled past them in the hall, a dark expression on his face, but Pater only rolled his eyes at him. "He'll get over the poetry eventually. But perhaps you should take them to your room to read."

Jason had intended to do just that. He couldn't imagine reading Vale's poems while his parents breathed down his neck, watching for his reactions and fretting. The words of the first poem danced on the page, and he started quickly toward the staircase before stopping and turning back to his pater anxiously.

"Yes, Jason?"

"I just wondered, before I read them, I guess I want to know—" He stroked his hair off his forehead and frowned, bracing himself. "Are they any good?"

"Oh!" Pater smiled, his hazel eyes crinkling around the edges. "I thought they were quite good. Beautiful work. He has a nice way with language and description. He's rarely rococo. He's honest." Pater's eyes went distant, obviously remembering something he'd read. "When you're older, there are some poems of his that you really ought to see. But not now. Not at this juncture."

"Miner!" his father's voice called from the study. "Join me, please."

Pater called over his shoulder. "Of course, Yule. I'm on my way."

"Do you think new information came in? About Vale?" Jason asked, torn between following his pater to see what was going on and rushing up to his room to read what Vale had crafted.

"If it did, you can wait until morning," Pater said. "But I think this is about the squabble he had to settle today at the shipping yard. He likes to relive his heroics for me, you know. So I can be impressed by him all over again." His eyes gleamed, and Jason laughed. "Go on now. Up to your room. Be enthralled by your Vale's words."

Jason dashed up the stairs, locking his bedroom door behind him. He paced for a few seconds, trying to get the energy out of his legs. The room still smelled of Xan, despite having changed the sheets and leaving the window open.

He picked up the bookmark he'd gotten from Vale and pressed it to his nose. He could still smell Vale's house and even the sharper note of mint from the garden, but the musk of Vale's slick and the perfume of his skin was gone now, stamped over by the heavy scent of the sex he and Xan'd had earlier that day.

Frustrated, he tucked the bookmark into his pocket. He shouldn't have fucked Xan. Or maybe he should have. He didn't know. It was all so confusing. He didn't owe Xan anything, but in that moment, buzzing with alpha expression, he hadn't been able to tease out what he wanted from what he *wanted*. And Xan was so desperate, and, if he was honest, so in love. It'd been a heady mixture, and he'd given in. He couldn't really regret it…though he did.

He sat down at his desk, but the microscope and slides were still out. He didn't want to take the time to put them away before reading. The scent of Xan's jizz floated by him again, and he stood up, gripping the sheaf of papers tightly. The window opposite opened onto the sloped roof below.

Jason stepped over to it, climbed out, and settled on the slates. The night breeze flowed over him, chilling his bones. His nipples ached from the cold and his nose burned, but it was better than reading Vale's poems in a room reeking of his mistakes. Was being an adult alpha always going to be so confusing and so hard? He hoped not. What had been fun and games in the dorm now seemed like so much more with so many more potential consequences.

He hoped Xan was okay tonight. He hoped he wasn't alone.

A layer of clouds obscured the stars, but the moon, determined as always, broke through, pale and judgmental. Jason shuddered at the scarred, all-seeing, all-knowing eye of the wolf-god.

Two alphas weren't supposed to lie together. Not even as a favor to a best friend. Not even as alpha expression. Not unless you meant to leave the other unmanned.

To kiss and caress, to *care*? That wasn't the way of wolf.

According to the Holy Book of Wolf, omegas had been created to prevent unnatural acts like that. And they'd been created for breeding, of course. To carry on the race. And because reproduction was the most sacred duty to wolf-god and to the world, spending seed in another alpha wasn't something that could be borne by religious or secular law.

Under the cold, watchful eye of the moon, Jason wondered if

he'd been grievously wrong to have thought it so silly a rule before. Now he'd hurt his best friend, broken his heart, and disappointed his pater. And if Vale found out, he'd be *unhappy*.

A strange swell of emotion pummeled Jason—joy and grief combined. He didn't ever want to make Vale unhappy, it hurt him to the quick even imagining it, but the idea that he *could* hurt Vale? That his actions with Xan might provoke feelings in his smug, older omega, feelings that cracked his cool, mature exterior? That made him nearly giddy.

Not that he deserved strong feelings from Vale. Not after what he'd done today.

But he would deserve them one day soon! He'd be a better man, a better alpha, and he'd earn Vale's devotion, love, and submission.

Just as soon as he was allowed to do so, as soon as they'd settled all the frustrating preliminary issues in the presence of attorneys.

Jason sighed, closed his eyes, and let go. He allowed the night breeze to carry off the events with Xan, the awkward conversation with Pater, and the jealousy and fear that Vale might be spending time with another alpha while everyone else forced Jason to follow 'protocol'. He released the impatience burbling inside and waited for calm, drifting with the alpha quell.

When he lifted his eyes the clouds had parted and the stars shone down. He shifted his attention to the papers in his hand, the sheaf of them ruffling with each sigh of wind.

The opening lines of Vale's first poem cut into him like glass, beautiful and shiny. He pressed a hand to his throbbing heart as he read the next line, and the next, and the next.

Every word chosen by Vale.

Every word a prism through which to know him.

Every word perfect.

Just like his omega.

He memorized them all with ease and then lay back in the darkness, staring up at the sky, pondering the meanings for hours.

# CHAPTER NINE

"DO YOU THINK bringing Urho was a good idea?" Rosen whispered into Vale's ear as they waited on the sidewalk for Yosef and Urho to climb out of the backseat of the car the Sabels had sent to collect him.

Vale glanced over at his handsome friend. Rosen wore his hair down in a long, flat wave across his shoulders, the brown turtleneck and creamed-coffee jacket fit him well, and he looked casual and relaxed in comparison to Vale's own deep green suit and white shirt. At least Yosef was equally dressed up in a berry red suit, which alongside his white hair and trimmed beard, made him look like a lean, handsome version of the Old World's fairytale of Santa Claus.

Vale peered up at Jason's house—no, mansion—wondering where on earth the old Sabel family had found such large pieces of granite for the front and just how they'd transported it all here. The house looked cold on the outside, but Jason hadn't seemed like a cold man, nor had his pater seemed cold over the phone when issuing the invitation.

"Urho is the muscle of the group," Vale murmured. "I doubt I'll need to employ him, but I don't want them thinking I'm helpless."

"What do you think they're going to do? Kidnap you and force you to consummate the imprint?"

Vale snorted gently.

Rosen went on, "And they'd perpetrate this crime during Autumn Nights first feast?"

"No, but I don't want to take any chances. Besides, Urho is part of my life. Miner, Jason's pater, said to invite my closest friends. That's the three of you."

"Yes, but Urho is an alpha. The alpha you've written poems about. The alpha who's helped you through heat how many times now?"

Vale shrugged, hoping his unsettled stomach didn't lead him to vomit in the bushes. "If they want to contract with me, they'll need to accept all of you. Isn't that what Yosef told me just a few days past?"

"You're scared." Rosen slung a protective arm around Vale's shoulders. "It's okay. I've got you."

Vale rolled his eyes and dumped Rosen's embrace. "Jason's on alpha quell. Everything should be fine."

"Even with Urho here?" Rosen asked again, clearly thinking Vale had overstepped in bringing him.

"*Especially* with Urho here," the man himself said, his voice deep and comfortable by Vale's ear. Vale turned to see him straightening his simple gray suit and black tie. "Come along now, gentlemen. Let's not dally."

Vale led the way up the path, Urho directly behind, and Yosef and Rosen followed at the rear with their arms linked together. Always the couple in love. If they weren't such dedicated friends, Vale's envy of them might turn poisonous.

The house loomed despite being only three stories high, with the top floor appearing to be an attic. It was the granite front and the wide windows staring down at them like blank eyes that gave it such an imposing air. At least the windows at the bottom were lit up with warm lights, like honey pouring out onto the well-tended lawn.

The front door opened before they had a chance to ring the bell. Vale didn't know what he'd been expecting—possibly a beta servant or even Miner himself—but for Jason to be the one in the doorway took him by surprise. He froze on the front steps, heart thumping against his ribs, and he groaned as he felt a small, hot slip of slick wet his asshole.

Could Jason smell it? Could Urho? Wolf-god, how humiliating that just the sight of the boy made him respond so helplessly. With luck, he wouldn't embarrass himself further by making more. One little bit to acknowledge the presence of his alpha and *Érosgápe* ought to be enough. He begged his body to hold itself in check.

Jason swallowed hard, the prominent Adam's apple in his throat bobbing. "Welcome," he said, his voice gruff with effort. "Come in. My parents are waiting in the living room. We're happy to have you here."

Vale strode forward when Urho gently pushed him. "Thank you." He moved to unwrap his scarf as he stepped into the warm, luminous foyer of the Sabel house. "We're grateful for the invitation to visit informally before we sit down with attorneys."

Jason looked dizzy as he stared at Vale's throat and then dragged his eyes up to Vale's face. "Of course. The Feast of Alpha's Blessings is to thank wolf-god for all the wonderful things he's bestowed on us." He smiled shyly and took Vale's coat and scarf. "Finding one's *Érosgápe* is usually considered a wonderful thing. Something to be grateful for."

"It is."

Vale's stomach tumbled at the darling way Jason ducked his head to surreptitiously sniff Vale's scarf before hanging it on the rack by the door. Then Jason hung Vale's coat gracefully and with the same reverence a priest shows a saint's relic. Vale's lips twitched with a small smile. At least he wasn't the only helpless one here tonight.

Vale introduced Urho, Rosen, and Yosef as Jason took more jackets and scarves, hanging them with less care but still neatly. He smiled warmly at everyone but Urho, whom he met with an expression that more closely resembled a show of bared teeth. Vale had to admit there was something charming about the effort, though. It was more than he might have done had Jason shown up on his doorstep with an ex-lover in tow, expecting him to grin and bear it.

He frowned. What was he thinking? Of course he'd handle it well. He barely knew this boy. He hoped for Jason's sake he'd had a lover or two, or whatever omega he contracted with would be stuck teaching him *everything*. And who the hell wanted to do that? Yet the idea that Jason had been with someone else pricked inside him.

*If he opts for a surrogate, which he rightly should, then he'll be with someone else forever. Make peace with it now.*

"Have you helped everyone out of their coats, love?" Miner Hoff said from the doorway of what appeared to be a well-appointed living room. He stepped into the hallway wearing a plaid suit of autumnal colors and carrying a tumbler of amber liquid and ice. He was tall, almost as tall as Jason, and thin.

"Yes, I have," Jason said, his eyes gobbling Vale up and his breath coming in sharply. Vale wondered what he saw—whatever it was, he seemed to like it. "And we were just on our way to join you in the living room now."

Miner stepped forward and shook Vale's hand warmly. He noticed Miner didn't seem to follow the recent bonded omega fashion of wearing a circle pin on his collar. In his experience, eschewing the trappings of submission denoted a more independent mind. And just like that, and definitely against his will, a kernel of hope rooted into his heart.

"Vale, hello." Miner smiled warmly. "I'm happy you came and even happier that your friends came along with you. We look forward to getting to know all of you."

Maybe Jason's parents weren't going to push for a surrogate after all? It seemed an unlikely, even costly, choice, but how else could he explain the warmth in Miner's eyes and his sincere reassurance?

"Come along, we'll complete the introductions in the living room with Yule. He's eager to meet you, too." This last bit sounded less honest, and Vale's nerves tightened again.

But as if he sensed that Vale needed him, Jason stepped nearer, not touching, just closer.

He said, softly, "They really are happy you're here. Both of them." He grinned, and Vale's heart, for lack of a better description, squished. He marveled at his own ridiculous reaction to seeing a set of teeth. "And I'm very glad you're here, too," Jason went on. "You look amazing."

Vale despaired as that vicious kernel of hope grew green shoots. Wolf-god, his bumbling-but-adorable baby alpha was simply too delicious for words.

"So do you."

Jason's eyes went wide and he sputtered, losing his cool completely.

Vale laughed. "Oh, my. I forgot how lovely you are and how young."

"I'm old enough for you. Don't worry about that anymore."

Vale tilted his head. There'd been a command in that tone, something he felt in his gut and knees, something that made him quiver inside. "Well, well," he murmured, fascinated, but that was all he had time to say because they entered the living room and everyone fell silent.

Yule Sabel stood by the fireplace, his arms crossed behind his back and chest puffed up like the king of the castle. Which, Vale supposed, in a way, he was. Vale almost expected the man to lift his chin and say, "You may kneel before me."

Instead, Yule gave them all a good once over, relaxed his arms, and broke into a gorgeous smile. It was Jason's bright grin on a different face.

"Welcome," Yule said, striding forward with his hand out-stretched. He took hold of Vale's hand and shook it soundly. "It's good that you're all here. Can I get anyone a drink?"

"Wolf-god, yes." Rosen swept his long hair back from his shoulders and shot Yosef an amused smile. "I'll have a lot of whatever you've got."

Miner laughed and Yule followed suit. Jason scooted closer to Vale, taking deep breaths, clearly scenting him, though trying to be delicate about it. Vale's stomach did another tumble and another embarrassing slide of slick wet his asshole. He shifted, and Jason let out of soft gasp. Vale's neck burned hot.

"Yes! Let's drown this tension in liquor, why don't we?" Yule said, grinning. "Everyone will feel more at ease after a drink or two. Not you, Jason."

Jason flinched at being singled out as too young or too out of control for alcohol. Vale sympathized with him. It wasn't fair to the poor kid that their ages were so different, that they couldn't just contract quickly and neatly, and put their bodily urges to rest.

"Alcohol negates the effects alpha quell," Vale whispered.

Jason nodded, but he didn't meet Vale's gaze.

"Introductions first." Miner sipped at his own plentiful glass, obviously nervous despite his warm greeting.

"Of course," Yule said as he moved toward the bar and the rows of sparkling crystal glasses and liquor decanters.

"You've met Jason. I'm Miner Hoff, his pater. Please, all of you, call me by my first name."

"Yule Sabel," the king of the manor said, turning his gaze to Vale again. "Yule is fine. And who all have we here?"

"Feel free to call me Vale, of course." He hated that his heart fluttered anxiously. He was a grown man. He had commanded classrooms of young alphas less than a week ago. He could deal with meeting the parents. "Yosef Deckel is my attorney." He touched Yosef's sleeve. "Rosen Mann is my friend, and Urho Chase is—"

"Your muscle?" Yule said, a sparkle of amusement in his eye.

Vale wondered if he'd somehow been overheard on the front walk. The windows had been closed, he'd thought, but perhaps not. "Urho is a friend. A clearheaded friend with my best interests at heart."

"I see." Yule's voice made it clear that everyone *saw* exactly what Urho had been to Vale.

Staring at the wall across the room with a clenched jaw, Jason held very still, as though trying to ignore a strong, unwanted urge. Abruptly, he crossed the room to the window and opened it slightly, letting in some fresh air. No one rebuked him.

Vale was relieved when Rosen put out his hand to Miner and said, "I'm Rosen."

Similar statements were issued by Yosef and Urho, hands were shaken all around, and the introductions, awkward and quick as they'd been, were done.

Everyone but Jason gathered around the bar, making requests and accepting drinks. The liquor was potent and high quality, burning nicely as it slid down Vale's throat.

He hoped alcohol-induced loose-limbed relaxation would kick in soon. He didn't know which way to turn. Toward Jason standing by the window with eyes only for him? Toward Jason's parents who mingled with his friends kindly? Or toward the restroom where he could deal with the annoying seepage of slick that refused to entirely stop?

The question was resolved for him when Miner sidled over with a refreshed drink and an eye on his son. "How have you been this week?" Miner guided Vale toward a set of chairs by the bar, but neither of them sat.

"Bored mainly," Vale answered honestly. "I'm accustomed to

full days. I need to find a new, suitable schedule for myself. I lazed about quite a lot, I'm afraid."

"Rightly so. You've had a lot to think about, I'm sure. There's so much to consider."

"Yes, so many unknowns. Like what will become of my properties, my retirement accounts, and the inheritance from my parents."

Miner paled slightly, his eyes glowing with empathy. "I can only imagine the worry this is causing you. I promise we won't pressure you to make a quick contract."

"Now, now, you're getting dangerously close to negotiation talk," Yule interrupted with a soft smile for Miner. "Let's just get to know each other tonight, shall we? We don't want to get off on a stressful foot."

Vale didn't know how Yule couldn't see that all the sharp-toothed uncertainties swimming around them were what made everything so tense. If Vale had some sense of whether he was going to be able to continue his life mostly unmolested, he'd be happier. Or at least less worried. It was always better to know than to be left wondering.

"Jason," Yule called out, moving across the room toward his son who still stood by the window. "Have a glass of water." He pressed it into his son's hand and watched as Jason sipped it. Vale noted the gentle way Yule slid an arm around Jason's shoulders and whispered something into his ear, making Jason's cheeks flush as he nodded with a grateful smile.

"I see where Jason got his looks," Vale said to Miner. "With your height and build and Yule's blond hair and blue eyes, you've made quite a handsome son."

"I'm glad you think so," Miner said with a proud gaze across the room to where Yule and Jason talked quietly. "He's a smart young man as well."

"I'm sure he is."

"He loves science especially. All types, but he's majoring in biology." Miner turned to Vale. "What about you? What did you study?"

Vale almost laughed at the question. He knew Miner and Yule were both entirely aware of his education and employment history. A private investigator would have supplied them with most of the facts of his life by now. But small talk was small talk, and there was no way around it. "I studied Literature, and took a Creative Writing minor with a focus on poetry."

"I see. What drew you to poetry?"

Vale sensed Jason was moving closer.

"I'm not sure. I've always been interested in it, since I was a small child."

Jason came to stand behind the bar, sipping his water, and listening with a greedy expression, like Vale's words were sex and chocolate rolled into one. He turned slightly to allow Jason to feel part of the conversation.

"Did your pater or father read poetry to you then?" Miner asked.

"No, but when I was old enough I used to read my father's poetry books. I was six the first time I tried my own hand at iambic and trochaic."

"Were they any good?" Jason spoke quietly. Vale heard an echo of his adamant statement that the poem Vale had won the bookmark ribbon for must have been good.

"For a child? Perhaps. But they were, in fact, terrible of course. I believe my first poem was called 'The Teddy Bear's Tea Party'. The milk spilled and the stuffed animals mourned. It was quite dramatic."

Jason's smile was sun-bright and Vale's heart clenched, desperate for more of it. He cleared his throat and looked away, an unexpected shyness gripping him.

"That's adorable," Miner offered. "Jason was much more into bugs and spiders as a child. Tea parties with stuffed animals was more my idea of fun, but he always had me down in the dirt."

Vale caught Jason's eye, remembering the photos of him as a child—robust, healthy. He could imagine the boy he'd once been wearing short pants and rolling in the grass, laughing. It was a beautiful image.

"Do you still write?" Miner asked.

Vale couldn't help the scoff that broke through.

Miner laughed. "All right, I admit to knowing the answer to that."

"Your poems are amazing," Jason said and then hastily swallowed a giant gulp of water, his cheeks pinking and his eyes darting down to the floor.

"You read them?" Vale's guts twisted up. He knew his scent had changed because Jason's nostrils flared slightly with alarm.

"I, uh…" Jason gaped.

Miner took up the slack for his undone son. "I read through one of your books and allowed Jason to see the ones that were suitable for this stage of events." He tapped his glass against Vale's own in a small toast. "You have quite a way with words. Your work was very beautiful."

Jason frowned, as though disappointed he'd been shown up by his pater. "Beautiful," he murmured. "I agree. Powerful, too. And smart."

"Thank you."

Jason looked as if he might melt into the floor. The power Vale had over him was intoxicating, and Vale's pulse picked up in excitement.

Miner went on, "I admire that you've done so much with your life. A respected professor of alphas and an accomplished poet, no less." He threw back the last of his drink and sat it down on the bar, motioning for Jason to make him another. "It would be fair to say I envy you."

"But you have so much here to be proud of…" Vale looked to Jason, who was listening with an air of astonishment. He remembered the age well. It was strange coming to know your parents were human, with dreams fulfilled and dashed, with foibles and resentments. It'd been his first loss to know his own weren't the perfect creatures he'd imagined. And then he'd lost them both entirely.

"I do. Of course I do." Miner waved an elegant hand. "But I always wanted to be a musician, myself. When I was young, I dreamed of playing with the symphony here in the city. But my Pater-in-Law would have none of it." His smile went brittle.

"I didn't know that," Jason said, a frown creasing his brow. "Grandpater Derak wasn't very nice to you, was he?"

Miner shrugged. "It's all in the past now. I settled for composing and teaching Jason to play." He gazed at Jason fondly. "He's not gifted, but talent can't replace hard work. That's something Jason has never been afraid of. He's more than passable on the guitar and not terrible on the piano."

Jason laughed, blue eyes sparkling. "And believe me, that's high praise from him. He's usually less generous. I'm working at getting better, though." The words *for you* were somehow implied, and Vale felt them like warm fingers pressed over his heart.

"I look forward to hearing you play."

Jason smiled again and Vale nearly swooned from his white teeth glittering in the soft light.

"What about your family?" Miner asked. "Where do your people live?"

Another question he surely already knew the answer to, but it was fair to assume Miner wanted to hear Vale's take on the events himself.

"Father and Pater are both deceased. There was an accident. I didn't have any other family."

"They were *Érosgápe* or…?"

Contracted alpha-omega relationships were legally every bit as valid, but culturally they were still looked down on as less-than. Vale straightened up, sipping his drink before answering, "*Érosgápe.* Though I was born quite late."

Miner nodded, already aware.

"You were?" Jason asked. "Why's that?"

Vale swirled his liquor around in his glass, schooling his features to thoughtfulness, ignoring what he knew about Miner's problems with conception and carrying to term. "They didn't find each other until they were both in their thirties. It seems my family line is full of late bloomers." He took a long swallow and grimaced at the burn. "So perhaps I shouldn't be so surprised by our situation."

"Your parents didn't contract with someone in their youth?" This was from Yule who'd turned from his conversation with Urho, Yosef, and Rosen to listen to Vale.

"No. They were both romantics. They believed their match was out there, and it turned out they were right."

"Amazing. That's quite the risk to take," Yule said.

"Maybe, but there's always the risk of finding your match after you've contracted with someone else, and that's its own kind of hell, from what I understand."

"Oh, indeed." Yule's eyes went wide.

"Going it alone is brave," Miner said. "Believing in destiny even braver."

"Speaking of a special kind of hell, your pater must have been a madman," Yule said. "Enduring heats without an alpha as he must have done before finding your father is a very bold choice."

Vale lifted his brow, and Miner grew pale. "Oh, I doubt he endured heats without an alpha. I'd wager he did what any sensible omega would do and found someone to help him."

Jason let out a soft noise, almost like a growl, but when Vale gazed his way, he went silent; the only indication he was unhappy was a flush up his pale neck.

Yule's jaw twitched, and he glanced at Urho before smiling tightly at Vale. "Of course. I understand it's preferable to make such arrangements, but I still believe that a contracted situation is a better option. More civilized."

"And if I'd taken such an option, we'd have been in quite the mess when Jason grabbed me at the library, wouldn't we?"

Yule tensed but inclined his head in acknowledgement.

"The ridiculous weight alphas have historically placed on their omega having never known another is absurd." Miner's eyes shone darkly and anger crackled in his voice.

"I agree," Yule said, quickly. "While I think omega freedom groups go too far, it's clear to me that omegas deserve more leniency and understanding than they've had in the past. And that includes taking lovers when necessary, such as in cases of interminable heat, or to endure an uncontracted and unbonded existence."

"*Endure*," Vale whispered under his breath, after Yule turned back to the more palatable conversation Rosen was carrying on about the breakthrough he'd had in a recipe for crab legs and cornbread stuffing.

Jason stared toward Urho with a black expression, but when Vale reached out his almost-empty drink and asked for a refill, he came back to him with a sweet smile and a gentle, "Of course."

"You and I aren't that different in age," Miner said thoughtfully, as Jason poured more scotch. "What class were you at Mont Juror? I was Class of Wolf-moon, and you were…"

"Class of Wolf-storm."

"Ah, my friend Miles had a younger brother in that class. Rasmus Beck?"

"I knew him well." Vale had found him boorish, but he didn't volunteer that information.

Miner smiled. "Jason will graduate in a Class of Wolf-Rain. I've always liked the sound of that. It reminds me of the Old World saying about raining cats and dogs." He broke off. "I'm babbling. I apologize. Discussion of omega rights often makes me anxious."

Vale smiled, his heart softening toward Jason's pater even more. "Me, too."

"Normally, I'd smoke a cigarette, but it's a habit I'm trying to break."

"Don't let me stop you."

"Jason doesn't like it. You don't smoke, do you?"

Vale shook his head.

"Good, he'll be relieved." Miner gave Jason a wink.

"Jason, come sit with Vale's friends," Yule called, steering everyone toward the plates of hors d'oeuvres set out on the tea table next to the sofa. "You should get to know them, too."

Vale smiled encouragingly as Jason stepped from behind the bar and moved to sit in a plush chair near his father. Rosen, Yosef, and Urho took the large leather sofa, fresh drinks in hand.

"This has to have been a terrible surprise," Miner said as he and Vale moved slowly across the room toward the group. "You probably thought all *this* wasn't in the cards for you."

"I had given up hope for it, yes."

Hope wasn't the right word, but Miner's eyes showed he understood he'd accidentally backed Vale into a corner. He took Vale's arm, pausing several feet away from the cozy seating area where Rosen was complimenting the caramelized onion tarts with apples. "I do understand more than you might think."

"Omegas have a kinship," Vale agreed.

"Yes." Miner's eyes searched his. "We all spend our youth in suspense, waiting for the match or the contract that means our lives can begin now. You must have gone a long time thinking it would happen any moment."

"Anytime. Anywhere."

"Yes." Miner tilted his head. "And just when you'd probably given up, gotten comfortable, built a life of your own, Jason comes along."

Was this a trap or did Miner truly feel for him? Vale chose a wry smile as his only response.

"He's a loving boy." Miner smiled.

"And I admit I'm fond of surprises," Vale offered.

Miner clinked Vale's glass again. "To surprises, then, and to wolf-god's blessings."

Jason offered his seat to Vale, going to stand by the fire instead. He was a quiet young man, from what Vale could tell. He didn't insinuate himself rudely into conversations the way many alphas did, or insist on Vale's attention being directed at him. Though his gaze devoured Vale greedily at every opportunity, he grew shy when Vale caught him.

Where was the desperate baby alpha who'd shown up outside his window, eager to know anything about him, driven by the impulse to get closer to his omega? Right there, Vale bet, beneath the layer of shy distance he kept. That was the Jason he should get to know, the one he became when he was alone.

The conversation shifted from Rosen's recipes to their preferences at the theater, and Vale wasn't sure if Yosef or Yule was a bigger fan. They discussed the latest plays and musicals, both holding vibrant and well-considered opinions of everything from the leading actors to the pacing and the book. Vale enjoyed theater, but not with the same intensity. He didn't mind if the lead bungled a line, so long as the hour and a half took him away from the world for a little while and the experience gave him something new to write about.

He wondered if Jason liked the theater. He turned to gauge his interest.

Jason didn't seem to be paying any attention. Instead, he looked mouthwateringly gorgeous leaning against the wall with his heart in his eyes, and his lanky body encased in that sweetly tailored suit that showed the spread of his shoulders and the bulge of his alpha cock.

Vale's heart tripped over a tangle of feelings, both primal and surface, a mess of things he wanted and didn't want, longed for and feared. He cleared his throat and pretended to study the painting over the sofa, a riot of color and form that made little sense. His pulse raced and his mind whirred from the contact high of Jason's stare.

"Dinner will be served shortly, sir," a voice said from the doorway.

Vale turned to see a beta-for-hire, recognizable by the traditional black pants and white shirt. Apparently, the Sabels didn't have regular servants. Betas-for-hire were only arranged for when someone didn't have help of their own. Vale had used them on more than one occasion to cater a party.

Surprised, he looked to Jason who shrugged and straightened up from the wall.

Rising, Yule gestured toward the door. "Why don't we all take a seat in the dining room?"

Miner led the way from the room, and as they headed down the hall together, Jason sidled up beside him. "Is everything going all right so far?"

"I should be asking you that."

"Oh?"

"It's typically believed that it's the job of the omega to please and charm the alpha."

Jason rolled his eyes. "Old fairytales."

"Agreed."

Jason smiled and then said, "Usually, my father does the cooking in our house, but tonight we hired someone in. I hope the food is good. I can't vouch for it personally. We've never had this chef before."

A bubble of optimism settled in his gut at the idea that Yule Sabel, the alpha of this mansion and wealthier than many a man could even dream, made dinner every night for his family. If that was the kind of alpha who'd raised Jason, then maybe it wasn't entirely stupid of him to let his hopes flourish.

"It'll be wonderful," Vale said. "Better than anything I could make. I'm a terrible cook. Just ask Rosen."

"How could you be terrible at anything?" Jason asked.

Vale laughed and shook his head. "Omega persuasion is powerful stuff, darling. Beware. I'd diagnose you with pheromone delirium for saying something as sweet as that."

Jason was about to deny it when Yule gripped him by the shoulder as they entered the dining room and steered him toward a chair to the right of the head. "Sit by me, son."

Then Miner closed in to whisper to Vale, "I thought it best to put some space between you so you can both think more clearly. Would you take the seat next to me?"

Vale almost protested. The truth was, he felt more clear-headed when interacting with Jason than when not. The pheromone attraction went both ways; his body seemed to know he was meant for Jason and relaxed.

Yosef and Rosen sat across from Vale, leaving Urho to sit across from Jason. The instant tension between Urho and Jason was palpable, an almost-violence that quivered over the table. Vale could see Miner trying to calculate the risk of leaving Urho seated where he was or asking him to switch with Rosen. If he did that, he'd be placing him closer to Vale than Jason was, and that wouldn't be a good choice, either.

Inviting Urho might not have been such a good idea. Vale hated it when Rosen was right.

Eventually, Miner seemed to abandon the idea of changing the seating. Vale hoped for the best.

"Jason," Yule said, after catching Miner's insistent expression. "Urho used to be a doctor in the military."

"I'm still a doctor," Urho interjected. "But I've retired from the military. I only use my medical skills for volunteer work now."

"Very admirable," Yule said.

Jason bristled.

Yule went on obliviously. "Now he partners with Professor Minze and Dr. Obi to study omega heat and breeding at the university. I was telling him about your interest in genetics earlier." He smiled at Miner, clearly hoping his omega would approve of his conversation-starting skills.

Miner sighed and drank deeply of the wine beside his place.

Vale lifted his glass to his nose and sniffed curiously. It was a good vintage. It reminded him of some he'd opened from his pater's wine cellar.

"Oh?" Jason smoothed his face with obvious effort and met Urho's gaze. "Biology with an emphasis on genetics is my major. I've been a fan of Dr. Obi's work for years now. I'd even considered asking him to sponsor me for some research ideas I have for my independent study next year. What's he like?"

Urho swirled his wine glass and smiled indulgently. "He's brilliant, of course, but stern. I can put in a good word for you with him if you'd like, but I should warn you he doesn't suffer fools lightly."

Jason smiled tightly. "I'm not a fool and, thank you, I'd appreciate that."

Yule asked Urho, "So what is it about heat that you study specifically?"

"Omega presentation and its ties to the wolf genes versus our more ancient human ones."

Jason's brows lifted slightly. "That's pretty close to the area I want to study."

Urho leaned back in his chair, allowing the hired beta who'd entered the room to place a full dish in front of him. "Wolves don't tend to present with such a deep back arch. That's more often seen in primates."

Vale sighed. Once Urho got going on his research, it could be hard to shut him up. He smiled gratefully at the beta laying a delicious-smelling plate down on his placemat.

"Broiled lobster tails with garlic and chili butter," the beta whispered.

Vale's mouth watered. Money wasn't a bad thing to have if it afforded a chef who could make a meal like this one. He couldn't remember the last time he'd had lobster. Not since he and Urho had been on vacation near the sea several heats ago.

Vale was relieved his potential in-laws weren't the kind to pray to wolf-god before a meal. He'd never been very religious, and it would be awkward to pretend now. The lobster was heavenly, and it was all he could do to stifle his moan around the mouthful. Jason shot Vale a happy look before taking another bite of his own lobster.

"How do you test your theories?" Yule asked Urho, seemingly the only person still paying attention. "Surely you don't tweak the genes of omegas to see if it changes their heat behavior? I didn't think we had the technology for that yet, though I know many are working on it."

"Of course not. That would be unethical, though you're correct that we don't have that kind of technology either," Urho agreed. "Right now, our studies are limited to finding omegas who volunteer. They must admit to a failure to demonstrate lordosis behavior—" He turned to Jason and explained, "That's the stereotypical arched back—"

"I know what lordosis behavior is," Jason snapped.

Miner groaned softly, shaking his head.

"Good, then you'll understand that it's one of the most identifiable positions of the beginning stages of heat. It sparks a reliable response in any alpha who sees it, *Érosgápe* or not—"

Jason's cheeks grew red and his eyes narrowed on Urho, his hands clenching on his silverware dangerously. Miner cleared his throat, but only Vale seemed to notice.

"—leading them to instinctively mount and knot."

Miner whimpered softly, trying to get Yule's attention.

Yule asked, "So what happens if an omega doesn't present?"

"They usually—"

Vale interrupted before Urho could continue. "An omega who fails to present with the lordosis behavior often seeks out medical help, worried something is wrong with them."

"And then?" Yule asked, oblivious to his son's tension.

"At that point, they often volunteer for genetic analysis," Vale replied. "He takes their blood, runs some tests, and tries to draw conclusions based on that information."

"And what have you found?" Yule asked.

Miner gave a stern nod to Yule, his Adam's apple bobbing as he swallowed nervously.

Noticing this time, Yule abruptly looked to Jason and placed a hand over his, squeezing until Jason released his lobster fork and, thank wolf-god, his knife.

"It fits my hypothesis well," Urho said around a bite of lobster. "Those omegas with higher rates of wolf-gene markers in their blood don't present as often or as thoroughly. They are more wolf-like in their behavior, which strangely has the effect of *not* triggering the knotting instinct in their alpha to as strong a degree." He grinned. "There's nothing like seeing an omega in full presentation to bring out the animal in us."

Jason shoved back from the table, and Yule stood up, too, to grab his son by the shoulder and push him back into his seat.

Vale cleared his throat, but it sounded like a squeak. Yosef put his hand on Rosen's arm, and Urho wiped his mouth with his napkin. Eyes downcast in shame, Jason murmured something that sounded liked *sorry* but it didn't quite carry down the table.

"No, please accept my apologies," Urho said. "I forgot what it's like to be a young alpha. I should have been more thoughtful. I didn't realize my research would be a dangerous topic, but I should have."

"I hadn't considered it either," Yule agreed. "That was short-sighted of me. It's been too long since I was so young and driven by so much instinct. The impulse toward alpha expression is to be expected."

Jason shifted in his seat, like he couldn't decide if he wanted to shrink away or sit up taller to prove himself. Vale cleared his throat again, and Jason's eyes were on him in a heartbeat. He smiled comfortingly. "Everything is fine here."

Jason swallowed hard and nodded. "I'm sorry about that. It won't happen again." Then he went back to his dinner, though he didn't seem to truly enjoy the lobster any longer.

Urho smiled reassuringly at Vale but it seemed pale. Vale wanted Jason's smile instead. Hands trembling, Vale found his own lobster tasted less delicious than it had before the awkwardness.

# CHAPTER TEN

"LET ME WALK you in," Urho said as the hired car pulled up in front of Vale's house.

They'd already dropped Rosen and Yosef off at the apartment they shared in a renovated house near the river. Vale's house was the next stop.

"If I let you do that, you'll want to stay for a drink, and if you stay for a drink…" Vale smiled coyly.

Urho's eyes brightened with interest. "Why shouldn't I stay for a drink then?"

"You'll make this hired car wait out front for far too long. We wouldn't want to anger the driver. I'm sure he'd like to get home at a decent hour tonight."

Urho leaned closer. The scent of his expensive aftershave filled the space between them. "I can call another ride."

Vale sighed, pulling his scarf tighter around his neck. "You know you can't come in, Urho. Not like this. Not anymore."

"We didn't get a real goodbye." The words were gruff with sadness, and Vale swallowed against his own.

"That's the way of life, isn't it?" He hadn't gotten to say good-bye to his parents before they'd gone. Endings were often sudden. Goodbye was a gift not everyone received. "I couldn't go against my instincts on this matter. If Jason chooses another, well…arrangements will need to be made for my heats. Who knows what lies ahead?"

"You're a fool. That boy and his pater have their hearts set on

143

you. The alpha? He's another story. But we all know who really rules the roost."

"Let's not argue. I'm tired."

Urho pressed his thumb into the dimple in Vale's chin. "One drink as friends."

"Not tonight. I know that look in your eye. I've seen it for years and always gave you what you wanted—yes, what I wanted, too—but I couldn't look at myself in the mirror tomorrow if I allowed it now."

"So sure of yourself, aren't you? Maybe I just want a drink."

"I love you dearly, Urho, but you lie terribly. Another night we'll share a drink when we aren't both feeling so strange."

"I'm going to miss us."

Vale smiled and touched Urho's cheek. His stubble scratched at Vale's fingertips. "Me, too."

"Who will you talk to about tonight?"

Vale shrugged. "I have a telephone. Maybe I'll call someone. I have friends."

"Rosen and Yosef and me."

Vale gasped in mock offense. "I've got other friends. And who says I need to talk about tonight? It was what it was, he is who he is, and that's all there is to it."

"He's a pup."

"You've said that before. It changes nothing." Vale opened the car door and climbed out. He leaned in and smiled at Urho one last time. "Have a safe ride home."

Heading up the walk, he studied his house objectively. What would Jason think of it? How long would he be allowed to keep it once they contracted? *If* they contracted? The front yard was tidy enough, he hired out for that, but the back and sides looked like an unruly mess. Jason would likely want to sell it. He couldn't blame him.

Vale stopped in his tracks at that thought, remembering the house in earlier years. His pater had been much better at housekeeping than he was and everything had always looked fresh and bright. He studied the oak tree by the fence, remembering his father's strong arms swooping him up to the lowest branch, and his pater's voice calling out, "Climb carefully, baby. There's only one of you in the whole wide world."

Life had seemed so easy before his parents had passed away. This house was all he had left of them. But if they contracted and Jason wanted to sell the place, he had no legal right to object.

Vale swallowed down the tightness in his throat and headed inside.

JASON FIDDLED WITH the microscope slide, attempting a wet mount of a droplet of wine. Usually it was easy enough, but he felt unfocused and his fingers were clumsy. He resented the cool alpha quell running through him. Missing Vale already felt like a sickness deep inside, but at the same time, he'd been glad to see him go.

The night had been awkward and strange, and he hadn't been alone in that assessment. He'd been able to tell through subtle changes in scent and expression that Vale had been uncomfortable at times, too. It wasn't right. None of this was how it was supposed to be. *Érosgápe* were supposed to fit perfectly from the start, right? Did the age difference between them really matter so much?

He sighed and pressed his thumbs against his eyes. He would be strong. Be the alpha Vale deserved.

Jason consulted his biology book again for the directions on making a wet mount. He'd done it plenty of times before, but he just couldn't seem to get it right tonight. Frustrated when he read the same sentence for the sixth time, he leaned back in his chair and looked around his room.

What would Vale think of it? The walls held framed paintings of sailboats Pater had chosen for him when he was moved from the nursery into this room as a boy. In addition, fluttering on the walls were pictures he'd drawn of the wonders he'd found beneath his microscope lens and the occasional life drawing he'd made while bored in the park or while waiting in Father's office at Sabel Motor Parts or the shipping yard. Childish things in Vale's eyes, he was sure.

Vale's own bedroom was probably the one he'd spotted with the lace curtains billowing in the breeze. He'd have his own furniture, chosen himself, and paintings on the walls he'd specifically bought to his own taste. To suit himself. Because he hadn't needed to suit anyone else. And there probably wasn't a single hand-drawn fluttering bit of paper taped up anywhere. Or if there was, it was probably one of his own handwritten poems made up of devastating words and sharp little sentences that tore into the reader with meaning and light.

Vale was a marvel, and Jason had so little to offer him that was his own. He squeezed his eyes shut. Why did he have to be so young? Why hadn't he been born when Vale needed him? Then they could have grown up together, developed their tastes as one, and lived the entirety of their lives, side by side.

The slide he still held slipped from his sweaty hand and landed on the rug, smearing the carpet with a small red stain. He stared at it morosely before gripping the stem of the full wine glass on his desk and taking a large swallow. He'd stolen it from the bar when his parents were distracted paying the beta help in the kitchen. Drinking interfered with alpha quell—but it also interfered with unwanted thoughts of his inadequacy, so he took another big swallow.

He remembered Vale putting on his coat at the end of the

night, the musky smell of his slick entirely dried up. The night air had rushed into the foyer through the open door, stealing the sweetness of his skin away from Jason, too. He'd been so proud when Vale had produced slick on sight and then he'd been humiliated as it'd dried up over the evening. Of course he'd been unable to hold Vale's thrall as his alpha. He shouldn't be surprised by that. He'd barely spoken to the man.

He closed his eyes and remembered the worst moment right at the end.

Father had thanked everyone for coming as he shook everyone's hands. Pater had followed suit, but Jason had hung back, unsure of himself. Vale had wrapped his scarf around his neck, obscuring his beautiful throat, and then turned to Jason to say with a sad smile, "It's been a pleasure."

Jason slammed his fist against his desk remembering. He hadn't been enough. He should have been dashing and strong. He should have told Vale that he had...that he wanted...wolf-god, he still didn't know what he should have said to the man, but it should have been *something*.

Vale's guests had made noise about how it had been a lovely evening and they'd enjoyed themselves immensely. Lies. It'd been weird and strange, and every single one of them knew what a little twit he was now. It was horrible to imagine what they might have said about him to Vale on their drive home. Even now they might be with him, filling his ears about how Jason wasn't old enough to give Vale the life he deserved.

The sole good thing about the way the evening had ended had been when Vale had turned to Father and said, "We can start negotiations when you're ready. There's nothing more I need to know before moving ahead."

But then Father had ruined it by saying, "I should warn you that there are several items I won't budge on."

147

Vale's eyes had gone inhumanly cold. Jason felt his heart shrivel just remembering that look. "Then I should warn you of the same."

Jason's breath came raggedly remembering his father's stern glare and irritable growl. Jason had instinctively stepped between them but remained silent. For that small bit of gallantry, he'd been rewarded by Vale's genuine smile, and the soft touch of two fingers on his own. "Thank you, Jason. It's been a lovely evening."

Jason groaned, his cock growing hard against his leg. Such a small touch, but it'd burned into his memory. He could still feel the tingle on his knuckles. No other man could ever be satisfying again. He pressed the heel of his hand to his dick, closing his eyes and imagining Vale was there.

Instantly, he cringed. No, Vale couldn't be here in this room so full of Jason's boyhood. Better to imagine them in Vale's room instead. The fantasy shadows of Vale's bedroom seeped into his mind, calming him.

In Vale's room, he could take and own and claim without worry or shame. There was nothing of his past there. It would be just the two of them.

But just as he moved to unbutton his pants and free his cock, he froze. Urho had been in Vale's room. Taken him there. Seen him exhibit lordosis behavior, heard him beg for a knot, and satisfied his needs. Urho had helped *his* Vale, his own omega, through heat.

He growled and pressed his head into his hands.

Ridiculous, Pater had called this reaction in alphas. Even Father had agreed jealousy was primitive and undesirable in a modern man. And yet Jason hated the idea of Urho's hands on Vale. Hated Urho. Hated how much he hated him.

What if Urho was there now? What if he was touching Vale, pleasuring him, while Jason sat alone and tortured in his room? They weren't contracted. Vale might not care a whit for the protocols. He might not care at all that they were *Érosgápe*.

Jason bit back a scream. Desperate, he grabbed his wine, tossed all of it down, and shuddered as the burn battled the cool of alpha quell in his veins.

He couldn't stand it. He wouldn't stand it. He had to make sure.

Heart hammering, he slid the window over the roof open and put one foot out.

At the sharp knock on his door, he jumped and bumped his head against the window frame. How could his parents have possibly known what he was planning?

"Jason? There's a phone call for you."

Father's voice sounded annoyingly smug to Jason's ears. How could Father sound so calm when Jason's insides were shredding apart?

Father went on cheerfully. "You can take it in my study."

"I don't want to talk to anyone." He was sick of the calls from his school pals trying to ferret out gossip about his situation.

Father laughed. "I think you'll want to talk to this person."

Jason rolled his eyes, took a deep breath of the cool night air, and pulled his foot back inside. "Tell Xan I'll return his call tomorrow."

"It's Vale, son," Father said with an amused huff. "Come on down and speak with him."

*Vale.*

His heart leapt and his knees went weak. "Yeah, um, hold on. Just a second."

He paced over to the mirror by his closet and looked himself over. His pants were wrinkled, his shirt a mess, and his hair scrubbed every which way. Unacceptable. He patted desperately at his hair and tried to hold back the excitement inching up his throat.

The door opened and his father peered in at him, laughing. "It's a phone call, son. He won't have any idea what you look like. Calm down."

Jason ran his hand over his hair one last time and darted past his chuckling father and down the stairs, practically running to the study. After shutting and locking the door, he collapsed into the large leather chair behind his father's massive wooden desk, before gripping the phone receiver in one hand.

"Hello?"

Could he have sounded more breathless and wild? Probably not. He cleared his throat and prepared to try again with a more even, steady tone, when Vale spoke.

"Are you surprised to hear from me tonight, Jason?"

The buzz of his name in Vale's mouth zipped up his spine. "A little. But I'm glad, too. I think. I mean, I don't know why you called. Maybe I shouldn't be glad." He was babbling like an idiot. "I hope I should be glad?"

"I'm not calling with bad news if that's what you're worried about."

"Oh, good." Jason clunked his forehead down on the desk and rolled it back and forth. Wolf-god help him, he was a failure at this. A total failure.

The wine climbed through his veins, undoing the alpha quell's work a little more with each breath. He was too hot; he unbuttoned the top of his shirt so he could breathe better.

"We had so little privacy tonight." Vale's voice was delicious. Jason wanted an entire bathtub filled with it so he could luxuriate in that honey for hours. "Do you agree?"

"Yes," Jason said, his heart lurching. "Did you want privacy with me?"

Vale laughed. "It would be imprudent to be entirely alone right now. But I did wish I'd had more of a chance to speak with you one-on-one. I don't know that we exchanged more than pleasantries all night."

"I wanted to talk with you, but Pater kept interfering. I think he wanted you all to himself."

Vale hummed. "Omegas do enjoy each other's company more often than not. There's a certain shared experience that comes from being sent away to omega schools so young, among other things."

Other things like heat. Submission. Pregnancy. All things an alpha couldn't ever truly know or understand.

"I read your poems. The ones Pater gave me."

"I know, we discussed it earlier."

"Not really. You just found out that I'd read them, but we didn't talk about them."

"Do you want to talk about them now?"

"Yes," Jason said, ecstatic with the opportunity to pose the questions he'd longed to ask when he'd read the poems alone on the roof.

"All right. What would you like to know?"

"Have you truly seen a whale at sea, or was that something you wrote from your imagination?"

Whales had been nearly extinct for so long that sightings were unbelievably rare. Jason didn't know if he'd ever met someone who'd seen one with their own eyes.

"What do you think?"

"I don't know. I could picture it so perfectly with your words that I thought for sure you must have seen it. But then I remembered how impossible it is to describe my favorite microscope slides to Xan. I can't ever find the words for what I see. So I end up just making him look for himself. So maybe it's easier to make up words for something you imagine than to describe something you've experienced yourself."

"Xan is your friend from the library?"

Did he hear a hint of jealousy?

"Yes, he's been my roommate since high school, and we'd

planned to room together at university. But I guess not anymore."

"I see. He wasn't at your house tonight," Vale said slowly. "I was asked to bring my closest friends. I'd have liked to meet yours, too."

"Yes, well." Jason's mind tumbled. How to explain what was happening with Xan? He couldn't tell Vale the truth. "He's...We...I don't know. Maybe you'll meet him soon? I can't promise, though. It's complicated."

"So much about this situation is," Vale murmured. "To answer your question, I've never seen a whale, but I've read about them from recovered Old World texts, and when I was a young boy my pater took me to a theater showing a salvaged Old World film of whales in the southern seas."

"Really?" Jason's inner scientist perked up. "There were so many animals that went extinct before and after the Great Death. It's amazing to see old photographs of them. I can't imagine how compelling a film of so rare an animal might be."

"I can ask Professor Bitar about it. He's a friend of mine who presides over the film archives at the university. If there's a copy in their vaults, he'd know about it."

"But will he show it to me?" He opened a few more buttons on his shirt, still feeling hot and shivery all at once. Vale's voice seemed to do that to him, especially with the liquor beating up the alpha quell quite handily. "I'm just a first year, and I don't have a good reason to ask him about it other than curiosity."

"Intellectual curiosity should always be rewarded. I can put in a good word for you, of course, and I can't see why he'd say no. You'd have to make some effort, too."

"Oh, I *will*," Jason agreed heartily.

Vale released a soft sound that went straight to Jason's dick. He squirmed as he grew hard again, and he pressed the receiver to his ear, trying to capture Vale's every breath.

"Was there anything else you wanted to know about my poems?"

"'Snowflake burn in heat of night'. That was a reference to alpha quell, wasn't it?"

"Did it seem like it was?"

"Yes, because the speaker in the poem is really into viscosity and so-called 'slippery slopes', but he's held back from it all by this snowflake burn. Cold burn. That's how it feels at first, slipping into my veins, chilling me from the inside out. I think Pater just didn't get the symbolism."

Vale laughed. Jason gripped the edge of the desk as lust roared in him. He breathed through it, edging open his pants to let his cock pop out to the cooler air of his father's study.

"Well, I'd like to say you're reading into things, but, yes, it was a poem featuring lines from a friend's description of his first experience of alpha quell."

"So it's about sex."

Vale laughed again. "Yes, in many ways, almost all of them are."

"I knew it! The lines in 'viscount, are you dreaming?' with the cherries and the burst of flavor over the tongue is described as 'pumping summer's glory' are totally about oral sex. Tell me I'm right."

"You're right."

Jason went a little lightheaded and he squeezed his eyes close. "Wolf-god, you're a filthy man."

Vale purred, "Is that terrible?"

"No, I love it."

Vale choked quietly, his breath coming in strange gasps. "Darling, are you hard?"

Jason stared down at his throbbing, red dick with pre-come slipping from the head. He gripped his fist around it, squeezing until another drop slipped down the side. "Yes," he growled. "And

I've got my dick in my hand."

Why had he said that? Vale would probably be offended and end the call. What kind of out-of-control alpha was he that—

"Jason, I'm hard, too, and I'm unbuttoning my pants now."

Holy wolf-in-heaven, was this happening? Was this actually *happening*?

"What's it look like?" Jason asked, needing to know. "Tell me. Now."

"Mm, well, it's not terribly thick, but it's longer than average."

Jason whimpered. "Yeah?"

"And I'm cut like they used to do to so many boys in the Old World before the Great Death."

"Why?" Jason's cock thudded against his palm, arousal undeterred by this news.

"Childhood issue. The foreskin was too tight and wouldn't draw back. It was deemed for the best."

"Huh." Jason closed his eyes, holding the receiver tight against his ear. He tried to picture a cock without foreskin. He'd heard of such a thing but never seen it.

"Does that seem strange to you?" Vale sounded—could it be?—vulnerable, and Jason rushed to reassure him.

"I can't wait to see it."

Vale moaned. "I hope you like it."

"Do you? Really?" Jason grunted and had to bite his cheek to keep from falling over the edge.

"You sound wonderful, darling. You sound like you're about to come for me."

"You'll come for me first," Jason gritted out. It was an order, because that was how it was done. Omegas first, alphas second, and he wasn't the kind of man to fail his omega even over the telephone.

"Will I?"

"Yes."

Vale whimpered. "Oh, I think I might."

"You will." Jason closed his eyes, listening to the heavy breathing on the other end of the line. His balls ached, and he was ready to come as soon as he'd secured his omega's pleasure.

"Talk to me," Vale whispered, strained and breathless. "I'm so slick and wet for you."

"You want to make your alpha proud, don't you?"

"Yes!"

"Then come for me," Jason muttered. "Now. Let me hear you."

Vale cried out. The noise of his pleasure broke Jason's fragile hold against his own orgasm. It tore him open like a pleasure-wound. With his muscles spasming, semen pumping in harsh, thick ropes out onto the wood floor, he shuddered and shook, his moans uncontrollably harsh and desperate. A moment of strange clarity crashed over him, a vision of himself as a quivering, shattered boy sweating and coming painfully hard in massive spurts all over his father's office. And then he snapped back into himself again. Panting through tears of desire he gazed at all the come. Wolf-god, he'd made a mess.

"That's it. That's beautiful."

"You're beautiful," Jason murmured. "And mine. You're mine."

Vale moaned. "Only if you want me to be."

"I do. I want you so much."

Vale sighed, his own pleasure seeming to calm while Jason still trembled with need. "This wasn't the reason I called," Vale said, a hint of embarrassment in his tone.

"It wasn't a mistake." Jason sat up, gathering command into his voice despite the way his thighs and arms shook. "Don't say it was a mistake."

"I won't. Not yet." But he sounded sad. "I can't. It was too perfect, listening to you, feeling you through the phone. Did you feel me, too?"

"I can almost taste you," he growled. And he could. Vale's voice was a sweet grit on his tongue, and he swallowed it down. "Don't be sorry. I won't allow you to be sorry."

"I'm not," Vale said softly. "I just regret I didn't accomplish what I'd set out to do."

"Which was?"

"To know you better."

"Well, now you know what I sound like when I come."

Vale laughed. "Indeed I do."

"That's one thing you didn't know before."

"No, I didn't." Vale's voice went breathy again. "Thank you for sharing it with me."

"I should thank *you*."

"Yes, you should. Tell me what you liked best."

"You really are dirty."

"Does it bother you if I am?" Vale sounded naughty as he asked.

"No. I like it. If you were a prude, then we'd have a lot of problems."

Vale chuckled again, his tension coming and going in waves over the phone with every question. "We should clean ourselves up."

"I don't want to stop talking to you."

"Let's have one more question and then we'll say goodnight. You can call me again on Monday after school."

"But I didn't call you at all."

Vale snorted. "Don't be pedantic. I'm giving you permission to call me on Monday."

"I will. Absolutely. On Monday."

"After school."

"Yes."

"Okay, one last question for you, Jason Sabel. Do you believe you're capable of being my alpha?"

Doubts that he'd ever convince Vale that he was old enough plagued him, but he lifted his chin, remembering the sweet sound of Vale's climax. "I know I can be."

"And if your parents don't approve?"

"It's my choice, not theirs."

"You don't know everything about the situation. I'm not asking for promises from you tonight. I just wanted your honest gut feeling. A surrogate might still be—"

"Don't talk about that. We just...the two of us... We were together." He fought to untie his tongue. It'd been over the phone, but it meant something. "We just made love together. I don't want to hear about surrogates. Not now. Not ever."

"I agree it's poor timing, but—"

"No," Jason cut him off. "Stop. I have one last question for you."

Vale hesitated. "I'm all ears."

"In your poems, what do you have against capital letters?"

Vale giggled softly, sounding young and embarrassed. "It's a ridiculous affectation I started in my youth and has now become my signature style, that's all. Do you prefer capital letters? I can start using them if you'd like."

"Do whatever makes you happy. Your words are beautiful just the way they are."

Vale was silent for a long moment. "Goodnight, Jason. Sleep well."

"Goodnight. Sweet dreams."

They listened to each other's breathing for a half-dozen heart-beats and then Jason hung up first, determined to show his strength of will and exert his power.

# CHAPTER ELEVEN

"**Y**OU JERKED OFF together?" Rosen's dark brown eyes flew wide and his red mouth hung open. His hair was twisted up into one of his artful buns, and he wore a paint-spattered shirt as he prepared a canvas for another of his 'expressions', as he called the art he produced when he wasn't teaching at the university or playing at being a chef.

Vale sighed, scratched at his unshaven face, and paced the messy room over the detached garage near Rosen and Yosef's apartment. Rosen rented it as his studio. The floors were tacky with half-dried oil paint and spilled turpentine, and the astringent scent of the place filled Vale's nostrils completely despite the open windows. Colorful canvases lined the walls and leaned in small stacks a foot or more deep. Glass jars, smeared with paint, were stacked on a counter.

"It was a mistake," he said finally.

"Huh."

He frowned and pulled up short next to Rosen where he mixed a blue very similar to Vale's favorite color on a large, wooden pallet. "What do you mean by 'huh'? Your expression said everything about what a disastrous move it was."

Rosen shrugged. "It's done now. Who cares if it was a mistake? Onward, I say."

"Onward into what, though? That's the real question. Now I've given him hope." And he'd given himself hope. That was the worst of it, really. Jason was a child; his parents could break him easily enough. It was Vale's own heart that he'd stupidly risked.

"Was it good?"

"Don't be ridiculous."

"Amazing, then," Rosen murmured. "You'd tell me everything if it sucked. There wouldn't even be a problem if you'd hated it. You'd just decide that you didn't want to contract with some alpha who couldn't even hold his own for phone sex, force him to take a surrogate, and be done with him."

"Wolf-god, you're almost as impossible as Urho."

"You didn't tell *him*, did you?"

"No. He's so old-fashioned at heart. He'd find it all 'improper'."

Rosen smirked. "You're so cruel to him."

"I can't do anything about his feelings for me."

"At least don't deny you have them for him, too."

Vale groaned. "You're missing the entire point of what I came to talk about. When will Yosef be back? He'll understand."

"He's travelled to see his pater today. He's not doing well. Hasn't since Yosef's father passed."

"*Érosgápe* suffer," Vale murmured, crossing his arms over his chest and imagining a future where Jason faced so many years alone. Like Urho. "I'd die long before Jason. Another reason he'd be better off with a surrogate his own age."

Rosen rolled his eyes. "You can tell yourself that all you like, but it doesn't make it true. Just like eating moldy cheese sandwiches won't make them a decent dinner."

"Speaking of, you need to feed me before I go home. I'm out of everything civilized. This morning I almost resorted to eating Zephyr's food before I found a hunk of cheese in the bottom of the refrigerator."

"It was molded, wasn't it?"

"I scraped it off."

Rosen sighed. "I'd be much more worried about how you're going to feed your alpha than whether or not he'd be better off with a surrogate."

"A surrogate would probably know how to cook," Vale said mournfully. He knew he was whining now, but wasn't he allowed a little self-pity? This was a big change no matter what happened.

"And a surrogate would never satisfy him deep down and you know it. It would never be the same. You're *Erosgápe*. He'd long for you regardless. Besides, what would you be cursing yourself to? A life of knowing that he's out there, miserable with someone else, and that you can't have him? Ridiculous. Put your best self forward. Convince him to contract with you. Be happy."

"That heat... You remember the one?" He looked at Rosen meaningfully. "When you found me? And then after..."

Rosen threw his paintbrush down and grabbed Vale into a hard hug. "Now *that* was a mistake. An honest, tragic, horrible mistake."

"The scar tissue from the abortion would make a birth too dangerous. Even if Jason and I contract, if we consummate, and bond, he'd always have to hold back during heat, never give in entirely. He'd have to keep his wits about him to use a condom when I'm begging for his child. He'd be better off with someone he can just fall into heat with and screw blind."

Rosen went still but held him even tighter. Eventually, he whispered in his ear, "Rumor has it his pater has access to abortifacients."

Vale jerked out of Rosen's embrace. "What?"

"Drugs that prevent pregnancies from taking. That's why he's so fragile." Rosen pushed a hank of loose dark hair out of his eye, but it felt back almost immediately. "Or at least that's what I heard."

"Who told you this?" Vale's heart beat faster, cold seeping into his gut.

Rosen shrugged. "Betas gossip just like anyone else. The chemist's lover told me."

"Which chemist?"

"Delta section."

"Anton? The chemist with the red beard who hands out balloon animals for the sick children while they wait for their medicine to mix up?"

"The very one."

"He makes abortifacients for Miner Hoff? You're certain?"

"And other omegas who won't survive a birth."

"No!" Vale's mind whirled. "It's too risky."

"It's true. Shankar only told me because he wanted to know if Yosef would be willing to represent Anton if he should ever be discovered and arrested. I told him Yosef would be happy to, of course, but we all know those laws are airtight. The man would swing."

Vale swallowed hard. "You can't tell anyone about this, Rosen. You know what would happen to Miner."

And to Yule if it was determined he was complicit. Anton wouldn't have a prayer in the world. If it was uncovered, an investigation would no doubt be launched, and who knew how many other omegas might be sussed out using these illegal drugs? Wolf-god, it could be horrific.

Rosen's eyes darkened angrily. "I'd never put anyone at risk. I only told you because, well, perhaps he can help you if the worst ever happens."

"Anton or Miner?"

"Either. Both. I can't imagine the omega we met the other night would ever want you to suffer a birth at the risk of your life. He was a good man."

Vale nodded.

Generally, he agreed, but a jittery fear rode his nerves. He didn't want Jason to lose his parents to something so scandalous. The family name would be forever tarnished and their lands and business forfeit to the state. Jason would be left destitute. His parents would be imprisoned and possibly executed for crimes against humanity. It made Vale's stomach turn.

How could Yule be so selfish that he'd impregnate Miner when he knew the man couldn't handle it? He'd played the devoted alpha at The Feast of Alpha's Blessings. Vale never would have suspected he'd be so cruel. He wondered if Jason knew. He couldn't imagine those wide, innocent eyes knowing anything about it at all.

"It's too much to be believed," Vale breathed.

"Some people play the hero to the point of idiocy," Rosen observed. "But I don't think either one of us would accuse Anton of that. Not given what we know and what we've seen."

Vale rubbed at his mouth and said nothing.

Rosen returned to his painting, and for a while Vale watched in agitated silence. Eventually, the quiet in the room coupled with the breeze calmed him. The pace of Rosen's work was soothing as well. The progress was similar to how Vale wrote poetry: he relied on creative flow to get a draft of his initial inspiration, and then he took away from the piece a little at a time, narrowing it, focusing it, until the words were perfect, like blades of grass, sharp and green.

Rosen painted broadly first, and then used a scraper to narrow bits that were overlarge, adding details with smaller brushes and a lighter hand. Perhaps all art started out as a mess and was refined gradually to something worth sharing with another person.

"Should I not have told you?" Rosen asked after almost an hour had passed.

"Admittedly, I'm not sure what to do with the knowledge, but I'm glad to have it."

"I thought you shouldn't contract without knowing. Not only because he can help you, but it's only fair that you understand the risk of association."

"Yes, getting more deeply invested with a family that could be extinguished in one swoop of the executioner's blade does seem precarious."

Rosen shrugged. "True. But I know you don't think what they're doing is wrong."

"I do, actually," Vale said. "Yule Sabel didn't strike me as the kind of man to lack in self-control, but to consistently impregnate his omega despite his health? That, I judge him harshly for."

"We don't know the whole story. There might be a good reason."

Vale raised a brow. "Lack of will is the only explanation I can think of."

Rosen shot him a glance from beneath his strong eyebrows. "The world is vast," he said in his philosophy-professor voice. "There are things we can't know unless we ask. And sometimes we can't ask."

Vale watched him outline a yellow square with a thick line of the blue. "Perhaps you're right, but I'll have a hard time shaking this knowledge when we start negotiations on Friday."

"Maybe you'll be stronger for it. You'll know going in that Yule is a man like any other, hiding his own terrible flaw. It can help you stick to your principles knowing that your past doesn't hold the worst sins at the table."

Vale chewed that thought over. "I have one absolute going into the meeting. Anything else, within reason, is open to negotiation. But you and I both know what I can't deliver on. And that will put an end to the whole thing."

"Will it?"

"You know it will. Jason will want children and his parents will make sure his imprinting and my 'omega persuasion' doesn't get in the way of that."

Rosen didn't seem convinced. But he slipped his brush into a jar of mineral spirits and sighed, turning from his canvas. "I wish I could have a child sometimes."

"You do?"

"Sure." His lips quirked in a bittersweet smile. "A little Yosef would be very cute, don't you think?"

"Especially if he had a little white beard."

Rosen rolled his eyes. "It's hard to understand, probably, as an omega, what betas miss out on. Our culture is set up to glorify the alpha and omega connection, the consummation and the intoxication of a heat-fueled mating." He rubbed his paint-spattered fingers together. "I know that's all designed to disguise the danger and precarious nature of breeding, to make the peril and lack of control seem romantic and worth it. But I can't help thinking that having a child, a baby of your very own, would be a beautiful thing."

"Yes, I suppose it would be." Not that he'd ever know. In that way, he was doomed to be as barren as Rosen and Yosef. Still, it was true that he'd never thought of how it must be from a beta's point of view—to not even have the option of a surrogate for breeding. He'd always assumed that most betas didn't want children. After all, he'd envied them their carefree lives without heats to handle. They could be anything, do anything…well, so long as they didn't get designs on proper alpha positions. And so long as they never fell in love outside of their gender.

He supposed there were probably all kinds of ways a beta felt hemmed in by the laws of the country and the Holy Book of Wolf. He'd just never bothered to truly consider them. Perhaps he was a good match for Jason after all. It was shameful to discover how often he suffered from the self-centeredness of the young.

They lapsed into silence again, and after watching Rosen paint for another half an hour, Vale said, "You need to feed me soon or I'll die of starvation."

Rosen laughed and dumped all of his used brushes in a mason jar of turpentine. "All right, come along to the apartment. What would you like? Something from scratch or a quick meal?"

"As much as I'd love one of your creations, I'll take the quickie, please."

"Are you sure? I could use the company over dinner." Rosen washed his hands in the deep sink stuffed into the corner.

Vale stretched with a sigh. "I have to go soon. I told Jason he could call me after school."

Rosen laughed, his eyes sparkling as he cast a glance over his shoulder and rinsed his hands off. "Are you going to ask after his homework?"

"You're an asshole worse than Urho."

"Are you going to jerk off with him again? You know he'll expect it now."

Vale's cock twitched to life and he glared. "I will absolutely tell Yosef how you've tormented me today."

"Oh, good. Maybe he'll spank me." Rosen grinned, wiping his hands and then tossing the towel into a bin next to the door. "Why don't you see how Jason feels about that? Would he like it if you turned him over your knee? Or would he like to spank *you*?"

Vale shook his head and jerked his hand up in a rude gesture before following Rosen from the studio. The smell of oil paint dragged along behind them.

"If I wasn't so hungry, I'd go home," he said to Rosen's back.

"You could try this thing called grocery shopping. It's not as hard as it looks."

The blue sky stretched overhead and Vale shrugged. "But it's better when you take care of me. It makes me feel loved."

Rosen slowed his step and threw his arm around Vale's waist. "Oh, we love you. Even when you serve us moldy cheese."

Vale smiled and a knot inside him unwound. He had friends. No matter what happened with Jason. He had people who loved him.

"HOW WAS SCHOOL?"

Vale's voice was delicious. Jason squirmed in his father's big leather chair, wishing he had a phone extension in his bedroom for privacy. Cleaning up the mess the other night hadn't been easy, not with Father's sensitive alpha nose. He'd opened all the windows and sprayed lemon-scented freshener everywhere, but he'd still worried that Father would know what they'd done. Or at least, what *he'd* done.

"Don't ask it like that." He opened a desk drawer to grab a piece of paper and a pencil. Maybe doodling would keep him focused this time.

"You don't want to share your day with me?"

"Sure I do. But not when you ask like you're one of my parents." Jason frowned.

"How should I ask then?"

"I don't know. Tell me about your day first. I bet it was more interesting anyway."

"Highly doubtful. You probably learned something or interacted with someone at least. Aside from a trip over to Rosen and Yosef's for lunch, it's just been me, Zephyr, and a pile of old magazines I'm trying to sort through."

"Is Zephyr a beta servant?" It was an unusual name, but betas liked to be a bit flashy sometimes to make up for not being alphas. At least that was what Father said.

Vale snorted. "No, I'm afraid I'm not of the income class to hire servants."

"You can be now."

"Let's not get mired in that discussion. That's for our lawyers to help us figure out."

"Fair enough. Who's Zephyr?" he asked again.

"My cat."

"Oh, you have a pet?" Due to Pater's allergies and fragile state, he'd never been allowed one. He'd always envied Xan his fluffy dog and his classmates all their various cats, gerbils, and birds. "Is it a boy or a girl?"

"A girl."

"Wow. That's amazing. Can I look at her sometime?"

Girls were fascinating beasts. It was stunning to Jason that once upon a time there had been human females, too. He'd seen pictures of them in Old World art.

Vale's tone held a smile. "If Zephyr wants you to see her, then you will. She's a magician and a marvel at hiding if she's nervous."

"What color is she?"

"Silver."

"Oh, she sounds lovely."

"She can be. She's also very good at knocking things over. She has a true talent for that. And sometimes she bites. She's either a doll or a demon."

Jason laughed. "Changeable. Like the wind."

"Very much like the wind."

"So, today at university was strange," Jason ventured, answering Vale's initial question now that he didn't feel like such a child about it. "Everyone had heard about me imprinting on you."

"I imagine your cohorts had a lot to say about it."

Jason frowned, remembering Wilbet Monhundy's taunting. *Your omega's a slut. Your omega's all used up.* If it hadn't been for the massive amounts of alpha quell in his system keeping him unnaturally calm, he might have punched him.

"You don't have to save my feelings, Jason. I'm sure you were teased about my age."

Jason sighed. "But you're beautiful and perfect and smart and talented. They're just jerks. Jealous jerks."

But he knew that wasn't entirely the case. Sure, they were assholes, but none of them especially envied Jason for imprinting on an older omega. Most of them wanted the usual experience of finding an age-mate match, even if they *were* titillated by the idea that Jason might have already consummated with Vale.

At least he only had to put up with them for two more days before the University closed so students could be home in plenty of time for the second Autumn Nights feast on Saturday. As the Feast of the Expectant Wolf, it was the most holy of the three.

"Mm, well, omega persuasion is a bit blinding. But I'm glad you're not entirely dissatisfied with me." Jason had a strange sense that Vale had left off the word *yet*. "And your professors? How are they treating you? Some might have some trouble reconciling that one of their colleagues is now your *Érosgápe*."

"They've been fine." Though Professor Shriner had suggested he watch ahead of the class on the educational films in preparation for consummation. Jason had broken out in a cold sweat at that. "All my teachers are being really generous about giving me enough time to complete my make-up work."

"I'm glad everyone's being fair."

"Well, professors are for sure. The others…well, I can't blame them if they're acting a little different from usual." His stomach shriveled as he remembered the way people whispered when he walked by and how he'd been shunned at lunch, like mere contact with him would make them imprint on the next random professor to walk by. "They probably didn't mean the things they said." Though he suspected Wilbet Monhundy absolutely did.

"Do you want to talk about that or how it made you feel? I don't think it's likely to change as time goes on. People will talk about us this way forever if we contract."

Jason grimaced. "It doesn't matter what other people say. I've never cared about that anyway."

"But you're Yule Sabel and Miner Hoff's son. You'll have a role to fill in society when you inherit your father's company."

"I want to be a scientist. I'll let someone else run Father's company."

"You'll be expected to be the figurehead, attend the right parties, schmooze with the right people."

"You saw the other night how bad I am at schmoozing."

"You were charming."

"I was silent and I let you down."

"You are entirely too hard on yourself. You're nineteen. Give yourself some time to grow into your puppy feet. You'll be fine."

"Puppy feet?"

Vale laughed. "Just something I thought of the first time I saw you. You're still filling out, not quite entirely grown. You move like a puppy, all big feet and hands. It's sweet."

"I need to be more than sweet to you."

"Oh, believe me, you can be. You are."

Jason's heart raced and his cock grew semi-hard. Determined not to let Vale think he was an out of control alpha by making this phone call all about sex again, he changed the topic. "What are the magazines you're sorting?"

"A stack of poetry and creative writing magazines from about five years ago. I always meant to look through them, but never found the time. That's something I've got plenty of now."

"What about poems? Are you working on any?"

"Some are percolating, but nothing's grabbed me by the throat and insisted I write it. I've scribbled a few words here and there, but nothing good. Why?"

"I loved what I read. I'd like to see more."

"You can just re-read those for now."

"I've memorized them. I have a photographic memory."

Vale was silent for a long moment. "That's unusual. I'm sure that serves you well in your classes."

"It does. I honestly think it's unfair. But it's not like I can turn it off." Jason listened to Vale's breath for a moment and then recited, "'breath of light that falls on sweat soaked skin, wolf-god sings his prayers.'"

"I haven't thought of that poem in a very long time."

"I liked it. And this one, too: 'salamander eyes glisten in time to a pulsing heart i cannot find'."

"Truly, that's abominable. I should be ashamed of calling myself a poet!"

"It's beautiful. No one else would ever think of those words. Only you."

"Maybe it would be better if I hadn't."

"Stop." A bubble of irritation filled his voice with command. "Be happy that you please your alpha."

"Oh," Vale said, a bit breathlessly. "You're going to tell me how to feel?"

"If you're being wrong-headed, yes."

"And if *you're* being wrong-headed, oh, mighty alpha?"

"Feel free to point it out." He nodded firmly. "I can handle being told I'm wrong. But I'm not wrong about the poems. Have you ever seen salamander eyes?"

Vale still sounded breathless when he replied, "There used to be a variety of salamanders in my pater's garden. He would capture them sometimes to show me the different colors and variety. I imagine they've made quite the home out there now that I've let the place go."

Jason closed his eyes, soaking in the tenderness of Vale's tone when he spoke of his pater. "No green thumb on you?"

"Urho says I'm lazy and maybe he's right, but if it comes between reading and gardening, I'll take reading. Though reading in a garden is always a nice compromise."

Jason tapped the end of the pen he'd been doodling with against his chin. "It wouldn't be hard to clean up your garden. I could hire a few betas to help me. We could put in a beautiful winter theme for now." Excitement pierced him. He'd never been allowed to have any say in Pater's gardens before, though he'd wanted to. "And we could lay in brighter colored bulbs for spring."

Vale was quiet a moment but eventually said, "It's almost too late for that."

"Then I should get started right away."

"This isn't a good idea. We haven't contracted."

But he sounded uncertain. Jason could hear the longing in his tone. Vale wanted his garden to look nice again, and moreover, he enjoyed the idea of his alpha doing that for him. Jason puffed up a bit. Father always said that omegas respond well to being cared for. "Give an omega some tender care, son, and he'll be putty in your hands." Though Jason also recalled that Pater rolled his eyes at that, chiming in with, "Any man likes to be cared for, Yule. Alpha, beta, or omega."

Regardless of who was right, Vale sounded tempted.

"I'll start tomorrow," Jason said firmly. "It'll be no trouble."

Vale made a soft noise but didn't reply.

"There's no reason not to agree to it. No matter what comes of the contract, my family will owe you an allowance and the care of your estate for the rest of your life." Vale's quiet became somehow brittle like Jason had said the wrong thing. "But that's not why I want to do it. It's not about any of that. I *want* to make it beautiful back there. I could see the bones of it that day when I spoke to you through the window. It could be so handsome. I want to make it nice again. For you."

Vale was a tough nut, though. "It wouldn't do for me to agree to anything without your parents' approval. After all, it's their money you're talking about spending."

"Not really." Jason grinned, twirling the pen between his fingers and thumb. "I have an allowance of my own and this won't make a dent in my trust fund."

Vale sighed. "You sell this idea quite nicely."

"All I need to do is talk with the betas who work Pater's gardens. They'll be happy to help me."

Vale was quiet again and then said, "I should tell you that I'm not fond of red tulips."

"Do you like pink and orange ones, though?"

"They're preferable by far. Though purple irises are my favorite. Aside from red roses, of course."

"Of course. They're my favorite, too." Wondrous joy swept through him. "And what about daffodils?"

"The ones with the white centers are always sweet."

Jason started making a list on the paper he'd gotten out to doodle on. They discussed the garden for some time until Pater knocked on the study door and stuck his head in. "Dinner is ready, love. It's time to get off the phone."

Shocked to see that over an hour had passed since he first called Vale, he pleaded, "Already?"

"I'll give you a moment of privacy to say goodbye, but your father is waiting." His tone brooked no argument. Pater shut the door again and left Jason alone.

"I have to go eat dinner now."

Wolf-god, he sounded like an infant, being called to the supper table by his parents.

"Oh!" Disappointment laced through Vale's honey-rich voice. "I didn't expect you'd have to end the call so soon. Though I suppose we did talk a long time about the garden."

"Were there other things you wanted to talk about?" Jason asked, his breath coming quick.

"I suppose I thought…" Vale trailed off. "Never mind. It's for the best that we don't repeat what happened the other night. It was smart of you to come to this conversation with a level head."

"Oh, my head isn't level," Jason assured him quickly, his skin prickling in excitement. "I just didn't know if you wanted to—"

Vale cut him off. "You need to get to dinner and I need to find something in a tin for me and Zephyr here."

"From a tin? That's awful." He wanted to ask Vale to come across town and eat with them. There would be more than enough. It was ridiculous that he couldn't. Not without asking his parents' permission and they'd have to issue the invitation. Then things would be awkward again.

"I'm accustomed to it," Vale said. "No use preparing big meals for one person."

Longing and frustration squirmed in Jason's gut. "Can I call you again after? I want to talk with you more."

"We shouldn't—"

"Not for that!" Jason hastened to explain, but then he softened his voice. "Well, for that and other reasons. I want to talk to you about anything really." He'd settle for listening to Vale breathe. "Anything at all."

"Not tonight. You need to do your homework. I know you have quite a lot to make up."

"Yes," Jason admitted reluctantly.

"But I'll tell you what, Wednesday, maybe you could come over to my house."

"What?" Jason gasped, unable to believe his ears.

"I'm having Rosen, Urho, and Yosef over for dinner. It'll be an early Feast of the Expectant Wolf. Since we're negotiating on Friday, and my friends have to travel for their other plans on the actual feast day, I wanted to spend Wednesday in their company. Would you want to join us? Rosen will be cooking, never fear. I'll ask your parents' permission of course. But with the three of them here, nothing untoward will happen. I can promise them that."

"Yes! Of course! I'll be there."

"I'll call your parents in the morning."

"No, I'll ask them tonight. They'll say yes. I'll make sure of it."

"Don't, Jason," Vale said with a hint of disapproval that made the thrill in Jason's gut shrivel. "I should arrange the meeting through your parents. Protocols are cloudy with our age difference, but if we were age-mates my parents would arrange the invitation with yours. I don't think it would do for me to overstep. Your father isn't someone I want on my bad side. Your pater, either, for that matter."

He didn't want to admit it, but Vale was probably right. His father wouldn't take it as a good sign at all if Vale failed to follow protocol for arranging meetings. Jason just hoped his parents didn't insist on tagging along.

"I'd come over after school on Wednesday?" He hoped the answer was yes. He wanted all the minutes and hours in Vale's presence he could hoard at once.

"Well, not directly. You should go home, of course, and change into something suitable for dinner, and then, yes, come to my house. Oh, and use the front door this time." Vale's voice lifted with the tease. "While I've no doubt you're limber enough to crawl in the study's window, there really isn't any need."

Jason grinned. "But there's something romantic about that idea, isn't there?"

"Oh, you sweet young thing. What am I going to do with you?"

"I think you better start asking what I'm going to do with you," Jason growled. "Because *that* answer is much more exciting."

Vale gasped, and Jason took the opportunity to end the phone call. He leaned back in his father's leather chair, grinning like a wolf. Yes, he wanted Vale on his toes. And on his knees. And in his bed. And bent over desks and tables and countertops. And down in the dirt of the garden Jason was going to plant for him.

He wanted him everywhere.

Jason stood up, grabbed the list, and shoved his semi-hard dick into a more comfortable position in his pants. Then he left his father's study in a much better state than the last time he'd taken a phone call from Vale.

# CHAPTER TWELVE

"JASON! WAIT UP!" Xan jogged toward him, cheeks flushed with exertion. His coat flapped behind him and his scarf slipped, revealing a polka-dotted bow tie.

Jason reluctantly slowed his steps. He didn't want to be late to Vale's house party, but he couldn't afford to blow Xan off. They were at a crucial juncture in their friendship, and if he wanted Xan in his life at all, then he couldn't make an excuse to him now.

"Hey." He pushed his hair out of his face. The dry air of the heaters in the classrooms had sucked the humidity out of his usually full-bodied hair, leaving it a flat, overlong veil. He needed to trim it. "I didn't see you in Alpha-Omega Relations today."

Xan's cheeks flushed even darker, and he used the opportunity to rewrap his scarf to evade Jason's gaze. The weather had turned frigid the night before. It was unseasonable and would be disappointing if it remained, because then the ground would freeze and Jason would miss his opportunity to plant bulbs for Vale. Jason wrapped his coat tighter over his thick burgundy sweater and khaki school pants.

"Yeah, I didn't feel up to it," Xan said dismissively. "Did you take notes?"

"Of course." Jason dug around in his bag full of books and notepads until he brought out some pages he'd scribbled in class. He handed them over to Xan.

"What'd we cover?" Xan asked, not meeting Jason's eye.

Jason wrinkled his nose. "Pregnancy."

"Yeah?"

"Specifically the rate of fetal development in modern omegas compared to Old World women."

"Why do we have to learn about that?" Xan groaned.

"Because that, combined with a smaller hip-size and lack of flexibility in an omega's ligaments, all contribute to the danger omegas face in birth. It's why, during pregnancy, they have to take synthetic hormones to help their bodies handle the rapid expansion of the baby and to help ease labor." Jason rattled it all off in an neutral tone, though his heart had skittered wildly in class imagining Vale with their child growing inside, his body struggling to accommodate their creation. He'd sweated with fear and a strange arousal he simultaneously loved and hated.

"The Old World babies grew slower?" Xan tugged at his scarf, pushing it back into place, still not looking Jason in the eyes.

"Yes. Apparently, human women gestated their fetuses for four months longer than our omegas do." Jason shifted to his other foot; an eagerness to get home so he could go to Vale hummed inside him, but he kept his tone open and friendly. "It's all there in the notes. But you'll have to go watch the movie about heat Stage 3 and impregnation in the library. It was intense."

His mind supplied him with images of the same dark-haired omega in all the educational movies he'd seen so far. In this one, the man crowed with joy and pleasure, quaking visibly, as his alpha's knot swelled and filled him with bursts of semen. The film had explained in dispassionate tones that the head of the alpha's cock was lodged in the omega's descended womb, which would be filled with the alpha's semen. This would hopefully result in insemination of the egg that had dropped earlier in the week and which the hormones of heat had readied for fertilization.

Jason's fevered brain had barely been able to process what he was hearing. As the omega had come on the alpha's knot, writhing with an anal orgasm before shooting a sticky white load of his juices from his brutally hard penis, Jason had almost jizzed his pants in class. Several of the other alphas around him actually *had* come, their moans and musk bombarding him along with the images from the film. Just thinking about it all flustered him again. Heat rose up his neck.

"You should make sure to watch it," he repeated. "There'll be questions about it on the next test for sure."

Xan nodded and examined the papers in his hand before hesitantly meeting Jason's gaze. "So, how are you?"

A cold breeze blew past them and washed away Jason's renewed arousal. He was able to smile genuinely when he answered, "I'm all right. How about you?"

Xan shrugged, his mouth wobbling a little before he ducked his head. "Not so great."

"Yeah?"

"I miss you and…things aren't the same."

Jason threw his arm around Xan's shoulder. "C'mon. I have half an hour before I have to leave or risk being late for another obligation. Let's head back to the dorm and talk." Xan tried to shrug him off, but Jason just held on tighter. "You can still talk to me, you know. Just because we aren't roommates doesn't mean we aren't best friends."

Xan's attempt at rejection collapsed miserably under Jason's insistence, and he let Jason steer them to the dorms.

Once in their old room together, Jason released Xan to remove his coat and flop down on the stripped mattress that had once been his. "Wow, it looks weird in here without my stuff." They'd hired beta movers to come in and gather all of Jason's belongings. The boxes were still untouched in his closet at home.

Xan didn't say anything, taking his time unwinding his scarf and neatly hanging up his jacket in the closet.

"So what's up?" Jason asked finally. "Why did you skip class today?"

Xan sat down on his bed opposite Jason's. Covering his face with his hands, he was silent for a long time before coming out with, "I get too turned on by the movies."

"We all do." After class, he'd had to make a long stop in the bathroom, along with half the alphas in their year, to deal with his problem.

"It's different," Xan whispered.

Jason cocked his head, considered Xan's creeping flush, and winced at the pain in his voice. "Because you like to play omega?"

Xan choked on a sob, nodding desperately.

Jason sat up and leaned forward, trying to understand. "When you watch the films, Xan, do you never imagine yourself as the alpha? As the one on top?"

Xan shook his head and his shoulders quaked. Sobs spilled from him. "I'm made wrong, Jason. I'm unmanned. I've always been this way, even before we started. I'm a disgrace to my family name. I hate myself."

Jason's heart twisted, and he shook his head. "No, it's not like that." He moved over next to Xan and gathered him into his arms, kissing the top of his head. Xan trembled against him, stinking of fear. Throat tight, Jason whispered the only thing he knew to say. "It'll be different when you find your *Érosgápe*."

Flinty rage poked through Xan's misery as he hissed, "And if I don't find him? If I don't have one?"

"You'll feel differently about whatever omega you contract with."

"And if I don't? Then what?"

Jason held him tighter. "I don't know. We'll figure it out, though." His chest ached. "You're not unmanned. You're Xan and you're my best friend."

Xan turned slightly, his face wet with tears as he nuzzled against Jason's throat. He pressed an open-mouthed kiss where Jason's collar rubbed and moaned softly.

Jason didn't want to let go, but he wasn't going to do this again. In the long run, it'd just hurt Xan more anyway.

"Don't." Jason pulled back far enough to tip up Xan's tear-wet chin. "I can't do that with you anymore."

"Why?"

"You know why. But it doesn't mean that you're a bad person to want that. It just means…"

He didn't actually know what it meant. Xan was in danger if he continued to pursue that kind of activity. If he asked the wrong alpha to help him satisfy his urges, being ashamed of himself was the least of his concerns. He could be beaten or reported to the authorities as unmanned—as unnatural. Jason didn't know what consequences might come of that, but they couldn't be good.

"I wish I'd been born an omega," Xan murmured, tugging away from Jason and wiping at his eyes.

"But why? Omegas have to give up everything to their alpha once they contract. They don't have any social or financial control. And then there's heat and childbirth." Jason shuddered thinking about all that his pater had suffered over the years. "I wouldn't want to be an omega for anything."

"Because you don't want what I want!" Xan shouted, standing up. He paced the room, blue eyes wide and wild. "You don't understand how much this hurts! All this hiding. All this lying. You were the only one I could be myself with and now you're gone."

"I'm right here, actually," Jason said, as patiently as possible. He didn't know how to keep a grasp of Xan and his slippery fears. "I'm here listening to you."

"But you'd rather be with him."

Jason sat up straighter, putting some firmness into his voice.

"He's my *Érosgápe*. You're my best friend. There's no comparison. But I'm not going to leave when you're this upset." He reached out, but Xan avoided his grasp, so he patted the bed next to him. "Calm down. Sit with me. It's going to be all right."

Xan ignored him, opened a window to let in some fresh, cold air, and pushed his head out. He took deep, gulping breaths. When he'd settled, he turned back to Jason, arms crossed over his chest.

"It's going to be okay," Jason said again.

Xan shook his head. "It's easy to say that when everything in the world is going your way."

Jason sat quietly for a few moments, until Xan left the window to sit down on Jason's old bed. Tension and anxious despair were all that seemed to be holding Xan together. Tears leaked from his eyes in a steady stream.

"Everything isn't going my way," Jason said. "I've got struggles, too."

"I know," Xan murmured, palming away a tear. "You've got omega troubles. Everyone's weirded out by you now."

Jason hiccupped a laugh. "Don't sugarcoat it, asshole."

"Okay, everyone's been talking about your old, used up omega and how you'll have to take a surrogate and—"

"Shut up." His fists tightened. "Why are you being this way?"

"I'm being honest." Xan's blue eyes flashed hard and angry. "That's what they're saying. If you contract with him, that's how it will always be. You've seen how they've treated you lately, acting like you're a leper, acting like you're going to give them all bad luck just by being near you."

The other alphas were distant with him now, it was true, but he figured it was something that would pass sooner or later, just like everything in life did. But maybe Xan was right. Maybe if he contracted with Vale—*when* he contracted, rather—he'd be ousted from the better parts of society forever.

It hurt, but so what? He'd have more time for gardening, micro-scope slides, and scientific journals. More time for his planned research into the wolf genes that had created the alpha, beta, and omega genders. More time to spend with Vale and whatever family they made together.

Screw society. He wasn't a big fan of it anyway, and neither were his parents, though they skated the edges, always going to the right events and parties to keep from being deemed outcasts. He came by his avoidance naturally.

"We're the same, you and me," Xan said. "For different reasons, maybe, but it doesn't matter. What we instinctively want isn't up to the standards of our culture, and because of who we are, we're screwed."

Jason didn't know what Xan wanted him to say. As far as seduc-tions went, convincing him that they were both doomed to a life of isolated misery wasn't a compelling one. As far as anything else, well, what was he supposed to do about it? He couldn't change his attraction to Vale any more than he could change Xan's desire to be fucked like an omega.

He took the opportunity of Xan getting up to close the open window and adjust the flow of air from the heater to check his watch. He needed to leave soon if he was going to get home, get into nicer clothes, and make it to Vale's before the rest of the dinner party arrived. He'd wanted to be first in hopes of capturing a few precious moments alone with Vale. Even if it was on the front porch for propriety, it'd be amazing to have his undivided attention.

"How's it really going, by the way?" Xan asked, calmer now. "How are things with Professor Aman?"

It was a step in the right direction for Xan to refer to Vale by his title at the university rather than the sneered 'your omega' he'd tended toward before, or the veiled way he'd tried to keep from saying his name at all the last time they'd seen each other.

Jason pushed the flop of hair off his sweaty forehead again. The intensity of the last few minutes had left him clammy and in need of a shower. "I'm going to a dinner party alone at his house tonight."

"Your parents allowed it?"

"Yes."

"Alone? Really?" Xan's eyebrows rose toward his hairline.

"Oh, not alone-alone. I mean without my parents. Vale's friends will be there."

The nasty sneer came back. "That alpha he's been screwing?"

Jason tensed. He wished Xan wasn't so determined to make him hurt as much as *he* was hurting. As Jason's closest friend, Xan sure knew which stick to use for the most painful poking. But Jason had taken his alpha quell and wouldn't be provoked. "Yes, he'll be there. And two beta friends."

"I'm surprised your parents agreed anyway."

"Me, too."

It hadn't been easy. Father had been especially wary, but Pater had eventually pointed out, damaging Jason's pride a bit, that Urho seemed more than up to the task of taking Jason down if necessary, and they'd make sure he was dosed with plenty of alpha quell before he left. "He'll be fine," Pater had said. "They both will."

Jason shrugged. "They know I'd never hurt Vale."

"Ha! You didn't see yourself in the library. You probably left bruises. I hope you apologized to him."

"Of course I did."

He had, hadn't he? He couldn't remember. He hoped so.

Jason glanced at his watch again. "Are you okay? I need to get going, but I don't want to leave if you're still upset."

"Oh, I'm going to be upset forever," Xan replied with wide-eyed cynical honesty. He waved toward the door. "Go on. I'll still be an unmanned mess tomorrow, and next week, and next year, and when

I'm trying to get an omega pregnant." He smiled with a grim misery that made Jason's stomach hurt. "No rush to make me feel better about the shit show of my life."

Jason hesitated but, as awful as Xan's predictions sounded, he was probably right. He rose slowly, brushed the wrinkles from his pants, and grabbed his discarded coat and scarf. As he put them on, he wracked his brain for something soothing to say.

"See you next week," Xan said, standing. His eyes were puffy and his cheeks were still red. "I'll try to make it to Alpha-Omega Relations next week. Old Shriner will flunk me if I miss every class with films on the syllabus."

"Yeah, he will."

Xan reached out a hand and then let it fall. "Hey, I'm sorry."

Jason paused with his hand on the doorknob. "For what?"

"For being an asshole to you. You're a good friend. And I…" Xan looked away, the words clearly stuck in his throat. "I can't help the way I feel, but you *could* still shun me for it. No one would blame you. Not even me. But you don't. You don't even try to make me feel bad about it."

Jason let go of the knob and pulled Xan into a hug again. "I love you. I wish it was the kind of love you needed."

"Why? Then we'd both be in this mess."

"But we'd be in it together. I'm sorry I can't go through this with you as more than a friend."

Xan crumbled, gentle sobs shaking his shoulders. Jason held him tight until he'd calmed down again.

"I take it back. You're a terrible friend. You were supposed to go and leave me with some dignity." Xan shoved at Jason's chest. "Don't say another word. Just go."

Jason kissed the side of Xan's head and left without looking back. If his friend needed him to pretend he didn't know he was in love with him, then he could do that. He could pretend it all day long. And as far as protecting Xan's secret went, he could do that, too.

Jason would do whatever he could for Xan. He loved him that much.

JASON RANG THE doorbell at Vale's house three minutes past the time he'd been asked to arrive. He straightened his tie and used the reflection in the tall window by the door to make sure his hair looked all right. The extra alpha quell he'd been dosed with before his parents would let him out the front door left him feeling distantly calm, like there was a space between his excitement and his experience of the excitement. He could almost step into that space, dance a waltz in it, hum a tune, and then return to himself before the emotion touched him. It was weird.

Still, he *was* excited. He hoped that he'd arrived before the others, but he doubted it. Not only had he spent too much time with Xan, but he'd gotten waylaid by Wilbet Monhundy and his pals again on his way to meet the car that waited to drive him home.

They'd teased him, of course, mocking his omega as sad and 'used up'. But with Vale waiting for him, he hadn't let them get under his skin. Vale was much more important than idiot alpha schoolyard posturing. He wasn't going to be late because he got into fisticuffs with some dummies who didn't understand what it meant to imprint yet.

The door swung open, and much to Jason's disappointment, Vale's friend Yosef stood in the doorway. His smile was wide and welcoming.

"Jason! Happy Autumn Nights!" He stuck out his hand and Jason took it, his fingers enveloped in a warm, dry palm. "Vale wanted to greet you, but Zephyr tripped him on his way down the stairs earlier."

"Is he all right?" Jason's heart leapt into the space between his feelings and the alpha quell.

Yosef released his hand to wave away his worry. "Oh, he's more all right than not. Rosen's coerced him to elevate his twisted ankle while Urho's forced him to ice it. It's all been very loud and dramatic." He tugged on his beard and smiled. "The usual for our group. Come on in."

As Jason stepped into the foyer, dust motes swirled around him. Piles of books were lined against the baseboard to the right, and dusty ceramic figurines of alpha-omega pairs paraded around on a table to the left. Voices rang from deeper in the house, one of them Vale's, full of laughter and annoyance, the other two clearly Urho and Rosen disagreeing with him.

A silver streak darted across the hallway while Yosef relieved Jason of his coat and scarf.

"That's Zephyr," he said calmly, hanging Jason's things on a rack near the door already laden with many coats and scarves. "Demon cat. Only likes Vale and Rosen. Bites Urho whenever she gets a chance. Tolerates me." His eyes twinkled at Jason. "I'll be curious what she makes of *you*. This way. They're in the kitchen."

The ruckus from the back of the house seemed to have calmed. Jason tried to take in as much of Vale's home as he could—everything from the rose-patterned wallpaper in the hallway, to the furnishings in the rooms he glimpsed looked dated and out of fashion. In a darkened room they passed, there was a piano and a guitar. He wondered if there might be an opportunity to play for Vale tonight. Pride puffed in him at the thought, pleased with himself that he'd been practicing more often.

Everywhere and everything was dusty. The rooms were stacked with newspapers, magazines, and books. As they passed an open door there was even a giant pile of what looked like socks and underwear next to another pile of clothes—dirty or clean, Jason couldn't tell. But Yosef rapidly shut it as they passed, saying, "Vale won't want you seeing his laundry room just yet."

Then they passed an open room near the back that Jason recognized as Vale's study, the one he'd seen from the window. They turned down a short, warm hallway, covered in dusty photographs of various tourist destinations and two men Jason didn't recognize, but both of whom looked enough like Vale for him to assume they were his pater and father.

"I'm fine, Urho. Back off before he comes in. He doesn't need to see you looming over me like this."

Jason bristled beneath the alpha quell, but in the space where there was room to dance, he kept it from showing as he stepped into the kitchen.

Rosen was at the stove, adding seasoning to a pot. Vale sat in a chair with one long leg hooked up on top of the rectangular dining table taking up much of the kitchen. His ankle above his bare foot was smothered in a small bag of ice. On the floor by his other bare foot, his black socks and shoes were abandoned.

Urho hovered behind him but moved away when Jason flicked a hard look at him.

Vale was beautiful, of course, but different, too. He obviously hadn't shaved in a few days, possibly not since Jason had last seen him at his parent's house. The beard was coming in scruffy, and Jason's fingers itched to touch it.

Jason slid his gaze over Vale entirely, noting his nicely tailored aubergine pants and the much lighter purple shirt he wore with the shirtsleeves rolled up, exposing a tantalizing glimpse of a tattoo on his right arm. Small dark hairs gathered beneath his collarbones, visible where his collar was left open.

A quick glance around the kitchen showed that everyone else

was dressed similarly—tailored pants and relaxed shirts. Jason fidgeted with his suit jacket and wished he'd known the dress code was going to be so informal.

"Are you all right?" Jason asked Vale, eschewing greetings to make sure his omega was safe. He started forward and brushed Urho's shoulder as they passed in the narrow space between the counter and the head of the table.

Vale's pale skin on top of his foot and his pink sole looked soft, except for the callus on the big toe and pinky where his shoes must have pinched over the last thirty-five years.

"I'm fine," Vale said, rolling his eyes. "Zephyr tripped me and my friends overreacted."

Jason leaned close enough to smell Vale's skin and shampoo, and his heart rang with pride when he scented the musk of Vale's slick, too. Just a small amount, subtle. But released for him all the same. It hadn't been there until he'd drawn close.

He wished he could run his hand through Vale's hair. It seemed absurd that he didn't feel free to touch yet when they were meeting with attorneys in a day and a half to negotiate a contract to fuck, mate, and be bonded together until death.

He cleared his throat. "May I?" he asked, indicating the ice on Vale's ankle.

Vale smiled. "Certainly, have a look for yourself. Oh alpha, my alpha." It was a tease, but it brought heat into Jason's neck and a smile to his lips.

Jason lifted the ice off Vale's ankle, noting the redness of the skin beneath. He touched the slightly swollen place beneath the bumpy anklebone, and he ran his finger along the skin there, testing it softly. "You twisted it a bit."

"Yes," Vale said, but his voice had gone breathy and the smell of slick intensified.

Full of pride to have garnered such a reaction from so simple a touch, Jason added a few more fingers to his cautious probing. He slipped them over Vale's skin, allowing the black hairs of his leg to scratch against his fingertips. "Yes, it's twisted," he said again.

"But not badly," Vale reiterated. "It'll be fine, though probably still tender, by tomorrow morning."

Jason lowered the ice pack down on Vale's ankle and then touched his cold fingers to Vale's cheek. Their eyes held and Vale's mouth opened, a soft sound escaping. It zipped up Jason's back, and his lips turned up in a small, smug way.

Jason pulled his hand back and turned to the rest of the men in the room. "I'm sorry I was late."

"Not a problem," Yosef said, coming around the table with his arms out. "Why don't you give me your suit coat, too? I'll put it with your other. You'll be more comfortable. Our little group doesn't engage in much formality."

Urho handed Jason a cup of hot tea enlivened with traditional Autumn Nights spices. He sipped it softly, letting it soothe his throat and keep his mouth busy so he didn't have to talk. He stood near Vale but not too close, taking in the lay of the land.

The room was sparsely decorated for Autumn Nights. A centerpiece had been made from a fat candle of sweet beeswax, several gourds and a small pumpkin, along with a handful of mint clippings from the garden. Nothing like the ornaments Jason's pater decorated with, and nothing like the massive centerpiece the Sabels ordered from Sanz's Floral if they were entertaining. It was rustic in comparison, but everyone's tastes were different. He liked Vale's simplicity.

Jason hoped he might get another peek at the garden again before he left, so he'd have a better idea of what to plan for it. But with sunset coming earlier and earlier as the year aged, he doubted he'd get that chance. Not unless they finished dinner in a hurry.

"How was your day?" Vale asked.

It was better than being asked outright about school in front of Vale's friends, but it was too close for comfort, too. "It was all right. You're growing a beard?"

Vale's fingers rubbed over his chin, releasing a scent into the air that went right to Jason's dick, making it tingle and threaten to engorge. "Shaving was part of my routine for going into work. Now that I'm on this extended sabbatical"—the sarcasm was light but still evident—"I seem to have let it go. I noticed it for the first time tonight when I was dressing and decided it didn't look half bad."

"I like it," Jason said, licking his lips. "It suits you."

Urho chuckled. "It reminds *me* of the camping trip we took last year. You came home exhausted, bedraggled, and bearded."

Vale sent Urho a small glare and then said, "Perhaps lay off the wine, Urho."

"Why? I've only had a glass and a half."

"Because I said so."

Yosef clucked, and Urho raised an eyebrow but put his wine glass down. Vale turned to Yosef and Rosen, asking, "What grooming products do you recommend? You've both had beards for years now and they always look so well-kept."

Yosef launched into a discussion of trimmers and beard oils that Jason didn't imagine he'd need to know much about anytime soon, since he could still get away with shaving every third day if he wanted. Leaving his tea on the table, he decided to put himself to use rather than stand around gaping at Vale's beauty. He crossed to Rosen as the other three began a quarrel over whether chypre or aromatic scented oils were better in a beard. That was yet another subject he wasn't versed enough in to offer an opinion.

"May I help with something?" he offered. "I'm happy to chop or wash. Whatever you need."

Rosen lifted a brow, considering, and then shoved four onions his way. "All right. Have at it. Let's see how pretty you are when you cry."

Jason took the knife Rosen offered and began to dice the onions.

"Were your parents reluctant to let you come tonight?" Rosen asked, smiling.

Jason shrugged. "They had their concerns, but Vale had reassured them. And they trust me." Mostly. Sometimes. Not enough to live on campus, but enough to let him come tonight. "They know I want what's best for Vale, and they know that I won't be able to make good choices during negotiations if we aren't allowed time together to be our real selves."

"Wise of them."

"My parents are good people."

"Their reputation precedes them," Rosen said with a smile. "But really, what is 'good'? Not that I doubt your parents are, but don't you ever wonder what makes a person or a thing 'good'?"

"Philosophy professor, right?" Jason said, smiling. "Sorry, but I'm out of school for the long holiday weekend."

Rosen laughed. "We can continue this conversation on Monday then."

Jason chopped the onions and soon his eyes watered freely. He let them flow and didn't stop until he had reduced all four white globes to a pile of tiny beautiful squares.

"Lovely," Rosen said when he was done. "And prettier than Vale when he tries to chop onions. He goes all red and snotty, usually ends up wiping onion juice in his eye, which becomes a calamity of epic proportions. Then I burn something helping him wash it out, and Yosef snacks on whatever vegetables I've brought along and watches the show."

"That sounds ridiculous," Jason said.

Rosen laughed. "And loud. Your omega has quite the voice on him when he's unhappy." Then he steered Jason toward the sink to wash his hands again before moving ahead with preparing the meal. "Now go sit with Vale and be your real self so you can make good decisions during negotiations."

Jason washed his hands twice, though the scent of onion lingered. He thought about Rosen's assessment of Vale's voice when he was unhappy, and he wondered with a combination of joy and dread just when he might have the opportunity to hear it. Anger seemed such an intimate thing in a way. Something new to learn about Vale.

He retrieved his now-cold tea and sipped slowly, joining the other three at the table. Sitting across from Vale so he could see him better and keep a bit of distance between them so he could concentrate, he listened avidly. He was intent to learn about Vale— his likes and interests, the things he found funny—but the longer he sat in silence, the more uncomfortable he became.

Urho knew exactly what to say to draw Vale out of silence and rouse him with irritation. His cheeks would pale and his eyes grew a brighter green at every annoying word out of Urho's mouth. It was a reaction so beautiful Jason burned that he hadn't been the one to provoke it. And Yosef was so easy with everyone; it was like he was born knowing what to say. And Rosen would chip in when he felt like it, relaxed and at home in Vale's kitchen. And Jason...didn't know how to be a part of their group.

His tea slipped down his throat in cool, spicy draughts as the distance between himself and the rest of them grew. Bigger than the space held by the alpha quell. And as childish as he knew it was, he resented Vale's friends for their inside jokes and easy rapport. He hated them for their education, travel, and life experience. He hated that he was a child in their presence. He even hated that he drank spiced tea while they drank wine. Wolf-god, he hated them all.

Except Vale. He didn't hate him. Couldn't even if he wanted to.

Stupid *Érosgápe* urges.

"Jason, do you tango?" Vale asked suddenly, turning to him with a smile that flashed bright in his dark beard. "I've been meaning to learn and, if you do, maybe someday soon you can teach me."

Jason did not in fact tango, but he was absolutely going to learn to do so as soon as possible now. "I'd love to dance with you. We can take lessons together if you want," he said. "That would be fun."

"So you like to dance?" Vale took a sip from his wine glass, his moss-colored eyes glowing. "I *love* to dance and haven't had anyone to dance with in a very long time."

"It's not my fault you have two left feet," Urho said. "Don't dance with him, Jason. You'll live to regret it."

Jason smiled tightly. "Vale is too graceful to be anything other than a dream on the dance floor."

They all laughed like Jason had purposely made a joke, so he laughed, too. But he'd been sincere. How could a man who moved like liquid, and who made Jason's insides quiver just by walking, actually be a bad dancer? Vale had surely only ever had bad partners if that was the case.

And if by some chance Vale's friends were right, then Jason would wear the bruises on his feet with pride.

# CHAPTER THIRTEEN

"HOW DID YOU meet each other?" Jason asked what felt like hours later, after Rosen announced that dinner would be served in five minutes.

"Who? All of us?" Rosen asked over his shoulder.

"Yes, all of you."

"Well, Yosef and I met first," Vale said, smiling softly and taking the ice off his foot. He lowered his leg to the floor and tossed the ice bag onto the counter without rising to his feet and nearly hit Rosen with it.

A furry silver slinking animal caught Jason's eye, and he turned his head to see Zephyr skulk into the room with a dark gleam in her green eyes. She kept to the wall for a bit, and then hustled toward Rosen with a plaintive meow.

"Whore," Vale muttered and rolled his eyes. Rosen gave the cat a hunk of meat he'd carved out of the duck he'd prepared earlier. "Yes, Yosef and I met on campus," Vale went on. "He was helping out a graduate studies law professor, another omega, actually, who'd gone into an unexpected heat and needed to take a sudden leave. The only person willing to step in was Yosef. We met over the last apple dumpling in the commissary. He wanted it and I wanted it, too. So we shared."

"That's nearly a meet-cute for one of those sweet romance novels Rosen's always reading," Urho muttered.

"Romance is the language of happiness," Rosen said, opening the oven to check the giant bird inside. Zephyr had climbed up his body and now perched on his shoulder, her nails digging in, peering into the oven with him. He didn't utter a word of discomfort. "You should try it sometime."

Urho snorted.

"Urho's right, though," Vale said. "Why didn't you fall madly in love with me on the spot, Yosef? I'm offended now."

"I was with Rosen already," Yosef said. "Or no doubt I'd have swept you off your omega feet and been utterly useless when your heat came on. A match made in heaven."

Vale laughed and winked at Jason. "So then Yosef invited me out to dinner at the ever so trashy but delicious Cinco Manzanas."

"Half-naked dancing boys and enchiladas are always an enjoyable combination," Yosef said, a white smile gleaming between his lips.

"Rosen met us there, and he was his charming self. We've been friends ever since."

"Urho came later," Rosen chimed in, using massive gloves to pull the roasted duck from the oven. "He met Vale on campus, too, I think."

"Campus seems to be the nexus of all my most important relationships." Vale shot Jason a teasing look.

An awkward silence descended for a terrible second, but then Rosen bustled over with serving dishes full of delicious smelling food.

"This looks amazing, Rosen," Jason said. "Are you a chef?"

"Rosen is a philosopher, an artist, *and* a chef," Vale said, smiling at Jason while Urho cut the roast duck and Yosef passed the bowl of fragrant stuffing.

"Yes, Rosen is quite talented," Yosef said warmly. "I hope you're not opposed to ordering out for food, Jason. Your omega here is a terrible cook."

"Oh, don't start," Vale said.

"He's worse at cooking than he is at keeping house." Urho dug into the bird with the carving knife.

Father made prettier cuts and so did Jason, but he wasn't going to say anything negative about Urho. Everyone probably already thought Jason was resentful of him for having been Vale's alpha during heats. And he was. But he wasn't going to let that rule the rest of his life with Vale. Clearly Urho wasn't going anywhere, so he might as well make peace with it.

"I like to cook." Jason took the stuffing bowl from Rosen and added a pile to his plate. The scent of rosemary and sage wafted up, making his mouth water. "Though I can't claim to be as skilled as Rosen, I'll be capable of keeping us fed, I think."

Vale's brows lifted in interest. "Oh?"

"As I told Vale the other day, Father doesn't keep house servants all the time. Too many people in his space, Pater says. They like their privacy. Father only hires them in for parties and special dinners. Otherwise, we take care of ourselves."

"So your pater is a good cook then?" Yosef asked.

"No, Father is the one who makes most of our meals. Pater is sick a lot and…" He wondered for the first time if Pater's weakness would reflect badly on him. "Pater doesn't cook."

"So your Father learned to in his place?" Urho asked.

Jason frowned. He hated the implication that it was always the omega's job to provide for the alpha in the home. Certainly alphas were usually the main breadwinners, and most well-to-do omegas ran the household, but those of lesser means often worked outside the home in whatever way they safely could. Besides, even the wealthy omegas did more than simply run a house. They were people. They had interests of their own.

Take Vale, for example. Left to his own devices, he was clearly not the stereotypical omega alphas were taught to expect, and Jason had it on good authority from Pater and Father that omegas came in all stripes of human, just as alphas did. Pater had always argued that it was appalling to strip omegas of everything but house duties. Father had never demanded it of Pater, and Jason wouldn't demand it of his omega, either. If Vale wanted to return to teaching after they'd contracted, consummated, and bonded, then he'd make sure that was an option for him. He'd make sure Vale got whatever he wanted.

"Not exactly. Father loves cooking and Pater loves to eat what he makes. It made sense for them to stick to the part they most enjoy."

Vale grinned at him and Jason's heart grabbed hard like a fist. He wanted to see that pleased smile again as soon as possible.

"Did your father teach you, then?" Rosen passed a basket of bread while Urho finished piling a massive serving plate high with half-destroyed slices of duck.

"He did. Whenever Pater is ill..." Jason trailed off again, but Vale caught his eye and smiled warmly, encouraging him to go on. "When Pater is ill, which is more and more often, unfortunately, Father calls me in to assist him, and I've picked up a lot. When Father is away for business, I cook for Pater and myself." He shrugged. "I make a lot of casseroles because they're easy for leftovers."

"My pater used to make a divine hot crab casserole," Vale said. "It was my favorite." His plate was filled with Rosen's cranberry sauce, the stuffing, a huge helping of duck that Urho had placed there directly, green beans, and several rolls.

Jason accepted the serving plate of duck, put several thick pieces on his plate, and sent it on to Yosef.

"If you lend me the recipe, I'll make it for you, Vale," he said, stomach tightening. He hoped Vale would accept his offer—as a courting gesture, and as a promise of what he could expect if a contract between them was made.

"Would you?" Vale's smile crushed every beautiful thing in the world into a glorious, aching ball in Jason's chest. He was going to break from joy if he wasn't careful.

"Of course."

"I'd have made it for you if I'd known," Rosen said, a disgruntled note in his voice, and his dark brows lowered.

Vale waved his suggestion away, not taking his eyes from Jason, making that beautiful ball in Jason's chest glow and grow. "You're a wonderful cook, Rosen. Too good for casseroles."

"Are you calling your alpha's skills and tastes plebian?" Urho asked with a laugh in his tone.

"It looks that way," Vale said, grinning and twinkling at Jason.

Jason smiled back, and as his cheeks and neck grew hot, the ball in his chest exploded in shimmery, screaming joy. He tore his eyes from Vale's before he did something stupid like shove back his chair, stride over, and kiss his smiling mouth.

Distracting himself, he took a bite of duck and stuffing. The flavors melded perfectly. "This is delicious," he said to Rosen. "Would you teach me how?"

"Of course. I'd be happy to," Rosen said warmly.

Yosef sipped his wine and said, "Why don't you come over to our place one night next week and Rosen can show you a few things? Vale could come over, too. And Urho," he said, extending the invitation to Urho last, as though he didn't want to offend him by leaving him out.

Urho shook his head. "Why would Jason want to spend time with us when he could be with alphas his own age? Obviously, Vale's another matter. But it's like we discussed the other night: we aren't of interest to him. It isn't as though we will be his friends."

Yosef frowned at Urho, and Vale leaned forward with anger bright in his eyes, but Jason interjected, "It's okay. I'm sure I can learn by following the recipes if Rosen wouldn't mind sharing them."

There was a conversation with eyes between Rosen and Yosef, which Jason refused to acknowledge, returning to his plate. The food didn't taste quite as good now that he realized none of these men truly anticipated becoming friends with him. But what did he expect? Vale's friends didn't want to hang out with a teenager. They didn't owe him anything.

"I think we should let Jason determine who he's interested in spending time with," Vale said icily. "If he wants to know Rosen and Yosef better, I don't see them refusing his company. They're the ones who extended the invitation after all. A very kind invitation at that."

"You can come train with my cook, if you want." Urho wiped his mouth and ignored Vale's scolding. "That would be a better use of your time."

Jason bristled. How had Vale been intimate with an alpha who'd discount his opinion so easily?

Oblivious to Jason's irritation, Urho lifted his wine and took a large gulp before adding, "He's worked in my family for years. He was the chef when my pater and father were alive."

Jason said nothing. Had his invitation to Rosen and Yosef's house been rescinded? He wasn't sure and didn't feel capable of accepting it with so much uncertainty in the air. He desperately wanted more time with Vale and, despite what Urho had said, he did want to make friends with them. Well, with the betas anyway. Urho himself was another issue.

"Ah, yes, your chef is quite good," Rosen said, nodding with a thoughtful expression. "What's his name again?"

"Mako," Urho answered with a self-satisfied smile. He took another sip of wine.

He'd taken up drinking again shortly after Vale had scolded him earlier, and Jason had counted that this was his sixth glass. Despite a loosened tongue, he didn't seem especially inebriated. In fact, he seemed as sanguine and calm as ever.

"He makes a delicious linguine with clam sauce. I believe he's going to make it next Friday, Jason, if you want to come over after your classes. He'll be happy to teach you. Vale enjoys it."

Vale sighed, irritation bristling him from head to toe, and he narrowed his eyes at Urho as he took another sip of his wine and then slowly chewed a bite of duck.

Urho didn't seem to notice, though. "Oh, and my housekeeper, Warren, will be happy to show you how to vacuum, dust, and do laundry." Urho chuckled, his handsome face breaking open with a wide smile at his own joke. "Because I promise Vale has no idea how to do any of it."

"Pampered Urho with all of his servants," Yosef teased.

"I manage just fine," Vale snapped.

"Oh, yes, we all see that." Rosen gestured toward the door leading from the kitchen out to the rest of the house.

"I cleaned!" Vale's voice was tight and one dark eyebrow rose archly.

"Indeed, we can tell."

"Leave him alone," Jason said, a tone of authority swelling in his voice. "He doesn't think it's funny."

Vale flushed above his beard. "Normally, I don't mind, but..." His eyes didn't leave Jason's face. "My ankle hurts. My patience is low."

"And Urho has insulted your alpha and your friends, and we've razzed you about your housekeeping," Rosen added. "Let's all agree to behave better before Jason gets the wrong impression of us."

Too late, Jason thought. Or at least it was too late for Urho. Rosen and Yosef were nice and seemed open enough, but Urho, for whatever reason, was not. That hurt Vale and pissed off Jason. But he'd have to deal with it all another night. The first time a new person entered any group, it always threw things off. Urho probably resented Jason as much as Jason resented him.

"Speaking of housekeeping, didn't you have to let someone go recently, Urho?" Rosen asked. "Who was that? The gardener?"

"Oh?" Vale's eyes flickered, like he was trying to decide if he wanted to forgive Urho yet or not. "I thought you liked him?"

Urho rolled his eyes. "I didn't fire him. He took leave. It's a shame because Zim was amazing with Riki's roses. Kept them as healthy as the day Riki passed away."

"How did you run him off?" Vale asked carefully. There was a hesitation to his tone that Jason tried to understand. Maybe it had something to do with the man who'd passed away, this Riki. "Did you tease him until he hated you?"

"Believe it or not, it wasn't me." Urho sighed. "His younger brother is an omega and a nymphomaniac. Unable to be satisfied for more than a few hours at a time and during heat he's utterly insatiable. His alpha sued to break their contract. They weren't bonded, of course, just contracted. A terrible mistake. Contracts often are."

"Urho," Yosef said warningly, but it didn't seem Urho had heard him.

"Zim's brother kept slipping the ropes, so to speak, and heading out to the Bowery looking for alphas. Such a shame. Ruined the family name."

The table went still, everyone staring at Urho. Vale wiped his mouth on his napkin and took a deep breath.

"Wolf-god," Rosen whispered.

Urho nodded. "Terrible. But yes, my best gardener, my old pal Zim, took leave to help the family during his brother's upcoming heats. They can't find a surrogate, of course. Not now. And it's going to be painful. They'll need all hands on deck to keep the boy locked away." He clucked his tongue. "That's what happens when omegas get sullied, though. No alpha wants to help them." He shook his head like he was sorry about it, like there was nothing he could do.

"That's ridiculous," Jason burst out, his fists clenching next to his plate. "It was his alpha's job to satisfy him, and if he couldn't handle it he should have hired a surrogate. How can you blame an omega for seeking what he needs during heat? Or any other time?"

Rosen and Yosef's brows went up, darting glances between Jason and Urho, but Vale's eyes didn't leave Urho; they were needle sharp.

Jason went on. "He did what his instincts drove him to do. No more. No less. It's the alpha's job to make sure the omega is satisfied no matter what. Interminable heat or no interminable heat." He pounded the table with his fist as he repeated that fundamental truth his parents had drilled into him from childhood. "Did the alpha he contracted with bring in help? Or was his pride too wounded to make the right choice for his omega?"

Vale shifted his gaze slowly to Jason.

Urho frowned. "I'm not sure. Perhaps he couldn't afford a surrogate. Decent alpha surrogates can be expensive. But the contract has been dissolved, or shortly will be, and there's nothing anyone can do about that."

"What about his upcoming heat? The one Zim took off for?" Jason asked. "There's no one to help him with it? No one at all?"

"Apparently not."

"That's a lie. There *are* alphas everywhere, and plenty are widowed or otherwise not contracted." He stared at Urho. "There's one at this table."

Urho stared at him. "Are you suggesting…?"

"Yes, I'm *suggesting*."

From the corner of his eye, Jason saw Vale lean forward, bearded chin on one elegant hand, and a smug smile gracing his lips.

Urho sputtered. "Our society has expectations. There are protocols that provide clear instructions for situations like—"

"Oh, sure, the protocol for when an alpha is too cheap or selfish to help an omega in heat is to just let the omega suffer. I'd say that the uncontracted alphas of the seedier parts of town are better men than those who follow such a cruel protocol. They heed an omega's need, at least."

"For their own benefit!" Urho exclaimed. "You can't claim that those filthy alphas who brawl to breed desperate omegas are actually heroes. They're in it for their own pleasure. They're in it to screw and come and knot."

"And what's the omega in it for?" Jason challenged. "What are their choices? Sweat it out and suffer? Or pay dearly for a surrogate?" He cocked his head, venom sliding into his veins. The space where the alpha quell kept him separated from his emotions provided room for a little victory dance as he pressed the point home. "Did Zim's salary from you allow him to hire a surrogate for his brother? As you said, the good ones are pricey. What about the financial circumstances of the rest of his family? It sounds to me like they love this brother very much. I'm sure they'd take any decent surrogate who offered."

"Now you're saying I should fund a surrogate for this boy? That his ruined reputation and pain are my fault? Absurd. Vale, are you listening to this?"

Vale just smiled wider, though, and his eyes burned brightly.

"If you're going to have servants then you should know what's happening in their lives, and if you can help them in any reasonable way, you should." Jason nodded firmly.

"Spoken like a boy without servants," Urho muttered.

"I think you mean, spoken like a boy with a conscience," Yosef corrected.

"And plenty of money to back it up," Rosen added.

Zephyr leapt suddenly into Jason's lap, purring and circling, her claws prickling his nice pants. Then she curled up and began cleaning between her toes on his lap. Jason stared down at her in shock.

"Oh." He patted her back and she stopped licking, shot him an annoyed look until he removed his hand, and then went back to licking again.

"You're all wrong. It was spoken like a boy with an admirer,"

Vale said. "Or two." A mischievous smile danced on his lips. "*I* was impressed anyway."

Urho snorted. "You would be with all your liberal ideals."

"Some of us want to build a better world, my friend," Vale said, but the endearment held a bite to it. "Alas, you're too old-fashioned and uptight to understand."

"Old-fashioned," Urho repeated, stabbing his fork into his bird. Jason wasn't sure why that was the bigger insult of the two. Personally, he'd rather be old-fashioned than uptight.

Zephyr purred and settled more deeply into Jason's lap, giving up her cleaning. Jason ran a hand over her back, and this time she allowed it. His heart plucked a happy chord.

Urho's gaze fell to Zephyr with a frown. After a long moment, he nodded. "Fine. I'll show you old-fashioned." He sat up straighter. "I'll deal with the boy's heat then."

Jason blinked in shock and Vale's smile nearly blinded him. Rosen winked at Jason and nodded. Yosef applauded as though he was at a dinner theater show.

"Bravo. Delightful joust. I've rarely seen Urho concede so quickly."

Vale's cheeks flushed as he smiled at Jason. "Me, either."

"Sometimes even old-fashioned assholes can see when they've been bested." Urho shrugged. "And as much as I hate to admit it, maybe the boy is right. It would be easy enough for me to deal with Zim's brother's heat, pleasurable even. Assuming they take me up on the offer and the boy isn't utterly repulsive in some way. And then I'll have my gardener back working with Riki's roses where I need him."

Jason stroked Zephyr's head and down her back. She purred, a warm, furry weight in his lap. He'd barely touched his dinner during his argument with Urho, and so he started in again, surprised it was still warm.

Zephyr tried to swipe the duck off his fork, and he laughed.

"Hungry?"

"She's had plenty of food," Vale disagreed, waving at the cat. "Shoo, off! Unhand him, Zephyr. He's mine."

Jason's heart clenched and released, blood rushing through him in a dizzy whoosh. But Zephyr ignored him. He fed her a piece of duck, and she ate it like she was starving before settling back down into his lap. Her paws, kneading and grabbing at his thigh, were ruining the wool of his pants, but he didn't care at all.

"Zephyr likes Jason," Yosef said with a laugh of surprise. "And with her deciding vote being cast, I think we should move away from this topic and onto something less exciting. Like the weather. Or winter holiday plans." Vale caught Jason's eye and held his gaze as Yosef went on, "Rosen and I are considering the seaside. Has anyone been at winter holiday before? Any advice for what to pack?"

"JASON, STAY BEHIND a moment, if you please."

Urho paused in slipping on his coat and gave Vale a sharp look. "Is that wise?"

Rosen and Yosef had left fifteen minutes earlier in a taxi, burdened with the serving dishes, cutlery, and cookware Rosen had used. Either Vale didn't own any of his own or what he had didn't meet Rosen's requirements. Regardless, once they'd loaded in the bags of kitchen items, there hadn't been room in the taxi for Urho, too.

Jason leaned back against the wall, rolling his shoulder blades flat so that he didn't slouch, but still trying to give a loose, casual impression. Calculated, sure, but he wanted Vale to feel safe and if he stiffened up, he'd be sent out into the cold with Urho for sure. The alpha quell was waning, and he felt the tug of the imprint stronger than he had in days.

Vale glanced his way and smiled with that secret warmth Jason had seen in his eyes ever since he'd bested Urho at dinner. "Your taxi is waiting, Urho."

One of Urho's dark brows lifted and his strong jaw clenched. "I've been charged with delivering him to his parents safely."

"His parents never asked you to provide that chivalry."

"No, you did."

"And I've changed my mind. Just call me an indecisive omega."

Urho's eyes widened. Jason almost felt sorry for him. But then he remembered that Urho'd had his cock up Vale's delicious ass, and he hated him all over again. But he refused to let that show. Vale needed him to be an adult, someone who got along with his friends, and that's the person he was determined to become. Jealousy was instinctual in an alpha, sure, but his intellect was too strong to allow his most base nature to rule him.

"Don't forget your hat," Vale said, plopping the black, pompous-looking beret on Urho's head with a smirk. Urho hadn't been forgiven for his remarks over dinner yet. Vale was going to make him work for it, and Jason was okay with that.

"I think you should reconsider, Vale. This isn't a joke and it—"

"It isn't your concern unless I make it your concern." He tilted his head, pale neck gleaming in the low light of the hallway lamps. Jason wanted to lick it. "I'll see you soon, Urho. Thank you for coming to dinner."

"Thank you for having me," Urho murmured, voice tight, and his expression tangled.

Jason worked to keep his own face neutral. He fought the urge to sneer, all smarmy and mocking. Yes, no matter what Urho wanted, it wasn't his call. Jason would stay here and speak alone with Vale. It was his right as Vale's alpha. His right to be with him and to touch him—

No.

He wasn't going to let himself go down that mental path. He

was strong and intelligent and his instinct wasn't half as important as Vale's smile. Which now turned to him as the door shut on Urho's reluctantly retreating back.

"It's snowing," Vale said softly.

"Yeah?"

"Big fat flakes." Vale's lashes touched his cheekbones and then lifted slowly, the tiniest hint of seduction in his gaze.

Jason clamped down on his urge to straighten up from the wall, grab Vale, and kiss his gorgeous, lush mouth.

"Is it sticking?" Jason asked huskily.

Vale tugged aside the long, skinny curtain blocking the view out the narrow window beside the door. "It's gathering on the grass now. The streets are probably too warm for it to stick on the pavement. Maybe if it keeps snowing on into the night." He turned back to Jason, lips parted slightly. "Do you like to go sledding?"

"Sure. If there's enough snow, my friend Xan and I usually head out to the hill behind the post office. It has the best slope."

"I know the place," Vale said, inching closer hesitantly, almost like he was second-guessing his movements. "If it sticks and if there's enough accumulation, would you take me sledding?"

"You'd want to go?"

Vale's eyes twinkled. "I admit I'm old for it, but—"

"Is your ankle all right? It was swollen earlier, and I wouldn't want it to get hurt worse sledding."

"It's fine." He put his weight on his foot. "See? All better."

"If you're sure?"

"I am."

"Then of course you can come with me," Jason said, sounding too eager even to his own ears. His hot cheeks flushed even hotter.

But it wasn't a mistake this time, because Vale smiled widely, the small wrinkles next to his eyes going deeper, and Jason's heart fluttered in his chest. God, he'd never survive the happiness, the *utter bliss* of pleasing Vale.

"Wonderful. I'd like that very much. We'll see in the morning how the weather has shaped up."

"I hope it snows heaps."

Vale grinned, ducking his head like he wanted to hide. "Me, too. I haven't been sledding in a long time."

"I'll help you. It's like riding a bike, you don't forget how. And it'd be my pleasure to take you out. Really."

Vale's breath came in shallowly as he crossed the last few feet to Jason, standing within easy touching range. "You were... Tonight at the table..." he gazed into Jason's eyes. In the low light of the lamps, his irises were the green of mossy ponds. "You made me proud."

Wolf-god, Vale meant to obliterate him from the world with this immeasurable, uncontainable joy. Jason's heart tumbled so hard and fast he felt dizzy, and he clutched at the wall behind him to keep from reaching out. He knew Vale wanted to decide when he'd be touched or taken.

*Not taken. Don't think about taking, Jason!*

"I want to make you proud always," Jason whispered, his lips trembling and his knees weak.

"You're so earnest." Vale reached toward him, his fingers halting just beside Jason's cheek, and it took all the self-control Jason could muster not to lean the half-inch into the touch.

"You're so beautiful," Jason breathed.

"So are you."

Jason *wanted*. Desperately wanted. But he forced the words from his mouth anyway. "I should go."

The wrench in his chest hurt as much as the joy had, but he couldn't risk it. He'd done so well. This time with Vale was a test, he knew it was, and he refused to fail. He'd make Vale see he was capable of controlling himself, of being in charge, of taking care of them both.

Then Vale would invite him back. Maybe without the buffer of other friends.

"Yes," Vale said, stepping even closer. "You probably should." His body heat touched Jason like a caress, and Jason's cock throbbed. He knew if he looked down he'd see the tent his arousal had made in his trousers. It probably came within millimeters of touching Vale's hip; the distance between them was so small.

"I'll call in the morning if the snow sticks," Jason said, closing his eyes and slipping sideways, trying to escape temptation.

Vale's hand on his was a shock of pleasure he couldn't have anticipated. He gasped aloud, a sweet 'oh' of bliss, and almost came in his pants. He stopped, motionless, gathering himself from the roar of instinct that rose up inside him.

*Claim him. Now.*

"I should go," he croaked.

"Yes," Vale said again, but didn't let go of his fingers.

That was when Jason smelled it—the sweet, musky aroma of Vale's slick. Lots of it. He groaned, his restraint near collapse. He pressed Vale's fingers to his lips, kissing them greedily, tantalized by their cool, firm lengths. Then he forced himself to pull away, pushing Vale back firmly by the shoulders when he seemed to instinctively follow him.

"Goodnight. Thanks for inviting me," he said, voice thick with lust. He threw open the front door. "I'll call in the morning if the snow sticks!"

He ran down the front porch stairs, out to the sidewalk, and down the street toward his side of town. He heard Vale's voice behind him and his alpha instinct begged him to stop, to listen, but he knew if he did, he'd go back inside, kiss Vale's mouth, take his plump ass in his hands, and rub against his body until he creamed his pants.

And then he'd use that cream to further slick Vale's sweet hole, and—

He couldn't think about it.

# CHAPTER FOURTEEN

V ALE SIPPED HIS tea, gazing out his study window at the sodden brown leaves of the garden. The snow from the night before hadn't accumulated at all. The pink light of mid-morning left no indication of the fat, beautiful flakes that had spun joyfully through the air. The skies were clear, and the day looked like it would be sunny eventually. Strange to be irritated by something he normally enjoyed, like good weather.

His phone remained irritatingly silent, too.

Vale turned to shoot a glare at it, as though it was responsible for Jason not calling. Zephyr perched on the desk, legs spread wide, licking her asshole in a very impolite manner.

Vale rolled his eyes. "Shameless beast," he muttered her way. "I enjoy having my asshole licked as much as any omega, but even if I *could* do it myself, I wouldn't display it to the world."

She ignored him, licking even more intently.

Vale sighed and turned back to the window, his mug warm against his cool hands.

The night before with Jason had been a close call. He didn't know what had come over him, but if Jason hadn't taken off like he had, then Vale had no doubt he'd have ended up on his hands and knees, presenting himself and being mounted.

When he'd asked Jason to stay, it'd been partly to praise him, to let him know that he'd enjoyed seeing him rise to the occasion in the confrontation with Urho, but he'd also meant to subtly investigate the subject of Miner and the abortifacients.

Even now he wasn't sure what he'd been hoping to ascertain from Jason about the situation, but with pheromone delirium touching Vale, and Jason's alpha quell no doubt wearing off, things had gone so sideways he hadn't been able to corral his thoughts. Then Jason had luckily run off into the night forgetting his coat and the recipe for hot crab casserole Vale had carefully copied out for him.

Now he wasn't sure when he'd get another chance. He'd go into the negotiations tomorrow not knowing if Jason knew about his parents' alleged criminal behavior, or how he felt about it if he did. Given his own history, Jason's thoughts on the matter were rather important to Vale.

He built a fire, considering his options as he struck the match. When the flames took hold, he rose, dusting small pieces of bark from his trousers and the soft, long-sleeve pink shirt he'd pulled on that morning. He supposed he'd sort through another old stack of magazines or possibly finish reading the novel he'd begun the day before. Neither seemed particularly appealing, though, not when he could have been sledding with Jason, acting like a kid again. It was a relief when the doorbell rang.

Placing the mug of tea on his desk, he gave Zephyr a firm look and said, "Don't knock it over. Understand?"

She meowed and turned her back on him.

Anticipating a delivery or perhaps the early post, Vale gasped when he opened the door. "Oh!"

"Hi," Jason said, grinning cheekily.

Vale raised a brow, his stomach swooping like a bird in flight. "I thought you were going to call me this morning," he scolded. "Not show up on my doorstep."

"I was going to call if it *snowed*," Jason said, a bit smugly. He wore a pair of rough-looking pants, a thick, heavy, long-sleeved shirt, and held a shovel in one hand.

Three men stood on the lawn behind him in similar garb, carrying garden tools. There was a work truck in the street behind them. The side of it read *Garden Grow – Betas for Hire*.

Jason pushed a hunk of blond hair away from his eyes. "It didn't snow."

"No. It didn't."

"We'll have to go sledding another time. But the cold last night got me to thinking. If I'm going to do anything about your garden, I need to get started before the ground freezes. Mox, Jim, and Roe, the betas my parents hire, agreed to come over with me and get started today if that's okay. We have a lot to do. If I remember, the place is pretty overgrown."

Vale blinked at Jason in the pale light glinting through the trees. His blue eyes glowed like the sea in high summer, and his cheeks were pink from the chill. "Do your parents know you're here?"

"Of course. They dosed me extra, don't worry." Jason grinned.

Vale flushed, a wave of heat rising through him as slick dampened his asshole.

Jason's nostrils flared and his eyes glinted dangerously. "Oh."

Vale groaned, wiped a hand over his beard, and said, "Hold on a minute." He closed the door in Jason's face and took a deep breath in and out, trying to still his pulse. Ridiculous pheromones. He was a grown man, for wolf-god's sake.

He turned to the coatrack by the door, grabbed Jason's coat, took a long sniff of it, reveling in the hints of pencil, earth, and something spicy. He opened the door again. "You left this last night."

Jason took the coat from him, smelled it, too, and smiled. "Now it smells like your house. And you."

"I thought it smelled like you, actually."

Jason gazed at Vale with such intensity it made more slick spread around his asshole. "Did you like that?"

Vale groaned again, glancing over Jason's shoulders to where the beta gardeners stood talking quietly in a huddle in his front yard. "I did." At that admission, his body betrayed him even more. His cock thickened and rose, and his hole grew sopping wet. He'd have to change his underwear.

Jason's jaw clenched, and he leaned the shovel against the side of the house. Pressing his coat back through the doorway, he said, "Keep it then. I won't need it today. I'll be plenty warm once I start working."

Vale took it without argument, and he quivered as Jason's scent wafted over him again.

Jason glanced over his shoulder toward the men he'd brought with him. "I could send them away. I can smell how you're opening for me. And if you consent, I can do something about that." He gestured down where his hard cock distorted the front of his work pants.

"Protocols," Vale rasped, his own dick throbbing now and his nipples grazing the front of his shirt, roused by more than the cold air outside.

"Who cares? We're already wrong by cultural standards. You want to feel me. I want to feel you." He took a step forward, pupils dilated and mouth open as though he was going to bend for a kiss.

"Stop," Vale whimpered. He squeezed his eyes closed to get himself under a semblance of control. "I thought you said they dosed you."

"They did. Maybe they need to dose *you* with something, though, because you're soaked for me. You shouldn't suffer when I know what I want." But he hesitated just at the threshold. "It's up to you."

"Impudent brat."

Jason's eyes glinted. "I should spank you for that."

Vale's knees quivered, and he shut the door until it was just open an inch. "Yes, you may clear out my garden," he said through the crack, trying to get some dignity back when he wanted nothing more than to pull Jason in the house, fall on the floor, shove his pants down and get spanked—then fucked—until he couldn't see straight.

"If you're sure." Jason's eyes sparkled.

"I'm sure," Vale said, his heart racing.

Wolf-god, Jason was so young, so inexperienced, he was probably all talk anyway. He wouldn't know what to do if Vale let him in the house. He'd have no clue where to start with a proper spanking and fucking. Right? *Right?*

Vale had to believe that or he'd go mad.

Jason nodded and blew a strand of his blond hair out of his eyes, but it only landed back against his cheekbone again. "We'll be around back. It'll probably take most of the day."

"I'll have lunch ready for you by noon then."

Jason cocked his head doubtfully. "*Can* you make lunch?"

"Don't believe everything my friends tell you. I'm perfectly capable of sandwiches for four men." His dick beat with his pulse as he fought the urge to throw the door wide and drag Jason inside.

"I look forward to it then," Jason said before adjusting his cock to be more inconspicuous and turning to the men behind him. "This way. There's a lot of work to do. Oh, and Mox, will you let me know your thoughts about what we should plant? We'll discuss it with Vale before we make any purchases, of course."

"I'll be here all day," Vale said faintly, before shutting the door completely, locking it, and clutching Jason's coat to his face. He felt to his knees, wrestled his pants open, and gripped his throbbing cock. With his eyes squeezed shut, thinking of Jason's intense blue gaze, he shoved his hand in his mouth to stifle his grunts. His hips jerked and his body convulsed as he painted white streaks on the worn brown planks.

When it was over, he rose shakily, hung Jason's coat back up on the rack and grabbed a handkerchief from the pocket of one of his own to clean up the mess. Heart still pounding and asshole quivery and wet, he headed upstairs to shower. A glimmer of worry pestered him despite the post-orgasmic haze. His arousal was barely sated at all.

Alpha imprinting might be instantaneous and violent, but the omega counterpart was nothing to scoff at! His body craved Jason and wasn't about to let him forget it. It took another orgasm in the shower, complete with his asshole stuffed full of an alpha-sized dildo he rode when Urho needed a break during heats, for him to return to his senses.

THE REST OF the morning passed calmly enough.

Vale pottered around in his study, all loose-limbed and relaxed, sorting through a few piles of magazines. Then he settled in for reading on the sofa with a blanket pulled up over him. Zephyr slept on his legs, and he faced away from the fire, so he could appreciate the view out the now-open windows, where Jason and the betas worked unimpeded. He sipped tea, read a few pages, dozed a bit, dreamed of Jason's fingers in his ass, and woke aroused all over again. He groaned and turned on his side, dislodging Zephyr, and took slow, deep breaths until his erection went away.

As he came back to himself, he heard four voices raised in song, and the words drifted into him on the breeze. Curious, he rose and stretched, and then crossed the room for a better look. Sure enough, Jason sang along with the other men, his voice a sweet, tender baritone as he crooned an Old World song of love for a human female named Roxanne.

Vale smiled fondly, leaning against the sill and gazing out to where they'd cleared away nearly a truckload full of debris. It was already shaping up to look more like his pater's old garden. They'd uncovered the old statue of Wolf in Extremis near the back.

The men sang about the beautiful Roxanne selling her body as her lover pleaded for her to understand that with him she had other options. Vale wondered what life had been like for human women. He'd considered the question often from the time he first understood as a young boy that he was destined to be an omega.

Had women suffered like omegas did now? He knew they didn't experience heats but instead endured a monthly menstruation that signaled the end of fertility for a period instead of the beginning of it. But otherwise, he knew little of their lives.

Did they die in childbirth? Had they also been required to submit to their alpha and subsume their lives to his whims? Had the deity who'd created them, wolf-god or whatever had come before, require them to do so?

Probably not. But there was no telling for sure. Artifacts from the Old World were incomplete at best and confusing at worst.

When the song ended, the beta Jason had called Mox started a new one. Vale recognized it as something he'd heard performed at the theater several months back. He'd attended the show with Urho, and afterward they'd returned to Vale's house to make love.

He'd always enjoyed Urho's careful, serious intensity in bed. He should miss it, and maybe eventually he would, but for now he wanted something else entirely. He wanted Jason. A boy who hadn't even been on his radar when he last heard this song. It was hard to believe it'd only been a week since his life had been turned topsy-turvy.

Jason turned, caught his eye, and wandered over to the window. "Do you like calla lilies? Mox says he can get them from a vendor in the Calitan district for a good price." Jason wiped a dirty hand over his sweaty forehead, peering in the window at Vale with a smile.

"Not that price matters. Don't let that worry you."

"I do like them, actually. My pater had them years ago. They died a few years after he did." Vale shrugged sadly. "I neglected it all very badly."

"It must have hurt to come out here and think of him. Of course it was too much," Jason said gently.

"It's hurt more over the years to look out and see how I let it go to waste. I'm afraid I'm quite lazy, oh alpha, my alpha. If I'm not teaching or writing, I'm fairly useless. I'm not sure what you'll do with me."

Jason's grin turned sly. "Oh, I have lots of ideas of what to do with you."

Vale's dick rushed with blood. He clucked his tongue. "Not now."

After casting a quick look over his shoulder, Jason leaned against the sill and said playfully, "You seemed excited by the idea of a spanking earlier. Would that make you less lazy?" His eyes twinkled. "A spanking a day keeps the dust away."

Vale's asshole grew slippery with slick, and he was glad the breeze was blowing into the room instead of out. He could smell Jason's sweat, though, and that made him even wetter and his ridiculous cock—hadn't it had enough already?—even harder. "I have a feeling a spanking would be useless for encouraging house-keeping."

"Why's that?"

"I'm very motivated by sex, as we've already discussed. Spanking will lead to fucking, and that will lead to an orgasm, and that will make me very tired and happy to do nothing but lay around reading books and napping while awaiting my next spanking." His nipples tingled, and he had to hold himself very still to keep from wriggling his ass. He chewed on the inside of his cheek for control.

Jason's eyebrows rose. "Good to know. I think I'll like living with you."

Vale's throat clicked as he swallowed.

"Stop flirting with your omega and get back to work," Mox called from where he hacked at a thick set of overgrown vines. He glared at Jason through a hank of dark, dirty hair. "If you want this cleared by this afternoon, I need all the hands I can get."

Jason called out, "I'm just negotiating lunch."

"We'll take ours out here. Right, boys?"

The other two betas nodded, not even looking up from where they cut, chopped, and tossed broken branches, dead bushes, and overgrown weeds into giant wheelbarrows.

"I'm eating inside," Jason said, turning to face Mox. "And then I'll be back out." His long fingers gripped the windowsill.

Vale closed his eyes as a flash of his dream hit him again. Dream-Jason had known what he was doing, nailing his prostate with every twist of his fingers and working his omega glands expertly, but this Jason couldn't know anything like that, could he? Had he even been with a beta? Wolf-god, he was going insane.

Mox huffed but only said, "If we don't finish today, I'm guessing you'll be giving us another day's pay. Go ahead, I say. It's your money."

Jason turned back to Vale and teased, "Should I climb in here or..."

"Come around to the kitchen door in fifteen minutes," Vale said, jerking his thumb toward the side of the house. "I'll have sandwiches for everyone then."

Luckily, Rosen had left behind leftovers and some staples, like bread, eggs, and milk, for Vale. If his friends didn't look out for him, he didn't know where he'd be in life. Hungry, for sure.

The brown bread was soft and easy to cut into sandwich slices. He slathered on some mayonnaise and dotted on mustard. The slices of leftover duck lay nicely over the bread, and the green spinach leaves gave a dash of healthiness to the offering. He rummaged around in his cabinet until he found the unopened bag of dried pineapple slices he'd been saving for a sweets craving, and put two on each plate.

He'd just finished when Jason's knock came at the back door.

"Come in," he called, and gathered three plates in his hands. He passed them out to the workers, who carried them toward the back yard with grunts of thanks.

"Don't they need something to drink?" Vale asked, watching after them, while Jason tugged to get his dirty work boots off before stepping into the kitchen.

"They have thermoses." Jason grunted as he pulled his second boot off. He stood with a grin and shut the door behind him.

The house felt quiet. A sense of *alone* fell hard. Vale's breath tingled in his lungs. The bubbly fizzy feeling lingered as Jason gazed down at him, his eyes almost obscured by the swoop of his blond hair.

"I should wash my hands," he said, but it sounded like seduction somehow. Gritty and full of lust.

Vale stepped back and motioned toward the sink. "I made sandwiches for us, too." They sat on plates on the table, along with tumblers of cold water, waiting for them to sit down.

Jason didn't say anything as he washed his hands thoroughly and then bent low over the kitchen sink, splashing his sweaty face with water. Vale's stomach flipped, an undercurrent buzzing between them. He stood frozen, waiting.

Jason wiped his face with a kitchen towel Vale had left out on the counter, and then turned to him. "Come here."

"Why?" Vale's gut squirmed and his cock thickened.

"Just do it."

Vale swallowed and took a step closer, his heart in his throat and skin prickling all over.

When he was close enough, Jason took hold of his chin gently. The room felt too small and too big at once, and so did his body. He wanted to run away, to lean up on his toes and take Jason's full lips, or to dissolve into a quivery, slick-damp mess all over the kitchen. He almost didn't care which, just so long as *something* happened.

"I'm going to kiss you," Jason announced, steady and sure. "Do you have a problem with that?"

*Where was his insecure baby alpha now?*

"No."

"No, you don't have a problem, or—"

"I don't have a problem with that."

He was thirty-five and he'd kissed many men, but nothing prepared him for the sweetness of Jason's lips on his. Soft and wet, determined but respectful, he felt the kiss in his toes, his dick, his gut, and his melting, aching, burning heart. His asshole gushed with slick, and Jason growled in reaction to the scent. Knees trembling, he wrapped his arms around Jason's neck and held on, tasting him over and over.

When Jason pulled away, he rested his forehead on Vale's, panting softly, his hard dick shoved tightly against Vale's stomach. "That's enough now." His mouth was wet and red, and his chin was scrubbed shiny pink by Vale's beard.

Vale thrummed with lust. His mind turned over a singular, wondrous question: how had his delicious, young alpha learned to kiss like that?

Jason's chest shook with the beating of his heart, echoing Vale's own inner pulsing.

"You taste so good," Jason whispered, his eyes drawing down to Vale's mouth. "Too good."

Vale groaned, fisted his hands in Jason's shirt, and shoved him back against the counter as he took his mouth again. Jason let him, and they moved against each other, hard and eager. Jason shook and moaned and then gripped Vale by the back of the neck, hauled him close, and kissed him until Vale's knees buckled.

Holding Vale up with one arm around his waist, Jason broke free of the kiss. "You smell so good. Wet and open for me. So easy. So ready."

"Always ready for you," Vale answered, like he'd been programmed to say it.

Involuntary. Compulsory. *True.*

"Yes," Jason hissed.

Vale's hole quivered. "I need you."

Jason's fingers clenched the back of his neck hard and he squeezed his eyes shut tight. "Wait, hold on."

Vale's heart hammered. Was his baby alpha going to back out now? Get him riled up and then fail to plug his desperate, opening hole with his giant, hungry cock?

Wait…giant, hungry cock? Wolf's-own lust, what was he *think-ing*? He was already so far gone.

Jason gritted out. "We need to make a decision. A smart one."

Vale hitched his hips against Jason's, his dick aching and his asshole soaked. It was all he could do not to demand Jason fuck him now. "I can't think when I can still taste your spit," Vale whispered, licking his lips for any hint of more.

"Fuck," Jason said, gazing down at him wide-eyed.

"But we shouldn't…" He couldn't even make himself truly protest. *This* was why they weren't supposed to be alone.

"Turn around," Jason said, flipping Vale to face the counter as he said the words.

It was hard and quick. Jason plastered himself against Vale's back and kissed his neck, his ears, and rubbed the crotch of his work pants against Vale's soft trousers, pressing against Vale's ass.

Vale arched back against him, eager and ready for whatever

Jason wanted to do. "Yes," he moaned. "Please."

Jason grunted, shoving his hard cock against Vale's ass. He kissed Vale's neck, sending shivery sweetness cascading over his skin. Then Jason cursed softly and ripped himself away from Vale.

"No," Vale whimpered, gazing mournfully over his shoulder. "Come back."

Jason shook his head. His eyes were glazed over and he panted, physically trembling, but he held himself away. "Let's eat."

Vale stayed braced against the counter with his cock thumping hard down the leg of his pants. "What?"

"Let's eat now," Jason said, voice gravelly, looking away from Vale and out the kitchen window onto the side lawn. "We'll finish this at a better time."

Vale turned around slowly to stare at him. "Are you insane? Or just an asshole?"

Jason laughed. "I'm trying to prove something to you. I can control myself. You're making it hard, but I figure if this is a test, I'm going to pass it, even if it's just barely."

Vale blinked at him, utterly lust-addled. He stayed silent as Jason adjusted his cock and then gingerly moved to sit at the kitchen table. It took several stunned moments to join him there. When he did, Jason still had the haze of lust in his eyes, but he smiled hopefully.

"So we're just going to eat now?" Vale hissed.

"Yes." Jason picked up his sandwich and took a bite.

"You're serious?"

Nodding, Jason chewed and swallowed. "Hey, this is good! Rosen didn't do your sandwich skills justice."

Ignoring the tease, he said, "Earlier you wanted to come inside and take me. Now that I'm willing you just stop?"

"Earlier I was going to take you up to your room and do it right," Jason said calmly, though his neck was flushed.

Vale gritted his teeth.

"It's a good thing I dosed up on more alpha quell before coming in here, huh?" Jason lifted a brow. "Or I'd have failed the test for sure."

"It wasn't a test." Vale stood up, his body a livewire of denied arousal. "I wouldn't do that to you."

Jason nodded warily. "I know. Well, I mean, I know you wouldn't do it on purpose, like in advance. But later, you'd be thinking about it, and you'd wonder how you could be with an alpha who took you for the first time in the kitchen, without care and preparation, and without following protocols."

"I don't give a shit about protocols," Vale said, gripping the edge of the table hard. "I'm not the kind of man who could demand you follow them."

Jason put his sandwich on the plate to give Vale his full attention. "That's not true. You do care. You insisted from the beginning we follow them."

"Because I was scared," Vale admitted. The wood beneath his palms dug in sharply. "I didn't know you."

"And now you do?" Jason's eyebrows rose.

He had a point.

Jason tried a grin. "I think you're suffering from pheromone delirium, Professor Aman."

Vale glared at him.

"Eat your lunch," Jason said, nudging Vale's untouched plate. "You need to keep your strength up for all that reading and napping you've still got to finish today."

Vale snorted but didn't take up his sandwich. "I'll be right back."

"Where are you going?"

Vale stood and waved toward the laundry room. His underwear was soaked again, and he wasn't going to eat lunch with the annoying, slippery wetness a constant reminder of how Jason had led him on. "I need to change."

"But I like the way you smell," Jason said, his eyes hooding. "Knowing you're wet for me, I like that."

"You would." Vale gritted his teeth and went to change his clothes.

He took a few minutes to clean himself up and get his head together, but when he returned to Jason and the table, his hands were still shaking when he picked up his sandwich. How long would Jason have this effect on him? Would his body calm down if he gave in to his desires, if they contracted and consummated? How long until they both relaxed into something more normal?

"So, what's new?" Jason asked like he hadn't just been the biggest tease in all of human history five minutes earlier.

Still on edge, Vale chewed his bite of sandwich and then shrugged. "Not much. I think I told you I saw Rosen the other day. He's working on a new painting."

"Oh, yeah. He's an artist/chef/philosopher, right? Is he any good? At the art part, I mean."

"In my opinion, yes, but everyone has their own tastes about art, of course."

Jason popped a loose piece of spinach into his mouth. "I like abstract better than figurative. What does he do?"

"A bit of both." Vale wasn't hungry for food. He shoved his sandwich aside. "What draws you to the abstract in art?"

Jason cocked his head, thinking a bit. "Are you going to eat that?"

Vale shook his head.

"Do you mind if I...?"

His growing alpha had been working outside. Of course he was hungry. "Go right ahead."

Jason took a big bite of his own sandwich and then added Vale's to his plate. His chin was still pink from the scruff of Vale's beard. "I guess I'm drawn to abstract over figurative because I spend a lot of time looking through microscopes, both at school in my studies, and at home for fun. Sometimes I pretend what I'm seeing is art. I try to imagine what it would be like to recreate the image in some other way. Sometimes I try. I wouldn't call myself an artist but I do some drawing sometimes. What I see under the microscope is usually a mess, but an interesting mess. And that's what I see in abstract art—the same things I see under the microscope. It's the makings of the world, you know?"

Somewhere in that little speech, Jason had been adorable enough for Vale to forgive him for insisting on following protocols (after *not at all* following protocols). Maybe it was his sincerity or the way his eyes shone when he mentioned the microscope. Vale said, "I haven't spent much time looking into microscopes. In fact, I'd say I haven't looked into one since I graduated from Mont Juror all those years ago."

Jason's eyes lit up like sun on the sea. "Oh! I'll have to show you my favorite slides sometime soon. I know you'd like them."

Yes, it was the way he glowed. That was why Vale forgave him. That, and the knowledge deep down, beneath the lust, that Jason was right. If he'd taken him at the counter, Vale would have judged him harshly later for it. He was an asshole that way. And somehow, already, Jason knew that about him.

"Maybe if I showed you my favorite slides you'd write a poem about what you saw?" Jason swallowed hard. "Or maybe you wouldn't. Either way is fine. But I'd like to show you, if you'd like to see."

"I'd love to see. And maybe I will write a poem. 'ode to jason and the art of science'. All lowercase letters, of course."

"Of course." Jason grinned. "Will you write a poem for me? Truly?"

"I'm sure I'll end up writing one about you someday," Vale said, cocking his head, curious at how eager Jason seemed for him to do it. "It seems unlikely I'd share this experience with you and not write about it at all."

"Good." Jason nodded sharply. "No matter what my father says about it, ignore him. It won't go into the contract. I promise."

Vale's blood slowed, suspicion squirming in his gut. "No matter what your father says about *what*, exactly?"

"Oh, poetry. He doesn't want you to write poems, especially about me. But I do. I want you to write loads of poems about me. Your best poems yet." Jason's nostrils flared, and he shot Vale a hot, possessive look. "So get to it whenever I inspire you. The sooner, the better. I don't care what they say, either. You don't have to flatter me. They can be ugly poems. Just make them as real as you can."

Vale swallowed back a burst of laughter. "Oh, Jason. Wolf's own hell, what am I supposed to make of you?"

"I don't know. Figure it out. In a poem." Jason grinned again, happily chewing on a dried pineapple ring. "When can I bring my microscope over and show you some of my slides?"

"Perhaps I can see them the next time I'm at your house. Wouldn't that be easier?"

Jason's nose crinkled and he darted a glance away.

"What?"

"I guess I could bring it downstairs to the conservatory or Father's study. It would be easier than carting it across town. But..." He shrugged. "I don't know."

Vale studied Jason's flop of hair and his flushing neck. "What are you worrying about?"

Jason shrugged. "It's not important."

Vale crossed his arms over his chest and fixed Jason with a glare that had him buckling within seconds.

"Fine. It's silly. I can bring the microscope downstairs, but then my parents will be there and it won't be private. If I bring it here, then we can look at it together without people around. I like it better when we're alone. Don't you?"

Aside from the way Jason had ramped him up and left him hanging, he did, yes. "I could come up to your room. If your parents don't mind, that is. We could leave the door open so they'd feel more secure and—"

Jason huffed. "Do you leave the door open when you go to Urho's room?"

Vale chewed on the inside of his lip for a moment, taking in Jason's hunched shoulders, and the gleam of embarrassment in his eyes. "What does Urho have to do with your microscope?" he asked softly.

"Nothing." Jason bit into the last of Vale's sandwich ferociously, and then, with a heavy sigh, tossed the final bit onto the plate and pushed back. "My room is a kid's room. I don't want you to see it. You'll think I can't be an alpha to you."

"For what it's worth, I've never been to Urho's room," Vale said. "Not in his home here in town, anyway. From what I understand, he keeps it exactly as it was when his omega was alive."

"His omega?"

"Riki. I never knew him. Urho was desperately in love with him. They were a bonded pair."

Jason's shoulders relaxed a little. "But he's been in your room."

"Are you jealous of Urho?"

"Yes, but I'm not going to lose control over it. And you can't pretend to be surprised by that, because you already knew I was."

Vale smiled. "I did."

"I just don't like that you think of me as a kid. Going into my room would only make that worse."

"Maybe I want to see your room." Vale reached out and took

hold of Jason's fingers, feeling their strength as he twined them with his own. "Look, nothing is going to make us the same age or even close. If you haven't changed your room much then that's because it still speaks to you, and I'd like to see it, just the way it is. You're my alpha, and if I'm going to contract with you, there's no use in pretending that you're not nineteen and that you're not exactly who you are, and who you have been." Vale squeezed his fingers. "Because I can't pretend that I'm not who I am and who I have been, either."

Vale's gut clenched. He didn't know how he could confess to Jason about what had happened during that second rebound heat, but he wasn't sure if he could morally contract with him while keeping it a secret either. He needed to know what Jason thought of his pater's situation, how he viewed such things in general before he came out with his own history, but how to ask without it being obvious?

"I'll think about it." Jason squeezed Vale's hand in return.

Vale closed his eyes and gathered courage. His hands went clammy, so he pulled his fingers free and sat back. "We're talking about being honest and real with each other, and I heard something the other day that makes me anxious."

"What?" Jason asked, his brows dropping low.

"It's just that it's come to my attention in a roundabout way that it's possible you're keeping something from me."

Jason's throat worked and he closed his eyes. "Oh, yeah?"

"Yes, and I need you to be honest with me, Jason. If any contract negotiations are going to be fruitful, then we have to bare ourselves to each other. An associate of mine said that there were rumors…"

Jason's lips trembled slightly, as he ducked his head blond hair fell in front of his eyes. "Is it about Xan? Does a professor friend suspect? About us?" He swallowed convulsively.

Vale blinked in confusion, thrown off course. "Xan? Your friend from the library?"

"Yeah." Jason frowned. "Did he tell you himself? Or did someone guess..." He scrubbed through his hair leaving it ruffled. "Whatever you heard, you don't have to worry. It won't happen ever again. I promise."

Vale's brain stumbled trying to change direction with Jason's words. He had no idea what Jason was talking about, but he decided to follow the end of the piece of yarn until he got to the whole ball. "All right. But I'm going to need you to explain a little more."

"It was just a game!" Jason's earnestness shone from his face. "For me, anyway. I think, for Xan, maybe it was more. I think he developed feelings for me." He cleared his throat. "No, I know he did. Which is wrong on so many levels, I know. But the Holy Book of Wolf doesn't leave room for someone like him, and it seems cruel, don't you think?"

Vale stared at Jason, a suspicion forming.

"He didn't choose to feel this way. It's not what he really wants to be! I don't know how you found out, but please don't judge me for it." He wiped a hand over his mouth, eyes darting around. "It was only a game. And no one was supposed to ever know. Did Xan tell you? I know he's jealous, but I thought he'd accepted this." He motioned between them. "Us."

"Xan didn't tell me anything. I've never met or spoken with him."

"Oh, thank wolf-god," Jason whispered. "He'd be stupid to tell anyone and I know he's upset, but he's not suicidal. He wouldn't want anyone to know he's unmanned." Jason's mouth clomped shut, and his eyes went wider. "No! I didn't mean that. He's not unmanned. He's just...different."

Vale took a sip of water, wetting his suddenly dry mouth, full understanding dawning. "Let me see if I understand. You're telling me that you've been having sex with your best friend, penetrating another alpha?"

Jason frowned, confusion marring his features. "But you knew that. You just said—" He flushed darker. "Oh. You didn't say."

"No, I didn't. You must have felt guilty about this and thought I was referring to it," Vale supplied.

"Yeah." Jason's foot tapped rapidly on the floor, and he looked like he would vibrate out of his chair. Even his lips trembled.

Vale knew there were all sorts of taboos about alpha-on-alpha sex, but he also knew that growing boys, wild with hormones, needed outlets. Indiscretions were to be expected. Omegas at Mont Juror didn't hold back.

"I didn't realize your family adhered so strongly to the Holy Book that you'd feel guilty for blowing off steam with your friend. Though obviously, it needs to be kept secret for his safety, and, to a degree, yours. But I'm not the man to judge you for it, either."

Jason ducked his head. "It's not that. I don't feel guilty about that."

"Then…?"

"We did it one last time. After." He met Vale's eyes with his lips twisted up and tears drawing at his golden lashes. "I'm sorry."

The blood drained from Vale's face and a sharp pain lanced into him, unexpected and strange. Why did he care? They barely knew each other, and it was clear Jason didn't intend to carry on with the other boy, so why did it feel like he'd just been stabbed? He had no right to that feeling.

One voice in his head whispered, *Get used to it. He should take a surrogate*, while another hissed, *No, I want him to choose me! Please always choose me.*

Jason scrambled up from the table and around to kneel at Vale's feet. "I'm sorry. Please forgive me. I'll never do it again. It was the last time and I did it for him, because he needed it. But there's no excuse. I wish I could take it back."

Vale's fingers shook as he threaded them into Jason's hair and tilted his head back. "Shh. Be quiet. You don't need to say anything more."

"Will you ever forgive me?"

Vale smiled gently. Oh, there was his insecure baby alpha after all. "If there's one thing I've figured out over the years, it's that I'm not good at holding grudges. I'm not thrilled, but we aren't contracted. I don't have any legal grounds for objection."

"Morally, though…" Jason trailed off. "I shouldn't have done it. For a lot of reasons."

"I'm more concerned for your friend." Vale couldn't resist letting his fingers trail down Jason's cheek, finding the skin smooth from a recent shave.

Vale had heard of grown alphas who enjoyed the taboo nature of sex with another alpha before. They were called unmanned and scorned by society, thrown into jail if caught in the open, and considered morally depraved. He'd never bought into those ideas but he'd never known an alpha who yearned for another alpha personally.

Over his years as a professor, there had been a few rare instances of an unmanned alpha amongst the students. But when it was discovered the unmanned was usually withdrawn by his parents and taken home for an attempt at so-called re-education, which, from what he understood, consisted of contracting with an omega and getting him pregnant as quickly as possible. A family life was supposed to cure the problem.

"Is he safe? Will he get into trouble seeking out another alpha in the future?" Vale asked.

"I don't know. I don't think so," Jason whispered to Vale's shoes. "He says he wishes he was an omega." Then he shuddered.

"Don't tell anyone. Please!"

"Of course not," Vale promised. "I'd never put a friend of yours in danger."

Jason looked up with wet lashes. "I'm scared for him."

"You have every right to be." Vale stroked his fingers down Jason's face again, wiping the tears before they fell, and rubbed his thumb along Jason's lower lip. The temptation to kiss him again was strong, and he fought it valiantly.

*He deserves an omega he can reproduce with. Stop doing this to yourself. Stop doing it to him. Stop wanting him to want you. And stop lying to yourself that he won't resent you later when you're contracted and you can't provide him with a continuation of the family line.*

*Stop, Vale. Stop.*

But his body didn't listen to his mind. He twined his fingers in Jason's hair, growled, and gave in.

Kissing Jason was too sweet and right. His asshole gushed and he moaned, begging with his body as he tugged Jason up until their combined weight toppled the kitchen chair and they landed hard on the wood floor.

Still they didn't stop kissing, and Vale's cock throbbed with renewed need. Jason gripped his ass and they humped together, kissing, moaning, and pawing at each other. Sweat broke over Vale's body, and he felt the tug of an orgasm drawing near.

"Yes," he crooned, moving against Jason harder. "Make me come, darling."

Jason gripped his chin, kissing him thoroughly, and Vale arched up, his cock flexing in his pants. He cried out as he spurted hard and his asshole overflowed with slick again. He trembled, his hole squeezing and releasing, seeking Jason's thick cock.

His body spasmed as he rushed up into the hotter, higher place omegas ascended to after the first shared orgasm with an alpha. Vale needed to be fucked and he needed to come again—this time he wanted the mind-numbing, earth-shaking orgasm that came from being plowed by a massive alpha-cock. It was one of the blessings of being an omega—multiple orgasms of several different kinds.

Jason moaned and hunched against him. "Fuck!" He buried his face in Vale's neck, going still, while Vale still shuddered against him. His panting breath tickled, and Vale squirmed.

"Come for me," Vale begged. "Give me your cock. Please."

Jason shook his head.

Vale moaned and shoved against Jason's thick dick. "Take me upstairs if it makes you feel better about it. But please, Jason. I need you inside me."

His higher mind, still silenced by the shock of orgasm, buzzed with a slight discouragement, a sense that he shouldn't be begging Jason to do this. Not yet. Maybe not ever.

Jason gently disentangled himself from Vale's arms and legs and sat on the floor next to him, pants distended by his massive dick. "No. We shouldn't. Not now."

Vale nearly screamed in frustration, but he opted for reaching up and trying to drag Jason back into the kiss again. Jason rebuffed him gently. "No, I just wanted to make you come. To see what you looked like during and after. In case…" he let it trail off.

"What?"

"In case you won't contract with me," Jason whispered. "Because I know you're not convinced you should yet."

"And shouldn't I get to see what you look like when you come?" Vale licked his lips. "What if that's a selling point, darling? For the contract."

"You want to see?" Jason's voice was gruff.

"More than anything." Right now, that was true, but as the seconds ticked past, Vale's higher mind was coming awake again. A hint of doubt that this was wise coursed with the rush of orgasm.

Jason held Vale down, one hand on his throat, owning, possessive, as he kneeled up and took out his cock.

Vale's eyes rolled back in his head when he saw the veiny thickness, loose foreskin, and great length, and then he forced himself to focus as Jason stroked it right beside his face. Vale put out his tongue, but Jason pulled back from it.

"Just watch," he whispered.

Staring down at Vale, Jason's cheeks went red and his lips ruddy as he worked his hand over himself. Vale wanted to join in, undo his ruined pants and stick his hand down past his still-hard cock to finger his wet hole while he watched Jason jerk himself off.

"Come for me," Vale whispered. "Show me what you look like."

Jason's eyes grew vulnerable and almost frightened, as he thrust into his hand again and again. "Vale," he whispered, and then his face crumpled, his hips spasmed, and white wads of come shot up into the air. It spattered the floor, the kitchen chair that lay toppled to the ground, and Vale's shirt and pants. A glob landed on Vale's cheek and another on his forehead, and Jason groaned, aimed, and pumped a huge spurt directly into Vale's open mouth.

Vale's tastebuds exploded with flavor and he convulsed on the floor, the weight of Jason's hand on his throat holding him down, as he came a second time. His alpha's taste triggered a cascade of previously unknown pleasure, an orgasm of an essence and texture he'd never experienced before. Quivering, sweating, and shaking, he swallowed Jason's come down, and opened his mouth for more.

But Jason was done.

Panting and moaning, Jason collapsed on Vale and kissed him desperately before licking the sticky come from Vale's forehead and cheek and sharing it in another kiss. Vale lay limply on the kitchen floor, letting Jason taste him and stroke him through his clothes. Then Jason sat back and tucked himself back into his pants.

"That wasn't supposed to happen," he said hoarsely.

"No, it wasn't," Vale agreed.

And while a skeptical part of him feared there were too many difficulties between them to rely on the idea that an agreement could be struck and a contract signed, he also knew he'd never regret having tasted his alpha's come and witnessed his pleasure.

Protocols be damned. His heart be broken. His hope turned to misery. No matter what came in the future, this he would not regret.

Jason stood slowly, shakily, and helped Vale to his feet. "We should clean up. Separately. Or this will start all over again."

Head still spinning, Vale nodded and waved toward the downstairs bathroom at the end of the hall just past the study. "That way. I'll go up to my room."

"And then I'll go back out to work." Jason swallowed hard. "You forgive me then? For what I did with Xan?"

Vale blinked at him. "Darling, a life lesson for you: don't bring up former lovers while your current one is still shaking from the orgasms you shared."

Jason ducked his head and blushed.

Upstairs in his room, washing and changing for the third time since waking that morning, Vale realized that he'd still never asked Jason about Miner and the abortifacients. How was he ever going to make an informed decision about whether or not he should throw his lot in with the Sabel-Hoff family if he couldn't keep his hands off the boy? This was why protocols existed. So that level-headed choices could be made before it was too late.

As Vale knelt in his shower with the alpha-dildo shoved into his still-needing ass, he wondered if he'd ever be level-headed again.

He closed his eyes and stroked his cock, rolling the lingering taste of Jason around in his mouth, and as he pictured Jason's face crumpling in pleasure, he came again with a tight cry that echoed on the tiles.

He kept the dildo shoved inside and slipped to the floor of the tub, letting the water beat down on his legs and rigid cock.

"Wolf-god! Coming five times in one day," he whispered. "I might as well be in heat."

He bit into his lip as a terrible thought formed.

Yesterday, he'd loaded up on Rosen's food, but he hadn't been hungry all day today. Even after several orgasms this morning, he'd eschewed lunch. Then he'd begged Jason to fuck him, to forget protocols and plug his ass with that beautiful cock. He'd wanted him to do it. Again and again. And even more telling than that, he was *still aroused*.

But it couldn't be...

Aside from the awful rebound heats, he'd never had an unexpected heat in his life. He shook his head firmly. He refused, absolutely refused to even entertain the idea. All his behaviors could be explained as due to finding his *Érosgápe*.

Nothing more. Nothing less.

Because there was no way he was going to be obliged to attempt negotiation of a contract while descending into heat. The universe wouldn't be that cruel. Would it?

He wasn't a praying man, but he closed his eyes and whispered, "Don't let me down on this. If you force me to suffer such an injustice, I'll never forgive you."

# CHAPTER FIFTEEN

J ASON FIDGETED IN his chair at the long dining room table, separated from Vale by four feet of polished wood, the company of their attorneys, and the presence of his parents. His cock was half-hard and had been since the moment Vale had entered the room smelling of musk and the beard oil he'd started using. If everything went well today, he might be able to consummate with Vale that very night. And if that was the case, he was glad he'd forced them to wait yesterday.

The day before he'd returned to work in the garden with the betas, making a great deal of headway despite their constant jeering over what they believed had taken place with Vale in the house while they'd been alone. They hadn't been far off from being right. If it hadn't been for the cool distance of alpha quell, he'd have fucked Vale silly while kissing him breathless, and then flipped him onto his stomach and done it again.

He shifted in his seat, watching Vale and Yosef read through the preliminary papers detailing the topics to be covered today. Vale glanced up at him, his cheeks above his beard flushing and his eyes darkening with arousal like he knew exactly what Jason was thinking, before he shook his head and focused on the paperwork again.

Jason licked his lips. He wanted to see Vale's dick. It was cut, he'd said, and he wanted to know what it looked like. If they could just get on with things, then he might have a chance to do that in just a few hours' time. Why hadn't he done it yesterday? Stupid.

He'd had every chance.

He sat forward, trying to concentrate when Bisme Freet, Father's attorney, a tall, thin beta with a bald head and narrow glasses, asked if everyone was ready to begin and started to read aloud from an outlandishly boring legal document. Jason already knew what it said. He'd insisted on looking over the proposed contract the night before and he hadn't seen anything wrong with it. Every word was stamped into his memory.

Father was asking for Vale's consent for Jason to consummate the imprint, consent for Jason to take control of Vale's assets (a courtesy gesture since legally the assets belonged to Jason from the moment of imprinting), and at least one live birth. There were other details too, like discussion of the potential disposal of some other assets, but everything else covered in the contracts described what the Sabel-Hoff family would do for Vale.

Jason's heart grew full thinking of all he had to offer Vale. Surely, since every request was reasonable and the attraction between them strong and mutual, Vale wouldn't turn him down.

But it wasn't long until the negotiations started to go pear-shaped. Vale, for all that he couldn't seem to help returning Jason's heated looks, seemed distant and brittle. Not at all the warm, passionate man he was on the telephone or had been while writhing with Jason on his kitchen floor the day before. His shoulders were tight by his ears and his jaw worked like he was gritting his teeth. Yosef noticed, too, and he kept rubbing Vale's back and whispering in his ear, which only made Vale grow stiffer. Jason wanted to tell Yosef to shut up, that he was just making it worse, but he had no idea what 'it' even was.

And because wolf-god didn't seem to be smiling down on them for this negotiation, Father was strangely irritable and unsettled as well. Worse, Pater didn't quite seem himself. Everyone was on edge, and Jason didn't understand why. After what he and Vale had done together the day before and the confidences they'd shared, he'd allowed himself to hope negotiations would be a breeze.

Maybe Vale had changed his mind about Jason and Xan's indiscretion? Jason sought out Vale's eyes again but didn't see anger or resentment toward *him* when Vale glanced back. He didn't hold his gaze, though.

Jason wished he could call the meeting to a halt and get some time alone with Vale to find out what the problem was, but that still wouldn't explain Father's irritation or Pater's. His stomach knotted and worry climbed ever higher.

As soon as Bisme was finished reading through the legalese, Father said, "Does that all seem satisfactory or do we need to belabor these issues?"

Vale's eyes glinted dangerously. "I get the feeling that negotiating with me is distasteful to you."

"It's not that it's distasteful." Father sighed and shook his head. "Your parents should be here to speak for you."

Vale's lips curled up in a nasty smile. "My parents have been dead for many years. I'm not a green omega with no experience outside Mont Juror. I'm an educated adult with a career and holdings. I deserve to be treated with the respect you'd show to a man you consider your equal." He tilted his head. "And if you won't, I wonder how Miner feels about that?"

"My apologies if I came across impatiently," Father said, glancing Pater's way. "Please understand it's not a reflection on you or my opinion of you."

Vale's brows lifted, but he remained silent. Jason's scalp grew damp with nervous sweat. What was going on? Nothing felt right at all. Why was Vale being so aggressive toward Father?

Yosef broke the silence by saying, "Most aspects of the contract are acceptable. However, my client requires a change to the clause regarding a live birth."

Bisme picked up a pen to take notes. "Go ahead."

"Mr. Aman will *not* contract for any births at all. None. The number must be reduced to zero and all other clauses pertaining to a live birth removed."

Father growled quietly, and Bisme sat his pen down without making a mark. Pater patted his shirt pocket for his silver cigarette case and matches. Jason licked his lips, opened his mouth, and was interrupted before he could speak a word.

"He is our only son, and the contract will stipulate one live birth." Father poked the table with his forefinger, his blue eyes glinting.

Jason started to speak again but was immediately forestalled by his father's hand raised in his direction. Yosef didn't get a word in, either. Before anyone could say anything else, Vale hissed, "Yes, he's your only son. Let's discuss why that is, shall we?"

Pater looked away, his eyes shuttering as he released a long stream of smoke from his lips. Quickly, he took another drag from his cigarette.

Father took hold of Pater's free hand, squeezing once to comfort him. He then shot such a malicious glare at Vale that it made Jason's hackles rise. He didn't want to fight his father over this, but if he so much as spoke out of turn to Vale, he'd show him how much he'd grown.

"There were health concerns," Father whispered. "And Miner did bear one child as his contract required."

"We all know the reasons for Jason being the only one left in the Sabel line," Vale said, sympathy swirling in his voice alongside the tight control he was wielding. "We've all seen the medical write up and know the history. But you've also seen my medical charts. You know this is a matter of life or death for me. Yet you'd have me risk the same—either my own death, or the death of a child, or both?" He sneered. "I wish I could say I'm surprised by that, but given everything I know about you, I'm not."

Jason blinked, wondering where Vale's animosity toward his father was coming from. Surely he wouldn't have been shocked by the live birth clause in the contract, and Jason understood why he'd refuse it, but why was he so *angry* in doing it? Sneering at Father wouldn't get them anywhere good.

"You think you can speak to me like that?" Father said, his voice low and ominous.

Jason's fists curled up, his body tensing, and he shoved his chair back from the table slightly.

"You have no right to address me in that manner," Father went on. "This contract isn't necessary, you realize. We can pay you an allowance for your entire life and not feel it touch us. We're doing you a favor by acting like this is a match that could work. But one more disrespectful comment from you and—"

"Stop, Yule." Pater spoke quietly, smoke ringing his head and drifting up to the ceiling. "Don't say another word."

Father turned to him, eyes wide in surprise. Pater met his gaze firmly.

Father's neck flushed, and he cleared his throat as he looked away.

Pater turned to Vale then and spoke calmly, his voice steady with his promise. "We understand your reluctance to contract for a birth. Believe me, I sympathize. I nearly died with Jason, and I've lost too many now to count. If it wasn't for Jason needing me, and knowing how adrift Yule would be, I might have given up and gone to the other side years ago."

"Miner," Father said Pater's name with fear tingeing his voice, but Pater just placed his hand over his and went on.

"So I understand. Birth is no laughing matter. It's serious. It has the potential to be deadly for us, especially as we get older, especially if we aren't formed right or have scar tissue as you do. A first live

240

birth at your age would be exceedingly difficult, and, with the scar tissue, potentially deadly. We won't risk your life for a chance at a grandchild—not when there are other options."

Father paled and gritted his teeth together.

The word 'surrogate' hung in the air so clearly Jason could almost see it. He snarled at the idea he'd ever take any omega other than Vale. He'd never impregnate some other man simply to carry on the family line. He'd rather die than breed with someone he didn't feel this pull for.

Pater went on, "However, should you come to care for our son as a life partner, truly bonded as his omega, and if, at that time, you discover you're medically capable and want to try for yourself, then we would be honored to have a grandchild from your womb."

Father deflated, seeing that Pater had made up his mind. He covered his face with his hand. Pater sucked his cigarette and blew out the smoke before offering Vale a smile. "We'll strike the requirement from the contract."

"I don't want a child anyway," Jason said, lifting his chin.

That wasn't entirely true, but if Vale didn't want to bear one, or couldn't, then Jason was all right with that. Betas lived childless forever and had happy, even enviously wonderful lives. Still, the idea of Vale never growing large with his child made his throat ache with all the tears he'd refused to shed since presenting as an alpha. But that didn't matter. Keeping Vale safe was more important.

He forced a smile. "So this is good. Vale and I are on the same page."

"Quiet, Jason," Father said gently. "We'll handle this."

"Actually, I'd like to know his thoughts," Vale countered.

The desire for Vale's approval pulsed through him hungrily, almost angrily. "It's only that…it's more important that you're safe and healthy. I don't need a child."

"You don't? Who will inherit when you're gone?" Vale asked, a needle in his tone. "Are you content to see all that your family worked for and accomplished go to charity on our deaths?"

Jason shrugged. "I don't know. I suppose so."

"You suppose so?"

"You've been so unhappy since we sat down," Jason pleaded. "If this is why you're upset then let's set it aside. I don't like seeing you this way."

Vale gazed at him hard. "You're nineteen. Of course you've never considered the implications of being childless. Before we make any decisions, you need to consider the reality of it, Jason. What it would mean for your family."

"You make it sound like you think I should take a surrogate!"

"It's not a terrible idea."

Jason gritted his teeth. "I don't want that."

"We all know what you want," Vale murmured, pressing his fingertips to his eyes with shaky fingers.

What he *wanted* was to sign the paperwork today. He wanted Vale on his knees, where he belonged, rubbing his face against Jason's leg in gratitude for the comfortable, happy life Jason would give him. He wanted Vale to be joyful.

"I won't let you sign a contract that risks your life."

Vale snorted.

Father snapped, "He's your alpha. Show him respect."

Vale shot Father a harsh look but then whispered, "Jason, respectfully, you deserve a family."

"*You* deserve an alpha."

Vale's pale cheeks went even whiter and he ducked his head. Yosef touched his back, but Vale went stiffer and Yosef pulled away. "I don't know about that." Vale's gaze met his, eyes sad. "I've lived a long time without one."

"Imprinting is special," Bisme interrupted. "It's not the kind of thing to shrug off. The bond you could share, *will* share if you

242

spend much time in each other's presence, contract or not, will be beyond your imagination now." He smiled gently. "It's not something to walk away from because you're not sure you want it. It's wolf-god's greatest gift. You can't shun it."

"I do want it," Jason said. "I want the bond, the contract, and you." There was more he wanted to tell Vale but couldn't with his parents listening. He couldn't say that he wanted to see Vale come again. He couldn't say it was more important to have Vale's submission than it was to have children. That what he most needed was to be sure that Vale *wanted* to be at Jason's feet, that he longed for Jason the same way Jason longed for him. That he lived for the chance to come on his knot, the same way Jason now lived for the chance to give it to him.

"Do you truly know what you want, Jason?" Vale asked. "You say you do, but do you understand the cost?"

He swallowed hard, gathering his courage, and kept his focus on Vale and Vale only. "I want you. Just the way you are. That's all that matters to me. I don't want your lands or your house or to force you to give me children. I want you on your knees begging for me to take you. The rest of this contract can go to hell."

His parents opened their mouths at the same time to speak, but Vale lifted his hand, an amused smile on his face as he studied Jason.

His eyes crinkled sweetly as his smile spread, and Jason's breath caught. *So beautiful.*

"And that sort of reckless, youthful eagerness is why your parents are here. To see you aren't led by your..." The slight pause let Jason fill in the word 'dick' before Vale carried on with, "*Purity of heart* into a contract that isn't satisfactory."

"I'll decide what's satisfactory," Jason growled. "Not you. Not them."

Vale shifted in his seat and Jason's nostrils twitched.

Did he smell…? Was that…? Was Vale getting wet for him? Here? In the middle of their meeting? It was the best scent in the world, sweet and musky, declaring that he'd made Vale want him with just his words alone.

Inspired by Vale's reaction, he added a rough grit to his voice like he'd used when playing alpha with Xan. "You're wrong that I don't know what I need. I want you. On your hands and knees, presenting for me. That's everything I want."

He was embarrassed to say these things in front of his parents, Yosef, and Bisme, but when Vale's eyes flared hot, and the scent of slick drifted even more strongly across the table to him, Jason didn't care who overheard. He meant every syllable down to his core.

"It's good your parents are here for you," Vale said again nervously, standing up from the table. "Imprinting, omega persuasion, and pheromone delirium being what they are, no one can really expect you to say anything else."

Jason knew he should be annoyed at being dismissed but he couldn't feel anything other than pride that he'd made Vale's voice shake.

"Excuse me. I need to…" Vale motioned toward the door. "I'll be back directly."

Vale was wet enough he had to go clean up. Wolf-god, *yes*. They just had to get these legal proceedings out of the way first. Then he'd claim him. Fuck him. And then fuck him again until they both passed out, sticky and sore.

*Yes.*

He admired Vale as he walked across the room, elegant and outwardly composed, even though his fingers shook and the scent of slick wafted in the air. His pert ass moved beneath his pants, muscled and juicy, and Jason licked his lips. He'd taste it eventually. He'd suck a kiss into every inch of those beautiful mounds of flesh, and then he'd lick Vale's hole until he begged to be bred.

Gritting his teeth, Jason wondered if he could leave the table to deal with his arousal, too. Vale wasn't the only one left needing. Wolf-god, why couldn't they deal with it together? He sipped the cold water in front of him and tried to get a grip.

If he left the table now, it would probably disappoint Vale. He still needed to be careful not to come across as too immature, too out of control. He knew he was on the verge of doing just that. Possibly already had.

Jason met his pater's eyes and found them sympathetic and a little amused. His father, though, glared after Vale, as though the predicament of his slick was a stalling technique to prevent having to sign the contract or agree to a live birth.

"If you give him a chance, you'll see that he's not being unreasonable," Yosef said once the door had clicked behind Vale's retreating form. "He wants to contract with your son, but he's fair. He knows what his physical limits are, and he's offering you a chance to make the smart choice." Yosef frowned. "Frankly, I tried to talk him out of giving you this option, but he likes Jason far too much to hem him in."

Jason frowned. "You mean he really *wants* me to take a surrogate?"

Yosef glanced toward Bisme and shrugged. "There are many ways to want, Jason. There's want and then there's *want*. And sometimes they contradict each other. Do you understand?"

He did, actually. He wanted a child, but he wanted Vale.

Both religious and state laws around reproduction were strict. Biologically, an alpha could breed with any omega in heat. The Holy Book of Wolf made it clear, however, that in the eyes of wolf-god it was imperative to cleave to one mate, through contract or imprint. According to the faith, it was to prevent the mistreatment of wolf-god's greatest gift to the world—omegas.

But historically, the guidelines in The Holy Book of Wolf

hadn't always been followed.

In the past, alphas, greedy for power and to replenish the population of the world, had forced omegas outside the claims of *Érosgápe* into a kind of breeding slavery. Some wealthy alphas bought multiple omegas to breed with, despite having an *Érosgápe* bond of their own.

They forced the dangerous breeding onto the purchased omegas, spreading their genes and priding themselves on the number of children they produced. Then they favored their *Érosgápe*'s children in terms of inheritance, leaving those from the slave omegas at a cultural and social disadvantage despite their paters' sacrifices.

Omegas rebelled against the unfair treatment and, eventually, there'd been an uprising from the Wolf Above Party, resulting in years upon years of religious law. This had the negative effect of squashing technological and scientific advancements, but it put an end to the use of omegas as breeding slaves. The *Érosgápe* relationship became exalted above all others, and the laws of the state were forced to echo these values.

Omegas remained the alpha's purview, whether the relationship was contracted or *Érosgápe*, but the alphas were leashed as well by requirements that they choose only one mate. Any child born outside of a contract would be a bastard denied any access to lines of inheritance. Any alpha dying childless was required to leave his belongings (after the death of his omega) to charities run by the state to prevent any attempt to subvert the laws.

These rules were sound on the surface, Jason knew, or at least better than what had gone before in that they prevented sick misuse of omegas, but they were rigid and lacked the nuance that negotiating life outside of theory seemed to require.

In his case, it meant he had to choose between having a child and experiencing the full bond of *Érosgápe* with Vale.

"Could we have a few minutes alone with our son?" Father

asked, nodding toward the door to the kitchen. "I've left refreshments on the table. Please help yourself while you wait."

Yosef and Bisme complied.

"Jason," Father said as soon as the door was shut. "You must carry on the family line. This isn't negotiable. Either he contracts for one live birth or you must consider alternatives."

"Listen to yourself, Yule," Pater insisted, striking a match to his second cigarette. "Do you hear what you're suggesting? You're telling Jason he has to put his omega's life in danger or give him up altogether."

"Sacrifices sometimes need to be made, Miner. For the greater good." He stared meaningfully at Pater, like there was something else behind his words. "You know that more than anyone."

Pater stabbed the air with his cigarette. "And who decides the greater good? You?" He snarled, "Don't you remember what it was like when we met? How you felt, how I felt, what it meant to us—"

"Yes, of course. It was bliss."

"It was *holy*," Pater snapped.

"Yes. But we were a good match. Appropriate. From comparable families. We were the same age. You had all the markings of a good breeder—"

"And if I hadn't? If I'd been like this man..." Pater sucked in a breath of smoke and poured it out. "If I'd refused to contract for a live birth from the start?"

"You wouldn't have done that. You wanted to be with me too much!"

"I didn't have any idea then that I couldn't carry! If I had, well, you might not like to hear what I might have chosen. If I hadn't contracted with you, I could have lived well on the allowance, continued with my music, played in the symphony, and never suffered all these losses!"

Silence fell hard. Jason shuddered at the chill. Father turned green as though he might throw up. "Are you saying you regret being *Érosgápe*?"

"Of course not. I'm saying think of all we've been through!"

"It's not the same!"

"It is!" Pater got up from the table, pacing away from Father and back again. In his long fingers, the cigarette shook. "You have no idea what it's like growing up an omega, spending your whole life knowing that you're going to be claimed by someone, taken over body, soul, and possessions." He took a puff from the cigarette, waving away Father's attempt to interrupt. Smoke followed him. "No amount of fairytale spinning from parents, teachers, and books can take that terror away. The uncertainty this man has lived with his whole life? The heats he's suffered through?"

"Oh, he fully admits he hasn't suffered—"

Pater growled, and Father backtracked immediately. "I'm sorry. I didn't mean it that way."

"You did. You meant it exactly that way," Pater said coldly, freezing in place and staring Father down. "I'm ashamed of you."

Father paled. "Miner, please. I didn't...I'm sorry."

"If you wish that man had even one heat without help, Wolf-god save you, Yule."

"Miner, I swear to all that's holy I didn't mean it that way." He reached out in remorse. "Forgive me."

Pater glared at Father until he lowered his gaze and ducked his head. Then he turned to Jason, pointing at him with his cigarette. "Remember this. This is the power he'll have over you. You may hold the assets, the legal rights, and be able to subjugate him during sex, but you'll never be satisfied a moment in your life if he's not happy. Do you trust him enough for that?"

Jason felt a trickle of sweat slide down his temple. He wanted to trust Vale. The idea of crawling to him, begging for his forgiveness didn't horrify him the way it should. He'd do it happily if it meant

Vale was his.

Pater touched Father's shoulder. "Chin up." When Father met his eyes, he said softly, "I'll consider accepting your apology when you've made me believe you hold this man in the esteem he deserves as a human being."

Father groaned and covered his hands with his face. "Miner, you're killing me."

Pater flicked a glance to Jason but then returned his full focus to Father. He stabbed his cigarette out before taking hold of Father's chin and whispering, "Nothing you say here today is going to change the outcome of *anything*. Do you understand me?"

Father shoulders curved. He tugged his chin out of Pater's grasp and rubbed a hand through his hair.

At that moment, the door opened from the hall and Vale entered, his face red above his beard, and his eyes wary. Seeing the attorneys gone, he raised a brow at Jason and then asked, "Am I interrupting? Should I go again?"

"No," Jason said quickly. "We're ready. Aren't we, Father?"

Father took hold of Pater's free hand and kissed his fingers gently. "We are. If you'll have a seat, Vale, I'll get Yosef and Bisme. We'll leave aside the discussion of births for now." He rose and paused before opening the door to the kitchen. "When I return, we'll begin with the next item on the agenda. The plan for your assets."

# CHAPTER SIXTEEN

VALE'S HEAD THROBBED.

He'd refused Yosef's offer for company the night before and drowned out the awfulness of the negotiations by consuming half a tumbler of gin. Now he felt like his nerves were on the outside of his skin, and his miniscule breakfast threatened to crawl out of his mouth.

Gingerly, he sipped tea and leaned back in his desk chair. The late-autumn sun filtered in through the windows as he watched a bird pick at lingering mulberries on the tree near the back of the garden.

Zephyr was curled in his lap, kneading the smooth material of his robe and pajama bottoms, putting needle-like pricks in the fabric. He didn't care. The allowance the Sabels would give him would buy him a dozen of these robes a week if he wanted. But that didn't quell his anxiety about the future or the magnitude of what signing the contract, or not, would mean for his life.

Poor Jason. He hadn't known what to make of the tension in the room. His was a good heart and he clearly wanted what was best for Vale even at the expense of his own desires. He must get that generosity from his pater, because his father certainly didn't share it.

Vale had wanted to strangle Yule Sabel's handsome neck when he'd tried to insist on a live birth with so much sanctimoniousness. As if he wasn't a monster knocking up his omega every heat and forcing him to endure the loss of it! As if he had any moral standing at all! He rubbed his temples and glared out the window at the cleared-out garden. Who did the man think he was asking Vale to risk his life for the sake of passing on his callous genes?

Zephyr stopped kneading, her ears perking up, and a meow wrenched from her throat as she bolted from his lap and out the door into the hallway heading for the kitchen. Vale hoped he'd put food out for her when he woke but couldn't remember now. His brain was packed with itchy cotton balls of irritable rage. She'd screech if there wasn't anything in her bowl when she got there.

He rested his head against the back of his chair. Paper lay strewn over his desk with unfinished poems he'd started the night before when he was drunk off his ass. Not a one was any good. They were all about Jason, and that was the worst thing they could be about. Because he didn't want anyone to know how the thought of not being with the boy made him feel like he was being sliced to ribbons inside. He hadn't eaten anything solid for dinner the night before, and his stomach rebelled against tea, even.

He rubbed sleep from his eyes and sat up straighter, grabbing all the paper from his desk and shoving it into an overstuffed drawer without looking at what he'd written. There might be something good to salvage later when he wasn't so raw about it all.

His mind slipped back to the negotiations the day before. He wasn't sure what had happened when he left the room to clean up the annoying slick that continued to plague him whenever Jason asserted himself in any way, shape, or form, but the atmosphere had changed when he came back. Not necessarily for the better, but not for the worse, either. They'd discussed the properties dispassionately—Vale refusing to give up his home and Jason backing him. Then he agreed to allow them to fix up the cabin his parents had left to him. They could decide to sell or keep it once that was done.

But beneath it all, despite the progress made, he'd felt the current of truth pulling him farther and farther away from a signed contract.

When it was over, they'd attempted to give him details for when he should arrive tonight for Feast of the Expectant Wolf, but he'd cut Miner short, saying, "I don't feel it's appropriate to share such an important feast when the negotiations are still so unsettled. It's intended for family members as a celebration of new life and family is something I might never be."

Jason had looked gutted, but he hadn't protested.

The phone on Vale's desk had rung several times last night while he'd been scribbling furiously and gargling mouthfuls of gin. He hadn't answered it. He knew who it was. But what would he tell the boy? "I've led you on. I've let you think..."

Wolf-god, he couldn't even complete the sentence in his own mind. Not even in the light of morning with a thundering headache proving he was sober. He wanted Jason so much, wanted desperately to contract with him, and yet...

A tap on his window startled him and his head jerked up. His heart somersaulted. He swallowed hard and rose slowly to go unfasten the lock and raise the sash.

"Hi." Jason pushed his hair out of his eyes. They were swollen and he didn't look like he'd slept all night. The cold breeze flowed into the room, chilling Vale through his pajama bottoms and robe.

"You should learn to use a phone." Vale crossed his arms over his chest.

"You should learn to answer one," Jason shot back.

Vale's cock rushed with blood, and he groaned as he fought to keep from getting an erection. Simultaneously, his asshole grew wet. "Fuck," he whispered. "This has to stop."

Jason's nostrils flared, but he said nothing.

"When someone doesn't pick up the phone, it usually means they want to be alone," Vale went on. "It doesn't mean come to their house and harass them."

"I'm here to let you know that Mox and the other betas will be here in an hour. We're working in the back again today like we planned. I'm sorry I bothered you." He stepped back from the window and headed out into the garden, where he picked up a shovel and started to chop through a matted mass of weeds.

Vale shivered in the breeze and lifted his hand to shut the window, but stopped. He could smell Jason's sadness, taste it in his mouth, and it hurt him deep inside like a thorn twisting in his gut. "Come here," he called out, leaning through the window. "Jason, please, come here."

Jason threw the shovel down and trudged over with a sullen expression. Vale hadn't ever seen his baby alpha looking so dispirited and it was all his fault. "I'm sorry I'm being unkind to you this morning. You don't deserve it. I'm a bit hungover."

*And confused. And scared.*

"What about ignoring my calls last night?"

"You didn't deserve that, either."

"What's wrong," Jason asked, stepping close with his hands out beseechingly. "What did I do? Was it the kitchen? Do you want me to apologize for that?"

Vale's throat grew tight. "No, it wasn't anything you did at all."

*It's what I did years ago. It's what you deserve that I can't give you. It's that I like you, Jason, and you deserve the best. And that's not me.*

Vale chewed on his cheek to keep the words inside.

"Talk to me. What went wrong between when we were together in the kitchen and yesterday when you showed up for negotiations? Was it my father's attitude? Pater took care of him."

Vale's heart skipped. "It does have a great deal to do with your father. But it also has to do with me."

Jason gazed at him warily; his eyes looked bruised. Had he cried during the night? Wolf-god, help him if he made this boy cry and he hadn't even told him the truth yet. He needed to confess the full reason why Jason should look for a surrogate. Jason deserved a better omega. That Vale knew for sure.

"Your father and your pater…" He rubbed at his aching head. Why had he nearly drained the tumbler? He could barely think.

"What about them?"

"I heard from a source, a *discreet* source, that your pater regularly uses…" he broke off. "Oh, for wolf's sake, you can't stand out there looking at me like that. Come around to the kitchen. We'll talk. But that's it. Nothing else."

His asshole quivered and he gritted his teeth. *Nothing else*, he repeated silently.

Jason nodded and turned without a word toward the kitchen. When Vale reached the door, Jason was already removing his shoes.

"They're not muddy yet," Vale pointed out. "You could wear them in."

Jason shrugged. "They're dirty enough."

Vale glanced over his shoulder at the dishes piled in the sink and the mess of kibble Zephyr had left on the floor. "It wouldn't matter."

Jason moved past him into the kitchen, his socks on inside-out from what Vale could tell. He hovered by the table, waiting to be invited to sit, and Vale motioned for him to do so and then grabbed the last clean teacup from the cabinet and poured the dregs from his teapot into it.

He handed it to Jason as he sat down next to him. It was probably too close to be wise, but he needed the closeness for comfort almost as much as Jason did.

Jason put the cup on the table without tasting it. "Thanks," he said, quietly. "So you heard something about my parents that you don't like?"

Vale swallowed. "I don't know how I feel about it, actually."

Jason waited, his perfect lips trembling, but otherwise he kept his expression neutral.

Vale summoned courage and spit it out. "Does your father impregnate your pater even knowing he can't carry to term? And then does he require your pater to use illegal abortifacient drugs to dispose of the baby?"

There. He'd said it. Now for Jason's reaction.

Jason hunched over the teacup, closing his eyes. "Yes. But it's not what you're thinking."

"What is it then? And how do you know what I'm thinking?"

Jason covered his face. "You think my father is a cruel alpha who cares more for his own pleasure than my pater's health."

Vale didn't say anything. He didn't have to.

Jason met his gaze and whispered, "My father would give his life for Pater. It's not like that at all."

"Then why doesn't he use condoms to protect him?"

"Pater is severely allergic to the government supplies and the alternatives are..." He spread his hands and shook his head.

The government's position on condoms was touch and go. They supplied them only because the outcry was too great when they didn't allow any at all. And they'd cracked down on what they called 'less safe' condoms over the last half-decade especially.

The ones they provided were made with a protein known to be problematic for many omegas, though he'd never had an issue, thankfully. And Urho reported that they dulled sensation significantly, especially during knotting. Of course, the government was much more invested in ensuring reproduction between legally contracted pairs than family planning. They didn't want condoms to be safe or pleasurable. They wanted their use to be rare.

"I see."

"Did you really think Father didn't care enough about Pater to protect him? That he'd impregnate him against his will?" His eyes filled with tears. "That he'd try to make me do the same to you? And that I would?"

Vale swallowed. "It had crossed my mind. Yes."

"I'd rather die than hurt you."

"Your death would hurt me," Vale whispered. "Irreparably."

Which was true but also said way too much about how far their bond had come already and the danger they were both in now. He had to come clean soon. He had to tell Jason the truth about his past. Then Jason would opt to take a surrogate—no matter how much Vale wanted him—no matter how sweet a game they'd been playing.

The doorbell rang, and Jason started. "That'll be Mox."

"He's early."

"He probably thought he'd beat me here." Jason headed toward the kitchen door. "Tell them I'm out back." With his hand on the doorknob, he said quietly but with an authority that made Vale's knees weak, "This isn't over. You will talk to me and we will fix this."

Jason walked out the door and shut it firmly behind him.

Vale wanted to go drag Jason back, fall to his knees, and tell him the truth about his past. He wanted to feel washed clean by Jason's unconditional acceptance and love. Then he wanted to suck Jason's cock in desperate gratitude, and present himself to be fucked. When Jason pressed into him, the shame over his past would finally evaporate. He'd be safe and loved. Whole and complete with his alpha, the way he was meant to be. His legs shook as his omega glands released a wealth of slick.

At least he hadn't showered yet.

After opening the front door to direct Mox and the crew to the back of the house, he went up to his room. Passing Zephyr sleeping in the center of his bed, he turned into his bathroom and stripped off. His body felt feverish from the hangover and he let the shower run cooler than usual to siphon away some of the heat.

Then he dried himself, brushed his teeth and hair, and slipped on a soft pair of loose pants and an old t-shirt. He climbed onto the bed by Zephyr, trying not to disturb her, and stared at the window over the back yard. The view was of tree limbs and a wide, blue sky. He couldn't see Jason and the betas out there working, but he felt him there.

Even though they were at odds, knowing Jason was outside his window working for him made him feel safe.

Tender.

His alpha wanted to make things good for him, make things right. Never mind that he had all the doubts in the universe clogging up his brain and heart. Right now, Jason was taking care of him. He'd never had that comfort in his adult life before. He'd always been alone. But for now he wasn't. He wrapped the feeling around himself like a blanket.

When the work songs began and he heard Jason's sweet baritone lifting with the rest, it was easy to drift off to sleep.

"SHOULDN'T YOUR OMEGA be watching you woo him?" Mox asked, shooting a sly grin Jason's way before nodding toward the obviously empty study.

"He's got other things to do, I guess," Jason murmured, darting a glance at the house.

"Trouble in paradise already?"

Jason glared at Mox and that shut him up pretty quickly. They'd managed to clear out everything they needed to get rid of and now they just had to trundle off the wheelbarrows and dump them in the truck before they could get to planting the bulbs and bushes Mox had brought.

As they pushed the wheelbarrows through the side yard and into the front, Jason froze. Urho stood on the walk halfway to the house, brows lifted in confusion and surprise. He wore a jaunty bowtie that made Jason think of Xan.

The air between them seemed to crackle and then Urho smiled warmly, like he had a right to greet Jason like a host in Jason's omega's front yard.

"Well, this is a surprise!" he called, motioning at Jason's filthy work clothes and the sweat running down the side of his face. "I didn't imagine you were the kind of alpha to actually *do* the work for his omega. I figured you'd try to buy his happiness. I'm impressed."

Jason abandoned his wheelbarrow and ignored the curious glances from Mox and his crew. He tossed aside his work gloves as he advanced toward Urho without a smile. "Is Vale expecting you?" He came to a halt in front of Urho and crossed his arms over his chest.

"No. I thought I'd drop by. I wanted to see how he was holding up after negotiations yesterday." Urho's brows lowered as he observed Jason closely. "Should I be worried about him?"

Jason glanced over his shoulder to where the men were dumping the content of the wheelbarrows into the truck and then looked toward the house at the lace curtains waving in an open window upstairs. Was it Vale's room? He didn't know. There was a lot he didn't know about Vale. And maybe Urho *was* his rival in one way, but in a much bigger way he wasn't. He cared about Vale, too, wanted him safe and happy, and he knew Vale better than most anyone. He'd been his lover after all.

Swallowing his pride, Jason met Urho's gaze. "I don't know if you should be worried, but I am. I'm worried about everything, actually."

Urho's brows creased even more deeply and he gripped Jason's shoulder, peering at him like he could see right into his mind. He shot a glance toward the beta workers, taking their measure, and then smiled gently down at Jason. "Are you hungry? Lunch time is coming up. I'd planned to ask Vale to join me, but you look like you could use some advice."

Jason peered toward the house. He'd thought he might get another chance alone with Vale to talk things through, but at this point he didn't even know what he could say.

Urho followed his gaze. "I was going to ask him to head over to Alamanga Avenue with me to eat at one of the filthy food booths he loves so much. I'm sure he doesn't have anything decent inside. Or if he does, it's barely enough for himself. Why don't we walk over to Alamanga together? We can talk and grab some lunch. Then you can win points with Vale by bringing him a grilled sundried tomato and goat cheese sandwich. That's a favorite of his."

A pang of jealousy rang in him that Urho knew Vale's favorites and he didn't, but he smiled and nodded his gratitude. "Yeah, that sounds good. Are you sure you want to? Wouldn't you rather spend the time with Vale?"

"If I know Vale, he won't let me help him without a fight. You're his alpha, whether I like it or not, and it's your responsibility now to handle his moods." He smiled at Jason. "Believe me, you'll need all the practice you can get."

Jason took lunch orders from Mox and his crew, chuckling under his breath at the size of some of their orders. They'd probably been barely satisfied by Vale's sandwich and pineapple slices the other day, he mused. And he'd been too distracted by Vale's *everything* to think about it.

The walk to Alamanga was enjoyable. The weather was brisk but not too cold, and the pale sunlight warmed their shoulders and the tops of their heads. Urho kept the conversation light on the way over, asking Jason about what he and Mox had planned for Vale's back garden.

"As a courting gesture, it's a nice one, but how long will it take to see the fruits of your labor?" Urho asked as they walked across the Middleton Bridge, passing into the part of town set aside for beta-run businesses. The colorful signs declaring sales on everything from books to wedding suits were their own kind of garden, holding onto brightness even as winter came on quickly.

"This spring and summer the garden might not be as beautiful as it will be, but by next year it should be more mature. I think Vale will enjoy it." Jason loved working outside even though Father complained that it made his trousers dirty, and he had plenty of ideas for cross-breeding experiments he wanted to do with various flowers of similar species.

"So you're planning to live in his house then?" Urho asked, obviously surprised. "It seems a step down for a man of your family's status."

"If Vale likes his house, I don't see why we should sell it. I'm only nineteen. I don't need to start worrying about my place in society yet. We can make our home happily in his house and then, when I'm older, we can move if we want to do that."

His heart twisted and a dread fell on him like a heavy blanket. It felt like bad luck to speak of his dreams of their life together to Urho when he hadn't talked to Vale about them yet. Especially when Vale seemed so hostile the last few days.

"Vale is a homebody for the most part. Not that he doesn't have a wild streak in him, because he definitely does." Urho's lips pressed together, and he cleared his throat. "So, what are your family's plans for the Feast of the Expectant Wolf tonight?"

"Vale was supposed to come, but after negotiations yesterday he bowed out, saying the feast is for close family only and he didn't know if we'd ever be that." The pain in his chest made him catch his breath. "What are your plans for the night?"

Urho sent him a sharp, perceptive look, but as he waved at a beta shopkeeper sweeping the sidewalk in front of a store, he let the moment go. "Since I lost Riki, I don't do too much on this night. But I've been invited to Zim's house for the evening as a thanks for helping with his brother's heat. It will start next week, and they are all relieved to have an alpha on standby to help. I've asked another alpha friend of mine to be on call, as well. If the young man does suffer from nymphomania, his heat will be too much for me to handle alone. It might even be too much for two of us to deal with. So my friend is looking for a third unattached alpha." Urho shook his head. "Nymphomania is a real shame. Not that it's the omega's fault entirely, of course. The gene manipulations of our forefathers have many unforeseeable consequences and sometimes nymphomania is one of them."

"Interminable heat," Jason corrected, surprised that Urho spoke so openly about genetic alterations. Religious adherents insisted that wolf-god alone was responsible. "Nymphomania is an old-fashioned term."

"Now you sound like Vale. The thing is interminable heat only applies to heat. Nymphomania applies to the entire sex drive of the omega and can continue outside of the heat itself. That's a distinction that the liberals don't want to acknowledge. Nymphomania is a compassionate term. Otherwise, the omegas are just…" he trailed off, thinking. "What's the Old World term? Sluts. I believe it was considered a slur even then. Promiscuous and overly invested in sex. That's a negative trait by our culture's standards and has apparently been considered so deep into the past. At least the idea of nymphomania allows us some pity, gives some leeway by acknowledging that the omega suffers from an incurable illness and simply can't help himself."

Jason didn't reply. He didn't understand why there were so many rules around sex. Why couldn't uncontracted omegas enjoy as much sex as they could physically weather with as many alphas as they wanted? Especially if they weren't in an *Érosgápe* pairing? And for that matter, why couldn't Xan be with other alphas? Who did it hurt?

He knew Pater would say it was about control and paternity. They only had to look at the relaxed rules with betas to understand how much childbearing came into play with the laws around omegas and alphas. And yet, while he didn't want to see Vale with other alphas if he could satisfy him himself, he didn't see why contracted matches couldn't make their own rules. They didn't have the same *Érosgápe* attachment. They didn't have to fight their own natures quite so much. They could be more like betas, who were known for non-monogamous matches. Why not? Who did it serve for sex to be so tightly controlled?

Before Urho could introduce another topic or carry on with the current one, they arrived at Alamanga Avenue and split up to get their own lunch from the different food booths of their choice. They'd agreed to grab Mox's crew's orders and Vale's sandwich after they'd eaten their own, so it would all still be warm when Jason arrived back at Vale's house. The street was colorful and hectic, with alphas, omegas, and betas bustling between booths, hawking goods on blankets and in stalls on the streets, and dashing in and out of stores on their lunch breaks.

With a pineapple steak-on-a-stick in one hand and a bag of sweet potato fries in the other, Jason followed Urho to a bench set back from Alamanga Avenue on a less bustling side street. The calls of vendors echoed around the corner, but for the most part, they were alone.

"Vale's bucking hard, is he?" Urho said around a bite of his beet salad.

Jason shrugged, popping a sweet potato fry into his mouth and chewing slowly. He took his time replying. "He seemed open to the idea of contracting until yesterday. Then everything at the negotiation table went wrong. My father was in a terrible mood and was short tempered. Vale tried to talk me into taking a surrogate." Jason gestured sharply with his steak-on-a-stick. "I don't want a surrogate. I want Vale."

"In all likelihood, he can't have children," Urho said matter-of-factly. "If you want children, then you should take a surrogate."

Jason groaned. "I'm nineteen. What do I know about what I'll want in the future? Children seem great and all, but right now, I want Vale."

Urho nodded. "And he knows all of that, of course. He knows you can't predict what you'll want and that you'd choose him right now. He wants you, too. That's the way of it."

The steak was delicious, perfectly flavored with pineapple and tender as could be. Jason took some time to chew and swallow before he said, "It doesn't seem right that we can't choose each other, the way wolf-god wanted, and deal with a family later."

"In the old times, there were so many babies that some were killed or left alone to be raised by whatever kind soul came along," Urho mused. "Now children are so precious it's against the law to end a pregnancy, much less abandon a child. It's chilling to think of a world where so many were unwanted."

Jason thought of his pater, who definitely *wanted* and yet couldn't have more children. He thought of Vale who, from what he understood, faced a future that was much the same.

"Are alpha condoms really so bad?" he asked softly. "Would impregnating a contracted surrogate make up for turning my back on the bond with Vale?"

"You're *Érosgápe*. That won't ever go away. You'll suffer without him, period. Perhaps a child would make up for it, but I'm childless so I can't speak to the experience personally. To be truthful, having been bonded with Riki, I can't imagine walking away from that for any reason at all. Not even for my own life."

Jason swallowed hard and shoved the remainder of the steak-on-a-stick into the bag of fries. He'd eat it later.

Urho went on, speaking casually between bites of his beet salad. "As for alpha condoms, the ones the government hands out do dull sensation to a degree. But sex is still pleasurable. Much of the enjoyment is emotional—seeing the omega you're with delirious with pleasure, the various orgasms they enjoy, and knowing that you're doing that to them."

Jason's fists balled up, but he held back the urge to punch Urho. He hated knowing Urho was thinking of Vale in that moment, remembering the pleasure he'd brought to him. He squeezed his eyes against the jealousy, reminding himself that it was better Urho had helped Vale than for Vale to have ever suffered.

Of course, Urho had helped him between heats, too.

A lot, from what Jason could tell.

But who was he to determine what a grown omega did with his sex life? Hadn't he just been mentally railing at the rules around sex? He'd have to work harder not to be a hypocrite.

"If you choose Vale over a family, I don't know that you'll have regrets." Urho frowned. "You will likely outlive him, of course. If, at that point, you feel you've missed out on a family, you could contract with a younger, widowed or uncontracted omega and reproduce with him. No one would blame you."

Jason felt sick at the very idea. "Why haven't you done that?" he asked, curious. "Do you not want children?"

Urho's shoulders slumped, and his eyes glinted with pain. "Riki wanted children very much. It was his dream to give me a beautiful son. We struggled to get pregnant. He wasn't as fertile as some omegas. But when he did conceive, he was ecstatic. I couldn't share that with someone I didn't love. Not having been so close to perfection." He sat his salad aside, his face grey.

Jason was quiet a few moments before he whispered, "I'm sorry."

Urho shook himself. "Nothing to be sorry about. It's in the past." He turned to Jason, his expression all business now. "So what will you choose? Vale or a surrogate? I'm sure your parents want you to take a surrogate. Carrying on the line becomes so important to men as they age. They forget, I think, the way the bond consumes."

"Pater wants me to choose Vale, I think. And Father wants me to take a surrogate, but that's because he doesn't want Pater's suffering in having me to be in vain."

"You're going to choose Vale," Urho said knowingly. "And that will be a beautiful choice. He's a good man. He'll make you happy. Though he won't clean the house. You can give up on that right now."

Jason laughed softly. "I do want to choose him, but he has to choose me, too. He's having doubts about signing the contract."

Urho huffed. "That sounds like him. He's not accustomed to commitments. He's been on his own a long time. Even our relationship wasn't a committed one. He had other dalliances." Urho rolled his eyes. "Not that he suffers from nymphomania," he clarified. "But he's never liked to feel locked in. For years, he had used the excuse that he couldn't let himself get too attached because he never knew when his alpha might turn up. But then he let go of that idea and claimed to simply enjoy the freedom. I think, deep down, Vale doesn't think he deserves a commitment. He sees himself as damaged goods." Urho gazed at Jason meaningfully. "But surely you've realized that by now?"

Jason nodded. "How do I reassure him?"

"What you need to know about Vale is that he really wants to be taken firmly in hand."

"What do you mean?"

"He likes to be in charge of his own life, sure, but he *loves* to be told what to do. In bed, especially."

Jason thought he might have to kill Urho if he said even one more word.

"So that's how you handle this," Urho said, eyes narrowing thoughtfully. "Tell him he's going to sign the contract because you both want it. *Tell* him to submit. *Make* him be your omega." Urho shrugged. "That's the attitude I took during his heats. He melted like butter every time. And not just Vale. It's how I've handled every omega I've ever dealt with. It's what an alpha does, Jason. It's what omegas need."

Jason tried to imagine Father telling Pater to submit to *anything*. But all he could picture was Father gently stroking Pater's cheek and whispering how much he loved him.

Urho picked up his beet salad again and took another bite. "Ever since his parents died, he's looked to his friends to care for him. Vale's hungry for a sense of safety. He gets annoyed with me for not sharing all of his liberal points of view, but when it comes down to it, he likes that he can count on me. He likes that I took care of him when he needed me. He depends on Yosef and Rosen for that kind of love, too. As his alpha, you can fill that need for him now. Prove to him that you're strong, consistent, and dependable, and that you have his best interests at heart. He'll give you what you want." Urho smiled, "Even if that means you'll have to accept a childless contract."

They hit the food booths again before heading back. Urho gathered Mox's crews' orders and Jason stood in the long line for the specialty grilled cheese sandwich for Vale.

Heading back across the bridge toward Oak Avenue, Jason asked, "Do you resent that I came along and took him from you?"

Urho stared into the middle distance, sucking on his teeth. "I've loved him a long time but he's never loved me quite the same way."

Jason thought of Xan. Guilt sat on his heart.

"I don't resent you, Jason. Not so long as you make him happy. That, of course, remains to be seen. But if you hurt him..." Urho shook his head and his dark eyes glinted dangerously. "Let's just leave it at that, shall we?"

A puppy ran past them dragging his leash and a young beta raced after him. Jason handed Urho the bags he was carrying and took off to help. Once the puppy was safely back in his human's hands, he returned, breathless, to Urho's side.

Urho lifted a brow. "You're too soft by half. Vale could tear you apart if he wanted." He clucked his tongue. "Don't let him. Be tough with him. Remember the Holy Book gives you command over him."

"I'm not very religious."

"Who cares? The last thing you want is for Vale to think you can't or won't hold him. All of him. Every part. Even the ugly bits. Remember, he's been lonely for a long time, mostly by his own design. Don't let him push you away now. Not if you truly want this."

The house on Oak Avenue looked as inviting as it had the first time Jason had laid eyes on it. He and Urho parted ways at the gate.

"I'll check in on him by phone later," Urho said, when Jason asked if he still wanted to come in and see Vale.

Jason juggled the bags of food and tried to put out his hand to shake goodbye, but Urho just laughed and caught a falling bag.

"Thank you," Jason said, taking it from him again. "For the advice. I don't really know what I'm doing."

Urho grinned. "You'll be all right. You've got a good heart. A strong, alpha heart." He gripped Jason's shoulder and then looked to the side of the house where Mox was rounding the corner with an empty planting crate. "Good luck."

# CHAPTER SEVENTEEN

VALE WOKE FROM his nap with an ominous prickling feeling under his skin. He recognized it immediately. No amount of denial would put a stop to what was coming. He was probably, at most, four days away from the beginning of his heat.

Juice cooled him down, and he drank the rest of the bottle Rosen had left in his fridge several days before. He sat at the kitchen table and stared at Zephyr's tail as it swished, swished, swished while she glared out the side window at several puddle-bathing robins.

What was he going to do?

He couldn't contract immediately with Jason just to have him around for the heat, and he couldn't ask Urho to help him when he was already feeling a growing bond with Jason. Wolf-god, was this going to be the rest of his life? If he didn't sign a contract dooming Jason to a childless future and tying himself to a morally dubious family that could be taken down with one indiscretion, would he spend the rest of his life torn about how to deal with his heats?

What about regular, day-to-day sex? Was this desire for Jason going to interfere with obtaining that, too?

He rubbed his eyes. The fact that he was thinking about sex instead of whether or not signing a contract with Jason was the right thing to do *in general* said everything he needed to know about just how close he was to the heat itself. He was always motivated by sex, but when a heat was coming, it was nearly all he could think about. He needed to stay away from Jason so he could think clearly about the negotiations and not fall prey to any more inappropriate sexual activity between them.

A knock came at the back door and he cursed softly. That would be the workers, or possibly Jason, expecting some kind of lunch. And he was fresh out of food options. Again. Zephyr meowed and scampered out of the room, skidding as she hit the smooth hallway, and then slamming into a wall. Zephyr picked herself up and continued on her path with a dignity Vale imagined only Old World royalty could muster.

"Coming," he called, when the knock rang out again, and glanced down at his loose pajama bottoms and equally loose t-shirt. He hadn't worn real clothes since the negotiations. Not having a job had some benefits, he supposed, like catching up on his sleep, but he wasn't sure that wearing pajamas constantly was really one of them.

"I brought you lunch," Jason said, as soon as the door opened. "And the crew, too. You don't have to worry about feeding them today." He thrust out a paper bag, and Vale's mouth watered as the familiar scent hit.

"Grilled sundried tomato and goat cheese sandwich? How did you know?"

Jason shrugged. "I'm your alpha. It's my job to know."

Vale blamed the coming heat on the fact that his knees went weak. "Thank you." He took the bag and nearly invited Jason in before remembering he needed to keep his distance.

"I'll get back to work now," Jason said, smiling.

"Did you eat?"

"At the food booths, yeah." Jason licked his lips and said, "You didn't watch us working this morning."

"I took a nap." He left off the fact that he'd done so in part because he felt so safe with Jason outside. "I needed the sleep."

Because his heat was coming on and his body was storing up

269

strength while simultaneously shutting down his digestive system and thickening his colon to make way for the stress of knotting.

"Watch us this afternoon," Jason said commandingly. "Be in your study. I want you there."

Vale's asshole went wet and quivery, and he had to grit his teeth to keep from issuing the invitation inside.

Jason smiled, the light of the early afternoon sun glinting on his teeth. "Say you will."

"I will." Vale's voice was rough.

He shouldn't. But he would. What harm did it do?

Vale shut the door on Jason's retreating back and then sat down at the kitchen table. The delicious sandwich tasted sufficiently good to overcome his reluctance to eat. He managed half of it before he couldn't stuff in another bite.

Four days.

If he was lucky.

He left the bag and the half-eaten sandwich on the kitchen table and trailed into the library. Tired again already, he flopped down on the sofa with a book, warm blanket, and a cat, angling his head so he could see out the open window. A chilly breeze blew in—the weather called for a fire, truly—but it calmed Vale's prickling heat and he stretched a bare foot out to feel it more fully.

Jason lifted a hand toward him but didn't approach, instead going back to planting and tilling, digging and smoothing, and generally getting dirty all over. His cheeks glowed and his hair shone in the sun. Vale's balls drew up and his cock grew thick just watching the way he moved so effortlessly. His alpha would be big and strong one day.

Drowsily, he marinated in low-grade lust, pretending to read while desperately searching his mind for a solution to the heat problem. Finally, unable to come to any reliable conclusion, he put the book aside and napped again. His dream was sweetly sexual:

Jason by the seaside sporting a tan. He stood naked where the tide raced in, his cock in his hand, jerking himself off slowly while Vale knelt at his feet, waves rushing over his thighs, mouth open, straining to capture another burst of that delicious flavor on his tongue.

He woke with a start as the word "Goodbye" drifted into his study. Zephyr meeped and jumped from her perch on his thighs, crawling beneath the sofa. The afternoon light shifted, gracing the room with a golden sheen. Vale stretched. His cock was still half-hard and his asshole was as wet as the waves in his dream.

"Thanks for your help," Jason's voice said, and Vale spotted him alone in the garden, shading the sun from his eyes with his hand. "Send the bill and I'll take care of it. And don't forget the extra you spent on the bulbs from Calitan."

"It's been a pleasure working with you," Mox's voice called from what sounded like the side of the house. "Too bad your pater would probably frown on you helping us out in his gardens this spring."

Jason smiled. "It's unlikely he'd allow it, but if I'm still living there by the time you start, I might sneak out and try."

"Good luck to you with everything, especially that omega," Mox said with a tone that somehow implied he thought Jason would need it. Vale couldn't argue with that opinion, though. They both needed luck and Vale needed some kind of clarity. Urgently.

Then there was silence. Jason stood in the garden, looking around proudly. Vale didn't know what all they'd planted but he had to admit that even from his position on the sofa the place appeared neat and held an air of promise it'd been lacking for years.

Jason's gaze fell toward the open window of the study and directly to Vale. He walked through the newly cleared paths and came to stand right outside just as he had that first morning.

"You smell amazing. Like slick and sweat." Jason's voice was husky. "What were you dreaming about in there, Sleeping Beauty?"

"Of the shore. I haven't been in too long. I miss the ocean."

Jason's grin was thrilled. "We'll go for our first heat together, then. My parents have a cottage there. We'll head over in the days leading up, when you know it's coming, and enjoy the water before we lock ourselves up in the bedroom for the duration."

Vale swallowed. "That sounds nice."

Jason leaned against the windowsill and glanced back over his shoulder like he was making sure the men really were gone. "Come here."

Vale rose from the sofa like a hypnotist's thrall, aware that he should resist, but powerless to disobey. His feet propelled him to the window. The smell of Jason's sweat drifting in on the chilly breeze made Vale want to lick him.

"Get on your knees." Jason's blue irises shone with purpose.

"Jason…"

"Do it."

Vale swallowed hard and submitted. The polished brick floor was tough on his knees, but it was a solid presence in the ocean of desire that claimed him. He stared down at the bricks, taking deep breaths and trying to find his sanity, but Jason's clean sweat filled his nose, and he trembled with need. His skin prickled and burned, a harbinger of the heat to come.

"Show me your dick," Jason said thickly, as though in a trance.

Vale's shaking fingers got his pajama pants loose, and he pushed them down around his thighs, baring his cock to the cold air from the window. It didn't calm his ardor at all. In fact, the breeze's touch made his cock flex and a bead of pre-come oozed from the slit.

"Oh, wolf-god," Jason gasped.

"It's cut." Vale stared down at his arrow-shaped flesh, a worry creeping into his lustful haze that it was strange. That Jason wouldn't like it. Another mark against him. Along with so many others.

"I love it. It's beautiful. Like a flesh mushroom." Jason's cheeks flushed deeper. "Your pre-come smells so good. Let me taste it."

Vale shivered, nipples aching.

"Catch it on your finger. Hold it out to me."

Vale flicked a glance up, and when he saw Jason's wide, lust-blow pupils, a whimper wrenched from his throat. He ran his index finger over the tip of his cock, gathering the drop of pre-come, and lifted his shaking hand toward the window.

Jason moaned, taking Vale's fingers, smelling them first. Then, staring into Vale's eyes, he sucked his forefinger into his mouth. Vale convulsed all over at the delicious, hot suction and cried out softly. His balls drew up hard and he nearly came on the spot.

Jason closed his eyes, greedy, slurping, and making Vale's entire finger wet.

"Please," Vale whispered.

Jason peeled his eyes open and released Vale's hand. "Finger yourself."

"I...we..." Vale's brain scrambled. There was a reason they shouldn't, a reason why he should make Jason go home—but he couldn't think of what that was now. He wanted him so badly. The growing bond between them wrapped Vale in weaving threads of pleasure, undeniable and needy.

"Touch your hole. Do it."

Vale shivered as he pressed his wet finger between his ass cheeks and slid it against the place where he craved Jason's dick. He moaned as he traced his clenching, wet anus, and more slick rushed out, slipping down his thighs and wetting his hand.

Outside the window, Jason worked open his pants, taking out his beautiful cock to tease the foreskin back and forth over the bulbous head before stroking it slowly. He gazed at Vale, as he jacked himself, his dick sticking in through the open pane.

Instinctively, Vale leaned forward, mouth open, lust consuming him. Jason studied Vale's needy urgency with hooded eyes as he jerked himself slowly and kept his cock just out of reach of Vale's seeking mouth. "Get yourself off," he grunted. "Show me."

Heat flooded Vale's neck, face, and ears, and coursed down into his body, making his cock ache and his thighs sweat. His asshole gushed and Jason moaned, leaning his shoulder against the windowsill as he beat himself harder and faster.

"Come for me," Jason ordered through gritted teeth. "I *will* see your face again."

Vale shoved his loose pajama pants down to his knees, his dick slapping up against his stomach. He jerked his t-shirt off over his head, tossing it back into the study. Shivering in the cold air, he shoved two fingers into his asshole as he worked frantically at his cock.

"Fuck," Jason gasped, eyes roaming over Vale's body "You're gorgeous. Perfect. Those tattoos! When did you...oh, god, you're so hot. Fuck." He bent at the waist, gripping the windowsill with one hand as he jerked off.

Vale's biceps were covered in tattoos he'd had inked on during several post-heat rebellions in his late twenties, along with a line of his poetry across his ribs. He'd almost forgotten Jason might have an opinion about them. Pleasure in Jason's praise surged with the lust in his veins, romping through his body and making him shake.

Jason babbled on, stroking himself. "So hot. Perfect nipples. That fucking treasure trail. Gonna make it all mine. Gonna cover you with my jizz."

Vale's pushed his chest forward, dying for Jason's come, wanting it anxiously. He released his cock to play with his nipples, trailing his slick-wet fingers around the aching nubs. "Do it."

"Look at me," Jason commanded. "Show me what my omega looks like when he wants me."

Vale gazed up at Jason, his heart clenching and flipping wildly, like a skydiving bird.

Jason was gorgeous, flushed cheeks, dirty shirt, and wet mouth working. His pants gathered around his trim, flexing hips. His strong fingers gripped his massive cock with assurance and power.

Vale's balls clenched hard. "Yes," he whimpered. "Please, oh, please." He arched forward begging for the come with his body. "Jason, please."

Jason growled. "I see you. Showing off for me. Making me so hard."

His baby alpha had a filthy mouth and it made Vale lightheaded with lust. He swayed on his knees, jerking his cock again. His ass clenched with every thrust into his grip, and his anus quivered hungrily.

Pre-come leaked from the end of Jason's dick, dripping onto the ground below. Vale whimpered at the loss. That cock and all its juices should be inside him, deep inside him, filling him, and making him come.

"Wolf-god, I want you." Vale worked his own cock viciously, shoving through the tunnel of his fist again and again. With his other hand, he reached toward Jason's fingers gripping the window-sill and clasped them. "Need you. Inside me. Now. Please, Jason. Fuck me now. Fuck me *hard*."

Jason growled and turned his hand around to grip Vale's fingers. They stared into each other's eyes as they held hands and beat their cocks roughly. Groans, growls, whimpers, and cries volleyed into the space between them. Slick slipped down Vale's thighs and dripped onto the floor.

Jason's eyes glinted. "Stop jerking off. Finger yourself again. Get them wet with your slick. Don't touch your dick."

Vale kept his eyes locked on Jason's as he reached around and shoved three fingers into his own ass. The squelching heat sucked them in, and Vale's eyelids fluttered as he jammed against his own prostate and tender omega glands.

"Harder," Jason ordered. "Let me hear how wet you are."

Vale fucked himself roughly while Jason's eyes burned into his, and their joined hands clenched tightly. The squishing sound of his wetness was raw and wild, and the scent of his slick and their pre-come swirled intoxicatingly around them. Jason's nostrils flared.

"Stop. Hold your hand out." Jason's cock flexed and leaked another gob of pre-come. "Let me see it."

Vale lifted his hand toward the window, the slick shining and thick on his fingers. Jason jerked him forward, rubbing Vale's fingers all over his face. Then Jason took all three fingers into his mouth, groaning and sucking on them passionately. Vale's balls drew up tight, and he ached soul-deep for Jason's cock. His asshole squeezed and his nipples burned.

Gripping both Vale's hands, Jason's jaw clenched as he stared down at him. Vale arched toward him, needing more, needing Jason's touch, his kiss, his command.

Jason's words hit Vale like slugs from a gun. "Come. Now."

Vale cried out. His orgasm pumped through his body, vicious, blinding, and unbidden, called out of him by his alpha's order. Hole spasming, his cock spurted and his limbs convulsed urgently. Jason let go of Vale's hands, aimed his cock, and cried out as his own climax hit.

Come spurted in copious, thick ropes, coating Vale's chest hair, his beard, his thighs, and spattering onto the floor of the study. Vale gathered what he could onto his fingers and shoved it into his mouth, quivering with the flavorful orgasm he'd been felled by the day before. He shuddered and shook, his body craving more, his skin tingling, and the thunder of oncoming heat rising hard in him.

Jason hitched his pants up and climbed in the window. Vale's heart knocked against his breastbone and his muscles turned to jelly as Jason knelt, took him in his arms, and kissed him until they both couldn't breathe.

JASON DIDN'T KNOW when he'd slipped his fingers into Vale's hole—sometime during the endless kiss they were engaged in, probably—but he was having a hard time convincing himself to pull them out again. Vale was so tight inside, hot and velvety with a grip different from Xan's or any beta's asshole. Vale would feel amazing on Jason's cock, and he wanted to flip him around and fuck him hard. Vale's urgent little noises seemed to encourage him to do just that.

But not today.

He had to stay in control. Stay in charge. Prove this was something he could handle and not lose his mind. Urho had told him to *make* Vale be his omega, and so far, the experiment was working. He couldn't blow it now.

Slowly, he slid his fingers free, and Vale's whimper of distress was the reward he needed for making the right choice. "Shh, baby. It's okay. We need to calm down now before we take it too far."

Vale's eyes were glazed and lust-filled, a promise of things to come, and he stared up at Jason in confusion. "What?"

"Let's get cleaned up."

Vale's entire body trembled. His come-splashed stomach quivered beneath Jason's touch as he dragged his fingers through the mess, proud of having marked his omega so beautifully. His beard was full of it, too, and his chest hair. He was covered with Jason's seed and scent. It was perfect.

"I…" Vale trailed off, confusion still warring with need on his face.

"We can't. Remember? Protocols." Jason felt a little evil that his heart swelled at the miserable frustration that swirled in Vale's sweet eyes. "We have to meet tomorrow with the lawyers and then we can finish this up."

"You...you're..." Vale's tongue sounded heavy. "You're an asshole."

Jason slipped his hand back around to toy with Vale's delicious, open, and ready hole. "No, you are."

Vale's thighs shook and he spread his legs, offering himself. Jason took his time, playing with the sweet wetness that clung and worked around his fingers.

Closing his eyes, he breathed in Vale's scent. He couldn't help but catalogue the ways Vale was different from Xan. Older, taller, and hairier for starters. But inside he felt different, too—stronger, more gripping, though the texture was similar, quite nearly the same. His wetness was intoxicating, another thing he'd never had with Xan. And the sensation around his fingers—Vale opening, loosening—was mind-numbingly sexy. He breathed in Vale's concentrated scent and come-covered skin.

"You're perfect," he whispered. "I'm so happy I found you."

Vale brushed the hair out of Jason's eyes and gazed up at him, seeking something.

Suddenly, he hissed, and jerked on Jason's exploring fingers. "Sorry, darling," he whispered. "That's tender there."

Jason frowned, tempted to touch the place again. It'd felt like a denser wall of less velvety-slick inside, a ridge that thickened deeper in. "What's wrong?"

"Scar tissue," Vale said, burying his face in Jason's neck. His beard tickled Jason's sensitive skin when he shook his head and sighed heavily. "You're right. We should clean up."

Jason tightened his grip on Vale, not removing his questing fingers. "How did you get it? Did someone hurt you?"

Vale shuddered in Jason's arms, his ass gripping against Jason's fingers. "Yes."

"Who?" A thunderclap of rage splintered his tenderness.

"What's his name?"

Vale gently pulled at Jason's arm, dislodging his fingers, moaning at the loss. "It was a long time ago. It doesn't matter now."

Jason's jaw tightened. Whoever had hurt Vale would pay. "My father's private investigator could find him."

"It wasn't anyone's fault. It was an accident." Vale's voice trembled, and he leaned against Jason for support. "Please. I can't talk about this right now."

Jason kissed Vale's pale neck, sucking a bright red mark at the tender juncture at his shoulder. "I don't mind. You're still perfect. I'll be careful with you."

Vale made a sound close to a sob and then pulled out of Jason's arms. He rose slowly, standing on shaking legs, and used Jason's shoulders to hold himself up. "The shower's upstairs. Help me get to it?"

Jason stood, wishing he was twenty pounds heavier and muscular like Urho. He'd lift Vale up and carry him to the shower. Instead, he kept his arm around Vale's waist and guided him, kissing his shoulder and forearm at nearly every step.

Zephyr raced up the stairs and then lurked in the hallway before darting into the bedroom ahead of them with an outraged yowl.

"Someone's jealous." Vale laughed tiredly. "She'd claimed you for herself." He pointed at her as they entered the bedroom and rasped, "I told you he was mine, demon cat."

"She's not a demon."

As if to prove him wrong, Zephyr jumped onto Vale's dresser, knocked over a framed photo, pushed an empty mug to the carpet, and then yowled at them again like it was their fault.

"She's rotten," Vale muttered, steps faltering. "But she keeps my butt warm at night, so I'll keep her."

Jason laughed. "She what?"

"I'm a stomach sleeper. She thinks my ass is a pillow. You can figure it out. I'm too exhausted to explain right now."

It turned out Vale's room wasn't the one with the lace curtains. Instead, his room was at the other end of the hallway, near the back of the house with a view of the garden. And there were no curtains at all, just dark shades that were halfway up, letting in the pale light of a fast-falling evening.

Jason was going to be late to dinner. Not just dinner but to The Feast of the Expectant Wolf. Pater would be upset, and that meant Father would be angry. He darted a glance at Vale who had let go of him and was now holding himself up against the doorjamb to the bathroom.

Jason took it all in quickly. There was a big bed in the middle of the room with a thick, decorative wooden headboard, carved with roses in bloom. The unmade bedclothes were plain, though: white sheets and a light brown comforter. Nothing patterned or ornate. There was a dust-covered matching chest of drawers with roses carved into the panels. A brown-and-cream round carpet lay across the exposed hardwood floor, along with puffs of silver hair that must have come from Zephyr. And lastly, there was a plush chair in the corner so covered with discarded clothing that Jason couldn't begin to tell what color it was.

"My friends weren't exaggerating about my housekeeping skills. Or lack thereof," Vale said, sagging against the doorframe and watching Jason carefully.

"It smells like you in here." Jason had to fight the urge to fling himself on the bed and roll around in *eau de Vale*. He tried to name the scent—mint, musk, and rose, and sweet skin, and slick—but there was something so delicious and indescribable in it that he finally gave up.

His cock was interested again, though, and he shifted so that it hung more comfortably in his pants.

"Youth," Vale said, laughing softly and shaking his head.

"You'll appreciate it during heat." Jason lifted his chin, trying to do what Urho had suggested. He wished the alpha quell wasn't seeping out of his system. He needed that cool space to keep his head on straight enough to function. "When you're begging for my dick again and I don't need to shove you full of an unsatisfactory alpha dildo while I recover, you'll be happy."

Vale's chest flushed and his cheeks above his beard grew red again. His cock twitched, like it was making an effort to rise. "You need to leave," he whispered. "Or else you need to fuck me on that bed. Make your choice. Do it now."

Jason growled gently at how Vale had wrangled the upper hand just like that. Now how as he supposed to get it back? "You're covered in my come. I've marked you. You're mine. Don't get smart with me now."

Vale rubbed a hand over his beard, grimacing gently at the come stuck in it. "And your face looks like you just made out with a scrub brush."

Jason touched his own chin, only just becoming aware of the stinging, raw pain. "That beard's a menace," he muttered, and then grinned. "I like it. You'll keep it. It'll feel good in all sorts of interesting places. Like against my asshole."

Vale stared at him and gulped hard. Jason's smile grew wider. There he was back on top again. Just the way he liked it.

"There's another bathroom in the hall," Vale said, pointing toward the door they'd come through. "It has a shower. Mine just has a tub."

"We can shower together."

"No, if you stay longer, there'll be problems with your parents. You'll be late to your family's feast as it is."

"Come with me to it. There's no reason you can't."

Vale sighed and pushed off the doorjamb. "Aside from the fact that I'm strung out on wanting you and unfit for company?"

Jason's heart waltzed happily. "Is that all that's holding you back?"

Vale ignored him. "Go on. Use the shower." He groaned and

wiped a hand over his face. "Your clothes are covered with come. I don't think we have time to wash them."

"I'll call my parents and say I'm having Feast of the Expectant Wolf here with you."

"Jason, no. That won't win me any favor with your parents, especially your father. Not to mention, the alpha quell has to be nearly out of your system as it is."

"So? You were just begging me to fuck you on the bed here. Maybe I don't need alpha quell anymore."

Vale frowned, looking away. Even that much disapproval cut into Jason like a knife. "Leave," Vale said, firmly.

"But you're shaking. I don't want to leave you alone."

Vale smirked. "I'll be okay. I've survived plenty of heats, after all. Just wait until you see me then. I'll be shaking like a leaf." He squeezed his eyes shut and shivered.

Jason's chest collapsed under the weight of joy. He could barely summon the breath to whisper, "So you will contract with me then?"

Vale ducked his head, breaking his joy into an equal measure of fear. "Darling, we can't discuss that now. Tomorrow we'll meet with the lawyers and then we'll see." He pushed off the doorframe again and collapsed onto his bed in a heap. "Run the water for me, if you want to help." Vale rolled around, smearing Jason's come across the exposed sheets.

It smelled so good. The evidence of the two of them mixed together. Jason's heart sang with hope and his cock twitched with renewed arousal. He went into the bathroom and started the tub running, before going back to the bedroom.

Tomorrow would be the end of this waiting, and he could claim Vale as his own. Then they could live together in bliss in this dusty old house forever. Or for as long as Vale was happy here. Jason would learn everything about him, he'd discover what he loved, what he loathed, and he'd uncover things about Vale that annoyed him, made him roll his eyes the way Father did when Pater ranted about omega freedom groups, and he'd learn to love it all. Every last annoying habit and wonderful trait. It was going to be beautiful.

Vale stretched out his long limbs like a cat, and Jason admired his sweetly concave belly dusted liberally with dark hair. The colorful tattoos on his arms beckoned to Jason like mysteries he could solve immediately, if he only asked just the right way. The tattoos appeared to be pink flowers, or maybe they were clouds, wolf-god's face, a star, and perhaps a sun on one arm, and echoes of those themes on the other.

"Your tattoos…"

"Go," Vale said, waving his fingers toward the open door.

"But—"

"The tattoos are a story for another time. You should go now."

"Not without a kiss goodbye."

Vale started to protest, clearly afraid of where it would lead, but Jason gripped his head firmly and kissed him hard. Vale melted and pulled Jason closer.

Panting, Jason broke free. "Goodbye. I'll see you tomorrow."

Vale released him but said nothing, falling back, still smelling of Jason's come.

Zephyr nearly tripped him as he left the messy house on Oak Avenue and headed home. Clearly, she didn't really want him to leave.

Alphas on the street sniffed and stared after him with gleaming amusement in their eyes, but Jason didn't care. Let them think what they wanted. He'd made Vale Aman come again, and he'd fingered his ass, and he'd nearly extracted a promise that they would contract tomorrow.

It didn't matter that he was going to be late to The Feast of the Expectant Wolf, or that Pater was probably going to be smoking, or that Father was going to yell. It'd been a damn good day.

Absolutely nothing could ruin it.

# CHAPTER EIGHTEEN

D INNER WAS STRANGE.
And it wasn't because of the mélange of odors Jason was sporting when he got home. It wasn't even because he'd been late. And it wasn't because he'd violated protocols with Vale. No, he'd managed to dodge all those bullets so far.

Both his parents had been holed up in Father's study when he arrived, the scent of dinner nowhere in the air. Confused, but relieved not to be bombarded with questions and knowing eyes, he'd dashed upstairs to take some alpha quell before wallowing in the bliss of the combination of his and Vale's aromas all over his clothes and skin for a few minutes before showering.

After the shower, and once he could think straight, he stuffed all but the shirt he'd been wearing into the new-fangled washing machine Father had bought several years back. He shoved the come-covered shirt under his pillow, hoping his parents would stay out of his room until he'd had a chance to enjoy it more.

But then he'd arrived in the dining room and discovered that not only was there no feast, but there were no seasonal decorations. The Expectant Wolf candelabra Pater always put in the middle of the table wasn't out. The arrangements were several days old and not nearly as nice as the ones they'd had for the feast last week when Vale had been a guest.

It wasn't right. It wasn't natural. But when his parents had finally arrived in the dining room with only a strange variety of reheated leftovers to dish out from their nicest serving plates, the air had been so thick and tense that Jason hadn't dared to ask what was going on for fear of hearing it *was* his fault.

Surely all of this strangeness wasn't just because of what he'd gotten up to at Vale's? Obviously, there was no way to cover the marks on his chin, but a few kisses couldn't bring on this kind of tension, could they? If his parents knew all they'd done, he supposed they might be angry enough to cause problems. But if so, where was the lecture? The yelling? The suggestions that Vale wasn't suitable? All he had was this aching silence.

Jason hoped if he was quiet enough, maybe they'd just let it go. After all, negotiations continued tomorrow, and if they went smoothly then it would all be a moot point.

His stomach tensed. *Negotiations.*

What if they'd uncovered something else about Vale? Something they didn't like? What if they didn't want to celebrate the feast because there wasn't anything good to expect from the future after all? What if they were trying to figure out how to tell him that he couldn't have Vale ever?

He steeled himself and prepared to test the water with a question about the next day's negotiations, but before he could, Father set aside his fork and met Jason's gaze with a strange shadow in his eyes. "We should all eat dinner and then go to bed early. You'll need to be well-rested and clear-headed in the morning, son."

"But it's only eight o'clock."

Yes, it was late for dinner to have just begun, but too early to turn in for the night.

"Pass the butter," Pater said, his brows furrowed tightly. He hadn't even dressed up for the occasion. He wore a soft-looking, loose sweater in grey, one of his least-favorite colors. Father, for his part, had at least put on his suit coat. Jason felt like an idiot in his usual feast night attire of a suit and tie. "Jason? The butter?" Pater snapped.

"Right." As he handed the red glass butter dish over, he frowned. Beneath the stale cigarette odor emanating from Pater, there was another scent, something strange and foreign. Sickness, maybe? It wasn't Pater's usual odor at all.

Pater focused on Jason for the first time all evening and asked softly, "How was your day in Vale's garden?"

Father looked up from his hostile study of the leftover chicken and rice he was picking at. "Yes, did it all go well?"

Jason's mind quickly supplied him with the image of Vale on his knees, shirtless, tattoos on display, nipples tight in the cold air through the open window, and spattered all over with Jason's come.

"Yes. Everything went great."

Pater smiled at him, but it was brittle. "Oh?"

"Mox and his crew finished the clearing out, and finished putting in the bulbs for spring. Vale seemed happy with it, too." Not that Vale had said anything at all, actually. But he'd be happy with it when the blooms came in.

Pater nodded and went back to pushing his food around.

Jason took a bite of leftover shrimp and pasta and chewed thoughtfully, trying to suss out the source of the strange odor coming from Pater.

"That's good to hear, son," Father said.

"He's a fan of roses," Jason went on, warming to his subject. "So Mox thought it would be good to plant a few more beneath the windows of his study to allow the scent to drift in during summer. He's going to head back over next week after he picks up a few rose bushes that are good for fall planting and get them put into the ground."

"That sounds very nice," Pater said, trying for a smile again and failing. "I'm glad you had a good day there."

Jason darted a glance between his parents. They'd barely looked at each other through the entire meal. It was starting to scare him.

"Are you feeling all right, Pater?"

Father glared at Jason then, his blue eyes going cold with anger. "Enough," he growled.

Jason's stomach shriveled, and his pulse raced. His father had never spoken to him like that in all his memory.

Pater put his fork down and snarled at Father. "It's not like he can't smell it, Yule."

Father shook his head hard, pressing his lips tightly closed.

Jason's throat went dry. Silence reigned as they all pushed their food around on their plates. Finally, Jason whispered, "I do smell it."

"No!" Father shouted, banging on the table.

"Yule, there's no getting around it."

"He doesn't need to know about this," Father barked, shoving back from the table. He pointed at Pater. "Miner. In my study. Now."

But Pater just sat there, staring defiantly up at Father, his fingers clenched white against the stem of his fork.

Jason's food heaved in his stomach. His heart pounded. What had Pater done?

Father gripped the back of his chair, his throat working convulsively.

"What do you smell, Jason?" Pater asked finally, his voice deathly quiet.

"Someone else mixed with your scent." He dared a glance toward Father and then whispered, "Did you...but why would you...?" His throat clogged, and he sounded like a child. "You love Father."

Pater's eyes glimmered with confusion before clearing. A strange, fragile smile broke on his face. "Oh, wolf-god, no. Oh, Jason, I would never." He frowned up at Father. "See? This is why we have to tell him. He thinks I've had sex with another man."

Father yanked out his chair again and sat in it. With his elbows on his knees and his head in his hands, the tension rolling off him was almost unbearable. Silence ruled the table again for a long time.

Jason swallowed back another surge of his barely eaten dinner. "What is it, then?"

"I'm pregnant," Pater said grimly.

"Oh." Jason stared between his parents, his heart pounding. "But that's dangerous for you. I thought you took medicines to stop that from happening."

"You told him about that, too?" Father lifted his head to stare at Pater in shock. "Wolf-god, Miner, he shouldn't carry that burden."

Pater clattered his fork against his plate. "He's going to be contracted soon enough. Possibly tomorrow, Yule. He needs to understand the burden *all* omegas carry. Whether you like it or not, he's old enough to know the truth of our family."

"All omegas don't have your birth defect."

"Semantics won't fix this situation. Let's not fight over the details."

"No, let's fight over your life!" Father's blue eyes bored into Pater with a desperation Jason had never seen in him. "You nearly died with Jason. No, you *did* die. They had to restart your heart!"

Pater's lips set more firmly and he stared back at Father. "I know that, Yule. I was there."

"What?" Jason said, blinking between them. He'd had no idea.

"And once it was barely beating again, if the hospital hadn't just happened to have several bags of your blood type on hand..." Father's eyes filled with tears as his voice gave out on him. "If we'd been anything less than wildly lucky that day, I'd have lost you."

Pater's eyes filled, too, and his lips wobbled. "You didn't lose me. I'm right here."

"Yes, you're here. Nearly twenty years older, and more fragile than ever after using those abortion drugs for so long, and you think

SLOW HEAT

you can carry this child to term?"

"I don't know. But I'll try." He closed his eyes. "He wants to be here, obviously. The drugs didn't break him free. He hung on through the cramps and the bleeding. He's a fighter."

"Who knows what effect those drugs have on a developing fetus!" Father shouted, covering his face again as the words rang in the room. Pater's eyes popped open and he trembled as he stared at Father, but he didn't flinch.

Jason sat paralyzed, icy cold fear tearing into his heart.

"What other choice do we have, Yule?" Pater's skin was pale, but his eyes glowed with determination. "The other options are just as illegal as the abortifacient drugs and much more risky. Without a competent doctor, an abortion is nearly as physically dangerous as attempting to carry. Besides, we don't even know where to start with procuring a procedure of that sort. Who could we even begin to trust?"

"Money can buy silence, and I'll pay any amount to keep you safe."

"I won't do it," Pater said, shaking his head. "This child wants to be born. And I want to have him."

Father's mouth worked, his breath came in great shudders. A heaving moan escaped him before he stood and left the room, slamming the door. Jason's mouth was dry, and his blood screamed through his body. He wanted to run away, too, but he didn't know where or how, and his terror kept him rooted to his seat.

Pater patted his breast pocket, pulling out a cigarette and matchbook. He shoved his plate away and struck the match, lighting up. Smoke spiraled up from his head and drifted toward the ceiling.

Jason's fingers and toes tingled, and numbness spread through him. The room spun. A black silence seeped in from the edges of the room, as if everything outside had vanished. As if only this table and the two of them existed.

And Father, somewhere in the darkness outside the room, in agony.

Waving away the smoke Pater exhaled, Jason asked, "Is that good for the baby?"

Pater laughed bitterly. "Wolf-hell if I know, love." He took a long drag. "Probably not. I'll quit tomorrow."

Jason poked his fork at the shrimp still on his plate, unable to imagine eating it now. He swallowed thickly. "I don't want you to die."

Pater groaned, reaching for Jason's hand. "Nothing is written in stone. I'm not well, but I'm not ready to break half a dozen more laws that could land your father or me in prison in order to terminate a pregnancy that, to my surprise, I want to see to term."

"But you said you wouldn't survive it, and Father says they had to restart your heart and give you blood with me, and you're older now, and you *aren't* well. Why are you doing this? You have me. You don't need another. The line's secure."

"Is it?" Pater asked softly. "Your Vale's medical charts don't look good for him carrying to term, either. And I won't put him through what I've endured. Another child—if it was an alpha or an omega—would open up a new possibility for the future of this family."

"I could get a surrogate." His stomach hurt and he thought he'd die. Choosing between Pater and Vale? His blood and bones ached at the thought. Still, he couldn't let his pater die. "If I need to do that I will."

"No." Pater's hazel eyes glimmered sadly. "I would never do that to you. Deprive you of the bond that's made my life so wonderful despite the pain?" He shook his head. "Absolutely not. I wouldn't do that to your Vale, either. It'd be a betrayal of myself as an omega to put carrying on the line above the bond you will share." Pater flicked ash into his uneaten food. "Besides, I always wanted another child. It wasn't as though I only wanted to have one, you know. I've loved being your pater all these years and now you're going to be leaving us soon. A baby in the house would bring us all a new joy."

"If you die having him, there will be no joy at all," Jason said, dropping his fork against the plate with a clang. "I don't want him. I want you for as long as I can have you, and I won't love him if you die having him."

"Jason…" Pater took a long drag of his cigarette before squashing it out against his plate. Then he stood and came around to kneel on the floor by Jason's chair, taking hold of his hands. "I know you're frightened and your father's reaction isn't helping, but let's not borrow trouble. For all we know, this pregnancy will be different from the others."

"Why would you think that?"

Pater shrugged. "I can only hope. Life is mysterious and stranger things have happened."

Jason stared at him with an open mouth, hot anger starting in his gut and pushing into his chest. He jerked his hands away.

"What?" Pater asked, sounding nervous. "What are you thinking?"

"You're giving up. It's like you said the other day, you knew I needed you, and now you think I don't need you anymore, and you're giving up."

Pater stared at him, his jaw clenching, and then he looked away.

"If you tell me I'm wrong, I won't believe you."

Pater rose and returned to his chair again, contemplating the ashy, uneaten food on his plate like it was a crystal ball full of the future. "All right. You're old enough for the truth."

Jason straightened in his seat.

"I'm tired of being in pain so often, of hurting and losing heat

291

after heat. I'm tired of putting your father through this. He's suffered, too. If I could give him one more child, maybe he'd forgive me for…for the rest."

"He loves you," Jason pleaded, hoping Pater would see reason. Though he was clueless as to how the illegal abortion procedure could be arranged, he had no doubt Father would find a way if Pater would only agree. "He's never been angry about any of that."

"I meant forgive me for dying," Pater said quietly.

A knife pierced Jason's heart. He could barely breathe but he managed to ask, "Did you do this on purpose? Did you even take the drugs this time?"

"What? Of course I took the drugs." Pater snapped. "The chemist who makes them for me has always warned they could fail. So far, I've been lucky. This time, though…" he trailed off. His expression softened. "You'll be in good hands with your omega. I can see in his eyes he'll care for you. And your father…" Pater's chin trembled.

"He can't raise a baby alone!"

"You and your Vale can help him."

"Stop calling him my Vale. He's just *Vale*. He's my omega, and he's not going to raise my little brother that you're selfishly insisting on having." Jason shoved his plate away, hard enough that it skidded to the other side of the table and almost toppled off.

"Jason…" Pater sounded just like he did when he'd scolded Jason when growing up.

"No. Stop." Jason thrust back from the table and stood up, pointing down at Pater. "And what if the baby doesn't make it and you die for nothing? For no good reason at all? What then? Please, Pater. This doesn't have to happen. Father said he could find someone to…to… handle it."

Pater shook his head and lit another cigarette, his fingers shaking. "That's so risky, Jason. You're young. You don't understand the consequences, but your father and I do. We've seen what can happen. My life isn't worth Yule going to prison. I'd rather die trying to do this for him than die in a prison cell, forced to endure heats alone, and knowing your father was miserable and frantic in a separate cell without me." Pater jabbed his cigarette Jason's way. "And let me tell you, prison is the best scenario if we're caught. I lost an omega friend when I was quite young. He was unbonded and fell into heat unexpectedly. He did what he had to do and ended up getting an abortion. He was caught two days later. Executed within a week."

Jason's mouth went dry.

But Pater wasn't done. "Not to mention the abortion procedure itself is risky. Doctors aren't trained in how to do it and so few good ones are willing. Omegas have been known to die from the attempt alone. Our anatomy is delicate. The instrument meant to save us can finish us." Pater sucked on his cigarette and then ashed in his plate. "So, again, I'd rather risk my life to give this child a chance, than to die trying to destroy it."

"Pater, please..." Jason whispered. "I don't want to lose you. Please don't do this."

"There's no good choice here, Jason. I have to take the least bad one. Like I said, this baby wants to be born. He's held on for seven weeks now. That's over a quarter of the full twenty week term."

"How long have you known?"

"A week or so. Your father smelled him for the first time yesterday. That means he's growing larger. He's healthy. If only I can hold onto him..."

The sound of shattering glass came from upstairs. Pater jumped up, knocking his chair over, as he rushed toward the dining room door. Jason followed, his heart aching like a horse-kick to his chest. Racing up the stairs, he passed his Pater easily and reached his parents' bedroom first. Jerking open the door, he found the room in darkness.

Their wide bed was made neatly and the other furniture in the room loomed like giant shadows. Father stood by a broken window, staring out into the night. Cold air poured in and whooshed past Jason into the hallway.

"I'm fine," Father said, in a dead, lifeless voice. "Go away."

"Yule!" Pater cried from the stairs, coming up as quickly as he could, but his face had gone pale and he was trembling.

Jason moved out of his way as Pater entered the room and took in the scene.

"I'm fine, Miner," Father repeated, leaning a bleeding hand against the window frame. He kept his eyes trained out the broken window into the front yard. The stars shone in the black sky, clearer without the glass to reflect the light from inside. They looked like pinpricks of white in a navy curtain.

Pater pushed past Jason and into the room. "What did you do?"

"I needed some fresh air and the window was stuck. So I broke it. But everything's fine now."

Jason's stomach ached and tears ran down his face. "Nothing's fine!"

Father kept his strong back straight and his face blank as he stared outside.

Pater moved toward him, saying over his shoulder, "Jason, go downstairs. I'll deal with this."

"But—"

"Go," Father echoed, his voice hollow and empty.

Pater mustered a reassuring smile, but it was bullshit, like everything else since dinner had started.

Jason shut the door on his parents and hovered in the hallway within calling range, but after a few minutes pacing, he didn't hear anything from behind the door. He pressed his ear to the wood and listened, making out only murmurs.

After a long time, he headed to his bedroom, but the scent of Vale and their come on the shirt stuffed under his pillow assaulted his nose like a surreal spike of joy in the midst of a funeral.

He backed out quickly and headed downstairs, turning toward Pater's conservatory. He tore off his tie and suit coat, throwing them on Pater's sofa. He rolled up his shirtsleeves, thinking he would practice guitar, but even with the instrument in his hands he couldn't rest. He paced the room, again and again. Finally, he took out a piece of paper from the desk to write a fast note. He left it on a table in the front hall, before exiting out the door into the night.

Jason didn't normally walk the streets after dark. It was a different world with the streetlamps glowing and the houses dark. The electric lights on inside most shone like melted butter. A few of the less wealthy houses flickered with candles, and Jason wondered what it would be like to have so little.

There were crowds on the street, surprisingly. Alphas, omegas, alone and together, and wads of betas who were dressed up for the clubs and parties. Those without strong family ties went out on the night of Feast of the Expectant Wolf, apparently. Funny, he'd never thought of what they might do to celebrate before.

He kept his mind focused on the goings on around him, like the fantastic outfits and the street performers with their songs and poetry readings. If he forced his attention on the moment, then he didn't have to think about his parents. He couldn't. If he did, then his heart thundered and threatened to explode. He felt lightheaded like his lungs had stopped working, and the world tipped around him crazily. He just kept walking, kept watching, and tried not to feel anything at all.

Into the city, down the familiar streets turned strange in the darkness, ignoring the questioning stares that came his way, he walked without ever looking back. His feet knew where to go. Before long, he stood outside Vale's fenced front yard, gazing up at it from beneath the big oak tree.

He opened the gate, walked up the path, and stood on the front porch. Music came from deep in the house, and he considered walking around to peer in the windows to make sure Vale was alone. If he wasn't…if Urho had returned to check on him? He felt sick deep inside at the thought of them together, but he squashed it down. Looking through the long, narrow side window by the front door, he saw Vale heading down the hallway toward his study.

Jason's breath caught in his throat. Vale was so handsome in a silver, satin robe, matching pajama bottoms, and fuzzy, gold-colored slippers. Zephyr followed at his heels, prancing with her tail up and her head high. Save for the cat, he seemed to be alone.

Jason knocked.

Vale startled but turned to the door, wrapping his robe more tightly as he approached. Cautiously, the door opened a crack, and Vale peeked out, one green eye checking who was disturbing him so late. Then the door flung open wide. "Jason? What in wolf's name…? Did you forget something?"

Jason lifted his head and said nothing, but Vale's eyes widened in his pale face.

"Oh, darling. What's wrong? Come in." He tugged Jason inside, shutting the door on the cold night. The sound of violin overlaying piano drifted from the direction of Vale's study and then a deep baritone voice spoke in the soothing beat of a radio announcer.

Vale's head tilted and peered questioningly at Jason. "What's the matter? You look pale as death."

Jason noticed the red mark on Vale's neck. The one he'd left there earlier when the world had been beautiful and full of possibilities. "I didn't know where else to go."

Vale tugged him deeper into the house, pulling him close. It was only when Vale whispered, "You're so cold," that Jason realized he'd left home without a coat.

"Talk to me. What's happened?" Vale's voice was tight in his ear. He leaned back enough to take in Jason's face again. "Is it your parents? Are they angry with you? With us? About earlier?"

Jason shook his head, but his throat was too clogged for words to come. He squeezed Vale closer, tucking his face against his neck, and held on.

Vale clucked in his ear, holding him hard. "Oh darling," he said soothingly.

Jason valiantly tried not to cry, but hot tears ran down his cheeks and wretched little sobs hiccupped out of him uncontrollably.

Vale rocked him back and forth as Zephyr wound around and around their legs. Vale hushed him and made promises Jason knew he couldn't keep. After all, Pater was pregnant and determined to have the baby. So no.

Everything was *not* going to be all right.

Jason cried harder, his throat aching as his childhood broke away.

# CHAPTER NINETEEN

V ALE TRIED TO parse all that had tumbled out of Jason as he
pushed him into the leather wingback chair in his study, and
then knelt at his feet. He pressed a mug of hot tea into Jason's
hands and murmured, "He's a stubborn man, isn't he?"

Jason had shared the bare bones of his parents' situation between attempts to quiet his tears in the hallway and then again in
the kitchen as Vale had boiled the water for the tea. He'd obviously
swallowed back the truly incriminating details about his pater's
habitual use of abortifacients, but Vale knew enough from his
discussion with Rosen and his talk with Jason earlier to put the
pieces together.

"Yes, he is," Jason said, wiping at his eyes with his thumb and
trying to manfully sniff away the evidence of his tears. "They're
going to be upset when they realize I'm gone."

"You left a note?"

"Yes, but they'll still worry."

Vale glanced toward the phone on his desk. "Let's call."

"No. If they're talking to each other, or fighting, or anything
else, I don't want to interrupt. I'm nineteen. Legally, I have the
right to be here."

"Technically, we've already violated a number of protocols…"

"Fine. You know what I mean."

Vale nodded and rubbed Jason's knee. "Drink the tea. It'll
help."

It was an herbal blend meant to bring calmness and peace.

Rosen and Yosef had given it to him for his birthday last year, citing his tendency to worry. He hoped it would ease Jason's distress. Plus, one of the components of the blend was the active ingredient in alpha quell, and so having Jason drink it made Vale feel it much less likely they'd end up fucking before the night was out. Though that remained to be seen, especially with the tremors of his oncoming heat rumbling beneath his skin.

Nothing about the day was going as he'd imagined when he opened his eyes that morning. He wondered if any day ever would again.

"He's going to die if he doesn't find a way to…" he glanced at Vale and then away. "If he doesn't have a miscarriage or find another way to end the pregnancy."

"I know you said your pater is allergic to the government condoms, an unfortunate number of omegas are, but surely they could have managed with them anyway?"

Jason shrugged. "Pater said no. He has a reaction internally that makes him bleed and tear during the constant intercourse of heat."

"I see." Vale resented that the new laws the government had introduced several years back surrounding condoms had led to a reduction in quality and variety of materials. Obviously, this left Miner with fewer options.

"I know I'm supposed to be strong." Jason rubbed the back of his hand over his mouth, wiping away his wobbly expression. "I know I'm failing you right now."

"You *are* strong. This is hard. It's normal to feel scared when scary things happen."

"I don't want to lose him. I love him."

"I know. I'm sorry, Jason." Vale rested his cheek against the chair cushion, gazing up at him. "Drink the tea."

Memories of the moment he'd heard about the accident that claimed his parents' lives bubbled up to the surface of his mind. He bit down on his lip. Jason needed him to stay calm. But it wasn't fair—losing a parent never was. He wished he could somehow spare Jason this pain.

"What does the doctor say about his chances?" Vale asked gently.

"I don't think he's talked to a doctor yet. I just know he almost died having me and he's never carried to term any other time. Once when I was three… I think they might have tried again. Pater was in bed for weeks and then I woke in the night to screams. I was scared." He cleared his throat and went on, "Grandpater came to stay with me. Pater was in the hospital, and Father stayed with him, of course."

Vale nodded.

"They love each other so much," Jason said. "I've never seen them really fight before. Not like that. Father was angry and scared. And Pater was…flat. Like he didn't feel anything."

"He's got to be scared, too."

"He says he's tired." Jason's eyes welled with tears again, and he set the tea aside. "I don't want to talk about it anymore."

"You don't have to." Vale rubbed his cheek against the seat cushion as lust whirled inside him, inappropriate and tempting. The beard he was growing scritched against the leather. Jason reached down and stroked Vale's cheek, running his fingers lightly over it. Vale kissed Jason's knee.

"I didn't think I'd have you at my feet so soon," Jason said, voice gruff and still muffled with his previous tears. "That's okay. I don't mind."

Vale sighed. "It's comfortable here."

Jason's voice was tender as he stroked Vale's beard and then lifted his chin to meet his gaze. "How many alphas have you been with?"

Vale's chest tightened and he turned his face, hiding it against Jason's thigh. Silence pulsed between them, and then Jason slipped his hand into Vale's hair, tender and calming.

"It doesn't matter. Forget I asked."

But it did matter. It was part of why he couldn't bear children. No matter what bond was growing between them, like glimmering ribbons he could feel tying them together even now, he had a past that determined the only possible future. It broke his heart to admit, but Jason deserved more.

"There was an incident in my twenties," Vale started, lifting his head to meet Jason's sad gaze. "I didn't have Urho in my life then and—"

Jason put his fingers over Vale's lips. "It's fine. Don't tell me. Not like this."

Vale's brows quirked, confused.

"One day you can tell me because you want me to know," Jason said. "Not because I asked."

Vale *did* want Jason to know, oddly. Even a day ago, he'd have declared that his alpha never needed to know what had happened during that second rebound heat, but now? After seeing Jason's heartbreak and tenderness for his pater, after sharing his kisses earlier, and being covered in his come? It wasn't right for Jason to grow more attached by the second without knowing the truth.

But those very things also made it impossible to tell him now. How could he hurt Jason while he was so scared for Miner? And how could he ruin the memory of their afternoon with a confession that would make Jason see him in a whole new light? It could wait. He shoved aside the niggling thought that negotiations were due to begin again in the morning and that he really needed to make up his own mind about what to do. But with any luck, and with all that Miner and Yule were going through, they might well be put off for another day or more even. He had time—he and Jason still had a little time.

"C'mere," Jason whispered, spreading his knees apart and patting his lap.

"You know what will happen if I do that."

301

"I'm just going to kiss you."

Vale's lips twisted in a smirk. "You're not a convincing liar."

But he climbed into Jason's lap anyway. It was a tight fit with both of them in the chair, but Jason held him firmly, making him feel small against his taller form. Jason wasn't thickly muscled like Urho—who made Vale feel almost breakable when wrapped in his arms—but he was solid, and his hair smelled amazing. Like rosemary and peppermint. He wasn't bony, either, despite being lanky. There was wiry muscle to pad and support Vale's weight.

Shifting, so his cock pressed up against Vale's ass, Jason smiled, his eyes less sparkling than that morning but still kind. "That's better."

Vale twined his arms around Jason's neck. As they kissed, blood rushed into his dick so fast it made him almost lightheaded. Jason's mouth moved down his neck, sucking soft and hard, and then back up to capture his lips again.

Jason's hand crept to the front of Vale's satin pajama pants, gripping his cock through the material.

"Show it to me again."

Vale shuddered. "Now's not the time."

"I need a distraction. Now's the perfect time." He slipped his hand under Vale's robe, gliding up and down his back. "Your skin is so smooth and soft." He moved his hand to the front, trailing through the hair over Vale's chest and across the words tattooed on his ribs. "I love your body. Soon you'll tell me about these tattoos. That'll give me something else to love about you."

Vale closed his eyes, trying to get control over himself, but his skin prickled maddeningly, and his asshole grew wet, ready, and wanton. "Fuck," he hissed.

"Yes," Jason whispered in his ear. "Fuck."

He kissed Vale again, throwing the world into a spin of breath, lips, tongue, and saliva. Vale clung to Jason, groaning, sucking and licking. His nipples drew up hard and tight, exposed to the cool air of the study, as Jason tugged his robe from his shoulders.

His cock leaked against his pajama bottoms, and his asshole loosened as more slick erupted from his omega glands. Jason kissed his neck and earlobe, teasing him with teeth, until he quivered and rutted against him in the chair. With surprising strength, Jason gripped him under the buttocks, lifted him, and rose to standing with Vale clinging around his neck and legs wrapped around his waist.

The sofa was the closest place to lie down and Jason crawled on top of him, his mouth never leaving Vale's skin or lips. "Yes," Vale whispered, hunching up to press their groins together. "Fuck me."

Jason pulled away long enough to stand up so he could unbutton and remove his own shirt and open his pants. His cock was fully erect. The veins Vale had noticed before were even more prominent now, and the whole perfect piece jutted out in hard, gorgeous inches that Vale couldn't keep his hands off.

Jason gasped, throwing his head back, as Vale leaned forward and sucked on the fat crown. The shaft was too big to go all the way in, stretching Vale's mouth wide until the corners burned. "Oh, yes," Jason said, voice shaking. "That's good. Use your tongue."

Vale closed his eyes and sucked and licked until Jason gripped him by the hair and pulled him off. "You're going to make me come."

Vale shuddered and wrenched his pajama bottoms away. "Come inside me."

Jason moaned, and dove down pushing Vale's legs back. He buried his face between Vale's soaking ass cheeks, licking and sucking on his quivering, wet asshole. "That's right," Jason murmured. "Get me soaked. Come on my face."

Vale whined and held his knees back to give Jason more room to work. Heat pooled in his pelvis and spread through his body. Pinpricks of brilliant, stinging need shimmered over his skin, stripping him of doubt and leaving him begging for more.

Legs trembling and heart hammering, he felt the first wave of a sweet anal orgasm descend on him. He crowed, arching his back. Jason worked his tongue harder over and in Vale's convulsing hole. And another wave crashed over him—an intense, fluttering, pulsing orgasm that left him cresting, riding the pleasure higher and higher, and craving Jason's cock.

Jason pulled away, rubbed the slick from his cheeks all over Vale's pubic hair, up his treasure trail, and into his chest hair. He captured Vale's mouth again and kissed him breathless, only moving away when he slid his fingers into Vale's quivering ass.

"I'm gonna make you come again," he whispered. "And then I'm going to fuck you."

Vale shook and writhed on Jason's fingers, his mind washed clean, purified of all doubt, as he succumbed to the perfect bliss of being finger fucked. Each pass of Jason's knowing fingers massaged his prostate and omega glands, and he moaned helplessly. Jason jerked them in and out, faster and faster, making Vale buck and cry out, making his nipples tingle and peak, until Jason bent to soothe them with his tongue.

"Darling! I'm coming!" Vale's limbs tensed and he breathed, "Fuck!"

His asshole convulsed at the same time his cock went rigid beyond belief and his balls drew up tight. He shot his load all over his chest, screaming and clenching around Jason's fingers, his whole body on fire for something thicker and *more*.

"Wolf-god," Jason whispered, sliding his fingers free and then bringing them up to his own mouth to suck. Vale whimpered, still twitching, as Jason licked the slick from his fingers and stared down at Vale with adoring eyes. "You're the most beautiful thing I've ever seen," he whispered.

Then he stood. "Come here."

Vale didn't know if he could sit up, actually, much less stand after that. But he managed to lift onto his elbows and watch Jason sit in the wingback chair again.

"Come here," Jason said again, this time command resonated in his tone.

Vale's shaky knees barely held him, but he rose and walked to his alpha, every cell in his omega body ringing like a bell.

"It's your choice." Jason said, motioning to his veiny, purple cock. It stood straight up, begging to be ridden. "I won't force you to take me."

Vale licked his lips, his heart hammering and his entire body vibrating. He could walk away now. Jason would let him. He'd just come twice and was floating on a buzzing high. He didn't need to break the last protocol. He didn't need to consummate the imprinting. He didn't need to take Jason's cock inside his body, upping the ante of all they both risked losing going forward.

But he did.

He settled his knees in the chair on either side of Jason's hips and stared into Jason's eyes. The blue was nearly obliterated by the black of his pupils. "Darling, you're perfect," Vale whispered, heart-blinded and falling hard. He impaled himself on Jason's straining cock.

The fat crown pulsed just inside his stretched asshole for a scary moment, feeling too big and painful, and then more slick released, coating Jason's cock in hot, slippery fluid. Jason thrust himself fully inside with a cry of joy that shook both of them.

"Oh wolf-god!" Jason shouted, gripping Vale's hips, his eyes rolled into his head. His body went rigid and then he shook all over, like a mini-orgasm gripped him. When it was over, he opened his eyes, met Vale's gaze, and lifted him until his cock had almost pulled free, and then shoved back in again.

Vale clawed at Jason's shoulders. Jason was so deep inside, Vale could feel his cockhead throbbing against the opening to his womb. He moaned, wishing he was already in heat and his womb descended, so that Jason could shove past that last boundary, fill him up, and impregnate him.

"Oh, darling, you feel so good," Vale whimpered. "You're going to make me come now."

And he meant *right now.*

He threw back his head, his asshole milking Jason's dick, his insides convulsing and squeezing as he lost control to another anal orgasm. His cock leaked between them and the room spun wildly.

"So right," he crooned, sweating and still greedy for more. "So good."

Jason dragged him down for a kiss, his cock rocking in Vale's hole, massaging his prostate and omega glands with each thrust. Somewhere in his mind, he knew it was just pheromone delirium talking, but he swore up and down and out loud that no cock had ever fit inside him better.

"Perfect. It's perfect. You're perfect, Jason. You."

His rambling seemed to inspire Jason because he shoved into Vale harder and faster, fucking him passionately, kissing his collarbones, nipples, and shoulders.

Jason sobbed out shocking things. "Gonna make you come so hard. Gonna flood you with my seed. Gonna fill you up with my babies. Make you mine. Keep you. Have you forever. Fuck, I want you so bad. Vale!"

His head flopped back and his hips jerked up, his cock expanding in Vale's body—a prelude to a knot during a heat—and then he came. His cock throbbed against Vale's prostate and omega glands sending another anal orgasm crashing through him. Harsh waves of bliss wracked him. He convulsed through it, weak as a kitten in its aftermath.

They panted together in the chair, with Jason's cock still deep inside. Seed slipped from Vale's body, and he shuddered, remembering what Jason had said about filling him up until he overflowed.

Jason quivered and quaked, whispering nonsense. Vale kissed his temple, trying to soothe his baby alpha down from the shaking, shuddering heights. But if he thought it was over, he'd forgotten the stamina of youth.

Jason lifted him with a grunt and guided him back to the sofa, then fell to fucking him again as soon as his back hit the leather. The next hour passed in a tidal wave of escalating, mind-destroying anal orgasms, and culminated in a screaming, pulsing, wrenching climax tugged from his cock by Jason's insistent hand.

When it was over, Jason lay sweaty and shuddering in Vale's arms. The space between them was slippery with slick, come, and sweat.

"How'd you learn to fuck like that?" Vale slurred, drunk on never-before-known pleasure.

"Instinct and practice," Jason whispered, lifting up to give him a proud grin. "You liked it?"

Vale snorted and rolled his eyes.

Jason laughed. "I'm good, huh?"

Vale groaned and struggled to shove Jason over so that he could breathe a little easier. "I don't have to tell you that."

Jason slipped his fingers into Vale's still twitching ass. "No, you don't. Because I felt it."

Vale groaned. "You've exhausted me. I'm finished."

But he wasn't. There was a burning itch in his skin. A familiar one that meant heat was on its way. If he was lucky, he still had a few days. And then...

He kissed Jason's shoulder and snuggled in to rest his head against it. He let his finger run over the golden hair growing sparsely on Jason's chest. Vale closed his eyes, enjoying the rise and fall of Jason's chest and the scent of his sweat and their come.

As Jason's breath evened out, Vale's mind gradually cleared, and as it did, a cold dread crept over him, chilling him despite Jason's warmth and the prickling, oncoming heat. What had he done? What had they *done*?

Vale swallowed convulsively as his heart rate kicked up. They'd

307

consummated the imprint. They'd violated the last protocol, and Jason would assume this meant they would contract tomorrow. Vale's gut wrenched.

But there was no way he could contract with Jason without telling him the truth about his past. Not after being with him this way. Not after sharing their bodies so fully, seeing the sweetness at Jason's core, tasting it, riding it to climax again and again. Not after what they'd done. It felt wrong to withhold the truth of himself from his *Érosgápe*.

Until this moment, he'd never fully believed it was possible that he and Jason would contract. He'd assumed that Jason would eventually take a surrogate at his parents' insistence. And when Vale had allowed himself to indulge in hope, he'd always pictured a future where Jason never knew the worst of Vale's history, where the blame for their infertility was never fully placed on his shoulders.

But now? How could he ever contract and enter a lasting bond with Jason if he was never honest with him? How could he take the future of this young man and wad it up in the trash with his own dreams of a family life?

He forced himself to realistically imagine Jason's reaction to a full confession. Jason's beautiful lips would twist in a snarl of repulsion and the blue of his eyes would go dead and cold. Vale's heart ached and his throat hurt as he clutched Jason's sleeping body and swallowed back tears. He *wanted* Jason, wanted to contract with him, but he couldn't fool himself. Once Jason knew the truth, there was no way such a romantic, sweet alpha would stay.

And if he did stay, how long would it be until he started longing for a child? Once Jason's age mates met their omegas and started reproducing, the reality of what he'd given up for Vale, and how little Vale deserved that grace, would be apparent to him. He'd start to loathe Vale then and resent their bond.

No. It was time he was honest with himself. He should save

some dignity and end the negotiations on his terms. Tell Jason's parents that he refused to contract because he knew deep down Jason deserved children. That would be sufficient for them and held the benefit of being true.

But Vale wasn't a fool. He knew he'd have to come clean with Jason altogether. The young man he'd come to know wouldn't let him go for any reason other than the pitiless truth. If Jason chose to tell Vale's secret to his parents, at least Vale knew they wouldn't turn him in. They had too many secrets of their own to keep safe.

His chest felt heavy and he stifled a groan. Why had he ever let himself entertain the idea that Jason didn't need to know about what had happened? He should have confessed his shameful secret at the beginning, no matter how it shattered his ego for Jason to know what he'd done. It would have saved them both the pain of severing this growing bond. They'd have never made the mistake of this beautiful, gorgeous night together. He'd never have known the joy of being in Jason's arms and therefore never would have had to fully grieve it.

He'd have to break Jason's heart tomorrow—and his own heart as well.

He'd already lost so much: his parents, his innocence, and now his career. Did he have to lose his alpha now, too? Now that he knew how wonderful Jason truly was, and how perfectly their bodies fit together? Now that he'd had a real glimpse of all they could be to each other?

The prickling burn of his upcoming heat stirred beneath his skin again. He shuddered against Jason who held him closer but slept on.

There was still the problem of his heat to resolve. Jason would revoke the contract offer as soon as he knew the truth, and Vale wasn't going to let him give his first knot to an omega who didn't deserve his bond.

# CHAPTER TWENTY

"YOU'RE NOT GOING to contract with him?" Yosef repeated Vale's words back to him, staring him directly in the eye. "Have you lost your mind?"

They were alone in the back of a hired car on the way to Jason's house to meet for what would be the final negotiations. The driver had put up the partition so they had some privacy. There was no time to spare; Vale needed Yosef to agree to do as he asked before they reached the Sabel residence.

Grief was a ringing, hollow thing. It was hard to believe relinquishing the tenuous hope he'd allowed himself to wrongly and dangerously indulge in could leave him so empty and raw.

"I've regained my mind," Vale whispered.

Yosef groaned. "What happened? What changed? Up until now, you were content to let them be the ones to conclude that a surrogate would be best, and I'd thought, or hoped at any rate, that you were willing to contract with him if they backed off on the birth requirement. Is that not accurate?"

"It is, but things have changed."

"What things?" Yosef's eyebrows jumped like caterpillars.

Vale hesitated. He couldn't explain how clarity had fallen on him as he'd held Jason sleeping in his arms the night before. How he'd understood with ruthless certainty that no matter what he yearned for, no matter how he wished for another outcome, he was never going to be the omega Jason Sabel deserved. He'd entertained the thought before. He'd known it was true. But he'd foolishly hoped he was wrong and allowed himself to imagine there might be a way…

Last night, though, he'd felt it in his bones: Jason was good, soul-deep good, and Vale was ruined, and he couldn't let Jason's life be tainted by that.

"What changed, Vale? Help me understand why you're sabotaging this."

"Last night, we…" Vale trailed off.

The bliss that'd washed over him and through him as they'd consummated the bond was hard to speak about. He didn't know that he'd ever be able to compose a poem that would capture those tender, perfect feelings. He probably would never try. Remembering so much unspoiled joy once he'd destroyed Jason's affection forever and rejected their bond would be soul-sickening. "We consummated the imprint."

Yosef's white brows twitched and he blinked in shock.

"I couldn't stop myself. I lost control."

"Pheromone delirium?"

"Yes, and…" He lowered his voice. "My heat is coming on. I don't have much time now."

"Wolf-god, Vale, then contract with Jason and be done with it."

"No. I have to put an end to this farce before I ruin his life."

"What farce? You're his *Érosgápe*. There's nothing farcical about it." Yosef took hold of his hand and said urgently, "Listen to me. I know you. You care for Jason. No matter what you say and what lies you're telling yourself, I know deep down you long for him to love you unconditionally."

"Why are you torturing me this way, Yosef? Don't you understand that it doesn't matter what I long for? I can't have him."

"You can. He's a good man! You could be happy with him."

"I could *never* be happy with him!" Vale exclaimed, his throat burning with the harsh lump lodged in it. "He'll hate me when he discovers the truth about that second rebound heat. He'll loathe me when he understands that he can't have children with his *Érosgápe* because I was selfish and stupid."

"How can you say that? It was instinct. You were in so much pain. Your suffering was unbearable. I was there." Yosef teared up. "I'd have torn out my own heart to help you if it would have changed a thing."

Vale clenched his eyes. "Excuses don't change outcomes."

"Fine then. Tell him. Give Jason the whole brutal truth and see what he does with it." Yosef's eyes pleaded with him. "Don't make this choice for him. Respect him enough as a man—as your *alpha*—to let him prove your self-loathing wrong."

Vale swallowed hard, his heart pounding ruthlessly in his hollow chest. The pain echoed inside, amplified with each word. "I *am* going to give him the truth. That's the whole plan, don't you see? It's the only way to make sure he accepts my refusal to contract and moves on."

"So you plan to break his heart? You want to hurt him?"

"I want him to be happy!"

"He'll never be happy without you."

Vale's eyes filled with hot tears. "Children will make him happy. He'll forget me when he looks into their smiling faces and hears them call him Father."

"You're so sure you're unlovable, huh? Absolutely certain of it. It's nearly an insult, after all the love Rosen, Urho, and I have thrown at you."

"Stop. This isn't about you. I know you love me. All of you. It's about Jason and what's right for him."

"That's a lie. It's about your fear. You're running scared. You're going to hurt that boy in reactionary terror that he's going to hurt you first. Why? He's a good person, Vale. And you deserve him. Do you hear me? You deserve his love."

Vale's chest was crushed with the weight of his longing. He yearned for Yosef to be right. He wanted—more than he'd wanted anything in his entire life—to be the omega Jason deserved.

Vale could still see the wonder in Jason's eyes as he'd entered him the night before. The awe he'd quivered in as they'd made love. He'd taken Jason's adoration like a hungry animal knowing full well he'd never be given it at all if Jason knew the truth. He didn't deserve him.

"I won't saddle him with the scars of my past."

Yosef let out a slow breath. "I beg you to reconsider."

"I'm going to end this today." The car neared the Sabel mansion. The houses around them grew bigger and posher. "There's no time left to indulge in longings that can never be fulfilled. I have to prepare for my heat."

"You'd take another after having Jason?"

Vale clenched Yosef's fingers hard and didn't address the question. "We're nearly there. I need your promise that when I dismiss you from the negotiations, you'll leave."

"What are you going to do?"

"I'm going to make sure that Jason never regrets this day. He'll take a surrogate and be glad to see the last of me. I'll say what I need to say—all true things, sadly—to make sure of it."

Yosef studied him closely as the car slowed in front of the Sabel's house. "All right. But I'm going to be honest with you, Vale. I think you're wrong, and, for what it's worth, my money's on Jason surprising you."

VALE SAT AT the Sabel-Hoff dining room table with Yosef at his side. He'd been mildly surprised negotiations hadn't been called off after the drama of the night before. But Yule and Miner were nothing if not dedicated to Jason and his future, so despite everything, both of them sat at the table, too. They looked like they'd been up all night grieving, yet they were dressed and ready for business.

All the better since it was time that Vale put an end to his and Jason's dreams.

Their attorney, Bisme Freet, had been there when Yosef and Vale had first arrived, but he'd excused himself after opening the meeting. "Yule and Miner would like to talk with you alone," was all he said. "I'll return later, if it's appropriate."

That'd been curious enough, but it became even more so once it was clear that Jason wasn't late. He simply wasn't coming. At least, not yet.

"Jason will join us later," Yule said, and his voice was a dead, raspy thing, containing none of the jovial warmth from the first time they'd met.

"He agreed to that?" Vale asked, surprised. When they'd parted ways the night before, Jason had barely been willing to go. Insisting that since they'd consummated the imprint, he might as well stay the night and they could go to the negotiations together.

Vale, desperate to be alone with this distress so he could grieve what was to come, had insisted that Jason's parents would be furious if they did that, and so Jason had reluctantly gone on his way. Now he wondered what had happened once Jason was home and if he'd even *need* to reject the contract. Perhaps Yule had plans of his own.

"Jason? Agree to let us talk to you alone? I don't think so." Yule smiled, and for the first time that morning, Vale saw a flash of warmth in his eyes. "He's set on you, and if he knew you were here, nothing would keep him away."

Miner met Vale's eyes with a cool appraisal. Clearly, he wasn't happy with Vale, either. "He thinks negotiations start at noon. He's been sent across town for refreshments, since we are quite suddenly out of anything decent to serve."

"I see."

"Miner isn't happy that I've arranged this meeting without Jason, but given how many choices he's made with regards to our son and our lives without consulting me lately, I think turnabout is fair play."

Vale raised his brows, and next to him Yosef cleared his throat.

"You have every right to refuse my next request, and if you do, then I'll disclose the same information as I would if you granted it, but I'd like you to send your counsel away for a little while. There are some things I'd like to talk over with you and you alone."

Yosef put his hand on Vale's arm and shook his head.

"Go on, Yosef," Vale said quietly. His heart ached, but everything was going to plan—better, actually. "I'll be fine here."

"I can't in good conscience approve of any of this, Vale."

Vale smiled at him reassuringly and insisted. "Go."

Yosef whispered in Vale's ear, "They could blackmail you or try to frame you in some way—"

Vale cut him off. "That's not what this is about. It's fine. I know what I'm doing. Please wait in the hallway."

Yosef packed up his stack of papers, muttering under his breath. "This is a fool's move and so is everything else you have up your sleeve."

Vale remained silent, blood cold and tongue ashen.

Yosef sighed. "I'll be in the hallway if you need me."

Vale waited until the door was entirely shut before he turned to Miner and Yule. "If this is about last night—"

"It is," Yule cut him off. "I don't know what Jason told you about why he left our house, but whatever he said, whatever you know, we'd like your assurance it will remain confidential, no matter how things turn out at the negotiation table today."

Vale stared at them. "This is about...oh. I thought...well, I see."

"You thought?"

"I thought you were going to confront me about what Jason and I might or might not have done when he was at my house last night." Through his misery, Vale patted himself on the back mentally for not completely admitting that they'd violated all protocols and consummated their status as *Érosgápe* without signing a contract.

Yule's eyes hardened slightly, but Miner's mouth turned up at the edges, his hazel eyes glowing a bit.

"I'm sure you and my son violated every last protocol in the bunch, but at this point, I don't give a damn about any of that," Yule bit out.

Miner looked at him approvingly.

Yule stared hard at Vale. "You see, we have a situation. Miner is pregnant."

Vale nodded and said, "Jason told me."

"And did he also tell you that we are at odds about it?"

"He did."

"And what will you do with this information?"

Vale frowned at Miner. "What do you mean? I don't understand."

"Will you go the authorities? Should I prevail over Miner's wrongheaded madness and convince him to terminate this pregnancy before it kills him, what will you do?"

"I..." Vale stared at him. "I'd do nothing. Why would you bring this up?"

If Miner's pregnancy terminated by unnatural means, he might never have known. Given Miner's history, he would have assumed a miscarriage. And given his own, he'd never have pressed for more information on the matter. His stomach churned slowly.

Yule raked shaking fingers through his hair. "Because if Jason told you what I think he told you, then you have my entire family in your hands now. You know about the abortifacients?"

Vale swallowed hard. If he hadn't already known, he did now. Yule was clearly out of his mind with distress for Miner and showing his cards all over the place. It was dangerous. For everyone. Especially Miner and Jason, and, subsequently, Vale.

"Wolf-god, man! Keep your mouth shut about such things," Vale whispered urgently. He wasn't going to give up his baby alpha just to lose him to the possible consequences of his father's wild panic. "It's too risky to talk about this openly."

"Tell me what you plan to do with the information you have on my family!" Yule demanded, pounding the table.

Miner frowned and put his hand over Yule's fingers, but he pulled away.

Vale's heart stuttered. "I have little room to judge you and your choices—past and present. And believe me, there's nothing that could possibly drag that information out of me. It would hurt everyone involved, including Jason."

"And you. If you sign a contract with him. It's only right that you know the risk."

If Yule was trying to scare him off, he needn't have bothered. "I don't plan to contract with your son."

Miner gasped, and Yule narrowed his eyes. "You consummated the imprinting last night," he said accusingly. "But you don't intend to contract with him? Why would you do that?"

"It will make it harder, for both of you," Miner said, his brows crinkled over his dark-ringed eyes. "Nothing can compare to being with your *Érosgápe*."

Vale wanted to dispute it, but he couldn't. The intensity of what he'd experienced with Jason was unmatched by any sexual encounter he'd shared with any other alpha—even during heat.

Refusing the contract felt like he was cleaving his soul in half. "At the time, it didn't feel like a choice." Or if it had, it'd felt like the only one.

Yule rubbed a hand over his face. "This is all going to hell."

"I shouldn't have allowed it," Vale said, apologetically, voice shaking earnestly. "I should have made him go home, but he was upset and…"

Miner nodded. "Omegas need to soothe their alphas."

Yule snorted.

"Yes, I wanted to soothe him," Vale agreed, rubbing his bearded chin. *And I wanted him to love me the way I know I could love him.* "But then things…"

"Enough. We remember." Yule sighed. "I can't believe I'm asking this next question. Two days ago, I was sure I wanted to convince Jason to take a surrogate, but…" He sighed. "Why don't you want to contract with our son? Is it because of this situation? Or our history with illegally procured abortion drugs?"

Yule's worry that he'd compromised his son's happiness was touching, but Vale didn't torture him by letting him cling to it. "No. I won't contract with your son because it will only lead to regret, resentment, and sadness in the end. He deserves an omega his own age who can give him children." The sob at the end of the sentence wasn't for effect. It tore out of him like a hand had gripped his heart and tugged it free.

Miner's jaw clenched and he leaned forward, shaking his head. "Nonsense. He'll never be happy without you. You'll never be happy without him. I don't know what you've done in your past that you think you need to be punished for, but please don't hurt my son out of your own self-loathing."

Vale's heart thudded dully somewhere outside his body. "You deserve grandchildren. He deserves a family. And I can't give him that."

"The word 'family' can mean a lot of different things," Yule said gently.

"But it shouldn't for Jason," Vale whispered, eyes welling.

Miner's shoulders slumped. "This isn't how it's supposed to be." He stared down at his own clenched hands on the table. "Jason wasn't supposed to end up like this."

"My point exactly," Vale said, rising from the table, legs shaking. He lifted his chin to show his determination, even though it quivered. "I'll make sure he doesn't. He'll have a good life. He's a wonderful boy, like you said, Miner. He'll make someone a wonderful alpha. I wish that someone was me, I truly do. But I won't end up being the cause of his future pain and sadness."

Miner sneered, patting at his chest pocket for the silver cigarette case and coming up empty. "You're a fool. Being *Érosgápe* is a blessing and a curse. You'll feel the pain regardless. So will he."

"I'm doing this for his sake."

"You're not. You're scared. You're hiding!"

"At least he'll have children. I understand they're compelling creatures, worth giving up one's own happiness and life for." Vale grimaced as his arrow found its way home and Miner went even paler and held his hand to his heart. "I'll keep your secrets, accept your allowance, and in return..."

"Yes?" Yule said, tightly.

"You'll keep your son away from me."

Vale's throat ached as he turned and left the room. Yosef waited in the hallway, but Vale shook his head at him, taking the stairs two at a time. He had one more thing to do before he could head home, curl up in his bed, and hope to die.

First, he had to break Jason's heart.

319

JASON RETURNED TO the house with a bag of groceries and a head full of bees. He felt strange and disjointed, as if the pleasure of being inside Vale last night had never happened and the only reality was the misery radiating from his parents.

He'd tried to put it all aside and focus on the fact that today Vale would sign the contract and they'd be officially contracted as *Érosgápe.* What that meant in terms of his day-to-day life, he didn't know. They'd discuss living arrangements today for the final touches of the contract.

He hoped he could begin staying at Vale's house immediately. He'd see about having all of his things sent to him over the next few weeks. He allowed himself to fantasize about taking Vale back home, making him dinner, and fucking him until they both fell asleep in Vale's big cream and brown bed.

Still, he couldn't get as excited as he wanted. He blamed his parents and this wolf-god forsaken pregnancy, but he also couldn't shake the goodbye he and Vale had exchanged the night before. He remembered how Vale's green eyes had filled with tears as he'd opened the door for Jason to leave.

"Don't cry. We'll just be apart for a few hours," Jason had said, wishing that Vale would have agreed to let him stay and for them to go to the negotiations together.

Vale had kissed him then, strangely desperate, and when they'd broken apart he'd said, "Keep that kiss in your memory forever. Promise me."

Jason had promised, confused, but he wasn't going to deny Vale something so simple. Of course he'd remember the kiss forever. He'd remember everything about Vale forever.

After he'd given his promise, Vale had steered him out the door and sent him on his way. Nothing had felt right since.

The house was oddly quiet when he came in the front door, and he blinked to see Yosef seated on the bench in the hallway with his briefcase and a stack of papers in his hands.

"You're early," Jason said, smiling. "I'd shake your hand, but I'm juggling a lot here."

Yosef stood, reaching out to take a bag. "Let me help get these to the kitchen." He glanced up the stairs then and said, "On second thought, why don't you just let me take them all and you go get dressed?"

Jason flushed. "Am I late? I didn't think I stayed away that long."

"You're fine." Yosef took the bags easily. "Go on upstairs."

"All right. Just leave those on the kitchen counter if you don't mind. There's nothing that will spoil. I'll make the platters when I've showered and dressed."

Yosef said nothing, disappearing down the hallway, heading to the kitchen with the bags.

Jason took the stairs two at a time. Adrenaline kicked through his system. He'd taken alpha quell that morning, but he grabbed two from his pocket and swallowed them quickly. He'd be calm and business-like through this negotiation and collect his prize as soon as it was over.

No matter how strange everything felt. Today was going to be a good day. He'd make sure of it.

The door to his room was open. He frowned, wondering who'd invaded his space and why. His parents better not have touched his come-covered shirt from the day before. He still hadn't had time to enjoy it properly. He stepped inside his room, his nose instantly recognizing that the shirt was still there, and something more.

Vale was there, too.

"What are you doing?" Jason asked, uncertainty enveloping him.

Vale jerked and nearly dropped the drawing Jason had attempted of sand as it looked under the microscope. "I wanted to see your room before it was over." Vale's voice trembled.

Jason's hope fluttered in his chest, beating against the strangeness he'd felt all morning with fragile wings. "Since we consummated already," Jason said shyly, "it's just a matter of signing the papers now. I would have shown you afterward."

Vale's eyes went distant.

Hope's wings shuddered with the effort to keep flying.

"Vale?" Jason asked. "What's wrong?"

"I've been thinking." His voice sounded cracked, honey that'd hardened and shattered.

Jason swallowed. He took a step forward, his heart seizing when Vale took a step back. "About what?"

"About consummation," Vale said quietly, keeping to his side of the room. "What makes it special? We'd already achieved orgasm together. Did putting your penis in my body really change so much?"

"Yes." Jason's voice quavered. "Didn't it change things for you?"

Vale shrugged, his pale skin going paler as he looked back down at the paper. "What exactly would it change?"

"It strengthens the developing bond," Jason said, closing the door to his room and leaning back against it. He hoped his father or pater didn't come banging. He didn't think they would, though. Something about the silence in the house told him they weren't going to interfere.

Vale sighed. "The bond. Right."

"Because we're *Érosgápe*." What was wrong with Vale? Why was he so distant, so different?

"What is it about sex that makes the bond grow?" Vale asked.

"I don't know. It's special between *Érosgápe*. It felt special to me."

Vale nodded reluctantly.

"And then during heat there'll be knotting," Jason offered.

Obviously, he'd never knotted anyone before. His cock grew hard just imagining being in Vale so tight and deep, knotted so big he couldn't pull out even if he wanted to. He wanted to feel Vale climax again and again on his knot. He wanted to wring him out with pleasure. "Knotting is special."

Vale gave Jason's now-distended pants a disdainful eyebrow. "Yes, knotting also helps with the bond. Or that's what they say." His words echoed hollowly, and he looked down at the paper in his hand one more time before placing it carefully on Jason's desk.

He cleared his throat and met Jason's eye. "I've had a lot of alphas, Jason. A *lot* of alphas, and I've taken a lot of knots."

Jason's throat went tight and he shook his head. "I don't care."

Vale held up his hand. "If you knew how many and if you knew the truth, you won't be able to help but care. Which is why I need to tell you now."

"Vale…" Stepping halfway across the room, he paused when Vale put his hand up to stop him. He stood still, anxious and waiting.

"You said the other night I should tell when *I'm* ready, and, while I think that's admirable, it's bullshit. See, the thing is, I need to tell you now, before we sign anything. It doesn't matter if I'm ready or not. It doesn't matter what I want or don't want. Do you understand?"

"No."

Vale's breath shuddered hard, but he straightened his back and went on, "Jason, once you know everything, you won't want me anymore."

"That's not true." Jason's stomach hurt and his knees shook.

"It is. And even if you tried to ignore what I tell you, pretend it doesn't matter? It *will* matter. It wouldn't be long before you came to resent me and regret what I'd stolen from you."

"I don't care how many—"

"Stop talking now."

Jason's mouth clamped shut.

Vale stalked toward him. "I was twenty-one when they took me off the heat suppressants after I graduated Mont Juror. Two weeks later, I went into heat for the first time and I had no one." Vale stopped a few feet in front of Jason, his eyes bright with anger. "It was excruciating. I begged my omega friend who sat with me to kill me. I screamed so long I lost my voice and then I still tried to scream some more. My body felt like it was on fire. Wave after wave of fire."

Jason's eyes filled with tears. "I'm so sorry. I should have been there for you."

"You were a child," Vale snapped. "Now listen to me."

Jason swallowed hard and nodded, trying to hear over the rushing in his ears. His legs quivered.

"After that, I hired surrogates for several years. Never the same one. They were expensive and they were strangers and I *hated* how I needed them. I loathed them." Vale clenched his fists. "When each event was over, I never wanted to see them again, and I made sure I didn't."

Vale's eyes dulled with painful memories. Jason wanted to say something to take away the hurt, to amputate his past, but he couldn't. He kept quiet and let Vale talk.

"In my late twenties, I was a new professor at Mont Nessadare when I realized my heat would arrive during midterms. I decided to try the heat suppressants the government had recently approved for adult omegas. I knew for many they weren't as effective as the strain they gave us at Mont Juror, but I had to try, for my career and for my students. It worked. My heat was delayed by almost a month, but then it came on hard."

"Rebound?" Jason asked.

Vale shuddered. "Yosef and Rosen had to enlist the help of four alpha friends to get me through it. Do you understand how intense it was, Jason? Four alphas could barely satisfy me. I was so worn out after that I had to take additional time off from work to recover. It was a disaster."

"Is that where you got the scar tissue?"

"No." Vale went so pale Jason was afraid he was going to pass out. "That came a year later when I tried the heat suppressants again."

The sun outside Jason's window shifted behind a cloud, darkening the room into a cool shadow.

Vale went on, his expression lost and distant. "Yosef and Rosen had gifted me with a trip to the beach for my birthday. I knew the dates would run up against my heat, but I didn't want to ruin their present." Vale hiccupped a harsh laugh. "I thought surely the rebound wouldn't be as bad as the time before, and I lined up a few alphas to help me out when I returned home." He ran a hand over his beard, fingers shaking. "The suppressants held my heat off for a week and a half. The day before we were to return, it hit me full force. There was no warning, no lead-up, and I went out of my mind with pain. Yosef and Rosen took turns watching me, while the other would go out to seek an alpha for help. But they couldn't find a decent one willing to help an unknown omega. They couldn't keep watch over me all the time. Eventually, Rosen fell asleep and I ran. I was desperate for anything to quench my need, to put out the fire inside."

Jason felt queasy. "What happened?"

"I don't know. I was missing for three full days. I have no idea how many alphas had me or how many times. I remember there were fights over me. I remember I let whoever wanted to fuck me do so again and again. I think betas even had me. I just cried for them to move off and let an alpha back on top, because I needed their sizable cocks to stop the fire. The alphas laughed at me and used me horribly. I cursed them, but then I'd sob with relief when the next one mounted me. The alphas were rough. I didn't care. I wanted it hard."

"Please stop."

"You need to know."

"Just stop!"

Vale licked his lips and spoke quietly. "When it was over, I was pregnant. That was clear very quickly."

Jason shook his head. "No, no, no."

"Yes. I was carrying a baby. Whose? I had no idea. Of the unknown number of alphas who'd fucked me, one lucky gentleman's sperm got to my egg and set off the chain reaction of cell division."

"Wolf-god..."

"I admit I was terrified." Vale's voice was steady now, like he was speaking words someone else had set down for him. "I had no one to turn to. Both my parents were gone and I couldn't risk telling many people. I'd lose my position at the university. Be ostracized. I had my inheritance, but how long would it last? And to what end?"

Jason felt lightheaded, but he couldn't seem to move or do anything other than stare at Vale as he talked on and on and on about this horrible thing that Jason didn't want to know.

"I confided in Yosef and Rosen, of course. They're the ones who'd found me in that broken down hovel, still wet with blood and come. They'd looked for me for days, scared that I'd been brutalized or murdered." Vale's voiced cracked. "I owe them everything for keeping my secrets."

Jason's gut churned.

"I knew I had a limited amount of time if I wanted to terminate the pregnancy. I confided in an omega friend of mine from school. It'd been rumored he'd experienced a similar event around an unexpected heat. That's when I met Urho Chase." Vale lifted his chin. "I *didn't* meet him on campus like I've let Yosef and Rosen believe. My omega friend referred me to him. You see, Urho had helped him once and, when I needed him most, he helped me, too."

"Urho?"

"Performed the abortion. Yes. That's how I came to know him and how he agreed to help me deal with future heats. Rosen and Yosef don't know he's the doctor who helped me. Until now, it's been Urho's and my secret."

Jason's mind spun, trying to process everything. "You aborted the baby?"

"Yes. It didn't go smoothly. Urho did his best, but I started seizing from a reaction to the anesthesia. His hand slipped, and he cut me badly. As the seizure went on, I start hemorrhaging and nearly died. He saved me. But the result is that scar tissue in my colon...my birth canal. That's what you felt the other day with your fingers."

Jason swallowed hard.

"I can't bear a child, Jason. Like your pater, in all likelihood I'd die." A bitter smile twisted Vale's beautiful mouth. "And call me selfish, but I'm not about to sacrifice myself for you. And I won't let you share my fate. You're a good man, you've done nothing wrong, and you'll make a wonderful father. You deserve a family. You should take a surrogate."

Jason shook his head, tongue numb and irresponsive.

Vale smiled tenderly, one hand reaching toward Jason but not touching. "You won't feel for him the same way you feel for me, but he'll be young and able—no, *eager*—to bear several children. And a surrogate omega can help you overcome the longing you'll have for me, and, if you choose wisely, you could be his salvation, too."

"How?"

Vale took another step forward. Tears welled in his eyes. "You could contract with a young widower, for example, and help him through his grief. You could help *each other*. And I'd be free to carry on as I did before. The way I prefer." Tears spilled over as Vale said, "And that's what I truly want, Jason. I won't sign a contract with you. It will be a mercy for everyone."

Jason's vision swarmed with small black dots as Vale stalked out of the room. Gulping air, Jason tried to breathe, but still the room spun. As the darkness got the better of him, he collapsed to sit on the floor. There he stayed—unable to fathom the stunning vacancy in his heart where so recently joy had lived.

# CHAPTER TWENTY-ONE

"H E LEFT YOU? That makes no sense!" Xan blew across the top of his mug of hot apple cider and then took a careful sip. "Are you sure that's what he wanted? Maybe you were supposed to chase after him, like in those romance books betas and omegas like to read."

"I'm sure," Jason said dully. His drink was a foamy one, the coffee shop's daily special. He didn't know what flavor it was supposed to be; he'd been so distracted when ordering it. He poked a knife at the flower the barista had drawn in the foam, disrupting it and sending it into a meaningless swirl resembling the mess of his mind.

"I don't know," Xan said. "Like I said, it doesn't make sense. He was lucky to have you." He glanced over the rim of his cup with heat in his eyes. "Really lucky." He shoved his hair off his forehead and shrugged. "Something else is going on. He doesn't *really* want you to take a surrogate. No omega wants their *Érosgápe* to do that."

Jason hadn't told Xan all the things Vale had said. He'd never betray Vale's confidence like that, but right now he wanted to. He wanted to lay it all out and have his best friend tell him what to think and feel and do. He wanted Xan to tell him how to salvage it.

"What if..." Jason trailed off.

"What?"

"This is purely hypothetical, of course."

"Right." Xan's eyes narrowed, smarter than his grades gave him credit for. "Hypothetically then, what if, what?"

"What if the reason he doesn't want to be with me is because he *does* want to be with me?"

"That's what I just said. He wants you to chase after him. Omegas love to be courted. Maybe you didn't do enough to woo him."

"No, not like that." Jason growled in frustration. "What if he wants me to be happy and he truly believes I won't be happy with him."

"Oh." Xan frowned, sipping his drink. "Well, he might be right. I mean, like I said from the beginning, he's—"

"If you say 'used up', wolf-god help me, Xan, I will punch you right here and now." Jason had been inside Vale and he wouldn't let that beautiful experience be cheapened. "There is no way for a human being to be 'used up'. Omegas aren't like pencil erasers— only so many uses before they're done."

"That was an asshole thing for me to say," Xan agreed. "Sometimes I'm like that. I can't help it. Especially when it comes to you, and, unlike your omega, I'm not selfless in my feelings, okay? If you told me right now that you wanted to start up again, I'd be ready for that."

"Xan…" They were never going to start up again. He didn't know how to be clearer without ruining the tentative peace they'd made.

"I know, I know. I need to stop pressuring you. You don't feel what you don't feel." A group of alphas from their school filed in, enlivening the coffee shop with noise and raw energy. "Shit, do you want to go? This conversation isn't going to be private for long."

"Look who it is," Wilbet Monhundy's voice rang out over the group lined up to order their lattes and mochaccinos. "Sabel, how's it hanging, buddy? How's your slutty omega doing? Sucking your cock and taking your knot yet?"

Jason gritted his teeth. "Ignore him," he whispered to Xan. "He's not worth it."

Monhundy and two of his friends, guys Jason had never bothered to learn the names of, broke free from the line and headed over to their table. Smirks and nastiness were screwed firmly on their faces.

"So are you gonna be in class at all this week, Sabel?" Monhundy drew up behind Jason, putting his hands on Jason's shoulders and rubbing like they were old pals. "Or will you be too busy screwing your nasty, used-up omega?"

Jason's fists clenched and he stood up. "Say that again."

"Yeah, say that again, asshole," Xan said, popping up, too, and getting in Monhundy's face.

"Aw, Jason, do you need your widdle pal here to protect your widdle feelings?" Monhundy laughed, but then his eyes grew beady and small, his lips drawing into a sneer. "Maybe the rumors are true then, yeah? I hear he's unmanned and you're the one who did it."

Xan growled and threw himself at Monhundy. He landed a solid punch, but it wasn't anything for solid Monhundy to grab small Xan and toss him against the table, spilling their drinks everywhere. Jason launched in to the fray, ready to fight, when a fist knocked his jaw, and the room went wobbly and dark. He fell to the floor next to Xan, pain radiating through his face, and his mind spinning.

Monhundy loomed over them, a foul grin on his face. "Let's stomp these unmanned bastards," he said over his shoulder to his brutish-looking pals.

"Hey, hey, no fighting!" Garth, the muscular beta owner of the coffee shop, flew out from behind the counter with a wet towel over his shoulder. He snapped it at Monhundy, thwacking his exposed forearm hard. Garth's dark red hair was a curly mess, and his red cheeks shone with irritation.

Jason struggled up from the ground, the floor unsteady beneath his feet. He pulled Xan up, too, and then regretted it when he had to hold Xan's arms to keep him from flying at Monhundy again.

"Take it back," Xan yelled. "Say whatever you want about me, but take it back about Jason!"

Monhundy laughed and said, "Hear that? He's as good as admitted it."

"Fuck you, I'm gonna kill you," Xan snarled, rearing against Jason's hold.

"Stop!" Garth clapped his hands in Xan's face. "Stand down, boy." Then Garth turned to Monhundy and his crew. "Get out. All five of you. And don't come back until you've grown some manners to go with your alpha posturing." He hunched his shoulders and flexed his arms, mimicking Monhundy's size and strength. Straightening, he poked his finger at Monhundy's chest fearlessly. "Don't make me call the police on you entitled alpha brats."

Monhundy and his clownish friends jeered and laughed, but apparently took Garth at his word. The courts, no matter how much money their father had, looked down on adolescent alphas harassing beta storeowners. So Monhundy and his friends vacated quickly, calling insults over their shoulders.

Monhundy, of course, had to get the last word. He shouted at Xan, "Unmanned alphas don't belong at Mont Nessadare. Better find a new school to prepare you for your upcoming career sucking alpha dick on a street corner for a nickel. Maybe Mont Juror will take you."

Xan snarled, but he'd given up trying to get free of Jason's hold.

"You boys all right?" Garth asked once Monhundy had gone. He looked them up and down carefully. "You come in here all the time and never cause problems. But as soon as these jerks turn up, suddenly there's trouble. You're not the first young alphas he's picked a fight with recently. I'm considering banning him."

"We're fine," Jason said, but Xan was trembling with rage, wordless and pale, his blue eyes trained on Monhundy's exiting back with a loathing Jason had never seen in him before. "Right, Xan?"

"Fine," he gritted out. "Just jolly, thanks."

Garth raised a brow at Jason and said, "You can both stay if you want to clean up the mess. Or you can go and leave it to me."

"We'll clean up." Jason didn't know if Monhundy and his pals might be waiting to continue the brawl in the street, and he was in no hurry to engage them again.

"No, let's go," Xan said, grabbing Jason's arm and pulling him with his surprising strength. "Sorry, Garth. I need some air."

Xan tugged him out the side door and onto a back street that led away from where Monhundy and his crew had headed. "That was rude. Garth's always good to us. We should have stayed to help him."

"I don't care. I had to get out of there." Xan set off toward the piers. "I hate Monhundy. I hate him so much. And I hate myself. I hate everyone." He darted a glance at Jason. "Except you. I just *wish* I could hate you."

Jason didn't know what to say. 'Me too', didn't seem quite the right response, but he did wish that whatever Xan felt for him was a lot less complicated and scary. But he couldn't change that any more than he could change what Vale had done in his past and what he'd said to him in his room. He just didn't know how to accept it yet, either.

He followed Xan down to the warf, vaguely aware that though he'd initially gone to Xan for comfort, now he was in the position of needing to comfort *Xan*. It wasn't an uncommon development between them, and so long as he couldn't be completely honest about the situation with Vale, maybe it was for the best.

The water at the wharf was briny and thick with oil on the surface. While they watched, ships came and went. One even docked at the pier used by Jason's father's company for shipping engine parts. He and Xan found a good vantage point out of the way, and watched a mixed work group of betas unload boxes from the cargo holds.

"What are you going to do about school now that Monhundy's targeting you?" Jason asked, when he thought it was safe.

Xan blew out a long breath and shrugged. "Without you around, I'm destined to flunk out anyway. I'd already decided to ask Father if I can start an early apprenticeship at his firm. It'd look better for him if I graduated, of course, but it's not like I need any special education to do his job. He's just a figurehead and that's all I'll need to be, too. I'll smile, cut ribbons at the groundbreakings for new building projects, and let Ray do all the hard work."

"Really? Ray?"

"He's a beta, but he's the one who got all the brains in the family. I'm a complete dud." Xan gave a sugary fake smile. "In every single way."

Xan's father and pater had been happy when Xan was born an alpha since their older son, Ray, had been a beta, and their third son had died from a childhood illness. Xan had been their bright light, their great hope.

In some ways, Jason thought Xan had more pressure on his shoulders than Jason did as an only child. At least Jason had a good relationship with both his parents. But Xan's father was cold and demanding, critical and harsh. He'd told Xan in no uncertain terms that he was expected to bring at least four live births into the world, and that two of them must be alphas to make up for Xan's pater's poor showing in that regard. Omegas were fine, as well, but betas would be unacceptable.

"Do you think your father will *let* you take on an apprenticeship?" He knew he should encourage Xan to stay in school, to get his education, but he didn't know how Xan would survive if Monhundy decided to target him. "Isn't there another way to prove you're not unmanned?"

"I *am* unmanned, idiot. Get used to it. I have." He turned into the salty breeze. "I can study at home. I don't need to put up with jerkwads like Monhundy to get an education. I can hire tutors. I can do whatever I want. The entire point of university was to be with you, anyway." He shrugged. "And that's over."

"Maybe not, since Vale won't contract with me."

Xan rolled his eyes. "You're ridiculous. He's your *Érosgápe*. He'll do what you tell him to do." He huffed irritably. "You were probably too nice to him. Did you tell him to sign the paper? No? Well, no wonder he left. Get a grip, Jason. You're the alpha. You're in charge, remember?"

"It doesn't feel that way." And how could he ever shake the images Vale had conjured up in his descriptive confession? How was he ever going to stop seeing Vale being fucked by hordes of men and then aborting the evidence? How was he ever going to unknow that the reason they were childless was because Vale had wanted to go to the shore without accommodating his heat?

He'd promised his pater he'd never hold Vale's past against him, and he didn't—not really—but he couldn't quite put it away. Vale's past impacted their future in ways Jason wasn't ready to accept.

"When I have an omega…" Xan trailed off.

"Yeah?"

"Wolf-god, I don't fucking want an omega." He groaned. "I'd do anything to be in Vale's shoes. He's an idiot. I hate him. It's official: he's lumped in with everyone who isn't you in my giant pile of people I hate."

"If I shoved you off this pier, you'd hate me. That could fix everything."

Xan laughed. "Oh, like you would."

With some effort, Jason grabbed him around the waist and hauled him toward the railing, hefting him up—Xan was surprisingly heavy for someone so small—and acted like he was going to toss him over. Laughter burbled up from his chest as Xan squirmed and kicked, screeching in outrage. It surprised him. He hadn't thought it was possible to laugh ever again.

Speaking of surprises…

He put Xan back on his feet and tolerated several of his irritated, retaliatory shoves before saying, "So, Pater is pregnant."

"What?" Xan's brows dropped. "I thought he couldn't or something. Since he hadn't in so long?"

"He's not supposed to. It's risky for him. He might die."

Xan's face twisted up. "Fuck, that's messed up. Your omega dumps you and your pater's gonna die? This is terrible. Jason, I think we need to go get drunk. I don't know how else to deal with all this. Do you?"

Jason laughed again. Xan's honest sincerity always had a way of pulling him out of the blue. He'd just never been this deep into it before. "Get drunk, huh?" He rubbed at the bruise forming on his jaw. "I could go for that. Where?"

"This way." Xan tugged Jason's hand and pulled him down the pier toward the street again. "Hollander's Haven. Gin for cheap. They don't check ID."

"We're old enough." Though just barely.

Xan shrugged. "Don't kill the thrill, all right? Just follow me and do what I say. You won't regret it. I promise."

VALE DIDN'T KNOW why he even bothered writing poetry. It was dreck. All dreck. Every single word was dreck, dreck, dreck.

And his skin *burned*. Relentlessly, horribly.

He knew what that meant. He didn't have three more days, or two days, or one day. He had no more days. This was it. His heat was here, and it was only a matter of hours before he'd be screaming and writhing, and—if not held back—bolting for the Bowery and any alphas he could find there.

He needed a plan. Which was why he'd called Rosen.

He scratched at his arms and rocked back and forth. Yes, Rosen. Who'd hopefully be here any minute, because he didn't know how much longer until the first wave hit. He threw his pen down on his desk and stared out the windows to the garden. *Jason's garden.* In his mind, it would never be anything else now. Before, it had been Pater's and now it was Jason's, and he'd see it every day and yearn. How stupid had he been to allow it?

"Vale?" Rosen's voice was a relief and an irritant at once.

Despite everything, despite saying exactly what he knew would work to drive Jason away, he'd held out a horrible hope that his baby alpha would appear outside the window, forgive him everything, declare the idea of all offspring anathema, climb through, and fuck him senseless on the study floor.

But that wasn't going to happen. Not today. Not ever.

Instead, he had Rosen in his house, arms laden with groceries, and that was as good as it was going to get. He'd be all right. He'd be wonderful even. Eventually. *Never.*

"I'm going to call Urho," Rosen said, dumping the groceries on Vale's desk and approaching with alarm in his eyes. "You can't do this alone. I won't let you. I won't go through that again and neither will you."

"No!" Vale shook his head desperately. "Don't call Urho. I don't want him. I won't consent. Don't."

"You're so close," Rosen said, sliding his cool fingers down Vale's cheek above his beard. "You're burning up."

"Do *not* call Urho," Vale repeated. "Promise me."

Rosen's jaw clenched and unclenched. "I won't promise."

"Yes!"

"I will not tie you to a bed and watch you suffer!"

"The basement," Vale said, nodding toward the hallway. "It will hold me. You won't need to tie me down."

"No. No way."

"It's perfect. There's water from the deep sink down there. And I've created a cozy nest with bedclothes and towels. If you lock me in and don't let me out, I'll be fine."

"There are spiders and ten years' worth of god-knows-what down there. And it's an unfinished *basement*, Vale! You should be in a comfortable bed, obeying nature, and submitting to the bliss of a rut. If you don't want Urho, let me call Jason."

"*No!*" Vale shuddered and scratched at his arms again. "If you're not going to help me then go."

Rosen's expression softened, and he tenderly stroked Vale's cheek. "I am helping you. This is what friends do. They help. Even when the other person is being a perfect idiot."

"I will not have Urho. I will *not*."

Rosen nodded slowly. "I understand." His eyes went thoughtful and then he drew Vale close. "The basement?"

"Yes. The basement."

"And if I were to bring Jason?"

"I would hate you forever."

Rosen hummed softly.

"What?"

"That's not a no, then. You'd consent."

"Fuck you and your loopholes," Vale snarled. "Oh, fuck. It's coming. Hold me through it. Please."

Rosen's grip wasn't enough. Nothing was enough when the heat came. Only an alpha could satisfy his body's needs. He writhed and cried out, the burning wave cresting inside him, breaking over and over again, until he was sweating and wailing, begging to be fucked.

"Shh," Rosen whispered in his ear, rocking him through it. "I'm here. I've got you."

Vale clung to him, whimpering. And when he finally came out the other side of the first wave, he was alone in the basement, rocking on his hands and knees, ass in the air, crying for Jason.

# CHAPTER TWENTY-TWO

J ASON DID REGRET going to Hollander's Haven with Xan. He regretted it very much.

He'd thrown up twice on the walk home, and he barely remembered dropping Xan off at his parents' house. He'd almost think he'd dreamed it, except he'd never dream of Xan's pater's horrified face when he saw the sick all over Xan's sweater. Or would he? No, he wouldn't. It'd been too hilarious. Or at least he'd thought so at the time. Now that he was sobering up, he felt a little bad about laughing.

He slunk up the stairs, head down, and hoped beyond hope neither of his parents would materialize and demand answers from him. He hadn't seen them since yesterday, before he'd gone out to get the refreshments for the negotiation that'd never happened.

After Vale had left his room, he'd locked himself in and refused to come out. While his parents had called to him from outside the door, he'd cried in his bed, holding the shirt he'd stuffed under his pillow. It'd been pathetic and sad, and he considered a repeat of it all now, but first he climbed into the shower.

He'd wondered where his parents were that morning over breakfast, but he'd just been grateful not to have to talk or see their sympathetic faces. Especially when he knew damn well Father, at least, had wanted this outcome from the beginning.

He turned on the hot water in the shower, leaned over the toilet, and puked again. Hopefully that would be the last of it. If the nausea stopped, he swore to wolf-god he'd never drink gin again.

Washing away the nasty sweat from his body and gargling the liquor taste out of his mouth, he scrubbed up quickly. After he brushed his hair and teeth, he got dressed again. Soft trousers and a loose, gray t-shirt he could lounge around in while he stewed in his misery.

Downstairs, on his way to get a glass of coconut water to rehydrate, he found a note on the front table.

*Jason,*

*I'm going to the shipping yards to check on a delivery. Pater is sleeping in the conservatory. Don't disturb him. He needs his rest. There are ribs thawing on the counter. Make something decent for dinner. And don't worry, son. We'll fix this. We'll fix everything for you.*

*All my love, Father*

Jason headed toward the kitchen to get started on dinner, but he paused by the mirror across from Father's study to examine the bruise blooming on his jaw. It was red and already shading toward blue. If it'd been much higher, it would have been on his cheekbone, and he might have gotten a black eye. As it was, it'd probably be healed up in a day or two and no one would be the wiser.

Except Monhundy would undoubtedly tell everyone at school. The jackass. Someday, someone was going to teach that jerk a lesson, and Jason just hoped he was around when they did.

Just as Jason turned away from the mirror, a soft, distressed noise drifted down the hallway from Pater's conservatory, followed by a sharp cry. And then another, louder, more wrenching sound, almost a scream, echoed against the walls.

Stomach churning again, Jason rushed toward the cries. The conservatory seemed empty on first glance, except for the swirl of cigarette smoke in the air, and the new, strange combined scent that was Pater's and the baby. Jason stepped deeper into the room to find his pater curled on his side on the sofa, his arms wrapped around his middle, and his face puffy with tears. Ash-filled plates circled him on the floor.

"Pater?" he asked gently. "What's happening? Are you all right?"

"I'm losing him," Pater whispered, his fists clenching and unclenching against his stomach.

Jason carefully crossed to him, nudging the ashed-up plates away with his foot. He knelt by the sofa and threaded his fingers into Pater's hair soothingly. "I know he's upset right now, but Father wouldn't ever leave you."

Pater hissed and curled into a smaller ball on his side, his face drained and white. "It's the baby. He's dying. I'm losing him."

Jason's heart wrenched. "Are you sure? What should I do?" He leapt to his feet. "I'll call for an ambulance."

Sweat darkened the hair at Pater's temples, but he shook his head no.

"Why not?"

"The drugs I use after heats build up in my system. They'll know. I can't go to the hospital, Jason." His eyes rolled back and he moaned again.

Jason fell to his knees beside him, moaning, "Then what do I do?"

Pater shuddered, his breath hitching as his body seized up. When he spoke, it was gasping and strained. "Nothing. We wait."

"I'll call Father."

"No. He'll worry. Leave it." Pater's teeth ground together. "I've done this before, you remember. Many times."

Jason remembered times when he was younger that Pater went to the hospital during miscarriages. But then, as time passed, he stopped. Now he knew why. The drugs in his system would give them away and prison would be the best they could hope for. He sat tormented by his pater's side, watching as he writhed and moaned, sweat dampening his hair and his limbs twisting up. "Is there something you can take for the pain?"

"Already took it. You don't have to sit here, Jason. I'm okay."

But Pater didn't look okay. He was gray and occasionally let out a muffled scream that twisted Jason's heart. He didn't know what to do, but he suspected his Father would lose his *mind* if he came home to find them here and Jason hadn't called him.

"I'll be right back," Jason whispered.

Pater thrashed on the sofa but didn't respond.

He left the door open in case Pater needed to call for him and ran for the phone in his father's study. When the call connected to the shipyards, it was hard to talk over the shouting and activity in the background, but he finally made it known to the beta who'd answered that he needed to find Father and send him home. "Let him know his *Érosgápe* needs him. He's...sick. Very sick. He's in pain. Please. Tell him to hurry."

Replacing the handset in the cradle, Jason took some slow, calming breaths, and tried to think. Pater was probably dehydrated. In the kitchen, Jason drew a cool glass of water and dampened a clean hand towel for Pater's forehead.

Halfway down the hall, Jason jolted as a scream tore through the house. The water glass shattered on the hardwood floor, sending water and shards of glass everywhere, but Jason left it, running toward the conservatory and Pater's cries.

Jason's heart filled his throat to find Pater with his knees on the floor, his torso on the sofa, and his hands gripping the cushions. The ashtrays all around him had been kicked over, sending dust into the air and scattering it over the floor. Jason flushed with cold dread as he took in the rest: blood stained the back of Pater's soft pants, the red growing larger and larger as Pater threw his head back, screamed, and pushed.

"No," Jason whimpered. "No, no, no." He rushed over and knelt by his pater, wrapping an arm around him. "Pater, what do I do?"

But Pater was too lost in pain to answer. The tendons of his neck stood out as he strained, pushed, and writhed, his body flexing and tensing. His formerly white face was almost purple from effort, and dark blood flowed from him below, staining his pants, and dripping to the carpet beneath his knees.

Jason soothed a hand over Pater's sweaty neck. "I'll be right back. Don't go anywhere. It's going to be okay."

*Don't go anywhere?* He chastised himself as he raced back to the phone.

He didn't know what to do, or who to call. He flipped open Father's address book and found a number for a doctor Pater had seen in the past, the one who sometimes came to the house after a rough heat or when Pater was sick, but the number wouldn't connect. He called the operator and asked to be put through to the doctor's office, but the line was busy and he couldn't get through. He skimmed through Father's address book for any other doctor's name and number. He found nothing.

Desperate and short on ideas, he dialed Vale's house and there was no answer. He tried again. Still no answer. From the conservatory, his Pater's screams raised goosebumps on his arms, as he pressed zero with shaking fingers. When another operator picked up, he asked for the only other doctor he knew for sure had ever dealt with this sort of thing before.

"I need the number for Urho Chase, please. Actually, just put me through. Ring until someone answers. It's an emergency."

VALE SWEATED IN agony, tossing on the basement floor. He'd

managed to drink some water from the deep sink's tap before the second wave started up, but he was still thirsty, and now he was too tired to crawl over and get his head under the spigot. That was part of what alphas were good for—taking care of their omega's basic needs in the throes of heat.

He heard footsteps upstairs. Two pairs of feet from the sound of it. He hoped it was only Rosen and Yosef, but, for all he knew, Rosen had disregarded him entirely and called Urho or, worse, Jason for help. If the door opened right now and either alpha descended the stairs, Vale knew he'd be helpless to refuse them.

The heat was too much. The endless need overwhelming. How had he thought he'd be able to suffer through this alone?

The alpha dildo he'd brought down barely took the edge off without alpha pheromones to soothe his need, but at least it pressed against his aching prostate and pushed against the slick-swollen omega glands that encouraged his womb to descend and open. It wasn't enough, but it might keep him sane.

It hadn't even been a day. How was he going to get through four more?

Voices rose and fell above him, echoing in the pipes and vibrating through the floorboards, but he couldn't make out the words or tell from the timbre just who was speaking. The phone rang upstairs and he shuddered as the shrill tone seemed to vibrate irritatingly over his overheated, oversensitive skin. It went on and on and he wondered why Rosen didn't answer it.

But then it didn't matter anymore because the next wave was coming. He desperately fucked the alpha dildo in and out of his ass, wishing Jason was here to do it for him, to lick his nipples, and suck his cock while soothing him on the dildo. Then Jason would throw the dildo aside, take his ass hard—

Oh, wolf-god!

He cried out, coming on the dildo and shooting a small load

from his dick. It wasn't enough. It couldn't be enough. Not without an alpha's sweet pheromones and their even sweeter knot to dilate against the glands and stop the shrieking need completely. He rolled onto his hands and knees and shook, shouting, arching his back, shoving his ass out, and senselessly seeking what wasn't there. Needing it.

And then the mind-numbing pain descended, crashing down on him like a fiery wave, sucking him under, reducing him to sweat and tears. Making him submit.

"MINER!" FATHER'S VOICE echoed through the front hallway and Jason nearly wept with relief.

"We're in the conservatory!" Jason yelled. His arms never left his pater's writhing body, trying to hold him together as he bucked and fought whatever was happening inside.

Earlier, the blood had become too great and Jason had stripped his pater of pants, covered him with towels, and tried not to scream in helplessness. He'd considered running into the street or banging on neighbors doors for help, but Urho was on his way and he couldn't bring himself to leave his pater, and what could the neighbors do for him anyway?

Father's face was pale as snow and his blue eyes burned as he entered the room and raced to Miner, shoving Jason aside to wrap his arms around him. "Miner? Can you hear me?"

"He just screams," Jason said, tears running down his face. "There's so much blood." He motioned to the soaked towels and the mess on the floor.

"Wolf-god, did you call his doctor?" Father asked, eyes wide.

"I tried, but—"

Father leapt up, turning toward the study door. "There's no

'but'. We need a doctor, Jason!"

Jason grabbed his arm. "Father, wait! There's a doctor coming. He'll be here any minute. I couldn't get through to Dr. Ruke, so I had to call someone else."

"Who?"

"Urho Chase."

"The alpha friend of Vale's?" Father sounded suspicious.

"Yes, remember? He was a doctor in the military and he's handled omega deliveries and miscarriages."

Father frowned. "I'd prefer Ruke. I know he's trustworthy at least." Pater screamed and blood seeped from him. Father went so pale Jason thought he might pass out. "We don't have time to be particular right now. How much longer until he arrives?"

"I don't know. I called him right after I called for you. I don't know where he lives."

Father lifted the towel Jason had used to cover Pater and swore. He reached down, trying to make some kind of adjustment, but that just made Pater scream again. Father fell over his back, soothing him and sobbing.

The doorbell rang and Jason left his parents, shoes slapping on the wood floor, as he ran to answer it.

Urho pushed him aside immediately and took off his ridiculous beret. "I assume it's bad if you called me. Where is he?"

Another cry from the conservatory turned Jason inside out, and he grabbed Urho's arm, tugging him in the right direction. Words were gone. Blind panic held him now.

"This isn't good," Urho said, as he entered the conservatory and took in the bloody spectacle.

Father snarled as Urho approached, the defensive instinct of any alpha with an omega in distress.

"Back off," Urho barked. Then he turned to Jason. "I need to wash my hands, but I shouldn't leave him. Bring hot water, and a lot of it." He gripped Father by the arm. "Get it together and move away so I can see what's happening."

Jason stuck around only long enough to make sure Father would allow Urho to help and then took off for the kitchen. He ran hot water and put a pot on to boil, too. Then he raced back to the study with the water, soap, and clean towels.

Urho looked grim but thanked Jason and quickly washed his hands. "He needs to be in the hospital. Call for an ambulance."

"No hospital," Jason whispered.

Urho lifted a brow. "Excuse me?"

Father draped himself over Pater again, soothing him.

"There are illegal abortion drugs in his system. He uses them every heat."

Urho grimaced but said nothing more about the hospital. "All right. From what I can tell, the babe is caught, possibly ensnared by some scar tissue from prior miscarriages. But he's small. It shouldn't be a problem to get him out. The real issue is the punctured colon. That's where the blood is coming from. He's probably gone septic." He frowned and shook his head. "Bring more hot water."

The next hour passed like a million years. Jason paced the room, his heart hammering and his mind racing. His father worked beside Urho, but Jason turned his back and stared out the window onto his pater's garden, tears streaming down his face, as his father and Urho did what needed to be done.

The sound of Father's sobs and Pater's screams of agony broke him.

"He needs a transfusion," Urho said eventually, once the screaming had stopped because Pater had, blessedly, passed out. "I don't have any bags of blood, but I have the equipment to go person to person. What's his blood type?"

"Wolf 3," Father said, his voice a dry husk. "I'm Wolf 2 and Jason is as well. What are you?"

Urho grunted. "Wolf 1."

Jason turned around then. Pater was unconscious, as he had been since the worst of it began, resting on his side with towels around his lower half. Father knelt by his head, soothing him with strokes over his brow.

Urho ran a hand over his face and cursed softly. "Who do you know close by? Anyone who might have Wolf 3? A neighbor? A friend?" His face brightened. "Vale's Wolf 3," he said urgently. "Call him. Now."

Jason ran to the study again to place the urgent call but once again there was no answer. He hung up and tried again. And again. And again. And again. Finally, the phone was picked up.

"I need your help," Jason blurted out. "It's an emergency."

"Jason?"

It wasn't Vale, though. It was Rosen.

"Hi, yes, it's Jason. I need Vale. It's an emergency. He needs to come to my house right away. It's life or death. We need his blood." He scrubbed a hand over his sweaty face. "My pater is… Look, Urho's here. He said for Vale to come. Please send him. We need him or my pater might die."

"Oh, wolf-god. Jason, Vale can't go anywhere right now," Rosen said urgently.

"But he has to!"

"I'm sorry, but he can't. Can you tell me more? What's going on? Can *I* help?"

"Isn't he home?"

"Yes, but—"

"This isn't a joke!" Jason's mind raced, trying to think of anyone else he could ask for blood. Knocking on a neighbor's door was still an option. They'd take anyone's blood. Anyone at all. So long as they were Wolf 3. "My pater needs blood or he'll die. Vale has the right kind of blood. I know he's upset with me, and I deserve that, because I should have told him everything in his past didn't matter immediately. But I was an idiot and I didn't say anything at all. I know I'll need to beg for his forgiveness and I will. But I also know he wouldn't want my pater to…to…" He couldn't say it again.

Rosen was quiet for a long second that lasted for an eternity. "Jason, Vale's in heat."

The room fell away and Jason sat in his father's chair, dizzy and helpless. "No," he whispered. "Not now. It can't be now."

Rosen ignored his denials. "Can I help you? What does your pater need? You said he needs blood? What type?"

In the background, behind Rosen's soft breathing, he heard shrieks and cries for help, and then, in Vale's ragged voice, somehow muffled and strange, he heard his own name. Over and over.

It was too much. Life was hot and heavy and coming down on him like a storm. He couldn't breathe. He was suffocating. He forced himself to whisper, "Who's with him?" Urho was here, so he knew it wasn't him.

"No one."

"He's doing it alone? He's suffering?"

"He didn't say he wouldn't consent to you, but he didn't intend for you to know."

Jason hung up the phone. He pressed his hands to his mouth, holding back the shout of agony. He closed his eyes, searching his mind desperately for a solution, and he burst into terrified tears when he finally found one.

He dialed Xan's parents' number, nearly weeping when Xan answered, sounding groggy but no worse for wear after their binge drinking. "I need your help. Now."

"Anything."

Grateful, Jason's shoulders dropped. "Thank you." Then he said, "Don't ask questions. Just do as I tell you. There's no time."

He hoped his friend could be selfless for once and do as he asked. Everything depended on it.

SLEEP WAS SO precious during the violence of an alphaless heat that Vale ruthlessly resented whatever had woken him from it. The next wave wasn't on him yet, and he'd managed to drink some water and collapse into the nest for rest. Earlier, at some point, he'd heard the phone ring some more and then there'd been a lot of pacing, but eventually as the heat wave passed, things had grown quiet again.

The sound of footfall on the steps brought him to full consciousness with a soft curse. "Go away, Rosen. I'm not fit to be seen like this."

"I've seen it all before," Rosen said, appearing at the bottom of the steps. He was annoyingly handsome with his dark hair swept back in a bun and his equally dark eyes burning in frustration. He had no right to look so good while Vale was a mess of suffering. "You'll want to come upstairs now so I can help you shower."

"What?" Vale shook his head desperately. "No. It's not safe. I could run off again."

Rosen stepped and pulled Vale up off the ground, supporting him when he stumbled on shaking legs. "You're weak as a baby right now. Besides, someone's going to help you."

"No." Vale shoved against Rosen. "No one can help," he slurred. "Only Jason. And he won't come. I made sure of that."

"Well, that's for Jason to decide, isn't it?" Rosen tugged Vale toward the stairs, and he considered resisting. But his muscles were sore from the makeshift nest on the floor and he felt filthy already, covered in sweat and slick.

"He did decide," Vale pointed out. "He didn't come after me."

Rosen sighed. "Come on, Vale. Help me out here. You're

heavy."

Giving in to Rosen's determined manhandling, Vale decided a shower would feel delicious. And then, if he was lucky, he'd have time to reason with Rosen before the next wave came on, and before whomever he'd enlisted showed up.

Dizzily, he let Rosen guide him up two flights to the bathroom in the hallway outside his bedroom, and then Rosen steered him under the warmth of the already-running shower. He moaned and leaned against the tiles, shaking in exhaustion, letting Rosen soap him up and wash away the grime.

"It's bad, isn't it?" Rosen whispered. "You're in pain."

"I'd forgotten," Vale admitted. "I've had Urho for too long now. It was dulled in my memory. I thought I just needed to be brave, but, wolf-god, Rosen, it's beyond endurance."

"I know."

He let Rosen wash his hair. "My omega friends who've given birth. They say it's the same. The mind forgets the agony."

Rosen smiled gently, taking time with the rinsing. "I take back what I said that day in my studio. I'm not sure any child is worth all this suffering."

Vale enjoyed the pampering, but then the prickling sensation started under his skin and spread deep into his muscles. It was coming back again all too soon. "Rosen, it's time. Help me."

Quickly Rosen grabbed a towel, and then dried him off before leading him, protesting feebly, toward his bedroom. "You have to get me into the basement," he whimpered.

"No, you deserve a bed, Vale."

Rosen maneuvered him onto the soft, cool blanket covering the mattress.

"I don't want Urho," Vale muttered and Rosen ran a hand through his hair.

"I know, darling. You won't have him. But you'll have someone, all right?"

Vale didn't know what Rosen was talking about anymore. The bed under his back was soothing but nothing could obscure the burn rising forcefully inside. He whimpered and threw his head back. "I need Jason," he said, voice clogged with tears.

"Jason's right here," Rosen said gently.

And then, somehow he was.

Blinking wetly, Vale reached for the tall, naked boy exiting his bathroom. He gasped at the sight of Jason's hard cock pointed right at him, and his tear-swollen, bruised face.

As the heat gripped Vale hard, he moaned, "Darling, you came."

# CHAPTER TWENTY-THREE

AFTER JASON HAD called Xan, he'd told Urho where he was
going.

Father was too distraught over Pater to notice Jason's absence,
and Urho could explain it all to him later when the danger had
passed. *If* the danger passed. That was yet to be determined.

After that, he'd taken a handful of alpha quell and stuffed more
in his pockets. He'd need to be in control.

Racing to Vale's house, the people on the sidewalks made way
when they saw him coming. Images of all he'd seen that day played
through his mind. He never wanted children. No matter what. Not
after that. It wasn't worth *that* at any price. He'd *never* take a
surrogate, and he didn't care what Vale had done in the past. So
long as Vale was safe now. Safe and not hurting. Which was Jason's
job. To make sure Vale didn't have to hurt anymore.

He was out of breath and sweating when he arrived at Vale's.
He hoped Xan had made it to his house half as fast. His pater
needed blood and Jason's photographic memory hadn't let him
down when it mattered most. As he'd been desperately casting
about for a solution, he'd remembered sitting next to Xan in
biology class two years prior, both of them pricking their fingers,
and scribbling down the test results. Wolf 3—that was what Xan
had written. And Wolf 3 was what Pater needed now.

Xan had been sleeping off his liquor but he'd agreed to come
over immediately when Jason told him the situation. Hopefully he'd
gotten there in time. Part of him wanted to call his house and make

sure, but a bigger part knew he couldn't control what was happening there. His duty was here with Vale. His pater was in good hands with Urho. Jason trusted him to do what needed to be done, even if it meant standing in the street and waving down drivers until he found one with Wolf 3 blood to volunteer.

Bounding onto Vale's porch, Jason reached for the bell, but Rosen pulled open the door before he had a chance to ring. His shirt was unbuttoned halfway down his hairy chest and his hair fell loose from the dark bun. His eyes were tired and weariness radiated from him in waves.

"Good. You're here." He tugged Jason inside, squeezing his hand reassuringly as he did. "You must be freezing."

Looking down at himself, Jason realized he'd again left the house without a coat. Since he was wearing only soft pants and a blood-stained t-shirt, he supposed he must be cold, but he didn't feel anything at all. There was so much distance between himself and the rest of the world—partially alpha quell but mostly shock— he could row a boat in it for hours and never reach shore.

Rosen rubbed Jason's bare arms, trying to warm them, and clucked his tongue. "You're quite the sight."

Yosef and Zephyr also lingered in the foyer. They'd all obviously been waiting for him. Zephyr wound between his legs in greeting and Yosef gave him a soft smile, his white eyebrows drawn low in concern. He reached out to shake Jason's hand and his grip seemed to lend strength. "Is everything going to be all right at home?"

Jason shook his head. He didn't know what to say or if he even *could* talk about what was happening at home. His faculties failed him.

"Come to the kitchen. Have tea and calm down," Yosef said, putting an arm around Jason's shoulders and hug-walking him into the hall.

"But Vale—"

"He's sleeping," Yosef said. "Finally."

"Thank wolf-god," Rosen added. "There will be enough time for you to warm up in the kitchen."

Settling Jason at the table, Rosen plied him with raisin bread he could barely taste and a cup of tea. He sipped it quietly and made crumbles of the rest. Meanwhile Yosef sat across from him and drank from a tall glass of water that made Jason think of the one he'd shattered in the hallway at home. He'd never cleaned it up.

Rosen took the open chair next to Jason and glanced at Yosef significantly.

"First let's address the bigger crisis," Yosef said, leaning against the table, lines creasing his forehead. "Tell us about your pater."

Jason did his best to explain the disaster at his house, the miscarriage, the blood, and the probable sepsis, without crying.

"I'm Wolf 3," Yosef said, as Jason drew to a close. He rose from the table. "I'll go now. If Xan hasn't arrived by the time I get there, maybe I can still help."

Jason was too grateful for words and his eyes filled again. Rosen pushed the hot tea into his hands, urging him to drink it.

After Yosef left, Zephyr leapt into Jason's lap. She nuzzled him and then settled in against him, her weight a comfort against his side. As he stroked her, the floodgates opened and the real tears came. Hot and silent, they slid down his face. He tasted their salt with each sip of tea.

Rosen squeezed his shoulder.

"I'm sorry," Jason said, wiping his eyes on his sleeve. "It's been a rough few days."

"Don't apologize." Rosen handed him a handkerchief from his pocket.

"How is Vale?" Jason asked, getting himself together.

Rosen shuddered. "It's been desperate. I thought I'd lose my mind listening to him. I was on the verge of calling you when..."

He trailed off. "Jason, be honest—are you up for this?"

Jason looked down at his blood-spattered clothes and shaking hands. "I don't know for sure. I've never handled a heat before." Gathering courage, he met Rosen's eye. "I guess I better be."

Quickly, Rosen outlined the plan and then led him up to Vale's bedroom bath, pointing out the towels, soap, and shampoo. He then grabbed fistfuls of alpha condoms from the giant box under the sink and took them out to Vale's bedside table.

Jason tried not to think of why Vale had an entire box of alpha condoms. Though of course he knew. Vale must have needed them plenty of times over the years, and it was good that he'd used them diligently. They'd kept him alive and safe for Jason to find him.

"I'll make sure there's plenty of food prepared in the kitchen. In between heat waves, you'll want to make him eat if you can. And you'll need to keep your own strength up."

"All right." Jason was exhausted. He had no idea how he was going to power through this. Only that he could. For Vale he would.

"You know how it works?"

A weird crack formed in his fear, allowing a bubble of his native humor through. Jason laughed. "I'm aware."

"Good." Rosen smiled at him and gave him a reassuring shake. "You can do this. You're his alpha."

Jason swallowed hard and nodded.

"Now, get cleaned up and I'll see about rousing him. He'll need a shower. I'll handle that in the other bathroom. You just get prepared. This will take a toll on you, too."

Jason nodded and headed into the bathroom to soak the trauma from his hands and skin. The warm water of the bath did a good job, but, even as he heard Vale and Rosen ascending the stairs, the racing fear for his pater didn't completely leave his bloodstream.

It was Vale's scent that broke him out of his panicked numbness. The sweet muskiness of Vale's slick drifted in to him from the other bathroom. His cock rose with a breathtaking rush. Vale's voice rumbled and Jason detected a raspy, spent quality to it, even through the bathroom wall. The coolness of the alpha quell battled with the rising heat of his lust. He took deep breaths. He could handle a heat. For Vale.

He dried off and set the rest of his alpha quell out on the bathroom counter for later. It would help keep him sane enough to remember to use the condoms, to not impregnate Vale, and to make good choices about how to spend the time between waves.

"I need Jason," Vale's voice rose pitifully from the bedroom.

"Jason's right here," Rosen answered.

As Jason stepped out from the bathroom, all he could see was Vale spread across the bed. He dragged his eyes from Vale's hard cock to his flushed nipples and then up to his red mouth and bright eyes. His skin was rosy from the shower and his hair glistened damply on the pillow. His eyes pierced Jason with a desperation that cut to the quick.

Rosen left, closing the door behind him.

"Darling, you came."

Jason approached the bed slowly, his heavy cock swaying in front of him. "You should have told me."

Vale shivered. "I didn't want you to know." He reached for Jason as his cock convulsed and leaked delicious pre-come. Jason's mouth watered and he moved closer, ready to lick it up. "But I can't recall why now."

Jason did. He remembered clearly how Vale's shame had driven him to try to burn the bond between them. But he didn't care anymore. Whatever Vale had done, whatever he'd said about his past—nothing was as important as keeping Vale safe. He couldn't do anything for his pater, but he could protect Vale forever.

"I'm here for you," Jason said. "You won't turn me away ever again."

Vale reached for him with his entire body, arching and calling to him, so wet, and open, and needy. Jason groaned, cock aching, balls twitching. The scent of slick was overwhelming and Jason wanted to bury his face there, licking and tasting that delicious fluid, but he also wanted to grab Vale's slim hips and drive into him the way he had on the sofa two nights before.

Torn between his impulses, it was Vale who decided for him.

"Oh, it hurts!" Vale gasped and arched up hard, crying out in pain, before flipping onto his stomach and lifting his ass high in the air.

Reaching for a condom, Jason rolled it on with shaking hands. It felt strange, a dull second skin, but through the material he felt the pressure of his fingers and the heat of his palm. He wiped nervous sweat from his eyes and crawled into position.

Vale pulled his ass cheeks apart, begging with his whole body, crooning for Jason to fill his hole. "Need it. Please, please, please. Need *you*, darling. It *hurts!*"

Nothing about this was how he'd imagined his first heat with Vale. He'd thought they'd take a trip to the shore, and they'd look forward to it for weeks with anticipation. He'd imagined nothing but pleasure for days.

But life kept proving to him, over and over, that it didn't give a damn what was supposed to happen. 'Supposed to' was for fairytales. No, Vale was here before him, on his knees, begging, after hours of pain. That was reality. Maybe it wasn't romantic, or dreamy, or sweet. But it was real. It was his. Vale was *his*.

To claim, and take, and soothe. To mark and fill. To forgive and love.

Screw contracts, screw the chomping teeth of death, and most of all screw the fantasies he'd spun before he knew any better. This was his life and his omega.

His Vale.

He aimed his cock and covered Vale's back, plunging deep and hard with his first thrust.

VALE CLAWED AT the bedding, pushing back to take more of Jason in. He moaned softly as his swollen omega glands released copious amounts of slick as Jason's huge cock pressed hard against them. The alpha dildo hadn't been enough—it never was. Vale reached back to grip Jason's hair and twisted to tug his mouth to his own. Jason's thickness expanded even more, milking his glands relentlessly with each thrust, and promising the knot to come. Vale quivered, anxious for it, greedy for the primal fullness that always left him awed and sated.

Jason broke their kiss, gripping Vale's hips and holding him steady and still with his cock buried deep. "Grip around me," he rasped. "Squeeze me tight."

Vale's mouth ached for want of Jason's lips and he tried to tug Jason down again, but a swift smack to his ass brought him to a gasping clarity.

"Grip me," Jason ordered again. Vale's stomach flipped over as he hastened to obey. "Tighter. Feel me inside you."

Vale squeezed all over, closing his eyes and moaning as his body vibrated around Jason's thickness. It felt more solid than anything in the world, and it felt so good against his tender, aching glands. Vale squeezed his fists, tightening as much as he could while the slick poured out, wetting their thighs and the bed, scenting the air with the musky smell of his need.

"That's right," Jason crooned, rubbing his hands up and down Vale's back soothingly. "Work your ass on my dick. Empty those glands on me. Such a good omega."

As Vale released and gripped again, his cock convulsed, drizzling pre-come to the sheets, and his eyes rolled up in his head. He wanted Jason to declare him good again—right now and every day, until the day he died.

"Mm, you smell so right," Jason moaned, leaning down to kiss Vale's shoulders and suck on his earlobe. "Want to roll in your slick."

Vale wanted to rub it all over Jason, too, make sure that every omega knew Jason was his man. He gasped when Jason placed his hand around his throat—gentle, but masterful—and murmured, "Grab hold of the sheets. I'm going to fuck you now."

Vale shouted as Jason thrust hard and fast, the bed banged against the wall, and the world dissolved. Their skin slapped in rhythm and Vale arched back, taking the thrusts hungrily, crying out for more, even as his cock exploded and shot wad after wad onto the bed. He shook in place, but didn't struggle against Jason's strong hand on his throat. He screamed as a second spike of pleasure pulled through him, and he convulsed and came again, his asshole gripping and releasing around Jason's pumping cock.

"Give me your knot," Vale begged.

Jason leaned forward, laughing in Vale's ear. "I took alpha quell. You're going to have to wait a while."

Vale gasped and Jason squeezed around his throat lightly.

"Take it. Open up," Jason murmured, rubbing his thumb up and down the side of Vale's throat. With each thrust, the head of his huge cock pressed against the mouth of Vale's descended womb, igniting the sensitive nerves there.

Vale cried out, clenching around Jason so that his glands gushed again. "Please, darling, knot me."

"I will," Jason whispered, kissing his earlobe before sliding his hands down to grip Vale's hips. "When I'm ready." He rested his forehead against Vale's shoulder blades, and thrust passionately.

Vale wailed and scratched at the sheets, coming again, his ass convulsing and his cock spurting. He whimpered while Jason kissed him, pushing back for more. He shivered and quaked, his heart somersaulting with each hard thrust, until he cried, "Please!"

But Jason didn't give him what he wanted.

Instead, he pulled out.

"No," Vale moaned, asshole gaping and ravenous.

Jason flipped him over onto his back with more strength than Vale knew he had. Collapsing beside Vale, he kissed his mouth and made soothing sounds, before reaching low and pressing three fingers inside.

"Fuck me!" Vale cried, humping up, riding Jason's fingers desperately. He'd suffered for hours and he wanted his reward *now*.

"I know," Jason murmured. "Just be patient."

Vale's skin prickled and his body ached. He needed Jason's cock. "Get back in me," he ordered, gripping Jason's chin. "Fuck me."

Jason tore his face free of Vale's grip, pulled his fingers out, and rolled up on top of Vale to restrain him. Vale pressed his hard cock—always so hard during heat—up against Jason's abdomen, and begged with his body, tweaking his own nipples, running his hands up and down his chest.

Jason groaned, bending down to lick the trails of pre-come from Vale's cock, and then he shoved Vale's legs up, burying his face between his ass cheeks.

Vale held his legs back, whimpering, as Jason rubbed slick all over his face and shoulders, mouthed his hole, and tongue fucked him. It was delicious but not enough. Never enough. He needed so much *more*.

Jason worked four fingers in easily and Vale squirmed, trying to make them hit all the right places inside, the places that Jason's cock easily rubbed against, making him come again.

"Where's the... oh," Jason whispered, as Vale cried out and arched. "There's the scar tissue. Does it always hurt?"

Vale clawed at Jason's hand between his thighs. Unable to talk, he spread his legs wider and rode Jason's fingers mindlessly, letting them glance against the scar tissue again and again. The pain was good, stretching and deep. Jason worked against the tissue with the pads of his fingers, and then he pulled back, lifted his hand to his face to scent it, and then smeared Vale's juices across his chest, leaving glistening streaks behind.

"Hold yourself open," he said. Vale gripped beneath his knees, spreading himself wide. His asshole gripped and released greedily, and he begged with every breath.

Jason stroked his cock, eyes raking up and down Vale's body. "Say it."

Vale moaned.

"Say it!" Jason ordered again.

"Alpha, with wolf-god's blessing, knot your omega," he whispered, invoking words he'd never spoken to any alpha, though some had tried to entice him. They were holy words, the start to the sacred bonding vow.

Jason's blue eyes glowed possessively and he plunged into Vale again, fucking him hard and fast, face buried in Vale's neck, muffling his cries. Vale clung desperately as his body was stuffed full of Jason's cock and then relieved of it, and then stuffed to the brim again. The scent of their union wafted around them in a heady musk.

"Fuck," Jason whispered, squeezing him so tightly that Vale had a hard time drawing breath. "Fuck...here it comes. Here's my knot."

Vale sobbed as he felt the tip of Jason cock press against the mouth of his womb, and then Jason thrust harder, popping the head inside. Orgasm claimed him again and he convulsed hard.

"Fill me," he begged, incoherent and reduced to instinct. "Fill me up!"

Jason threw back his head, a cry of gratification wrenched from him as he came. "Vale!" he shouted, his body twitching and convulsing between Vale's clinging legs. "Oh, wolf-god, it's…" Another teeth rattling convulsion gripped him. "It's too much."

Shudders clutched him, and then Vale felt it, too—the hard, bulbous knot forming at the base of Jason's cock, filling him up completely, pushing the last of the slick from his glands. He scrabbled at Jason's back, lost in pleasure, crooning and crying, his body spasming in bliss as his insides stretched around Jason's growing knot.

Jason twitched in his arms, lost in ecstasy, his knot stretching Vale open wide and locking them together. "Mine," he growled by his ear. "My omega, mine."

Vale squeezed around his knot and Jason howled, biting his shoulder, quivering and shaking as his cock pulsed deep in Vale's womb. Vale's eyes rolled up and he nearly lost consciousness as a cascade of orgasms rolled through him again. As he surfaced from the unbearable pleasure, he was sweating, crying, and still coming on Jason's knot.

A long time passed before Vale fully came out of the haze of bliss, the heat wave past, and the continuous orgasms slowing.

"Perfect, you're perfect," Vale whimpered when he could breathe again. He dared to squirm on the knot that held them together, and Jason almost broke the skin on his shoulder when he bit down again, convulsing through another orgasm. "Never been like this. The perfect fit."

Relaxed and sated for the first time since the first heat wave hit, Vale luxuriated on Jason's knot, squeezing it, and coming gently on it, never wanting it to soften. "Beautiful." His mind drifted in the lazy sweetness of the post-wave ecstasy of a knotted omega. "So beautiful, darling."

Jason moaned and sobbed gently against his shoulder, over-come. Vale rubbed his back and made soothing sounds, awed at the sweetness and the roughness of the boy who'd claimed him as his own. He kissed his neck gently, whispering, "Just hold me. I've got you."

Jason squeezed him tightly and shuddered again, tears wetting Vale's neck and shoulder. His heart swelled with tenderness and he whispered words of endearment.

As Jason clung to him, Vale licked his lips, suddenly sure, and whispered the rest of the omega's sacred words. "We are alpha and omega, the beginning and the end."

Jason lifted up to gaze down at Vale earnestly, sealing the vow with the alpha's response. "We are alpha and omega. The every-thing."

# CHAPTER TWENTY-FOUR

V ALE SLEPT DEEPLY, having finally passed out on Jason's knot as it softened, and after almost an hour of watching him sleep, Jason was famished.

Carefully, he extricated himself from Vale's grasp and pulled on a pair of Vale's soft pants. They were a bit short on him, but he wasn't about to put his bloody clothes back on. Then he chose a blue t-shirt, which fit fairly well. He checked that Vale was still sleeping before he opened the door to their room. There was water, fruit, and a package of cookies, but he was hungry for more. The scent of something spicy and warm wafted up from downstairs and he followed it to the kitchen.

Zephyr was on Rosen's shoulders as he stirred a big pot on the stove.

"Hey," Jason said, pulling at the bottom of his t-shirt hoping he didn't look ridiculous. "Is that for us?"

"It is indeed," Rosen said, smiling over his shoulder. "I went to the butcher and cheese shop when the screams started and, by the time I got back, the house wasn't shaking anymore." He winked at Jason. "I admit, I wasn't expecting you to have a great deal of skill, but from what I heard, Vale won't have any complaints."

Jason took a seat at the table as Rosen poured a bowl for him. "To be fair, I didn't do anything special. It was just intense. Together like that, during a heat, for the first time."

A sad smile crossed Rosen's lips. "I won't deny *that* part of the alpha-omega deal seems beautiful. But as for the rest? Well, listening to Vale this morning and afternoon did away with any notions I'd let myself develop since the last time I sat with him through a heat. No, thank you. I'll take being a beta anytime. Childless, and without a fairytale mate, sure, but free to choose who I love and fuck." He frowned when he looked at Jason.

"What?"

"Come here. I know something to help with that." He pulled Jason toward the cupboards and opened one to reveal a mess of liniments and ointments. He shuffled around inside. "Here." Then he carefully rubbed a soothing cream over the chafed spots on Jason's chin and face. "That beard burn is vicious. You should make him shave."

Jason felt his cheeks go hot but he didn't say a thing. There was no way he'd make Vale shave. He liked his body hair and loved the scrape of his beard. "My face will toughen up."

"Maybe. Eventually, you can grow one of your own." Rosen motioned at his own face. "It'll be a buffer."

Jason shrugged and sat down at the table again. Taking a bite of soup, he gathered his courage and asked, "Have you heard from Yosef?"

Rosen sat down across the table. Zephyr meowed and crawled down from his shoulder and settled in his lap. Jason was a tad jealous, he could use some comfort from Zephyr, but he supposed Rosen had been in her life longer, and he deserved her loyalty.

"He called." Rosen reached out to take hold of Jason's hand. "The news is cautiously good. Xan was there giving blood when Yosef showed up. Your pater's fever is stabilized, he hasn't gone septic after all, and he's stopped bleeding." He squeezed Jason's hand.

"Then what's the problem?"

"He's still very sick. Urho thinks his womb is infected. Perilously so."

Jason dropped the spoon, jerked his hand from Rosen's, and stood up. "How long will Vale sleep? Could I go home and get back in time?"

"Your pater is resting, Jason, and your father is with him. Yosef said to pass on the message from Yule that he understood why you'd left and he was glad you were gone during the worst of it."

Jason blinked at that. He'd missed the *worst of it*? How could anything have been worse than what he'd seen?

"He needs me, though, don't you think?" Jason asked. "If pater is that sick and his womb is infected, then I should go be with him, at least until Vale wakes up."

How had he let himself get lost in Vale when his father was suffering and his pater might be dying? He was selfish and stupid and—

"Whatever you're thinking, dear heart, you must immediately stop." Rosen tugged him back down into his seat and shoved the bowl of soup his way. "Eat."

Zephyr leapt from Rosen's lap, apparently inspired by the smell of the food, and headed over to the corner to pick at her kibble.

"This is the way life works. You're young, so you don't know that yet. But horrible things happen alongside wonderful things all the time. And if you let the horrible things detract from the wonder of the good things, you'll never really feel true happiness. You're allowed this time with Vale."

Jason didn't know what to say so he turned back to the soup. It was delicious now that he was paying attention. "Did you make this while we were...?"

"Not from scratch. I bought vegetable soup from Nix & Nots and then added beef from the butcher to make it heartier for you. You'll both need the energy. When you go back up, you should take a bowl and try to get him to eat."

Jason knew that, of course. He'd taken classes and his parents had given him the talks. But he just nodded, taking another bite, grateful Rosen cared.

"I made enough for a couple of meals. And I'll come back tomorrow with a casserole and some sides to hold you over. In the meantime, I'm going to head on home." His lips quirked up.

"But what if..."

Rosen shook his head. "You're going to be all right, Jason. And hopefully so will Miner. Urho is staying at your house until the danger has passed." Rosen rose from the table to refill Jason's empty bowl. "It was smart of you to think of him. Not many know, but Urho has a lot of experience in the field of omega health. After Riki died, he couldn't stand the lack of immediacy in his research at the university. He wanted to do something to help people in crisis. I think he saw it as penance for a crime he didn't commit."

"What sort of crime?"

"Failing to save Riki's life."

Jason thought of Vale and knew immediately if something had happened to him, something awful, he'd blame himself, too. Just like he knew Father would blame himself if Pater died. "Urho's a good man."

Rosen's dark eyebrows lifted. "Yes, he is. Annoying, but good." He smiled at Jason. "After Riki, Urho started volunteering his retired military medical skills to help the poor. Of course, one of the greatest dangers poor omegas face is childbirth. So he's handled a lot of births, along with miscarriages." He chose his next words carefully. "And rumor has it, maybe he's done a bit more at times, too, when an omega really needed it."

The oblique reference to Vale's past sent a sad shiver through Jason. He'd do anything to be able to turn back time and take those events out of Vale's history. Not because he wanted children, but because he hated that Vale had suffered so much, and that he'd blamed himself and felt so alone.

"I know about that," Jason said. "Vale told me."

"Good. I'm glad he isn't hiding it from you anymore." Rosen sighed. "Vale doesn't know that Yosef and I know what Urho did for him. He believes we think it was a stranger. But I think the time for keeping things from each other is past. We all know the truth."

Jason nodded. "I'm grateful Urho came when I called him. I didn't know what else to do." He flashed back to the panic he'd felt seeing his pater in agony.

"Urho is a sanctimonious jerk sometimes, but, like you said, he's a good man and a good doctor."

Jason finished eating, and Rosen showed him where Vale kept the silverware and plates. "So you can prepare things for yourself." He pressed a fresh bowl of soup into Jason's hands, a little less full than what he'd given Jason "Now take that up. He'll be waking before long."

Zephyr followed Jason from the room and he had to be careful not to stumble over her on the stairs. She hissed when he wouldn't allow her into Vale's room.

"We need privacy," he whispered to her.

She stared at him and then turned, tail in the air, to show him her ass. He chuckled.

"Sorry. It's just for a few days. After that…"

But the future was another scary thing he couldn't control, so Jason pushed that thought aside, too, and opened the door.

Vale sat up slowly, like his muscles ached and his ass was sore.

"You feeling all right?" Jason asked. "I didn't hurt you, did I?"

Vale puffed air through his lips. "Hardly, darling. I'll be ready for you again before we know it." He blinked as Jason climbed into bed with a bowl of soup. "What's this? Rosen made it?"

"He did."

"Maybe we should hire a beta cook for heats," Vale murmured, letting Jason feed him a spoonful. "Not to stay in, of course, but to prepare things to eat in advance."

His heart fluttered hopefully. "If you're planning for future heats with me, are you going to sign the contract now?"

Vale shrugged. "Maybe. Do we need one? Legally, everything that's mine is yours anyway. And the rest is details."

"Do you not want to contract with me? Truly?"

Vale's dark lashes touched his cheekbones. "If we don't contract, you could still take a surrogate and—"

"Stop, Vale." Jason held out another scoop of soup. "Eat more and then we'll talk."

Vale took several more proffered spoonfuls and then scooted back. "Enough."

Jason didn't argue. Omegas were notoriously hard to feed during heat so their colons could be put to a use better than elimination. "Listen carefully, now. I will never take a surrogate. Do you understand?"

"You are a stubborn man, Jason Sabel," Vale said with a dark glance through his lashes.

Jason put the bowl on the nightstand and then moved to a comfortable place on the pillow, gazing warmly at Vale's vulnerable expression. "Did you really think you'd scare me away with your confession?"

Vale rubbed at his beard, reminding Jason of the chafing on his own chin. It burned despite the ointment Rosen had rubbed on it. "I had hoped so, yes."

"Why? Is being with me so terrible? An hour ago, you were sobbing about the perfection of my knot."

Vale rolled his eyes, a fond smile on his lips. "You're an asshole."

Jason grinned. "No, you are."

"I think we've had this conversation before."

"And it ended with you begging me to fuck you. I suspect this one will end the same way." Jason puffed up.

"You're awfully proud of yourself, aren't you?" Vale asked.

"Making my omega cry with joy before he came so hard he passed out? Yes, I'm proud. I'm downright egotistical about it. I'm going take out an ad in the newspaper to announce it to the world and paint a big sign by the side of the busiest road in the Calitan section of town."

Vale giggled and it sent a ripple of joy up Jason's spine. "You silly, beautiful boy."

Jason cuddled Vale closer. "Vale, I need to tell you how sorry I am."

"For what?"

"I should have told you immediately, as soon as you told me, that what happened to you during that rebound heat wasn't your fault."

"It was my fault. If I hadn't—"

"*What happened to you wasn't your fault,*" Jason said again, authority filling his tone. "I want you to let that guilt go now. Do you understand?"

Vale swallowed hard. "Yes."

Jason kissed his mouth softly. "Also, thank you for telling me. That's what I should have said that first day. But I was an idiot and did everything all wrong. I'm sorry."

"I'm sorry I told you the way I did."

"You were scared," Jason said, softly.

"Yes," Vale admitted, his fingers digging into Jason's forearms. "But you deserve the best, Jason. You deserve better than—"

"We're *Érosgápe*. You are *my best*."

Vale lowered his gaze and nodded, and a tear slipped from his eyes. "I'm sorry I hurt you."

Jason kissed his forehead. "It was our first fight, that's all. I'm sure we'll have others."

"Wolf-god, I hope not."

"So you will contract with me, then?"

Vale lifted his eyes, bright with wonder. "I want that so much."

Jason kissed him until they were breathless. Then he pulled back and said, "Have you ever...I was wondering...during heat, have you tried..."

"Don't be shy with me now. I know what a filthy boy you are."

Jason cleared his throat. "Have you ever been fisted? I read at school that it can feel almost like a knot and that during heat some omegas are able to take a hand with some pretty amazing outcomes."

Vale shook his head. "I've never had anyone try that. Most alphas just want to get their knot and—" He broke off, frowning and shaking his head.

"It's just a thought."

Vale kissed him again, touching his face tenderly. "A generous thought. All about my pleasure instead of yours."

Jason shrugged. "I like to watch you come."

Vale shifted on the sheets, his body lithe and long, the tattoos glowing against his hair-scattered, flushed skin. "I'm not against trying it." Then Vale's brows crinkled and he sat up more fully. "What happened to your face?"

"You kissed me raw," Jason teased.

"No." He touched the bruise on Jason's jaw. "Who hit you?"

"Oh!" He'd nearly forgotten about Monhundy and those jerks. So much had happened since. "I was with Xan and..." he rolled his eyes. "It's hard to explain."

"I'm not sure I like this best friend of yours if he's hitting you. Maybe I'll punch *him* in the face to demonstrate my friendship as well."

Jason's heart glowed warm. Poor Xan, he'd probably be laid out flat by Vale if he ever followed through on that threat. "No, Xan didn't hit me. I was in a coffee shop with Xan and…" He groaned. "Unfortunately, it's a long story and honestly, I'm not sure we have time for it before the next wave of your heat comes."

Vale frowned. "All right. If you want to tell me about it later, that's fine." He curled up against Jason's chest, and played with Jason's nipples. Jason shivered as he tweaked them, and drew circles with his fingertips.

"Earlier, when I first saw you," Vale murmured. "You looked like you'd been crying. Was that because of me?"

Jason shook his head.

"No?" Vale sounded a little disappointed.

"I mean, I *did* cry because of you. Last night." He rolled his eyes at Vale's delighted expression. "Don't be proud about it."

"Oh, darling. I'd never be happy that my beautiful baby alpha cried over me. Never." But he glowed so brightly he was practically on fire with joy.

Jason jabbed Vale in the ribs. "I was done with crying over you by this morning, though. I was going to figure out how to get you back. But then…" He sighed and bit his lip. He didn't want to talk about this right now, but it couldn't be helped.

"Then what? Your friend Xan?"

"No, my pater." He took Vale's hands and said, "Now's not a good time to talk about that either. I want to be here with you and not…remembering."

"Jason, what happened?"

"He's going to be okay. Urho's with him."

"Oh. I see. The pregnancy." Vale's mouth turned down at the edges, understanding flashing in his eyes. "I'm sorry."

Jason gathered Vale close. "Me, too."

He pictured his future with Vale. This would be their room. He'd add pictures to the walls of his drawings from his favorite microscope slides. He'd go to school and come home to make dinner for Vale. He'd work in the garden, and Vale would write poetry and return to teaching his classes. It would be a regular, normal, everyday life. And it could be theirs.

"I don't want children," he said. "You're perfect for me just the way you are. We'll be fine on our own. We'll throw parties and invite our friends, and we'll grow old—"

"Some of us faster than others."

"—and we'll live our lives as happily as anyone can."

Especially when life clearly didn't follow the rules Jason had been led to believe existed. They could only do their best to be happy.

"You'll want children one day," Vale argued, nuzzling in close.

"After today, I don't think I ever will." He shuddered.

"But that wasn't the way it normally... I should really stop trying to convince you, shouldn't I? I'm not doing myself any favors here."

"And you're not making any progress anyway. I've made up my mind. I want you. And you want me." Jason nodded firmly. "When everything's said and done with this heat, you'll sign the contract—stipulating no births required—and I'll move in here."

Vale shivered against him. "Just like that? You're going to make the decisions for me then?"

"Yes. Because I'm your alpha and you apparently don't know what's good for you."

"Oh, I know what's good for me," Vale protested. "I was trying not to be a selfish asshole."

"And yet somehow you failed completely at that," Jason couldn't help but point out.

Vale snorted.

"Urho was right. I should have just told you what to do from the beginning."

Vale laughed, rolling up onto his elbow to gaze down at Jason.

"Oh, you've been taking lessons from Urho, have you?" He laughed again. "This will be fun. There's a reason, darling, he never appealed to me enough to consider a contract with him."

"I thought you were just waiting for me," Jason teased.

Any jealousy of Urho had evaporated while Vale had sobbed on his knot. He was quite sure Urho had never elicited that reaction or been declared so perfect. Though, if he had, Jason definitely didn't want to hear about it.

"Of course. Deep down, I knew you were out there." Vale rolled his eyes again. "No, darling. He's old fashioned and stuffy, and his ideas about omega-alpha relations are entirely backward."

"Hmm." Jason didn't say anything else, a bubble of amusement filling his chest at the memory of Vale's utter obedience to his every word during sex.

Urho was more than a little right about Vale, but Jason wouldn't push it. It wasn't his style to be bossy outside of the bed, and he didn't mind letting Vale have his way about, well, nearly everything. As long as Vale was happy, Jason would be, too.

"Oh, wolf-god," Vale said, shivering and curling up against Jason. "It's coming again. Did you want to try that thing you mentioned?"

"You've really never done it before?"

Vale shook his head. "But I'm curious."

Jason rolled Vale over and shoved his legs apart. "Get ready then, because I'm going to show you something truly amazing."

# CHAPTER TWENTY-FIVE

V ALE'S HEART PATTERED anxiously as he and Jason waited outside the door for admittance to Miner's sick room. When they entered, he was relieved to find Miner sitting up in bed.

"Pater," Jason whispered, and rushed into Miner's arms.

Vale hung back, watching as the family he'd agreed to be a part of clung to each other. Miner was pale but alive, and that was really all that mattered. Still, the dark circles under his eyes spoke to the trauma he'd suffered, and Yule's presence by his bed, hand held fast, did as well.

Vale looked around at Miner and Yule's bedroom. It was luxurious and fastidiously clean. He hoped Jason didn't think too much about the dusty rooms back at Vale's house, with the clothes tossed haphazardly on the chair. And on the floor. And in the corner.

Laundry. It was ridiculously annoying. Maybe he really should hire it out. Or not. He didn't care. He'd do whatever Jason wanted.

It'd been seven days since Vale's heat had begun and two since it'd ended. Afterward, he'd needed recovery time and Jason had, too. Over the phone, Yule had told them not to rush the aftermath. He'd said Miner was sleeping most of the time and he preferred to be alone with his omega.

But today they'd left for Jason's house after breakfast. They were both tired and somber, their bond sealed, but their hearts still wary about the future. Miner was doing much better, but there was still a lot of mending ahead before he'd be completely out of the woods.

As the family huddle broke apart, Jason took Miner's hand and sat on the bed next to him before motioning Vale closer. "Pater, look who came with me."

"I'm glad to see you here with Jason," Miner said, smiling and reaching out his free hand to Vale. "You both look exhausted, though."

"It's been a long week," Vale murmured, sitting at the edge of the bed next to Jason.

Miner smiled slowly. "For everyone."

"How are you?" Vale asked. "Everything is on the mend?"

Miner nodded and Yule spoke up, "Assuming he doesn't acquire any infection from the surgery, he should be able to go downstairs starting Monday, and Urho thinks he'll be his old self within the month."

"They won't let me smoke in here," Miner said, frowning. "Something about it being bad for my health." He shot Yule a glare and then smiled indulgently at him, reaching out to pet his hair. "It's time I quit that bad habit anyway."

Jason smiled and kissed his pater's hand. "I always hated it. It meant you were sad."

Miner smiled. "Maybe I'll have less to be sad about now. Dr. Chase removed my womb, did he tell you?"

"What? No!" Jason blinked rapidly. "Isn't that illegal?"

"Not if there's indication the womb was necrotic," Yule said, frowning and touching Miner's face gently. "Urho found evidence to that effect, or so he said, and once Miner was stabilized, he performed the operation. It was harder on me than on Miner. He was unconscious from Urho's anesthetics. I, however, watched the whole event."

"At your insistence," Pater said. "You refused to leave."

"I wasn't going to leave you alone. You might have needed me."

Vale's chest tightened as he watched Jason's parents dote on each other. His had been the same. He knew over time his bond with Jason would only strengthen, and, eventually, they'd be like that as well.

Jason's hand sought his on the coverlet.

Or maybe they were already there.

After they discussed a few more details of Miner's situation, they turned to the topic of Vale and Jason's contract.

"I'd like to apologize to you," Yule said quietly. "I never should have pushed the birth clause or suggested a surrogate. I was wrong."

Vale inclined his head to accept the apology and said nothing.

But Yule wasn't done.

"When I thought Miner... Well, when I thought I'd lose him…"

"You don't have to explain. I understand."

"I will say it," Yule said, lifting his chin. "And you will listen. All of you."

Jason stood up and moved behind Vale, wrapping his arms protectively around his shoulders.

Yule went on, "Jason had gone to be with you when the worst moment happened. Miner's heart stopped and Dr. Chase almost didn't get it started again. I was useless. Your friend, Xan, was helpful, though," Yule said to Jason. "He followed Urho's orders exactly, breathing into Miner's mouth while Urho pounded his chest."

"Wolf-god," Vale breathed and Jason's arms tightened around him.

Miner took hold of Yule's hand again, comforting him.

"And in that moment, I was so grateful that Jason wasn't here, that he was with you, and that he was, hopefully, happy."

Jason whimpered softly. Vale knew he'd felt guilty about their shared joy while his father and pater had been suffering so much. And he'd regretted personally that his own thankfully unsuccessful attempt to push Jason away had marred the bliss of their first heat together.

"I knew then how unreasonable and wrong I'd been. He'll be happiest with his *Érosgápe*, childless or not. It won't matter in the long run. Nothing lasts forever. No man, no relationship, no life. Death claims it all. So why try to defy that truth?"

"Love, you've gone rather deep and a touch morbid," Miner murmured, kissing his fingers. "I think a simple 'I'm sorry' was likely good enough."

Vale shook his head. "No, I appreciate your candor. It's a lesson you'd think I'd have learned after I lost my parents, but I didn't. Instead, I tried to push Jason away." He leaned back against Jason's tall form, happy for the strong, wiry arms around him. "I was afraid he'd find me lacking and resent being *Érosgápe*."

Part of him still worried, but Jason was so...Jason. Open, loving, ready to embrace their future together. He could only have faith in him.

Jason kissed the top of his head and murmured, "You're an idiot."

"You're an asshole."

"We've had this conversation before."

Vale's cheeks flushed and he rubbed his hand over his beard, looking away.

Miner yawned and Yule rose quickly. "You should go. Miner needs his rest. You two come back tomorrow. We'll discuss arrangements for signing a contract then."

"Tomorrow?" Jason asked, confused.

Yule glanced up from helping Miner get comfortable on the giant stack of pillows and said, "Aren't you planning to stay with Vale?" He blinked in confusion but went on rapidly, "You're welcome to continue living at home, of course. We love you and want you here if you want to be here. We just hadn't anticipated you'd want to stay."

"Oh! No, I…" Jason trailed off, turning to Vale. They hadn't discussed a timeline outside of Jason's declaration that they'd live together in Vale's house. They'd both assumed Jason's parents would want him to continue living at home until the contract was signed, possibly until Miner was on his feet again. But it was clear Yule had Miner's care well in hand, and no one seemed too worried about the contract anymore.

"You should pack a bag while we're here," Vale said. "You've already gone through the bag of clothes Xan dropped by for you. And I'm afraid I'm terrible about doing laundry."

Jason grinned at him. His blue eyes shone like the sun. "You want me to move in now?"

"Oh, yes. Don't worry. We can come back with boxes for anything else you need later."

Miner reached out a hand to Jason and he went over to kiss his pater again. "I'm sorry I scared you," Miner whispered, touching Jason's cheek. "I can only imagine what you must have felt seeing me that way, my sweet boy."

Jason smoothed Miner's hair off his forehead and kissed him there, too. "Father and Urho handled it. I just paced and prayed."

"That's not true," Father said. "You called Urho here. You arranged for Xan to come. You were a true man in the face of this crisis. We're proud of you."

Miner sighed. "And, luckily, we'll never have to face this sort of ordeal again."

"Thanks to Urho," Yule said. "He's the other hero of the hour."

"But Jason's the real hero for summoning him," Miner said, and yawned again.

"Enough talking for you," Yule said sternly. "You need to rest."

Jason hugged his father and kissed Miner one more time before taking Vale's hand and leading him from the room.

"YOU'RE TELLING ME those smiling faces aren't drawn on the slides?"

Jason laughed and shoved another shirt into his suitcase. He'd already balled up the t-shirt from the first time he and Vale had mixed their come and shoved it at the bottom of the bag, much to Vale's amusement, but he wasn't done with it. He might have Vale all for himself now, but he wasn't ready to part with such a sentimental item.

"I think you drew these smiles on here, Jason."

Jason zipped the suitcase and laughed again. "I swear. That's what sand dune grass looks like under the microscope."

Vale sounded incredulous. "Like smiling green babies?"

"Yes. But wait..." He crossed to the desk and pulled another prepared square of glass out of his slide box. "This is my favorite slide right now. Let me show you." Jason removed the sand dune grass slide and attached the other, bending over the microscope long enough to adjust the magnification. "There. Look."

"Oh! It's like one of Rosen's paintings."

"How so?"

"The colors and the strong lines." Vale leaned back from the microscope to look up at Jason with happy eyes. "What is it?"

"Dust. Like the stuff all over your house." He grinned. "Well, our house now, I suppose."

Vale laughed, his shoulders shaking, as he bent to gaze through the microscope lens again. "Just what are you saying, darling? I should dust more?"

"No, your...our house is a secret masterpiece. Everyone else sees dust, but not us. When we look around? We'll see this. Times a trillion."

Vale pushed the microscope away, standing up to capture Jason's lips in a kiss. "You're altogether adorable. What am I going to do with you?"

Jason smirked. "Well, I know what I'm going to do with you as soon as we get home and it involves your ass and my tongue."

Vale's dark eyes went glossy. "I see."

Jason waggled his eyebrows, a giddy bubble of joy popping and exploding in his chest. "You want me to demonstrate?" He gestured toward the bed.

Vale cleared his throat and chewed on his bottom lip, ducking his head almost shyly. "And if I said yes?"

"My door has a lock."

"I have to admit, my ass is very curious about this plan of yours. Will it make me come?"

"It better," Jason growled, slamming the door to his bedroom and locking it quickly.

Tossing Vale on the bed, he bounded on after him, kissing him hard and fast, rubbing his cheeks on Vale's soft beard, and nuzzling into his neck. His cock filled with blood and he humped against Vale's leg.

"Get your pants down," he ordered, holding onto Vale's jaw and licking behind his ear. "Now."

Vale squeaked and undid his pants, shoving them down quickly, exposing his hard cock. When he stroked it, Jason batted his hand away and straddled him. "Get your shirt off. I'm going to make a mess of you."

Vale moaned and shivered. "What if your parents—"

"They know what we did all last week."

Vale's fingers were already undoing his buttons, though, and his shirt came off quickly. Jason ran his fingers through Vale's chest hair, following it down his stomach to the treasure trail below his navel.

"Sexy," he muttered, bending low to rub his face against it all. "My gorgeous omega."

Vale let loose the sweet sound of surrender like he always did when Jason called him omega, arching into Jason's touch. He threw his head back when Jason smoothed his hands up to tease his nipples and then trailed his fingers back down to his cock.

"Tell me about these," Jason demanded, touching the tattoos on Vale's arms and running a finger over the line on his ribs. "When did you get them? Why?"

Vale shivered and sighed. "A long time ago. Post-heats. I was angry that I had to let those strange alphas fuck me. I wanted to reclaim my body. Make sure anyone who fucked me knew it was mine, not theirs."

Jason raised a brow. "And now?"

Vale lifted his brow in return. "Now?"

Jason laughed and kissed Vale's mouth before pressing kisses to each tattoo. "Now they're ours. No matter what we do, you're still Vale."

Vale reached up and grabbed Jason's collar, tugging him up to stare into his eyes. "You said something about your tongue and my ass. Don't be all talk, baby alpha."

Jason knocked his hand away and placed his own carefully on Vale's throat. "You're bossy for an omega." He squeezed lightly and then kissed Vale's red mouth. "I like you that way."

Then he flipped Vale over, shoved his legs apart, and rimmed his hole long and hard, until he came, trembling and gasping Jason's name.

AFTER THE SEX, Vale helped pack up the rest of Jason's things. He sang a little tune under his breath, something he'd heard his pater sing years before. Jason hummed along, providing harmony, and before Vale knew it, they had three stuffed bags worth of belongings to join the mess at Vale's house.

But as Vale turned to unlock the bedroom door, Jason gently grabbed Vale's hand and said, "Let me show you one more thing."

He opened the window that overlooked the beautiful yard and climbed out onto the roof beneath it. Kneeling on the opposite side, he stretched his fingers out to Vale.

Vale shivered.

The memory of their first interview through his study window rose, sweet and absurd, to the front of his mind. *"I'm here now."* Vale reached outside, took Jason's hand, and let him lead him out onto the slates.

Vale sat down, taking in the yard, the house next door, and the trees reaching up to the blue sky. "This is quite the view. I'm afraid there's nothing like it at my house."

"But you're there, so it will be perfect," Jason said, leaning back with his elbows against the roof and his knees pointing up at the sky. He tilted his head back, and the line of his neck was interrupted by the bump of his Adam's apple. Vale's mouth watered. He wanted to kiss it.

"I first read your poems out here," Jason murmured.

"Oh, really? Funny, because I'm writing a poem about you right now."

"You are?"

Vale chuckled. "Yes. In my head."

"Tell me." Jason sat up. "Do you need paper? Should I get some for you? I don't want you to forget it. You really should write it down."

Vale laughed, the sound echoing against the house and out over the autumn leaf-strewn yard. "You truly want me to write poems about you?"

"And publish them. Yes." Jason nodded excitedly. "I think everyone needs to know how much you love my cock. You need to tell them. In a very explicit but elegant way."

Vale laughed again. "I thought you were going to put an ad in the newspaper about it."

"But this is much classier. Much more upper crust." He winked and tugged Vale closer. "I'm going to be Jason Sabel, world-renowned scientist and heir to my father's company one day. We can't look cheap while letting the world know I'm the greatest alpha you've ever known."

Vale rolled his eyes before leaning over to whisper the opening line in Jason's ear.

"Yes, I love it," Jason said, taking Vale's chin in hand. "What comes next?"

The second line of the poem was swallowed by Jason's mouth. Vale didn't protest. Pressed back against the sun warmed slate roof, he tugged Jason down on top of him. The blue sky stretched above, the world spun on around them, but on the roof outside Jason's bedroom, they were all that mattered.

Alpha and omega, coming together, full circle.

The beginning and the end.

# EPILOGUE

"**A**RE YOU SURE it was wise to ask Urho along?"

Rosen poked Vale in the ribs, nodding to where Jason and Urho stood knee deep in the crashing waves, talking endlessly about *science*. Urho had agreed to take Jason on as a research assistant during his sophomore year at the university and now they were altogether too chummy.

Vale leaned back in the wooden beach chair, stretching out his pale legs, enjoying the first true warmth of summer. They'd descended on Jason's parents' beach house and planned to stay for two weeks. "If they don't stop discussing how omega anal orgasms and the lordosis behavior are tied to our spliced wolf DNA and theorizing on precisely *why*, then I might have some regrets. Yes."

Rosen laughed as he smoothed aloe over Yosef's shoulders.

"Those two have too much in common," Yosef muttered, irritable after having fallen asleep in the sun on the first afternoon of their holiday and suffering a sunburn for it. "You must hate when they both get going like this."

Vale shrugged. Deep down, he was happy to see his former lover getting along so well with his alpha. Yosef was right that they had more in common than they knew. Though if he said that to Urho, all he'd get would be a crass comment about how they'd both been in Vale's ass.

But it went so much deeper than that.

Both men shared a devotion to their friends and family, demonstrating their shared strength of character and loving hearts. Most days, Vale couldn't believe how lucky he'd been to have found Urho when he needed him, and then to have been found by Jason when he didn't *know* he needed him.

Vale couldn't be happier.

He glanced toward Xan, Jason's best friend, as he dug a hole in the sand and frowned out toward the sailboats in the distance. As far as happiness went, Xan was another matter. Vale pitied him greatly and wished he knew him better. Despite Jason insisting Xan was a bit of a clown, he'd been quiet on the holiday so far, but when he did talk, he was entertaining enough. His eyes lingered too long on Urho, though, for safety, and Vale worried what might happen if Urho noticed. But so far, everyone had gotten along swimmingly, and there'd been no fights.

Well, aside from Zephyr, who'd fought like hell to keep from being caught and put into the cattery for the duration. Vale still had a scratch on his forearm and a bite on his hand from that. Urho had fixed it up, though, and Jason applied the medicine he'd prescribed nightly.

"Are you excited to get back to teaching next fall?" Rosen asked.

"Or have you grown lazy and spoiled by Jason's attentions?" Yosef said.

Vale laughed, digging his toes into the sand. "I admit I've ended up enjoying my sabbatical more than I anticipated when it was forced on me. But, yes, I am looking forward to teaching. I'm not, however, looking forward to my students giving me grief about their classmate being my alpha."

Xan snorted, obviously listening, but not really contributing to the conversation. "Yeah, good luck with that," he murmured.

"I've been meaning to ask," Yosef said, pointing to a place on his side that Rosen missed with the aloe. "How is Miner doing?"

"Quite well. He still has heats, believe it or not. They aren't quite the same since the operation, but the hormones that trigger heats still happen. Now they can relax during them, though, and not have to worry, since he has no womb for carrying."

"That's fantastic."

"He and Yule are happier than they've been in years, Jason says. And I believe him. They act like they're on a honeymoon." Vale slipped his hand down to scratch at the hair beneath his navel. Part of him still yearned to carry a child for Jason, but he no longer worried that Jason would resent him for not being able to do so. The adoring way Jason cared for him in every way—physical, emotional, and financial—more than canceled out his fear. It obliterated it.

"Xan!" Jason called. "Come here!" He beckoned for his friend to join him. The sun poured into Jason's hair making him appear like an angel sent from wolf-god above.

Xan stood up and headed into the sea, splashing toward Urho and Jason. Vale grinned as Jason's laugh bounced off the water and straight to Vale's heart.

Vale swallowed his gratitude like a wad of joy and then stretched out even more on his beach chair, letting the sun warm his exposed chest and arms. He closed his eyes, safe among his loved ones. The sound of the waves and the cool breeze washed over him soothingly. He drowsed in happiness, jolting awake when Jason collapsed on top of him, wet and cold from the ocean.

"Wake up, baby. Come swim with me. The water's perfect." He kissed Vale's mouth. "Like you."

Vale laughed, grabbed hold of his happiness and didn't let go, splashing after his future into the cerulean blue sea.

# Philia:
## A Heat of Love Bonus scene

A PHILIA SOCIETY soirée was the last place on earth Xan ever wanted to be.

The Philia Club *itself* wasn't terrible. It was at the top of one of the new skyscrapers going up all over the city and boasted a view of the glittering electric lights in the Blue Vein neighborhoods and the warmer glow of candles in the Calitan district. The club itself screamed prestige and wealth. Beta butlers and waiters took care of every alpha and omega's needs, passing around alcohol to lighten the mood and loosen the tongue. Delicious food was laid out on multiple tables, everything from lobster to venison, and lemon tarts to pudding.

Everyone was dressed in their best, most fashionable attire, attempting to attract the right kind of attention from a special alpha or omega. Matchmaking was the name of the game, and anyone at a Philia soirée was desperate enough to be presenting only their very best selves. The diamonds and gemstones on display in alphas' cufflinks, and in the hair barrettes, rings, and other jewels on omegas, were almost obscene.

All of which conspired to dazzle some of the poorer, unmatched omegas present. Evidence of their poverty in their hunger-hollow cheeks, they gazed around with wide-eyed awe, and adjusted their threadbare clothes uncomfortably. Xan felt for them, but they were the lucky ones. Even poor omegas had every chance of making a match into a situation better than they currently endured.

Impoverished, unmatched alphas? Less so.

Luckily, Xan was not poor. Nowhere close to it. To him, the glitz of the Philia Club was downright commonplace, but, even so, his situation was fraught. He'd happily take the odds of one of the poor, unfashionable, unmatched alphas in finding a suitable omega in this mix over his own odds for the same any damn day.

He adjusted his bow tie, a red and black striped choice that he'd made to match the red of his waistcoat. But he now regretted choosing anything to make himself stand out. He tugged at his collar and then plucked a champagne glass from a passing waiter's tray and tossed the fizziness back. Several wealthy omegas eyed him with interest. A dark haired one with hazel eyes and an aristocratic chin, and a blond with blue eyes and the kind of nose that Jason would call snub, but Xan called piggy. The young men waved Xan over.

Ignoring the gestures, Xan turned his back on them both. He sidled into an adjacent room, hoping he wouldn't get cornered by any other hopeful omegas as he did. He was Xan Heelies, after all, heir to the Heelies fortune, and everyone in this room knew that. If he made it out of the party tonight without an omega stripping down naked for him to show off his goods, he'd be lucky. He shuddered at the thought.

The room he'd slipped into was darker, with little, secluded alcoves decorated with potted plants and covered in climbing ivy. Sheer curtains over the alcoves could be closed for a bit more privacy. The area was designed to be 'romantic' so potential couples could be alone to talk, find out if they were compatible, and, even, he guessed, make-out just to see if they could get into each other 'that way'. There were some rooms in the very back for omegas who'd already been through a heat, and who wanted to test full compatibility with a potential alpha.

Philia club meetings weren't for the prudish, after all.

In fact, Xan had holed up in one of those back rooms the last time his father had forced him to attend one of these events. He'd slept on the cushy bed until one of the organizers flipped on the light and told him the party was over. He'd considered the night a success. But he'd gotten into all kinds of trouble when he got home because, apparently, his father had spies everywhere.

"Your job is to reproduce and make an heir. I don't pay for you to attend Philia parties so you can sleep alone in a back room. Take an omega with you at least!" his father had snarled in disgust.

So, tonight Xan was doing his best to *look like* he was socializing, without ever talking to anyone.

As he casually walked around the room, careful not to peep into any alcoves, and avoiding eye contact with omegas and alphas alike, he kept his face carefully neutral. As he rounded a corner, though, he stopped dead in his tracks having spotted a familiar face. He blinked rapidly. Yes, there was no mistaking that handsome face. It was Wilbet Monhundy, smiling ingratiatingly down at a handsome, young omega, with dark eyes and longish, curly brown hair.

The omega was thin and moved with a sexy grace that distracted from his strangely concave chest. The deformity—if it could be called that—made him all the more interesting to look at. A hot, angry, not-quite-jealous pulse pounded against Xan's nerves, as his heart quickened, and his gut tightened. Worse, his cock grew slightly hard when Monhundy suddenly looked away from his quarry and gazed right at Xan, glinting a rageful smile at him, full of promise and hate.

Xan swallowed hard and turned on his heel, ducking into the shadows of what looked to be an empty alcove. He quickly pulled the flimsy, loosely tied curtain across the rod, sealing himself inside alone. The scent of roses and pepper tingled in his nose.

He wiped a hand over his suddenly sweaty upper lip, and squeezed his eyes closed. It shouldn't have been a surprise to see his bully here. He knew as well as anyone that Monhundy had not found an Érosgápe yet and that his family was urging him to contract, make a good match, and create heirs. The same as Xan's. But he hadn't imagined ever seeing Monhundy outside of run-down bars, the occasional business meeting, or the dark encounters they shared which left Xan in pain and full of self-loathing.

He'd imagined the dangers of attending the Philia Society soi-rees to be of an entirely different sort.

"Hiding from an especially aggressive omega, are we?" a soft, cultured voice asked from behind him.

Xan nearly came out of his skin, anxious as he was after spotting Monhundy. He swung around, eyes straining at the shadows of the alcove, spotting a man—an omega—with blond hair, cut to his cheekbones, pillow lips, and smart blue eyes. Sweat slipped down the small of Xan's back as he heard Monhundy's snarl of a laugh through the flimsy curtain.

"Just...hiding," Xan said. He snapped his mouth closed, an-noyed with himself for speaking at all. He should have simply fled. But to where? Not out where Monhundy would spot him again. He wasn't up for playing Monhundy's painful games tonight. And he knew, based on that gleam in Monhundy's eyes alone, if he didn't stay far away from the man, that was exactly how the evening would end.

"I see." The blond man said nothing else but gestured at the open space on the sofa beside him. There was a table, too, with several unused glasses and one that had some bourbon in it. There was a bottle of bourbon on the table, too. "Have a seat. I won't bite."

Xan rubbed his palms against his suit pants, and then nodded. "Thank you. I'll just sit for a few minutes."

"Until the danger passes?"

"Yes."

The blond man smirked but put out a hand as Xan sat next to him. "Caleb Riggs."

"Oh. I'm Xan. Uh, Xan Heelies."

"Ah!" He twinkled with recognition now. "And that's why you're hiding."

Xan blew out a breath, trying to cool his face. It shifted around his curls that were trying to stick to his forehead.

"Here," Caleb said, picking up the bourbon bottle and taking one of the clean glasses. "Have a drink. It'll calm your nerves."

Xan almost protested that his nerves didn't need calming, but he stopped himself because, obviously, they did, and he really wanted a drink, so… He took the offered glass and gulped half of it.

When he put it down on the table, he caught Caleb's eyelashes fluttering in horror at his gauche manners. "I swear my pater taught me better than this," he said. "I don't know what's come over me."

"Philia soirée panic," Caleb said smoothly. "I'm familiar with it. Intimately so. But don't worry. After a few years, it wears off."

Xan's eyes began to adjust fully to the dimness, and he saw Caleb's suit was all white, except for a blue waistcoat, and a blue pocket square. He wore blue-jeweled barrettes in his hair and was a bit older than Xan, that was obvious. But very unlike most of the older omegas, he was beautiful—tall, trim, and lovely from top to bottom. Xan wished that did anything for him at all, but alas. He also wondered what Caleb was doing hiding out alone in an alcove, instead of flirting with available alphas. He appeared imminently matchable.

"This is my tenth soirée," Xan said. "I hid during the first nine, too."

"Well, drink up. Fortify yourself. Then go find an omega."

Xan snorted, picking up his glass to try to cover it.

"No? None of the young things here tonight are to your taste?"

"They're pretty enough." Xan shrugged. Maybe that was part of the problem. He didn't like pretty so much as rugged. And he didn't like omegas so much as *alphas*. So… It was a problem. And forbidden. And, well, it explained a lot about what he got up to with Monhundy, he supposed. Not to mention why the omegas trying to catch his attention in the main room only made his head ache and his stomach whirl.

Caleb's brows went up, but he said nothing. They sipped their bourbon in oddly comfortable silence until Caleb refilled both of their glasses.

"I'm not trying to be an asshole, but why are you *here?*" Xan asked when the liquor had done its job of loosening his tongue, just the way the Philia planners wanted. He gestured at the little alcove they occupied.

"Same as you. Hiding out."

"Yeah, but *why?*" Xan rubbed a hand over his upper lip again, sweat remaining. Between the fright of seeing Monhundy, the liquor, and the closeness of the alcove, he was warm. He tugged at his collar and sighed.

"Go on," Caleb said. "You can take your coat off, undo your tie. Relax. I won't mind. It might start some tongues wagging, but that's all right with me, if it's all right with you."

"You're not worried about gossip?"

"Gossip that I made out with Xan Heelies? No. I'm not worried about that." Caleb laughed heartily, and it was a pleasant laugh. One that tugged a chuckle out of Xan, too. "Such sordid accusations couldn't do anything but help my reputation at this point," he added, lifting his drink to Xan, and then sipping from it again. "So thank you for giving everyone something to talk about when you ducked in here tonight. My father will be thrilled."

"I guess I don't mind gossip either," Xan said. His father would also be thrilled if he heard that Xan had touched any omega, much less one as beautiful as Caleb. This…this could be good for him, maybe for them both if Caleb was being honest. He tugged off his bow tie and his suit coat, throwing them over the back of the sofa. "You too. Get comfortable."

Caleb shrugged, but then removed his own white tie, and the coat. Then he took it one step farther by removing his waistcoat, and white button-down shirt, sitting back in just a short-sleeved v-neck. "That's better. Thank you. It's always far too hot in here."

"Maybe they want us to disrobe," Xan suggested.

"Probably." Caleb rolled his eyes.

"I'm not going to touch you."

"Good, because I wouldn't let you."

"Good." Xan nodded and they smiled at each other again. "So, it's weird, isn't it? Meeting strangers and trying to decide if we want to know them better."

"I don't mind making new friends, but too often alphas want to move faster than that." Caleb grew a bit tense and poured more bourbon. "I prefer to remain at the friendship level for a very long time."

"I don't know why that would be a problem," Xan said. "That's why it's called the Philia Society. Because most of us, if we find someone to contract with here, will have to start off learning to love each other as friends, and for some of us, even if we contract, there can never be anything more than that."

Caleb's eyes sharpened and he leaned forward with an imperious smirk. "And how do you feel about that potential outcome?"

"Relieved," Xan said, bluntly. Then he took a big swallow of the bourbon to cover it up.

"Me, too," Caleb said, like it was filthy secret. Caleb's lips twitched and he smiled. It was like a light in the darkness, and Xan smiled back with a strange flutter of hope in his chest.

Perhaps Caleb could be his friend. He thought he might like that.

Xan's smile widened and he lifted his glass to toast. "To friendship."

"To Philia." Caleb returned.

They drank and the evening slipped by in conversation that was both easy and amusing.

At the end of the night, they were both wasted and sloppy, slouching on the sofa, and laughing hysterically at some snarky observation of Caleb's. He was truly quite good at them, and Xan wished he had the same gift.

The curtain jerked back, and a flashlight swept over them. "Party's over, kids," a stern voice said, and behind the glare of the light Xan could just barely make out a flushed beta's bearded face. "You're among the last to leave. Get dressed. We'll call you both a cab."

Xan glanced down at himself. As they'd talked and drank, he'd taken off his shirt, too, and now he looked quite disheveled if he did say so himself.

"Can you make sure everyone knows we're back here?" Caleb slurred. "Tell them all you found me half-dressed with Xan Heelies."

Xan snorted, groping around for his shirt, bow tie, waistcoat, and jacket, while Caleb did the same. "Yeah," Xan agreed. "Spread some rumors about us."

The beta sighed. "You're both drunk enough I doubt anything happened at all."

"Not true!" Caleb said, tugging on a shirt. "Lots happened."

Xan nodded vehemently. He'd found a friend if nothing else. And maybe, just maybe, something more than a friend. "So much happened!" he enthused.

"Bourbon happened," the beta said, lifting the nearly empty bottle. "And you're both going to be sick as dogs later."

Xan burped. He might be sick as a dog now actually.

He and Caleb bumped into each other, laughing, as they managed to get dressed again. They stumbled out of the alcove and into the abandoned room. Xan took hold of Caleb's hand and said, "I'll be here next week. Will you?"

Caleb tugged his hand back, a small frown on his face. "I might be here."

"We can hide in another alcove together."

Caleb shrugged, glancing toward the beta servant, a strange, sloshy coolness descending on him. "I'm not sure that's a good idea."

Xan frowned for a moment and then shrugged. "If you don't want to be friends—"

"I do," Caleb said, gripping Xan's arm hard. "I want to be friends. But that's all. Understand?"

Xan smiled up at him. "Music to my ears."

Caleb's eyes flickered. "Really?"

"Next week. Same time. Same alcove. Bring gin."

"*You* bring gin. You're Xan Heelies. I'm afraid I have no fortune."

"All the better." Xan nodded. "Fine. I'll bring gin."

The beta guided them out into the main room where waiters and other servants were dismantling the party. A few omegas lingered, waiting for cabs, also obviously drunk. A handful of alphas stood alone by the elevator, a couple of them gazing at the drunk omegas speculatively.

"Omegas wait over there," the beta said, nodding toward the huddled group. "Alphas by the elevator."

"I could take you home," Xan said suddenly, a strange forlorn feeling coming over him at the idea of them parting.

"No," Caleb said. "Not tonight."

"Next week then?"

"Probably not next week."

The beta snorted. "Playing hard to get."

Xan glared at him until the beta backed away, hands raised. He turned back to Caleb. "I don't mind sharing a cab. I want to spend more time with you."

"Xan, I…" Caleb blew a piece of blond hair away from his cheekbone. "You'd be better off courting any other omega besides me, understand? This—" he gestured between them. "Isn't going anywhere."

Xan put his chin up. "I know. And I agree."

Caleb looked relieved.

"But I want to see you again all the same."

Caleb studied him for a moment, tilting his head, and he finally replied, "In that case, next week will have to do."

"If you insist."

"Gin," Caleb said, a spark in his eye, as he stepped toward the huddled omegas.

"Gin," Xan agreed, and repeated, "Same time. Same alcove."

Caleb smiled sharply but said nothing more. Before Xan knew it, Caleb and the other omegas were being hustled onto the elevator and taken down to meet their cabs home. A flutter in his chest told him something new had started. Something…not common, not perfect, not like *Érosgápe*, or even eros love, but the kind of friendship that was somehow destined from the start.

True philia.

He smiled, thinking of how much he'd hated the idea of coming tonight. And now Xan couldn't wait for next week's Philia Society soiree. He couldn't wait to get to know Caleb.

He knew they were going to be very good friends.

## THE END

Thank you for reading! If you'd like to know more about Xan and Caleb, read the story of their friendship and Xan's journey to forbidden love in my book *Alpha Heat*!

# Letter from Leta

Dear Reader,

Thank you so much for reading *Slow Heat*, the first in the *Heat of Love* series! I hope you enjoyed the bonus scene from Xan's point of view set some time after the end of *Slow Heat*.

If you enjoyed this book, look for more of Vale and Jason in *Slow Birth*. If you'd like to read Xan's full novel, his story can be found in *Alpha Heat*. Then the *Heat of Love* universe expands with the critically acclaimed third book, *Bitter Heat*.

Be sure to follow me on BookBub or Amazon to be notified of new releases in this series and others and look for me on Instagram for snippets of the day-to-day writing life. To see some sources of my inspiration, follow my Pinterest boards. I'm also on Facebook, so add me there, too!

If you enjoyed *Slow Heat*, please take a moment to leave a review! Reviews not only help readers determine if a book is for them, but also help a book show up in searches.

Also, for the audiobook connoisseur, the first three books in the series, *Slow Heat, Alpha Heat,* and *Bitter Heat* are available at most retailers that sell audio, narrated by the talented Michael Ferraiuolo.

Thank you for being a reader!
Leta

*Book 2 in the Heat of Love series*

# ALPHA HEAT
by Leta Blake

**A desperate young alpha. An older alpha with a hero complex. A forbidden love that can't be denied.**

Young Xan Heelies knows he can never have what he truly wants: a passionate romance and happy-ever-after with another alpha. It's not only forbidden by the prevailing faith of the land, but such acts are illegal.

Urho Chase is a middle-aged alpha with a heartbreaking past. Careful, controlled, and steadfast, his friends dub him old-fashioned and staid. When Urho discovers a dangerous side to Xan's life that he never imagined, his world is rocked and he's consumed by desire. The carefully sewn seams that held him together after the loss of his omega and son come apart—and so does he.

But to love each other and make a life together, Xan and Urho risk utter ruin. With the acceptance and support of Caleb, Xan's asexual and aromantic omega and dear friend, they must find the strength to embrace danger and build the family they deserve.

*Book 2.5 in the Heat of Love series*

# SLOW BIRTH

by Leta Blake

**Jason and Vale are back in this side story set in the *Heat of Love* universe!**

A romantic getaway turns dramatic when an unexpected heat descends on Vale, leaving Jason with no choice but to act. The resulting pregnancy is dangerous for Vale and terrifying for Jason, but with the help of friends and family, they choose to embrace their uncertain future. Together they find all the love, joy, and heat they need to guide them through!

**While this story follows the characters from *Slow Heat*, it would be most enjoyable if read directly after *Alpha Heat*, as it takes place contemporaneously with that book.**

*Book 3 in the Heat of Love series*

# BITTER HEAT

by Leta Blake

**A pregnant omega trapped in a desperate situation. An unattached alpha with a lot to prove. And an unexpected fall into love that could save them both.**

Kerry Monkburn is contracted to a violent alpha in prison for brutal crimes. Now pregnant with the alpha's child, he lives high in the mountains, far above the city that once lured him in with promises of a better life. Enduring bitterness and fear, Kerry flirts with putting an end to his life of darkness, but fate intervenes.

Janus Heelies has made mistakes in the past. In an effort to redeem himself, integrity has become the watchword for his future. Training as a nurse under the only doctor willing to take him on, Janus is resolute in his intentions: he will live cleanly in the mountains and avoid all inappropriate affairs. But he doesn't anticipate the pull that Kerry exercises on his heart and mind.

As the question of Kerry's future health and safety comes to an explosive head, only the intervention of fate will see these desperate men through to a happy ending.

# Winter's Heart

### Winter-fox always brings Tristan the best gifts

Tristan wakes every winter holiday to find a present that delights him or teaches him an important lesson.

Learn more about the character of Tristan, *Bitter Heat*'s Kerry and Janus's son, in this short winter holiday-themed story. This small bonus book doesn't contain the heat level of the full-length novels in this series, but it has all the cozy, hopeful warmth for a sweet holiday read. While it ends on a romantic note, the story does **not** contain a romance arc.

This story is **not a standalone** and is best read as an addition to the *Heat of Love* series, preferably after reading *Bitter Heat*. But if you should happen to read it out of order, you can find the rest of the books on Amazon and in Kindle Unlimited. *Another Heat of Love bonus novella by Leta Blake.*

# Winter's Truth

### Winter-fox brings Viro some surprising truths for the holiday

Viro Sabel is eleven years old and still entirely innocent about life. This year winter-fox brings him some surprising truths that alter the way he sees the world and his place in it.

Learn more about the character of Viro, *Slow Heat*'s Vale and Jason's son, in this **winter holiday-themed novella**. This medium-sized bonus book **features spicy scenes** between Vale and Jason, family scenes, and emotional moments. While the novella's epilogue teases a relationship for an adult Viro, it ends with a mystery regarding this person's identity.

This story is ***not* a standalone** and is best read as an addition to the *Heat of Love* series, preferably after reading *Slow Heat, Alpha Heat,* and *Slow Birth*. But if you should happen to read it out of order, you can find the rest of the books in the series on Amazon and in Kindle Unlimited.

*An Omegaverse by Leta Blake writing as Blake Moreno*

# HEAT FOR SALE
### Heat can be sold but love is earned.

In a world where omegas sell their heats for profit, Adrien is a university student in need of funding. With no family to fall back on, he reluctantly allows the university's matcher to offer his virgin heat for auction online. Anxious, but aware this is the reality of life for all omegas, Adrien hopes whoever wins his heat will be kind.

Heath—a wealthy, older alpha—is rocked by the young man's resemblance to his dead lover, Nathan. When Heath discovers Adrien is Nathan's lost son from his first heat years before they met, he becomes obsessed with the idea of reclaiming a piece of Nathan.

Heath buys Adrien's heat with only one motivation: to impregnate Adrien, claim the child, and move on. But their undeniable passion shocks him. Adrien doesn't know what to make of the handsome, mysterious stranger he's pledged his body to, but he's soon swept away in the heat of the moment and surrenders to Heath entirely.

Once Adrien is pregnant, Heath secrets him away to his immense and secluded home. As the birth draws near, Heath grows to love Adrien for the man he is, not just for his connection to Nathan. Unaware of Heath's past with his omega parent and coming to depend on him heart and soul, Adrien begins to fall as well.

But as their love blossoms, Nathan's shadow looms. Can Heath keep his new love and the child they've made together once Adrien discovers his secrets?

*Heat for Sale* is a stand-alone m/m erotic romance by Leta Blake, writing as Blake Moreno. Infused with a du Maurier *Rebecca*-style secret, it features a well-realized omegaverse, an age-gap, dominance and submission, heats, knotting, and scorching hot scenes.

# Gay Romance Newsletter

Leta's newsletter will keep you up to date on her latest releases and news from the world of M/M romance. Join the mailing list today and you're automatically entered into future giveaways.
letablake.com

# Leta Blake on Patreon

Become part of Leta Blake's Patreon community in order to access exclusive content, deleted scenes, extras, bonus stories, rewards, prizes, interviews, and more.
www.patreon.com/letablake

# Other Books by Leta Blake

## Contemporary

Will & Patrick Wake Up Married
Will & Patrick's Endless Honeymoon
Cowboy Seeks Husband
The Difference Between
Bring on Forever
Stay Lucky

### Sports

The River Leith

*The Training Season Series*
Training Season
Training Complex

### Musicians

Smoky Mountain Dreams
Vespertine

### New Adult

Punching the V-Card

### Winter Holidays

*The Home for the Holidays Series*
Mr. Frosty Pants
Mr. Naughty List
Mr. Jingle Bells

## Fantasy

Any Given Lifetime

### Re-imagined Fairy Tales

Flight
Levity

**Paranormal & Shifters**

Angel Undone
Omega Mine

**Horror**

Raise Up Heart

# Omegaverse

*Heat of Love Series*
Slow Heat
Alpha Heat
Slow Birth
Bitter Heat

*For Sale Series*
Heat for Sale

# Coming of Age

*'90s Coming of Age Series*
Pictures of You
You Are Not Me

# Audiobooks

Leta Blake at Audible

# Discover more about the author online

Leta Blake
letablake.com

# About the Author

Author of the bestselling book *Smoky Mountain Dreams* and the fan favorite Omegaverse series *Heat of Love*, Leta Blake's educational and professional background is in psychology and finance, respectively. However, her passion has always been for writing. She enjoys crafting romance stories and exploring the psyches of imaginary people. At home in the Southern U.S., Leta works hard at achieving balance between her writing and her family life.

Printed in Great Britain
by Amazon

23877536R00239